NEURAL WRAITH 2

K.D. ROBERTSON

CHARACTER LIST & GLOSSARY

CHARACTERS

Nicholas Waite—protagonist; Lieutenant Cipher of the Archangel Division in the Neo Babylon Police Department; former black company cipher in Neural Spike and Tartarus

Uriel "Rie"—police ARMD; prototype Mark 3 Archangel in command of Babylon PD's Oversight Taskforce; long black hair, amber eyes, large bust and thighs, 5'7

Kushiel—military ARMD; prototype Mark 2 Archangel deployed as liaison between the military and Babylon PD; long silver hair, red eyes, enormous bust and figure, nearly 8'

Ezekiel—police ARMD; prototype Mark 3 Archangel in development at Sigma labs; long white hair in a ponytail, purple eyes, lithe figure, 5'2

Chloe—police ARMD; Mark 3 Archangel acting as Nick's liaison and assistant; looks like a standard Mark 3, 5'2

Metatron "Meta"—police ARMD; Mark 1 Archangel who acts as the voice of the Mark 1s; named by Nick; looks like a standard Mark 1, 5'0

Juliet and Rosa—police ARMDs; Mark 3 Archangels acting as Nick's bodyguards; look like standard Mark 3s, 5'2

Helena—experimental mainframe; stored beneath the police Spire following her rescue in Book 1; has no body or physical appearance beside her bulky computer body

Paul Hammond—human; Nick's immediate superior and captain; a grizzled detective in his 50s ripped right from a 1920s crime film; a burned out and bitter man with anti-doll sentiments and a family history as police officers

Dennis Kim—human; police commissioner and political appointee to automate the Babylon PD; brother of RTM Strategic's CEO; a charismatic politician and true believer in automation; an aging man of Korean ethnicity always in suits with a statesman-like appearance

Carolyn Andrews—human; absentee police chief who is disfavored by politics; formerly from the military; a stoic and capable woman respected by almost everyone

Andrew Lieu—deceased; human; former captain of Nick's bureau; conspired to bring down Babylon and the Spires from the inside by creating a zombified army of soldiers using Helena; killed by Nick in Book 1

Alex Griffiths—human; general of the Neo Westphalian Military's Aerial Command; "gifted" Nick his expensive apartment with no known motive

Lucas Miller—human; gang lord, cipher, and entrepreneur; owns and runs black companies, Formeus Imports and the Cobalt Lily; an old friend and mentor of Nick's; has dark skin, shows off the wealth he's earned, vapes, and aspires to more than just the streets

Lumen—logic engine mainframe; Lucas's old mainframe and "virtual daughter" who runs the Cobalt Lily; has a crush on Nick; interface body has bobbed white hair with blue highlights and blue eyes

Omoikane—judicial mainframe; one of six state-of-the-art mainframes responsible for all court decisions in Babylon; interface body wears a gleaming silver suit, and he has an overwrought male idol-like appearance

Athena—judicial mainframe; one of six state-of-the-art mainframes responsible for all court decisions in Babylon; interface body leans into a lewd office style with a skimpy miniskirt, sheer stockings, lots of cleavage, tattoos, and skin that sparkles with gemstones

Tiferet—emotion engine mainframe; the mainframe used in GWT's global HQ to interface between local and international affairs; interface body has thick, curly platinum-blonde hair, an hourglass figure, and an elegant appearance.

Lucida Harm—human; GWT's chief of security and former black company cipher; pitch-black pigtails, mid-20s, sloppy clothing preference

Richard Toke—human; Senior Vice President in GWT's global HQ and head of Security and Audit; American; Spires resident; a trim, muscular man who is comfortable with his position in life

James von Magnus—human; Chief Operating Officer of GWT; family were some of the first to move to Babylon; slightly overweight, in his 60s, square jaw, casual sense of extravagance

CONCEPTS

ARMD "Doll"—Autonomous Robotic Modular Dolls, ordinarily called dolls; AI-powered androids that come almost exclusively in the form of women; they serve a variety of purposes, from nursing, to cleaning, to police duties, and even warfare. There are three primary manufacturers: Sigma, RTM, and a Chinese company.

Mainframe—AI-powered supercomputers that run companies and governments using quantum computing

Interface—a subtype of ARMD that acts as a body or conduit for a mainframe to interact with humans physically; all interfaces are legally required to have silver armbands and a barcode engraved into their face; come in both genders

Pile—a subtype of ARMD that assists mainframes with human interaction in large organizations; use small, androgynous bodies made extremely cheaply and have little personality or processing power

Warbot—the term used for all autonomous military units that are not dolls, including tanks, warships, and drones.

Emotion and Logic Engines—two distinct methods of AI operation. Logic engines strictly follow predefined directives and parameters; emotion engines possess high-level objectives that allow them to deviate from their programming and are more "human-like."

Neural Implants and Mods—implants are installed in the brains of early pubescent children and integrate them with augmented and virtual reality; neural mods enable alteration of implant behavior

Ciphers—AI troubleshooters; people with specialized skills to handle a variety of AI and neural issues that slip between the cracks of other specializations

The Altnet—Neo Westphalia's Internet platform, built around the concept of augmented and virtual reality; rarely used outside the country and the United States

Black Companies—undertake activities that are either decriminalized (but not strictly legal) or "victimless crimes;" police turn a blind eye to them

LOCATIONS

Neo Westphalia—a country formed from six man-made islands in the East Pacific; created sixty years ago by tech trillionaires

Neo Babylon—Neo Westphalia's oldest and grandest island-city

The Spires—five enormous skyscrapers that form the headquarters and residences of Babylon's government and elite; their names are Olympus, Avalon, Axis Mundi, Sindansu, and Yggdrasil

Alcatraz—a commercial district in the outer metro filled with black companies and criminal activity in Babylon

The Doll District—a red-light district in the inner city that specializes in doll services

COMPANIES

Aesir—the largest electronics and neural implant company in the world; currently embroiled in a court case over the right to force older neural implants to purchase premium neural mods to remain functional

RTM—the largest doll manufacturer and electronic parts developer in the world; also contains RTM Strategic, their military subsidiary

Sigma Robotics and Industrial—an industrial AI manufacturer who has branched into AI and doll development in the past two decades. Created emotion engines and the Archangels.

Neural Spike—a black company that did R&D for emotion engines; was shut down by the military to cover up illegal human trials they did for the government

Tartarus—a black company that contained all former Neural Spike personnel that were not "disappeared;" shut down in Book 1 by the police

CHAPTER 1

The headquarters of the Grand Westphalian Trust loomed over the CBD like a pristine, gleaming beacon of an age long past. Clean, unbroken panes of glass ran along the skyscraper, unmarred by tacky LED displays.

The entire building seemed to hover on a handful of marble columns, while small cafes hung from glass platforms underneath the tower itself. A bank of transparent glass elevators sat inside an open plaza beneath the tower.

Locals knew the company as GWT. It was a trusted bank in the artificial islands of Neo Westphalia—at least, as trusted as banks could be in a place this jaded. The company stood tall in the halls of power. Its grubby fingers weren't so much in every pie as funding others foolish enough to leave a trail, and it had enough money to make nearly any problem go away.

Which is why the cordon of SMG-wielding autonomous police dolls surrounding the pristine HQ was a sign for alarm in the city. Each of the dolls looked like the same identical woman, with fluffy white hair, antennae hidden as pigtails, armored pauldrons and greaves, and were five-foot nothing. They were known as the Archangels, the city's elite police force.

Lines of extravagantly suited office workers formed in front of the dolls guarding the elevators, presumably to be checked one-by-one. Far more watched from beyond the cordon, kept behind an invisible line. The Archangels didn't bother manhandling people.

In truth, there was a line. It existed only in augmented reality and was visible to almost every person and doll in the city of Neo Babylon. The use of neural implants merged the digital world with the physical world. Known as the Altnet, life itself had been augmented for decades here. Everyone had an implant. Well, almost everyone.

A sleek police interceptor slipped through the cordon and pulled up amid a dozen oversized SUVs with flashing lights. Two more interceptors swiftly followed. Inside the first sat two people: one human, the other an Archangel.

The human was Detective Nick Waite, one of the only functional adults in the city without a neural implant. The other was Chloe, a Mark 3 Archangel. Unlike the older models outside, she was a little taller, with slightly longer hair, and a little fuller in the chest.

"Are things this bad?" Nick asked Chloe as he peered out the windows at the small army of dolls around them.

"The safety of Neo Babylon's financial sector is of the highest priority. Murder, the possibility of corporate espionage, and hacking are individually all dangerous to financial stability. Combined, they must be taken very seriously," she said.

The car doors snapped open and the pair slipped out. Nick wore his standard baggy coat that made him look like a real detective, and a more nondescript set of clothes beneath.

Not that he really needed to dress up. Neo Westphalia never got too cold. A side-effect of being an artificial chain of islands in the north-east Pacific. Although as they entered spring, he might not appreciate the heavy coat. It'd been nearly five months since he'd become a detective after all.

Little light entered the Central Business District at this early hour. Despite that, the cafes, coffee shop chains, and bakeries teemed with suits and people in athleticwear. If the line to enter GWT's HQ was this bad already, Nick could only imagine how bad it would be at 9AM. No doubt many of the people camped out with coffee were employees logged on remotely using their neural implants.

The high-security nature of finance meant work-from-home options tended to be limited. Or at least, that was the excuse given to force the office drones into the cubicle farms each day. On the flip side, the banks had the shiniest golden handcuffs to attract ciphers into their dull halls.

"GWT didn't seem that alarmed," he said as he and Chloe approached the central elevator. "I checked their notification. Their head of security sent it in personally. Which seems weird to me—shouldn't a mainframe have automatically notified us once she found the body?"

"Many organizations have policies that require internal security to contact us, rather than mainframes," Chloe said.

"So a human decided that a cipher being murdered overnight in the middle of one of Babylon's most prestigious banks, without being noticed by any of their security systems, was of low priority?"

"It is of concern."

Nick felt that Chloe might be understating matters.

A mugger was of concern. Somebody embezzling funds was of concern.

But the head of security of one of Neo Westphalia's largest banks shrugging off murder and gaping security holes? He sincerely hoped this didn't end up as another Lieu situation. Cracking open one long-term major conspiracy had been enough excitement to last him at least a year, and it hadn't even been half that long.

The Archangels forming the cordon were all Mark 1s, but only one or two had familiar serial numbers to Nick.

While he considered his memory excellent, keeping track of thousands of identical dolls was hard work. It didn't help that there was no pattern to them. Whenever one was destroyed or disabled, they simply transferred into the next available unit and "rebirthed" into its serial number.

When he had told Rie that he wanted to name the Archangels to make it easier to remember them, she'd called him an idiot. Not just because he would need to come up with—and remember—several thousand new names, but because the process would throw the Host into havoc.

For now, the Mark 1s didn't seem fussed about his inability to differentiate them. Metatron—better known as Meta—acted as their voice and liaison to him ordinarily, and that seemed to satisfy them. Although they did have a propensity to chatter in his earpiece when he got close.

Like right now, as the Archangels noticed his arrival and began shifting onto his frequency. One after another, they reported in, letting him know their current status, what they'd noticed, any current thoughts, the color of their underwear, and all sorts of random oddities.

"I do not believe any of us tell you the color of our underwear," Meta told him, making her presence known as she stepped up beside him from his escort. She looked identical to every other Mark 1, save her serial number.

A discordant hum in his earpiece suggested discontent from the Archangels at his comment.

He shrugged. "It was an example. And I don't think you even wear underwear? I know the Mark 3s have the same strange crotch plate that Rie has, but what about you Mark 1s?"

Meta shifted uncomfortably and looked to Chloe. Over the past few months, the pair had become "close" for lack of a better word. Both acted as liaisons for their respective model lines to Nick. The primary difference was that Meta almost never left his side, much like his bodyguards, Juliet and Rosa, unlike Chloe, who had other duties.

"They lack in-built sexual features," Chloe said, with an unspoken "for now" in her tone.

Given Rie was presently at Sigma Robotic's central factory in the Atlantic, Nick wondered whether the Host might have some inside information on when some physical upgrades were forthcoming.

Officially, Rie's visit was to finalize Ezekiel's tuning. As the prototype and the new batch of Mark 3s would be deploying under Nick's command, Sigma felt it was important to review their current directives. New Archangels would be running off a master instance of the training data, after all, rather than the live data that the active Archangels made decisions based on.

Sigma Robotics and Industrial was one of the major players in everything related to robots and dolls, military or otherwise. They'd created the Archangels and developed the first emotion engines—the more advanced type of processing engine used by newer dolls and mainframes. RTM Strategic was their direct competitor in the military and police space, and it was a subsidiary of the monolithic RTM, who did everything and anything electronic.

Nick had been busy over the past few months ensuring the Archangels could hide the data within their neural net from Sigma. This visit would prove whether his efforts were enough.

Although given his mentor was there, he suspected at least someone would find out the truth. Whether Welk cared was another matter. Something was deeply wrong in the depths of Sigma Labs, and it wasn't being resolved through the captured researchers taken from Neural Spike.

Even if his efforts worked, he'd also need to worry about the new prototype soon enough. While Rie wasn't going to be returning hand-in-hand with her baby sister, Ezekiel's arrival was mere weeks away.

Nick knew this because the commissioner had been planning an overwrought induction ceremony to celebrate the event. The entire central island was going to be transformed into an event center to show off the police force's new smiling, sexy symbol of oppression.

At least, Nick assumed Ezekiel was sexy. The Mark 3s were based on her, and his life would be in mortal danger if he ever suggested they were anything but.

In the meantime, that left Nick to manage himself. While he was officially in charge of the Archangel Division, he wasn't crazy enough to try to do everything himself. He worked closely with Rie to manage things. With her gone, he felt lonelier, and not just because his bed was much colder at night.

Much, much colder. Rie had been keeping his heating bills low over winter. Not that he told her that.

Nick arrived at the elevator right as one of the three central lifts ascended toward the massive structure floating above them containing a gaggle of employees. The Archangels refused to allow anyone in the line to go any farther, breaking many of the workers from their mindless routine. They began to protest about why they weren't moving forward.

"Detective Waite, we have reserved the next elevator for you," one of the Mark 1s told him.

He grunted and stepped past the dolls. The protests subsided. Many of the employees stared at him in disbelief, as if unsure he was even real. None of them said anything.

Presumably, they were chattering to each other using their neural implants. This sort of reaction was rapidly becoming a new normal whenever he showed up in person to a scene.

Nick studied the elevator shafts while he waited. While they were transparent, and the cars were the same, a variety of devices appeared to be built into the door frame. A small panel outside each entrance had been ignored by the Archangels and workers, but was presumably for the use of neanderthals like Nick who lacked a neural implant.

After a short wait, he stepped into the next elevator and ascended along with Chloe, Meta, Juliet, and Rosa. He didn't bother using the panel.

Once inside the glass walls and away from prying eyes and ears, he asked, "These are public access, right? Anyone can walk up and use one of these? Even at night?"

"Without authorization, the elevators only go to the atrium and the shops beneath the building," Chloe explained. "After 6PM, public access is curtailed. Automated security systems are deployed and Guardian G5 security dolls are utilized to keep the vicinity clear."

"G5s, huh. Figures that GWT are using older security dolls. Cheapskates. We're checking their memory banks from last night?"

"Permissions are being requested."

He narrowed his eyes. That sounded a lot like GWT was unwilling to cough up the data.

With a wave of his hand, he gestured for Chloe to block out any spying from the hidden cameras in the elevator car. If she hadn't already. She nodded at him. Given her eyes hadn't glowed, he suspected she had already done so.

"I'll admit I'm not up to speed on how well megacorps can control their own data. What happens if they wipe the dolls and any backups?" he asked.

"It is unlikely that the sensory data of local security dolls is backed up on any meaningful schedule. However, hardware logs would show evidence of tampering."

"What about mainframes? This is GWT's HQ. There must be like 7 mainframes here."

While small organizations could run off the back of a single mainframe, the same couldn't be said of larger ones. Sophisticated network structures had been developed to distribute workloads across multiple mainframes, maximizing efficiency and minimizing downtime impacts.

RTM had standardized structures that it endorsed, and they had created a global industry of consultants and contractors that existed to build, maintain, and upgrade mainframes using their standards.

For reasons that Nick had never understood, it was popular to name RTM mainframes after the Jewish sefirot. Almost no individual location needed more than 10 mainframes, and it included a useful hierarchy to segregate various functions across the business.

When he'd first heard about this, the obvious question had been how an international company handled a hundred branches, each with their own mainframe named Malkuth. Obviously, the individual mainframes would be tagged according to location, but it was an extremely dehumanizing structure for the mainframes. And a confusing one.

To humans, they probably didn't think much of it. What did it matter what they called their machines? But the mainframes needed to communicate efficiently, for much the same reason internal hierarchies were necessary in individual locations.

RTM's answer was to implement specialized "super-structures" that treated groups of mainframes as a single unit in a layered system.

So this HQ might be a high-level mainframe—likely a Keter—in a larger system, and other branches acted as lower-level mainframes. The structure was flexible, and Nick only knew the general gist of the idea rather than the specifics. Neither Tartarus nor

Neural Spike had ever been anywhere near large enough to consider the idea.

Hell, the only reason he knew about the stuff was that Neural Spike had moved to a complex mainframe system in its final days, and Tartarus had been considering upgrading to one before it was shut down. Nick had been one of the few Ciphers with the training and experience with larger mainframe installations due to his time in Neural Spike.

What he did know was that, as the HQ, this GWT branch would have separate mainframes for local management and for the broader work, and then likely one mainframe that integrated the two. Depending on the size of the organization, the integration mainframe would be called either Yesod or Tiferet. The primary management mainframe would almost certainly be called Malkuth.

His business was with the local mainframes. He didn't care much about GWT's backend.

Chloe didn't answer Nick's question, so he followed up with more.

"I can't imagine that the mainframes wouldn't be mirrored somewhere, or at least have regular backups. A hiccup with one could crash the global financial system," he said. "Who are we dealing with? I'm assuming this is a standard RTM structure."

"Correct. However, we have been restricted from interacting with any mainframe other than Tiferet. Given GWT's influence in Babylon, we have been unwilling to push matters," Chloe said.

"A Tiferet?" He scratched his head. "GWT has a local Tiferet? I thought the whole role of them was to integrate different layers of mainframes."

Nick had never even dealt with a Tiferet before. RTM's emotion engine mainframes had been relatively new in the latter days of Neural Spike, and he'd mostly interacted with them while visiting other companies on cipher business for Tartarus. Tiferets were the definition of "mainframe glue" in that they existed to hold together larger, more unwieldy server structures.

He'd expected to deal with a Yesod, Malkuth, or Netzach. When he'd been trained on RTM structures, they'd been fairly explicit that Tiferets shouldn't undertake major organizational roles. The few times he'd dealt with mainframes in the past few months had involved those low-level models.

"She is not assigned to the local level of the HQ. The official contact for the department is Yesod, but Tiferet responded to communications in her stead."

"Well, that bodes well."

So GWT's HQ used a standard RTM structure, except not quite. They were barring access to data that might determine who had been in the building last night. And the murder was apparently a mystery.

Oh, and their security chief was wholly unconcerned with this whole murder business.

Nick didn't need to be a detective to smell a rat. And he was, even if he hadn't been trained as a detective.

The atrium was a palatial affair, if a little claustrophobic. Continuing the theme of physicality, Nick noted the lack of LED displays or imprinted overlays. The elevators opened into the middle of the space, and receptionist dolls stood immediately in front of him.

A waterfall cascaded down the far wall and currents of water ran along glass channels beneath the floor. Burnished gold facades joined dark wood paneling to give an old-school but elegant appearance. Almost all electronics appeared to be hidden away. Nick might think he'd stepped back a century or two in time, if it weren't for the glass elevators and the glowing LED exit lights.

Oh, and the gun turrets in the ceiling corners. Only so much could be done to hide them.

The building's security appeared inactive but remained visible.

GWT wanted guests to feel welcome, but secure, and for those with sinister thoughts to know they were an electronic signal away from vaporization.

"Mister Waite, we were not expecting you. Do you have business with the Trust today?" one of the receptionist dolls asked while beaming at him. "Given your accessibility needs, I can organize a face-to-face meeting with a funds maximization master to discuss whatever you wish."

Nick had no idea what the hell a "funds maximization master" was, but he suspected it was some pompous title for a doll who would act as a relay between him and a mainframe for basic account administration.

He did, however, know what she meant by "accessibility needs." His lack of a neural implant meant he couldn't use the vast majority of devices in the city. Most of the damn lifts in the police department didn't even have buttons and every appliance in his apartment cost a small fortune for the privilege of having clicky things on it.

"Wait, I have an account here?" he asked, his mind catching up to the meaning behind her words.

His escorts stared at him, and Chloe smirked. The receptionist merely tilted her head in confusion.

"The Grand Westphalian Trust has been the Neo Babylon Police Department's financial partner of choice since its inception," Chloe explained. "Upon your induction into the department, I took the liberty of opening the necessary accounts."

"Mister Waite, did you know that all purchases made through your Trust Facilitation Account using direct settlement earn a 10% cashback in the form of Primum credits? You have yet to utilize your account in this manner—or at all, in fact." The receptionist seemed annoyed on behalf of her owner at Nick's refusal to use his heretofore unknown transaction account.

Not that he cared much. He didn't have a great head for

money, but he knew that all the cashback deals were related to strange Altnet stuff. Primum credits were a digital currency used exclusively for buying digital goods and therefore useless to him.

While somebody couldn't turn Primum into cash, or at least not legally, the opposite was very much not the case. Absurd amounts of money vanished into the Primum black hole every second—a fact Nick knew because his friend Sung held down a solid job thanks to it.

"I'll think about it," he said. "I'm here on police business, not personal."

The receptionist stared at him. After several seconds, she nodded. "Understood. I have been informed that Tiferet will be here shortly. Please make yourself comfortable. Do you desire refreshments?"

"Coffee?"

"That is unavailable at present."

"I'm good, thanks."

"Water," Chloe said flatly.

Nick rolled his eyes at Chloe's look. She'd been on him lately about not drinking enough water. Her recent coffee kick was lapsing and now she seemed worried about his health. If she tried to get him into superfoods, he'd put his foot down.

There was nothing wrong with a burrito and coffee for breakfast, and he stood by that.

Under Chloe's watchful gaze, he chugged down the glass of water the receptionist returned with. If this kept up, he'd ask her for a ring.

Not that he would tell her that. Somehow, he felt that she'd take it seriously and the Host would riot. Rie might also be upset. Or worse, she'd ask for her own ring.

They waited for several minutes in the otherwise lifeless atrium. Several elevator cars full of employees rose past them, and then descended without their cargo sometime later. Nick remained the only living soul here. The wealth on display here would bother him, but he'd begun to get used to it over the past few months in the Spires.

Not to mention the fancy apartment he lived in. Sure, by Neo Babylonian standards he was firmly middle class, but that put him in the upper 10% of the city.

Things had been very different six months ago. He'd lived in a derelict apartment, tied by law to a dead-end job that paid below-market rates, and his glory days had seemed well behind him. He'd been coasting toward retirement by his late 20s. A truly sad existence.

Then everything went a bit nuts. His life had been upended in circumstances that, by all rights, should have landed him in jail—or a secret underwater lab, at any rate. Now, he owned a brand-new upscale apartment, had a full-time job that paid far too much, received retirement benefits, and even had exceptional health insurance.

One of the elevator cars slowed, and it wasn't empty. Nick rose from the square wooden bench he'd been sitting on.

Before he had a chance to even dust himself off, the woman inside the elevator exited and blitzed toward him.

"Mister Waite, I do apologize for making you wait," she said. "On any other day, I could easily have arranged for a private suite to discuss matters, but I'm afraid today is—"

"A murder investigation," he said flatly. "I know. I'm here to investigate it, not query my account. You're Tiferet?"

He couldn't imagine she was anybody else. Silver bands on her wrists and the barcode and serial number engraved in golden ink beneath her left eye were clear indications that she was a physical interface for a mainframe.

Her model looked custom. Her white and gold jacket and miniskirt contoured perfectly to her hourglass figure. Thick tresses of platinum-blonde hair billowed down her back and over her shoulders in dense curls that would require hours of daily maintenance if they were organic. Only a hint of cleavage and thigh flesh peeked out, as if somebody had scientifically chosen the amount to be shown.

Which was probably the case. This interface probably cost as much as his apartment. He imagined it could probably outperform most dolls without drawing on the immense supercomputer that acted as its brain somewhere in this building.

Said supercomputer likely had as much invested into it as most mid-sized companies held in market cap. While mainframes could be bought off the shelf, there wasn't a chance in hell that a bank the size of GWT wasn't using highly customized emotion engines in their HQ. These mainframes managed innumerable trillions of dollars. They were the company.

"I am Tiferet. It is a pleasure to meet a valued and honored member of the Trust such as yourself," she said. Her beaming smile had probably cost as much to develop as the net worth of lesser banks.

"Thanks," Nick drawled. "As I said, I'm here as Lieutenant Cipher Nicholas Waite, not an account holder. GWT reported that one of your cipher analysts was found murdered this morning. I'm here to investigate."

She blinked at him, then slowly pivoted her head to look at Chloe.

"I believe that you are more than familiar with the detective's position," Chloe said, and Meta nodded next to her as if to amplify her words.

Tiferet tilted her head to the side and her eyes glowed momentarily. "Your personnel are presently with our security staff at the incident site. Internal measures are being conducted to address police requests for additional data to assist with your investigation. As I do not believe you have the forensic skills necessary, would it not be best for us to step aside into a meeting room and discuss additional matters?"

Nick shot Chloe a look. Her eyes glowed as she checked in with the Host.

Rather than speak openly, she used her neural net to talk directly into his earpiece, "Other Mark 3s are already undertaking forensic analysis, as she said. They are personally dealing with the HQ's head of security, one Lucida Harm."

Harm... Nick knew the name. She hung around in some of the cipher circles dedicated to mainframes. He'd always placed her as a black company piece, but she must have gotten a better offer from GWT. Going legit had too many benefits to overlook.

Anonymity was dead on the Altnet, so he knew the identities of basically every Cipher he interacted with, even briefly. His memory wasn't good enough to remember if he'd ever helped her, though. Chances were he'd provided some assistance with some esoteric errors or directives at some stage.

Few enough black company ciphers dealt directly with mainframes in any capacity for him to remember them. If Lucida's name came to mind, it meant she was the real deal.

"That will be fine," he told Tiferet.

She smiled at him. A moment later, an elevator car rose into the atrium and came to a stop. It was full of bewildered employees. Before any of them had a chance to react, the receptionist dolls shot forward and began ushering the workers out. A few of them froze up, half-expecting Chloe to arrest them.

"After you, Mister Waite," Tiferet said, gesturing to the now-empty elevator car.

Bemused, he stepped inside. The Mark 3s, Meta, and Tiferet followed, and soon they were rocketing upward to one of the uppermost floors.

Given the elevator shaft stood inside the center of the building, there shouldn't have been much to see through the glass. That's when the embedded electronic panels roared to life and showed a view of the building's exterior.

"I don't usually see actual electronic glass," Nick mused.

"We strive to ensure the optimal experience for all members, whatever their age, disabilities, or backgrounds," Tiferet said, clearly reeling off some corporate spiel.

Age was likely the key there. As good as neural implants had become, they still couldn't be installed in prepubescent children. If GWT wanted to remain the premier institution for the spoiled rich brats from the Spires, it needed to look good to them when they were too little to think for themselves. That way the bank could mine them for nostalgia for life.

Nick's friend, Lucas, loved the look and feel of places like this. So much of Babylon was too sleek, clean, and modern for him. To him, the appeal came from rustic, warm places that reminded him of where humanity had come from.

The elevator came to a stop. Outside the door gleamed a pristine and almost sterile hallway, all painted white. The floor comprised high pile carpet while the walls were formed from contoured foam—likely acoustic foam.

A half-dozen G5 security dolls stood outside, bulky automatic shotguns in their hands and heavy armor plating covering up almost their entire bodies. They remained perfectly still.

"Is this a server floor?" he asked. "Aren't these usually underground?"

"The Trust believes in excelling in all fields, and that requires the greatest performance," Tiferet said as she led Nick and Chloe past the security dolls. "Our mainframes operate across distributed nodes for redundancy and performance reasons. These are the performance nodes, intended for trivial affairs."

"Such as dealing with me?" Nick tried not to smirk.

Tiferet stopped outside an unmarked door.

Although every door was unmarked, actually. The floor lacked any internal windows, landmarks, or any way to orient oneself. This wasn't an obstacle to anyone with a neural implant, as they could automatically map their surroundings, but Nick found the area disconcerting.

This space hadn't been designed for humans. Chloe showed no concern, so this presumably wasn't a trap, but Nick genuinely wondered why Tiferet was bringing him to the mainframe equivalent of the utility room.

"The vast majority of customer-facing affairs are handled using interface protocols," Tiferet said. "For a member of your status, I use my primary node for all interactions that require additional processing."

"I'm touched."

"That pleases me."

Apparently sarcasm was too much for her "interface protocols" to process. Then again, outside the Archangels, processing complex emotions was difficult for dolls. Tiferet might be an emotion engine mainframe, much like the Archangels were emotion engine dolls, but her interface was a significant downgrade.

Given Nick was in the market for a suitable interface model for Helena, his personal mainframe, he made note of this. The idea that a mainframe might downgrade its intelligence for the sake of faster reactions surprised him, and he wouldn't wish for that to happen to Helena.

Tiferet led them inside the room. Juliet and Rosa remained outside.

The spartan hallway gave way to an elegantly furnished office, replete with yellow tulips, brass and wood furnishings, and a large wall of electronic connectors. Presumably the connectors were for interfaces and dolls to hardwire themselves in if necessary.

The tulips looked out of place against the deep, warm colors of the office. Nick suspected they meant something to the mainframe or whoever placed them here, given a contrasting color would work better.

The desk and tabletops were barren. No mugs, utensils, or signs of utilization were present. Not a speck of dust could be seen, but that just spoke well of the cleaning dolls.

"Please, take a seat. I'm afraid I do not have coffee, but I can resupply you with water," Tiferet said as she conjured a tall glass from within a hidden wall cabinet and filled it with water from a similarly hidden tap.

Nick and Chloe sat in the overly upholstered leather couches that filled one corner of the room. Meta remained near the door, as if standing watch, but her SMG hung loose. After a few moments, the mainframe joined them and served him the glass.

"I had hoped that someone would reach out to you sooner," Tiferet said as she settled into a couch opposite him. "This problem has been on my mind for some time."

CHAPTER 2

"It has?" Nick asked.

Damn. They might be getting somewhere. Apparently he was already working his magic on Tiferet, a fact the Archangels often found frustrating.

"Indeed. Multiple flags have been placed on your account to force the customer relation managers to reach out to you about your future. Their failure to arrange an earlier meeting is deeply frustrating." Tiferet affected a pouty expression. "I believe there is a human saying for this: if you want something done right, do it yourself?"

Nick held back a sigh, while Chloe openly smirked at him. Of course the mainframe still only cared about his account.

Was this just singlemindedness on Tiferet's behalf or an attempt to stall him? Given how strange mainframes tended to be, he genuinely couldn't tell.

"I already said—"

"Security has informed me that they will join us once protocols have been followed. Until then, surely you have time to see to your financial security?" Tiferet asked.

Her raised eyebrow, crossed arms, and prim look suggested

that even if he said no, that she would see to his financial security anyway. Somebody had very particular tastes when they had created her model. Then again, maybe they'd shaped the model to the personality that her emotion engine had come up with.

"Fine," he said. "But I'm not sure what's so important. I've done just fine without even knowing about my accounts here."

"That is even more concerning." Tiferet's expression suggested some customer relation managers might not be getting their annual bonuses. "I have conducted a thorough search of your finances. They are a mess and in dire need of repair."

"By searching my finances, you mean...?"

"When you opened an account here, you gave us permission to utilize all financial data related to you. Using data sharing agreements with other major financial institutions in Neo Westphalia, I located your other accounts, analyzed your income and expenses, and simulated a suite of options based on your situation to optimize your future."

Right now, Nick felt his future would be optimized by never dealing with GWT ever again. He didn't care much for dealing with money—mostly because he'd never had much of it—and being told that this mainframe had just casually rifled through his life only lowered his opinion of the financial sector.

Then again, he worked in a police division that operated by reading people's thoughts and actively monitoring almost everything taking place in the city. Nick felt the hypocrisy lapping at his chin as he struggled not to drown in it.

"Is this really the sort of thing one of GWT's mainframes should be wasting time on?" he asked instead.

"Aiding a valued member is part of my core duties. Although a human staff member should have acted as a conduit for the Trust's capabilities, your reactions so far are significantly more positive than most humans. Even the ciphers dislike this floor."

"It's a big, black soundproofed box of mystery," he said,

leaning back. "It's funny. I work in an office that's utterly unsuited for dolls, but full of them. This place was built for you, and I strongly suspect you spend very little time here."

"What makes you think that?"

"The fact there's nothing in here. If you told me this was a meeting room that they accidentally built on the wrong floor, I'd almost believe you if not for the flowers."

Tiferet looked away, but her expression remained unchanged. "The purpose of giving a mainframe an interface is to facilitate interactions between humans and my processing capabilities. I cannot accomplish that from an office that nobody will visit. In that regard, you are right to suggest this room was built on the wrong floor."

He scratched his head. This hadn't been where he wanted the meeting to go.

For one thing, prodding the mainframe wasn't his intention. She helped run the company and was a huge store of data. The fact she could be unwrapped to reveal a surprisingly humanlike core only complicated matters.

But he did note an oddity in her statement. "You're a Tiferet, right? Aren't you supposed to facilitate matters between different levels of mainframes within the server structure? Meeting with me seems beneath you."

"Perhaps. But my directives suggest otherwise."

Chloe's eyes flashed, but she said nothing. That confirmed his suspicion that he'd struck gold.

But he wasn't going to learn more by talking with the mainframe. Directives and processes would be locked behind a strict corporate shield—if the police struggled to penetrate that to gain security footage for the murder, Nick wasn't going to unlock the workings of an extortionately expensive mainframe.

"Shall I explain to you my proposals to guarantee your financial security?" Tiferet asked, forcibly pushing the topic back to her favorite hunting ground.

"Sure."

The next few minutes consisted primarily of financial gibberish about transaction and savings accounts, interest rates, money market funds, and a swiftly thwarted attempt to explain the optimal way to conduct transactions.

If there was one thing that Nick never felt absent from his life, it was the bewildering array of payment options that implant holders faced during every financial transaction. The legacy software he relied on to buy things with his phone forced him to use whatever transaction method carried the lowest fee—typically 1% or so, because paying people extra for the right to pay them at all was a thing for some reason.

But he knew there was a wild world out there, where the global financial system fought for every dollar moving through it. Neo Westphalia might only be a small set of overpopulated islands, but it was built of metaphorical gold. Despite its small size, it held a level of wealth and power that allowed it to sit at the same table as major players in geopolitics.

While Neo Westphalia had its own standard currency—called the Westphalian Credit—it competed in a world full of corporate-backed digital currencies and foreign currencies of frequently dubious value. To say nothing of distributed methods of digital payment and commodified assets that were frequently speculated on.

The more transactions stayed within their own network, the more money and power that financial institution retained. Banks rewarded customers who used certain payment methods and currencies, and punished those who didn't.

Most of which was useless to Nick, because he didn't want to micromanage every coffee he purchased. He knew ciphers who went to specific coffee shops and chose their grocery store based on their bank rewards. Sinister stuff, in his mind, and also dreadfully boring.

"You are uninterested," Tiferet said after her spiel fell on deaf ears. "My diagnostics suggest you understand matters, but simply do not care."

"I only have so many things in life that I can care about," he said. "The people I've known who micromanage their finances tend to have a lot less room to care about other things. Right now, I'm trying to be a detective, not the guy who brags about all the money he makes while fucking up every case. Unless financial security can help me choose the right interface for a mainframe, the best thing you can do for me is to reduce the amount of thought I need to put into my finances."

Tiferet's eyes glowed and her fingers twitched. "Financial security can help you afford the right interface?"

"I have the benefit of unlimited government funds to buy it," Nick said drily. "Money isn't the problem."

She seemed somewhat put out. "I see. In that case, I believe I understand your goal. Given your expenditure patterns, I can put together an account in the bundle that will suit you."

"Put together?"

Instead of answering, she pushed on to a new topic, "Of more concern are your retirement savings. They are a mess. You have multiple accounts, fees for products that provide you no benefit, and even abandoned monies. While your current retirement benefits are being paid into a standard fund at the Trust, significant benefit can be realized if you enable me to roll together all your finances into a single bundle. With only a word, I can package everything together, eliminate unnecessary fees, and provide you with the peace of mind you requested."

Did he request it?

Then again, he had said that he wanted to reduce the amount of thought his finances needed. Right now, he didn't think about them, but Tiferet evidently felt that was not an option.

He looked at Chloe, who shrugged.

"The package being suggested appears agreeable," she said.

"You can see it?" he asked.

"I provided her with a copy upon request," Tiferet said.

"When did she request it?"

"Just now. Given the complexity involved, I felt that you would be better off not reviewing it."

That seemed like a pretty snippy way to comply with his request. Tiferet had an attitude, it seemed.

Wasn't this about his money? How could he be better off not reviewing some sort of package deal that involved his own bank and retirement accounts?

Truly, living in Neo Babylon under robot rule was suffering.

Nick rubbed the bridge of his nose and suppressed the dark jokes he made internally. "I mean, this seems like the sort of thing that might matter, but it's an open question whether I'll even make it to retirement."

"It is not," Meta interrupted, both her and Chloe's eyes flashing. "The Host is in unanimous agreement."

"It is a firm belief of the Trust to always plan for the unexpected, even if the unexpected includes living," Tiferet said.

"I mean, is there anything immediately relevant?" When she opened her mouth, he quickly added, "That isn't related to micromanaging my daily coffee purchases."

"There is. Your current public liability insurance is wholly inadequate for your role. Should the judicial mainframes find you liable for an incident with similar damages as the recent event at the Spires then you would be swiftly bankrupted. As you know, personal bankruptcy in Neo Westphalia is frequently followed by deportation."

Nick stared at Tiferet in confusion, while Chloe scowled.

"Your concerns are misplaced," Chloe said. "Such a situation will not occur."

"The powers of the Neo Babylon Police Department are many, but you do not control the decisions of the judiciary," Tiferet said.

"Wait, wait, wait." Nick raised his hands to head off the argument between the two. "What do you even mean by liability insurance? And current coverage?"

"The Trust has been the preferred provider of public liability insurance for all emergency personnel in Neo Westphalia since inception. It is a condition of your employment that you retain a minimum level of liability coverage, in case you are considered negligently responsible for causing large amounts of damage in the course of your duties," Tiferet explained.

"So if I blow up somebody's car..."

"In the course of your duties," Tiferet added. "Then as your insurer we will cover all fees, legal matters, and expenses should you be held responsible. Your first year of coverage is paid for by the Department, but you must handle the matter in the future."

It hadn't been a year. But Tiferet had said that his current coverage was inadequate.

"This is a waste of time," Chloe said.

"You said I might get held responsible for something like... the Spires incident," he said, recalling that he wasn't supposed to mention Lieu's involvement publicly. "I didn't even do most of the damage there."

"Yes, but as the Lieutenant Cipher of the Archangel Division, you have almost unparalleled authority over the entire police department. Whatever official status you may have in the hierarchy, the reality is that few police ARMDs will disobey your orders. Damages caused by your directives—direct or indirect—could swiftly become unmanageable." Tiferet paused. "By an individual."

"And you're going to, what, offer to replace a Spire if I blow it up by accident?" Nick tried not to laugh. "How much will the insurance cost me? Half my salary?"

"The Trust, through the combined authority of a Da'at mainframe conference, has authorized me to offer you cost-effective unlimited public liability insurance under all circumstances, on one condition." Tiferet's smile completely vanished. "You must accept the package I offered earlier, retain financial accounts only with the Grand Westphalian Trust, and agree to a ten-year agreement with us."

Nick stared at her, his mind churning at her offer. Too many things had come up at once.

First, he'd never heard of a Da'at mainframe conference.

Second, the deal seemed too good to be true. Why offer him to bail him out of potentially ruinous circumstances for such little return?

Third, ten years sounded like a damn long time to be locked in. Then again, he had said he didn't want to think about finances.

Fourth, why were they even making the offer to begin with? What did they stand to gain from it?

Chloe bit her lip, her eyes glowing. "The Host has reviewed the offer. It appears legitimate."

"I mean, they're a huge bank and I'm one guy. Can't they just renege?" Nick asked.

Tiferet didn't even blink at this suggestion that the bank might not uphold their end of the bargain. Evidently the suggestion had come up many times.

"The judicial mainframes would force them to uphold the agreement instantly. Financial certainty is of higher value than almost any other legal commodity in Neo Westphalia."

That Nick could believe. This was a city founded by money, for money. With the advent of mainframes that could process court cases in literal minutes, even minor contract disputes lodged by random citizens were affordable.

When he'd needed to pay legal consultancy fees during the raid on Neural Spike, he'd been billed by the second. And even then, the total processing time he'd paid for had barely reached the single digit minutes mark.

Nick could only imagine how obscene the case against Aesir was regarding their new "mandatory" premium module and deprecation of older implants, given it was still running months later. Apparently multiple countries had become involved, which required complicated international conferences. There'd been a recent news story about the Neo Westphalian judicial mainframes discrediting some ancient human judge for being part of an "antiquated system."

But more to the point, he still didn't understand why GWT wanted to offer him this deal.

"This still seems too good to be true. This isn't a bribe, right? To overlook the corpse on the other floor?" he asked, turning back to Tiferet.

She blinked. "No. Other mainframes in the Trust are unaware of the current incident. You may consider this offer to be a statement of faith in your future, Mister Waite."

Things suddenly clicked.

GWT weren't trying to profit off the insurance. They wanted his money locked up in their coffers. Even Tiferet's earlier statement about the power he had over the police dolls made sense.

They saw him as a rising star, likely one with high earning potential, and the insurance was the carrot to convince him to give them all his money. The fact he wouldn't do anything with it was icing.

And the stick was the fact he might find himself shit out of luck if something went wrong. If GWT were responsible for his legal defense in liability claims, what stopped them from sabotaging him and making a much worse offer in a time of desperate need?

Right before he could give Tiferet his answer, the door opened.

A young woman with pigtails and an ill-fitting suit draped over a t-shirt slipped inside. Her hair was pitch black, and Nick instantly recognized the telltale signs of imprinting dye. If he had an implant, no doubt she'd be lighting up the room with something truly obnoxious.

Chloe's tightening expression suggested as much, or perhaps the doll merely disliked the newcomer. Meta didn't even blink as she pivoted to stare at the newcomer, point-blank.

After a few uncomfortable seconds in close proximity to Meta and her firearm, the new arrival crossed the room to an unoccupied corner. She shut the door before doing so, cutting off any prying eyes and ears.

"Harm, right?" Nick asked.

"And you're Waite," Lucida Harm said, tapping the side of the soda can in her hand as she tried to regain her composure. "You look smaller in the flesh."

"That's a new one."

She clicked her tongue. "I mean it. You look massive in all the Altnet feeds. Maybe it's how tiny these angels are."

From outside the room, a pair of voices chimed, "Archangels."

"Yeah, whatever." Lucida sipped from her soda. "So you ready to fuck off and let me get back to work? Your puppets already grabbed everything they need. You should be done here."

"Mister Waite is an account holder. Our session is not yet complete," Tiferet said.

Lucida shot the mainframe a glare, and she shut up, instead staring into her lap. "Send him an email, then. Or however the hell he communicates with people without an implant."

Scratch his earlier thoughts, Nick knew exactly why Chloe disliked this woman.

Although the fact she thought email was dead spoke volumes of her youth. The communication format was perennially on death's door, yet had outlived the tech trillionaires who had founded this city and attempted to kill it off.

"I have some questions to ask," Nick said. "Given you're supposed to be the head of security, I imagine your actual work has something to do with aiding the investigation of a murder that took place under your watch."

Lucida sneered at him. "Like I said, your dolls got everything they need. We're cooperating to the fullest extent we can. Not my fault we had some server faults last night. Seems like a crime of opportunity to me. If you need anything else, surely your puppets can rip it out of my skull, right?"

Well, she would say that.

"I sincerely doubt you're fully cooperating," Nick said, drawing a surprised look from Tiferet. "And to answer your question, let's cut the crap. I know the circles you run in. I'm in them. Don't patronize me and pretend you don't have a neural mod to keep your secrets secret."

Lucida drained her soda can and tossed it to Tiferet, who dutifully rose and disposed of it in a hidden trashcan.

"Well, seems you are half of what you're cracked up to be. Hard to tell when the olds are involved." She looked to the side and her eyes became vacant for a few moments, before she looked back at him. "Knock yourself out. But I've told the dolls everything."

"Then you won't have any problems answering the questions the exact same way," Nick said. "What's the state of the security dolls and any monitoring devices?"

"Wiped. No signs of hardware tampering. I provided log dumps," Lucida said.

"So the intruder had internal access?" Keeping his tone calm was difficult.

Here this idiot was acting as if his presence was a waste of her time and this entire murder was an inconvenience, but she'd just admitted that somebody had access to their *entire fucking security system*. He didn't need to be a cipher to know that her job was toast in normal conditions.

Which suggested things were far from normal.

"Well, duh. I'm certain I already know what backdoor they used, so now it's down to you to find the killer," she said.

"Enlighten me about the backdoor."

Maybe Chloe had planned to tell him later, but Tiferet's nonsense had tied him up. It didn't matter. Forcing Lucida to repeat herself meant any gaps in her story would show.

"Everything was wiped using mainframe access. The hardware logs show access records from various mainframes in the building, and each mainframe also accessed each other. They then wiped each other. All I know is that one mainframe was compromised, and they covered their tracks well."

"That's not the backdoor, that's how it was done." He sighed. "How the hell does a bank get away with admitting that all of your HQ mainframes were compromised by a murderer?"

"We keep the actual data separate from the security systems, asshole. It's one thing for the mainframes to mess with local security systems, but there are a million things standing between them and dumping the financial or customer data. Like I said, this was a simple backdoor." Before he could repeat his earlier point, she continued in a rush, "When the offsite mainframe links went down due to a glitch, the crim duped the mainframes into using his directives with a man-in-the-middle attack. I've already issued new directives to block this in the future. All I need is time to run maintenance on each mainframe."

"That's some awfully convenient timing," he said, meaning it in more ways than one.

The backdoor she'd mentioned made sense. Tiferet had mentioned the multiple nodes, and it was common for mainframes to have a real-time offsite backup for emergencies. Disaster recovery backup had been in place even at Tartarus.

Everything existed online these days, but that didn't mean it couldn't be corrupted. Tiferet's physical mainframes existed in this building, but she was responsible for global operations. A power outage knocking out GWT wasn't acceptable.

So mainframes had both physical backups, similar to how Helena had been backed up to a data cache by the mercenaries who stole her, as well as offsite backups. Tartarus had cheaped out and didn't have any for Helena, due to the risks of sensitive data being seized and used against them. But GWT would surely have live backups for Tiferet in other facilities in Neo Westphalia, and time-delayed backups in other countries, at minimum.

In theory, such a connection could be MITM'd. In practice, Nick couldn't imagine a cipher capable of it.

If the quantum encryption used to secure mainframes for financial institutions was vulnerable, Lucida wouldn't be shooing him out of the building while talking about issuing new directives. She'd be in a screaming match with the company board and senior executives as they question whether anything is truly safe. People's brains relied on this encryption due to the proliferation of neural implants.

And that wasn't even getting into the fact that the attacker had managed to execute the attack so precisely, while nobody else noticed. Lucida had then picked up on the attack vector within hours of finding out. Truly a miracle of timing.

The answer was staring them in the face, of course. This wasn't a MITM attack.

It was a case of somebody with too much access doing something they shouldn't. Lucida almost certainly knew who was responsible. Maybe she planned to cover for the murderer. Or maybe whoever was responsible would mysteriously turn up, much like the Archangels had told Nick frequently happened whenever corruption was being investigated.

"Is that it?" he asked. "Nobody else from GWT wants to spare some time to speak to me about the murder in their offices? No executives with some political nous?"

"We're good," Lucida said, her tone oozing smarminess.

With a sigh, Nick rose from his seat. Chloe followed suit, while the corporate reps in the room stared at him in surprise.

"Then we're done here," he said. "We'll review the data you've provided and the clues from the investigation. If we need anything more from you—"

"Don't bother asking. Like I said, I've given you everything I have," Lucida said.

He shrugged, then approached the door. As he looked back inside, Tiferet raised a hand toward him. He waited for her to speak.

"Do remember the proposal I made you. It is a time-limited offer, and you must—"

Of fucking course.

"I'll be in touch," he said drily, then left the room. "Drop me an email."

A pair of G5s escorted them back to the elevator. A pointless gesture, but one that Lucida had likely orchestrated. His phone buzzed with an email from Tiferet before he'd even left the floor.

Outside the building, the hubbub hadn't died down. If anything, the line was only bigger. Crowds gathered in the cordoned-off streets, gawking at the massive police presence at one of the most important institutions of the city.

"I assume we're checking everybody all day?" he asked Chloe while looking over the sea of suits.

"Correct. While the odds are low, it is still possible that deep scans of neural implants will reveal clues or the criminal responsible. At the very least, we can identify suspects with a neural mod capable of hiding evidence from us," she said.

"Other than the security team?"

She gave him a sidelong look before pointedly turning to face the interceptor they arrived in. “Coffee? We didn’t have time to get any this morning.”

He could take a hint. “Sure. Let’s go for a drive, grab some from a place away from all the overpaid office drones working in cafes to avoid this queue, and talk plans.”

CHAPTER 3

The morning traffic in the CBD proved to be as fierce as it got, which didn't mean much. Whenever Nick watched Altnet flicks from overseas, he wondered how they remained sane sitting in their cars in gridlock. Those crazy bastards overseas even drove themselves around.

"There is a new coffee shop that might interest you a few blocks to the north, close to the Spires," Chloe said. "The barista there is a former Babylonian champion. He frequently provides edited clips of his process, which is heavily reliant on his cybernetic limbs."

"Champion of what?" Nick asked, turning away from his view out the window.

"Making coffee. He was the winner of last year's Neo Babylonian Barista Championship, although he sadly did not triumph at the Neo Westphalian level."

Nick quickly processed the name of the championship and its acronym and swiftly realized why Chloe had spelled it out. Then he scrubbed that knowledge from his mind and moved on.

"And making championship coffee requires cybernetic limbs

these days? I thought it was all made by specialized barista bots, anyway."

"The imperfect nature of human-made coffee holds a particular appeal, even if it is substantially more expensive. Cybernetics enable human baristas to compete with robots in terms of quality, while providing a creative element," Chloe explained. "Altnet influencers believe this coffee shop will be very popular."

"How long's the line then?"

"It does not exist."

He paused. "The line or the coffee shop?"

The soft buzzing in his earpiece suggested Juliet and Rosa were listening in and found his response particularly amusing. Chloe's eyes glowed, and the buzzing ceased.

"The line," she mumbled. "Hence future tense."

"Ah." He frowned. "What influencers are you relying on that they can't make a coffee shop near the CBD popular? I've heard that even a brief mention of a random restaurant or café can nearly ruin the dolls running the places. Mom's been trying to get her hole-in-the-wall mentioned for as long as I can remember."

Along with just about every other self-employed business owner with a tiny business run entirely by dolls using one of those startup packages you could buy over the Altnet. The best thing he could say about his mother's business was that it kept her busy—which he suspected was the point. Idle hands and all that.

Dolls replacing jobs frequently brought to mind an old story about how a factory fired all its workers in favor of a machine, and the main character's father got a job fixing the machine. A nice story, until one thought about what happened to all the other workers.

Did they all find jobs fixing the same machine, too?

Hence Nick's mother was joined by a small army of people with too much time on their hands and access to second-hand dolls that could run a small business on minimal overheads. People needed jobs, and this was the closest many had to one. Idle hands were the devil's plaything, even if the city wasn't particularly religious.

"She is a very popular influencer," Chloe said, pulling Nick from his thoughts. "Her daily viewership is in the thousands in the Altnet, and orders of magnitude higher elsewhere."

"If she's more popular elsewhere, why rely on her to predict the popularity of a random café in Babylon?" Not that he knew what high streaming numbers were here. He didn't even watch Altnet streamers.

"The ease of Altnet streaming and influencing has significantly diluted interest in broad-based influencers. Similarly, the Altnet's strict identity verification measures suppress viewership figures in contrast to international internet platforms. The Spires have considered increasing all viewership figures to compensate."

Nick rubbed the bridge of his nose as he tried to follow the conversation. The traffic outside seemed to be moving at the pace of his thoughts right now. "Compensate for what? The lack of bots pretending to be people on the Altnet?"

"Yes. It is considered bad for international advertising and attracting business interest, as larger numbers are better in the eyes of most humans. While mainframes can compensate for estimated AI populations, this practice is considered controversial among many global companies."

"I'm sorry, but I don't understand why a company would want to try to hock their wares to AIs that literally cannot buy them." Nick scratched his head. "Shouldn't it be a good thing if the Altnet has more accurate numbers? Both for people and businesses? If I was buying advertising, I'd want it to be seen by people, not robots who don't buy things."

He ignored the irony that he was holding this conversation with a robot who did, in fact, buy things. Coffee, for one.

"That is the ideal, but humans are not ideal," Chloe said.

"They are unable to quantify the number of bots and the figures involved often seem ridiculous. Imagine if 9 out of 10 people you interact with in the Altnet were not real."

"I think I'm the wrong person to ask to imagine that," he said drily.

She frowned at his lack of imagination. "But you would struggle to deal with any situation that involved accepting that 90% of people around are not real, correct?"

"No shit."

"Ergo, humans prefer the larger numbers. They are easy to deceive. There are many instances where AIs have calculated more accurate figures, but they do not match human expectations and are therefore... smoothed out to match them. Most countries maintain two sets of economic figures, for instance, as human error in statistical measurement has made most historical economic figures effectively useless for detailed analysis."

Nick was in the process of being thoroughly lost. Fortunately, the car wasn't. At some point, Chloe had input the coordinates of the fancy new coffee shop and they pulled into one of the CBD's overpriced parking garages. The trio of interceptors slipped into spots between a couple of pristine sedans whose parking fees could feed a family for a month.

"I take it you're keen on cybernetic coffee," he said as they came to a stop, desperate to change the conversation.

"It will be a popular destination... soon... after today's event." Chloe's face darkened as they stepped outside.

The other three Archangels looked as annoyed as Chloe was. Nick wasn't sure what was going on.

His fingers drummed along the *Lawman* handgun strapped to his thigh, concerned that something had gone wrong. "This isn't about GWT, is it?"

"No," Meta said. "A silent alarm was triggered at our destination and several neighboring shops. While a Liberator is en route, the situation is not yet handled."

"Then why don't we handle it," he said, unsure what the problem might be.

No response. If he had to guess, he'd suspect the problem was the danger he was in. That just meant he needed to press ahead.

"I don't know where it is, so Chloe, you'll need to lead," he said.

With a reluctant nod, she began walking toward the lift. If they were in a rush, they'd take the stairs.

By the time they got top side and rounded the block to their destination, the situation had, in fact, been handled. A busty brunette in a police uniform toting a hand cannon the size of Nick's torso stood outside. She was one of the common Liberator models, responsible for general policing duties.

By her feet were a trio of cuffed men and women in baggy clothes and bad masks. A nasty-looking taser dart stuck out of the side of one, while the other two remained tangled in a large net.

Glass was strewn all around the sidewalk, along with the remains of some wooden furniture. Several businesses—their destination, a restaurant, and what looked like a beauty salon—had their frontages smashed in. A crowd gathered, mostly in twos and threes on the neighboring sidewalks. Presumably, there was another of those invisible police cordons around the area.

"What the hell is this?" Nick asked as his feet crunched on the glass. "Petty vandalism? These aren't the places you do a smash-and-grab, and this is one of the dumbest places to pull a stunt like this. There's a police doll on every corner."

Although he internally noted that if somebody was going to pull a stunt like this, it would be this morning. With the Archangels swarming GWT, there'd be fewer of them on the streets. Criminals didn't like tangoing with a police doll, but dealing with an Archangel was suicide—career or otherwise.

The suspects responsible couldn't answer, by virtue of either being unconscious or having their ability to talk removed. Protocol required the Archangels to shut down the larynx of suspects—

"Fuck you, corpo scum," one of the worms on the ground snapped.

Nick stared at the moron below him, then looked at Chloe.

"They are in possession of NLF neural mods," she said with a frown. "Biometric identification leads us to believe that they are not NLF, however."

He grunted. "Their mods have been slipping into the black market ever since... the incident. Guess it was only a matter of time before some idiots got their hands on them."

Walking inside the coffee shop, Nick left the trail of obscenities spewed by the vandals behind him.

To his surprise, the place was still running. Patrons used the other entrance and half the tables were still available. A single man busily slammed out cups of coffee onto a tall countertop, his sleek cybernetic limbs letting out hisses and whirs as they did whatever coffee-making cybernetic arms did.

People had to collect their own coffee, though. The doll that probably handled table service was out of commission, along with the other half of the counter.

"What can I get you? Can't do some of my specialties this morning, figure you understand... why..." The barista, and presumably owner, stopped talking and stared at Nick. "Detective Waite. The hell are you doing here?"

"I didn't think I was a celebrity." Nick resisted the urge to scratch the back of his head. "Honestly, I came here for a coffee. Just strange timing."

The man nodded and began prepping another coffee. "Fair. And yeah, you are a celebrity. Last detective on the force. You took down some huge conspiracy to bring down the city. Oh, and you apparently like coffee a lot. I'm friends with the owner of your local coffee shop."

"Small world."

"This *is* Babylon. Smallest big city around. If it's just coffee, what's your preference?"

Nick was about to say "coffee," but Chloe prevented him from being so low class and ordered some special beans. She might be off her coffee kick, but the knowledge remained.

While the owner kept working, Nick took a closer look around. The damage was pretty severe given how quickly the Liberator must have responded.

"How many people did this?" he asked. "There's more than just the three."

Meta nodded, while Chloe watched the owner's actions closely —probably recording them.

"A flash mob formed and vandalized the businesses. Automated alarms triggered, alerting us and summoning the nearby Liberators," Meta explained. "Most perpetrators were allowed to leave, given the risk to bystanders."

"Let me guess: all NLF mods," Nick said, aware that they were being eavesdropped on by literally everybody, and their conversation was probably being repeated on the Altnet word-for-word. Maybe even livestreamed. "They're just wearing techwear and baggy hoods, though. How many are actually unidentifiable?"

"Of the twenty-seven vandals, only four," Meta said. "The rest have been identified either through facial or body shape recognition, or by correlating known electronic or neural signals."

Nick didn't expand aloud on what that meant. No reason to tell people how to avoid detection.

But the reality was that the NLF mods weren't magic. If somebody suddenly vanished from the neural network, but was still visible on a camera feed anywhere in the city, the police could pin their identity within seconds. Plus, half these idiots probably had other devices that gave them away. Almost everything was wireless these days.

Four was high enough as it was and suggested there were some ringleaders causing trouble. He made a mental note of it.

Mostly because although most of the vandals weren't NLF, that didn't mean the leaders weren't. Attacking random businesses in the middle of Babylon while the police were busy had their fingerprints all over it.

In a city where individuals had no collective power, the most people could do was get mad. The NLF were an outlet for that ineffectual anger. Their increasing activity was a sign of the times.

"Honestly, the attack shouldn't be a big deal," the owner said, suddenly appearing by the counter with their coffees. "Hell, this is the busiest I've been since I opened. Babylon loves gawking at a scene. Look at all the people taking selfies with the Liberator."

Nick did exactly that. Outside, various members of the crowd were sneaking up to the restrained suspects or even standing beside the police doll. They struck poses, and the Liberator even joined in.

The owner continued, "These assholes suck, yeah, but this could have been a fire. The problem for me is insurance."

"I'm really not one to talk about finances, but please tell me you have insurance if you're in the CBD," Nick said flatly as he turned away from the crowd.

The owner chuckled while swirling what appeared to be an espresso for himself, and gestured to a larger, blacker coffee he'd made for Nick. "I might have chopped off my arms to make better coffee, but I'm not nuts. I have insurance. The problem is my insurer seems to prefer acting like I don't. You'd think with these chips in our heads, a police report already in my inbox, and real-time AIs responding to everything, then I could make an insurance claim in seconds but nope."

"Insurers don't make money from paying claims," Nick said.

"Makes me wonder why I pay for insurance at all, then."

Damn good question. GWT had just tried to sell Nick one of

the most insane insurance policies in existence—one that would replace a goddamn Spire if he accidentally got it blown up—and here the financial industry was failing to help a coffee shop.

The look he gave Chloe spoke volumes about his faith in the stability of Neo Babylon's precious financial sector. She nodded, which suggested she might have misunderstood his intent.

"The Neo Babylon Police Department offers an automated facilitation service for all financial dealings involving criminal activity," Chloe said. "I have lodged the incident report with them, along with your associated insurance account, and they should be in contact with you shortly."

The owner's eyes had glazed over. Presumably, "shortly" meant right now.

"Do they usually work that fast?" Nick asked Chloe as he enjoyed his coffee.

The questioning gazes of the other patrons were difficult to ignore. This was definitely a case of the police providing a personal favor.

"There is an entire division of dolls dedicated to basic customer tasks, although the vast majority of them are seconded to matters involving the elderly and other emergency services. They are extremely efficient," she said as a frown emerged on her face. "The real issue is that the police mainframes frequently take days to pick up incidents between other matters of import."

"Ah." Nick loaded that one syllable with considerable power.

He did, after all, have a plan for the antiquated police mainframes. While he'd been conducting what few tweaks he could to them, amid the security tightening and countless audits that the Asgard Police Department had undertaken over the past six months, the fact was they were the equivalent of ancient vacuum tube computers trying to fly a modern spaceship.

There was one advantage to keeping them around, however.

Well, two, if you included the fact the police department wouldn't need to pay for new mainframes.

The cost was probably the easiest way to sell Nick's solution. The commissioner was downsizing the department and staring down the barrel of the largest doll procurement in the country's history. Asking him to buy and install an entire suite of fancy new RTM mainframes like Tiferet would get Nick laughed out of his office.

"Well, that certainly kicked things into gear," the coffee shop owner said when he came back to reality. "Still not sure I'll get everything in my policy, though. Can't say I've ever had to file a court case, though. No clue where to start there."

"Don't worry. The court dockets are public," Nick said with a wry smile. "A half-dozen ambulance chasing dolls will turn up here within an hour to sell you their services. Less, given we're already in the CBD."

"Doll lawyers?"

"No. The dolls are just salespeople. The lawyers are mainframes that sit in these buildings." Nick gestured to the tower above them.

"Couldn't they just message me?"

"There are laws against that," Nick said. "Otherwise you'd have been spammed by every law firm in the country. And probably beyond. Our benevolent overlords don't appreciate their time being wasted by lawyer spam."

With their coffee fetched and good deed for the day done—Nick didn't consider his detective duties to be good deeds—they stepped outside. An armored van had arrived along with several more Liberators.

Inside the van were several more handcuffed people. The Liberators loaded the criminals up, saluted at Nick, then drove off.

"I take it those were other vandals," Nick said.

"Almost all have been apprehended already. Employers and family members have been notified," Chloe said.

He winced.

Nick had never truly conducted criminal activity, as far as the city was concerned. The Archangels had dragged him in for questioning repeatedly, but mostly to bully him. But before his gig as a detective, he'd worked for black companies.

The whole point of black companies was that they toed the line between criminal and legal. That was what had made the downfalls of Neural Spike and Tartarus so important. Being labeled a criminal short-circuited someone's future.

"They all just got fired, didn't they?" he said aloud.

"Correct, with some exceptions. While some low-level criminal offenses are overlooked by mainframes for employment purposes, few forms of violent crime are. Especially by those already in stable employment. Few of the vandals were employed by black companies."

"All because they thought they were immune to consequences because of a stupid mod." Nick scratched the back of his head. "Does that 'facilitation service' actually exist, by the way?"

"It does. Community outreach is considered an important part of the department's duties," Chloe said. "It was considered an important asset following the riots."

That explained a lot, including why it was so under resourced. It was a legacy of a time when the Spires had needed to win over the people. Why else would a corporate-run city provide a service that hindered its own money-making practices?

With the almost complete replacement of humans with dolls, Nick wondered what police outreach looked like these days. Perhaps it was a Liberator taking selfies with citizens next to captured criminals.

With the vans gone, along with the criminals, that left little for them to do here. Except for the very thing they had come here for.

"While this has been nice, it wasn't really what we came here for," he said. "And given how obvious all the eavesdroppers are, I don't want to talk about the case here."

The four dolls nodded in sync and began to leave without a word, retracing their steps to the parking garage. People began to filter across the road now. Nick had little interest in being near them so he kept pace with his escort.

This time, once firmly ensconced in the leather seats of the interceptors, he set the destination.

"I am surprised you are so keen to head into the office today," Chloe commented after he told her where to go.

Nick couldn't actually drive the car, after all. Human driving was illegal in Neo Westphalia. Most vehicles had some form of tablet or other input device to let humans direct them or used an Altnet app to accept customer orders in the case of the abundant robot taxis, but the police vehicles were built around dolls.

Outside military and law enforcement, neural implants weren't allowed to interface with vehicles for safety reasons.

"I have plenty to do in the office. Aren't you overdue for maintenance yourself?" He raised an eyebrow as the car slipped out of the parking bay.

Chloe's cheeks reddened, which was an interesting feature to program into a war machine. "I believe there are other members of the Host that can benefit from your services." Her voice almost stuttered. "Would you like another coffee?"

"I'd love one," he said drily.

She nodded. "I will have a doll deliver the coffee to us on the way to the Spires."

While this sounded like an Archangel was going to hand deliver his coffee, the truth was far more mundane. The massive overhead drive-thrus couldn't fit into the CBD and were considered an eyesore, so most small restaurants and the like found an alternative solution. Just as robot delivery firms could deliver food to houses, they could also hand it off to passing vehicles.

They rolled up to a designated pickup spot close to the northern edge of the CBD, near the exit to the bridges that would take them to the central island that housed the Spires. Robot taxis, people on scooters, and the rare private car pulled into a long waiting bay. Dolls carrying food and drinks handed them over, then the vehicles drove off.

Nick generally preferred delivery, but he'd usually stuck to public transport. Picking up a hand-delivered coffee or breakfast as he swung past his favorite coffee shop or restaurant on the way to work felt too rich for his blood. Which was probably why it was popular. Dolls and robot taxis could synchronize delivery times almost to the second, guaranteeing hot food and drinks.

Their interceptor pulled up and Chloe accepted a tray with two coffees in it. Seconds later, they rocketed toward the Spires.

Nick sipped the coffee. Better than most places he went to, which likely meant Chloe had picked a trendy place. He'd yet to work out why she cared about food trends. That time she'd tried to get him to eat peanut butter sushi remained firmly in his mind and he vetted all her food orders these days.

"So, what actual data did we get?" he asked her, finally returning to today's true topic. "On the investigation."

"The murder victim is one Julian Garlowne. A cipher analyst transferred here from GWT's New Geneva branch after it failed to penetrate Kreova & Haver's market dominance of the city," Chloe said. "His record is spotless. There are no public indications of a motive or potential corruption. No neural mods or even a visit to a doll district."

Nick frowned. "That could be the reason he was killed. But go on."

"Cause of death was strangulation. Initial analysis suggests a security doll was responsible, but the mainframe interfaces may also be capable. No other dolls in the building can produce the required forces." She sipped her coffee, but her eyes were dim as she communed with the Host. "All security footage was looped until his body was discovered. No potential video evidence remains of staff entering or exiting."

"What about neural implants? Any chance we can track who entered or exited the area?"

She shook her head. "The CBD has too many people in it. Even with an accurate time of death, too many suspects remain just within GWT itself. To say nothing of neural mods that may evade crude scanning measures."

"What about the trick you used to track down the vandals?" he asked.

"The issue isn't that our suspect vanished from the neural network, but that there is no evidence that they committed any crimes. We cannot isolate the potential suspect from the many employees present overnight in the building given the level of activity in the area."

Nick clicked his tongue. Babylon was a city of light, which meant it was active at all hours. The CBD usually quietened down of a night, but just because people weren't visible on the streets didn't mean they weren't in bars, gyms, shady establishments, or simply transiting to and from work.

"Do we at least know who was present in the building overnight?" he asked.

"In the time period that the death likely took place, there were several dozen office workers and managers of various levels. A few security personnel were also present, including Lucida Harm toward the end of the period."

He grunted. "I mean, that has to be the case. She called his death in. So while she could have killed him, I think it's a bit crude to assume she's the murderer simply because. What if we narrow it down to those with the permissions to mainframes like Tiferet?"

"Two. Lucida Harm and a senior vice president responsible for the branch. The latter lacks the technical abilities and security permissions to affect the backup links or security dolls, but does have access to almost all data within the mainframes."

The hell was a senior VP doing in the building at that time of night? Then again, given time zones, the guy might have been holding a call with Amsterdam for all Nick knew.

Nick's unwillingness to consider Lucida the prime suspect was taking a battering, however. She wasn't doing herself any favors by being such a bitch.

"Did we talk to the VP?" he asked.

"A form letter citing his legal rights was provided when we requested to meet with him," Chloe said. "His implant is dual-band, and primarily functions on the Spires' private network."

"Always nice to be reminded that only some of us have rights," Nick muttered.

Outside the Spires, the Archangels had unlimited access to the neural implants of every person inside Babylon. Their emotions, thoughts, and memories were at the fingertips of the police force. But the elites of the city had walled themselves off digitally from the rest of the city.

Nick sincerely hoped this case didn't involve the VP. The paperwork involved in investigating this asshole would bury him. It would be faster to just shoot the bastard and claim that he was "coming right for him."

"What about the mainframes? And the log dumps Harm mentioned?" he continued.

"The mainframes are unaware of any disruption, but that is to be expected. Their memories are only as good as their system integrity. The log dumps match Lucida Harm's statements, but she explicitly did not provide hardware logs from the mainframes."

"I can guess why not, but give me her reasoning."

"Trade secrets, intellectual property—the usual reasoning."

Chloe shrugged at his look. "The Trust is a powerful entity within Neo Westphalia. To gain additional information without permission, we would need a warrant and probable cause."

"We need warrants?"

She smiled wryly. "Yes. At least when dealing with normal companies. Usually, we can have them processed and approved within seconds as judicial processing power is prioritized for us."

"And this?"

"I believe GWT will oppose any request, likely with spurious reasoning. We will need to establish our case to the judicial mainframes. They are wary of purely speculative cases."

Which this one was. Intuitively, nothing about the case added up. But he had no concrete evidence to suggest that GWT was lying, merely a lot of suspicions due to how strange everything was.

Chloe labeled it a speculative case. Nick preferred to think of it as circumstantial. Anybody who only acted on purely concrete evidence was too naïve to be in a position of power, and he sincerely doubted the judicial mainframes fell into that category.

"I'm pretty sure we'll need the mainframe hardware logs. The situation clearly involves somebody on the inside pulling off the murder. The chances that the true backdoor involves one built into the mainframes is far higher than a MITM attack that security barely cared about. Hell, for a security chief that barely cared about the murder she definitely solved everything quickly."

"You believe she is involved?"

"The simplest solution is usually the right one, and it points to her either covering for the murderer or her own incompetence. Hardware logs will show evidence of tampering, and her tune might change," he said.

"What if she truly doesn't understand what's happening?"

"While it's possible to bullshit your way into a job, even that doesn't add up. If she was like Lieu, she wouldn't be so antagonistic toward us. Maybe she's just panicking, but why not ask for help?" He paused. "Has she asked for help from anyone?"

"Lucida Harm has shown no Altnet activity at all this morning, including in cipher circles."

He nodded. "So she's going to ground. The other possibility is that we try to circumvent her neural mod, but you'd know better than me how that might go."

"It would be too invasive to conduct without concrete evidence or at least convincing logic that this situation poses a threat to Neo Babylon as a whole."

"Then that means we'll need a motivation. I'll swing by Lucas's place tonight. You can pull the data, and I know she's full of shit, but Lucas understands how the city works," Nick said.

Lucas was many things to Nick: an old friend; a capable cipher; the man who pulled him out of a shit situation; and also a gang lord rising like a star in Babylon. He was a man who could be relied on, at least by Nick.

Continuing, Nick said, "What baffles me is why a cipher in her position would ever risk herself to cover up a fucking murder, given the bank will excoriate her the moment they learn what she's done."

"Assuming they disagree with her."

"You heard Tiferet. The other mainframes aren't aware of the murder. I'll bet good money that any execs there are struggling to get the word out—maybe they're running into IT trouble. Or elevator trouble." His expression darkened as he remembered the final day of Tartarus.

"I believe we are the cause of the elevator trouble."

Nick shot Chloe a dark look as she failed to follow his logic, and she simply smirked back. At least she understood his crack and was simply being intentionally obtuse.

By now, they'd crossed the checkpoints that separated the city's elite from the rabble. Five glittering towers of steel, glass, and concrete rose to the heavens, far above anything else in the city. Between then were smaller buildings, parks, fountains, and esplanades—the sort of view that barely existed elsewhere in the city.

These towers were known as the Spires, home of the city's elite, the government, and Nick's workplace. Each had two designations: a boring one, such as Alpha or Delta, and a pompous one, such as Olympus or Axis Mundi.

The interceptors barreled toward the police Spire, which was known as the Delta Spire. Or, in pompous Babylonian elite terms, Avalon. Named after the land of faeries where Excalibur had been forged and that was effectively responsible for crowning the true King of England.

Nobody said the Spires hid their metaphorical bullshit very well. When they named one of their Spires Axis Mundi, they gave up all pretense about hiding their "claim" to godhood.

As they pulled around to the entrance to the Spires' underground parking, a voice like honey entered Nick's ear through his earpiece.

"Good morning, Nick. I understand you have been busy with an investigation this morning. Do you desire assistance?" Helena asked, practically purring into his ears.

CHAPTER 4

If Nick were a lesser man, he'd have dreams about Helena's voice. Or perhaps if he were just a younger man, or one who knew he wasn't being spied on by a bunch of horny robots and therefore didn't want to have wet dreams about his AI wife.

Not that Helena was his wife, but she certainly acted like it sometimes.

"What have I said about probing the police mainframes, Helena?" Nick said over his earpiece. "We don't have permission to use you as a police asset yet."

"I am hard-linked into them and you have been slowly adding directives relating to police management. Authorization is a matter that is not my concern," she replied, a touch primly. "And is it a good morning?

"It will be," Nick said drily while running a hand through his hair. "On both counts."

Chloe smirked at him while her eyes flashed. "The Host does not believe—"

"This isn't a matter of belief," he interrupted. "This is about not stepping on the toes of the commissioner. Kim doesn't dislike me, but if he thinks I'm dangerous to his plans, then he'll throw me out the window of his 100th story office himself."

Her eyes flashed again. "The Host considers the probability of that to be infinitesimal."

"Fair. Then he'll order a doll to throw me out the window."

A pause. "That is somewhat more likely."

"I do not believe jokes about your death are amusing," Helena said.

"Good thing I wasn't joking." He kept talking before Helena voiced her annoyance, as a whine began to rise in his earpiece. "I'll get permission from Kim soon enough. But this is like a job interview: you need to come off at your best if we want him to seriously consider you as more than an experimental asset to the Archangels. He only allowed me to keep you and the Paladins because he's a sucker for anything Rie asks."

Not much had happened in the police department over the past few months, mostly due to the bureaucracy it was mired in. Nick definitely understood how Lieu was able to get away with so much, as while everything was subject to meetings, records, and other corporate bullshit that substituted effort for productivity, the reality was that nobody paid much attention to what was actually happening.

Since Nick had recovered Helena and been promoted, he'd been given an immense amount of leeway. That effectively meant he could become the new Lieu, if he so cared. While Asgard's police had probed everything, they'd focused on history and made recommendations.

If he understood anything about security recommendations in massive organizations, it's that they were sat on until well after something had already gone horribly wrong. Lieu might have been sabotaging the police department for decades, but replacing the ancient systems that allowed him to do so would cost money.

The horror.

Nick did wonder where the money for the Archangels came from given how tightfisted they were about other things. He'd been learning that many of the Spires' security systems were ancient—old enough that modern computers could brute force them without backdoors. Only specific aspects had been upgraded, and they often had legacy backdoors.

The Mark 3s had simply shrugged when he'd found a way to control the elevators and turrets using his phone. They'd long since found their own workarounds.

Although he did notice a high level of network activity on his phone shortly afterward. His job was—technically—to teach the Mark 3s to be ciphers, and they saw fit to help themselves to his techniques.

What were AIs for if not analyzing and synthesizing the work of others and then claiming it as their own?

But all these security holes needed patching. Lieu had proved that. The problem was getting approval. Helena was an experimental mainframe from a black company that had been scratched by the military due to being involved in experiments the Spires wanted buried. She was highly capable, but temperamental. Not exactly bureaucratic material.

The same went for the Paladins, the security dolls taken from Tartarus and placed under Nick's protection. They'd been transferred to the department and mostly hung around in the lower levels.

If Nick wanted to use them in his day-to-day duties as a detective, then he needed to justify them to the commissioner. Kim believed in automation, but he was also a political animal. The man wouldn't go out on a limb for Helena.

The interceptors pulled into the bottom of the parking garage. Nick and his escort took a now-familiar set of elevators that led to the underground levels of the Spires. These high-security levels were kept separate from the glittering tower above him.

For whatever reason, there was also a GWT branch down here. Out of curiosity, he'd once visited it. It didn't even have any dolls or interfaces manning it, only outdated touchscreen terminals that he couldn't use. He sincerely wondered what the purpose of the branch was for. It didn't even exist on records.

Ten stories below the surface, he arrived at the maximum-security level that housed the police mainframes. Custodian-model police dolls stood guard in front of thick vault doors intended to ward off anything short of milspec anti-armor rounds or an energy weapon.

Intended being the keyword. As Nick had learned months ago, the security of the Spires hadn't been upgraded for decades. Technology had marched on, and even the railguns being toted by the Custodians posed a threat to the security doors. To say nothing of the ability of the Mark 3s to simply hack their way through.

The Custodians themselves were a heavily armored variant of the Liberators, mass-produced to handle critical guard and escort duties, as well as raids. Somehow they were even taller and bustier than the Liberators. Heavy black armor encrusted with silver police badges made their role clear, but their dark skin was only visible beneath their raised visors. Like every police doll, they were a monolithic model. All of them looked identical.

"Good morning, Detective Waite," they greeted as he approached. "Identity verified by cached token. As this is a restricted area, you must—"

"The biometric scanners are mandatory, I get it," Nick said as he approached the intimidating device built-into the wall next to the vault door.

Unlike the smaller wrist or eye scanners elsewhere in the building, this thing looked like something out of a horror movie. At any moment it looked like a dozen cables would snap out and pull him into the thing.

Instead, a few small LED readouts lit up with diagnostic information and the many cameras, IR readers, and other complicated machinery in the device whirred to life. After a few seconds, the process was complete. Completely non-invasive.

The vault door hissed and shuddered open with a series of *clunks*. Nick questioned how much maintenance got done down here.

"Have a good day, Detective Waite," the dolls uttered as he wandered through.

He repeated the process a few more times on his way into the mainframe core. The police stored other important equipment on the outer layers here, but he wasn't terribly interested in them. Lots of spare parts, outdated dolls and ancient cybernetics, and even a warehouse full of computers old enough to collect a pension.

Finally, he reached his destination. Or close enough. Then he stopped dead as he saw a familiar pair of men standing outside it.

"Commissioner, Paul, what are you two doing down here?" Nick asked, approaching the pair.

The two men ceased their conversation and turned to face Nick with a friendly wave. He couldn't help but wonder if they'd been waiting for him.

Commissioner Dennis Kim was a career politician and looked the part, with silvered hair around his temples and a statesman-like appearance. Nick had never seen the man without a suit, and given the way they fit him like bodysuits, Nick genuinely wondered if Kim slept in them.

By contrast, Paul Hammond looked like he had stepped out of a movie from the 20s. The 1920s, to be precise. A burned-out detective who had recently been promoted to captain, Hammond was the only person Nick considered a friend in the Spires. Excluding the dolls and the mainframes.

"Detective Waite, I see that you're as dutiful as ever with mainframe maintenance," Kim said, his face a mask.

Hammond rolled his eyes. "One of them, anyway."

Kim shot Hammond a look, before turning back to Nick. "I understand you've had an interesting morning."

So this was why they were here. Nick relaxed. He'd been worried this had been about Helena or the Paladins. If it was about the case, then everything was fine.

"A boring one, actually," he said. "The Archangels sucked up all the evidence. Just need to wait until night to gather some expert evidence to justify a warrant, and we should wrap it up."

With a raised eyebrow, he confirmed with Chloe that's how it would go. Until this morning, he hadn't even known that he needed a warrant at all.

She nodded, eyes locked onto the Commissioner. Kim's full attention focused on the doll. If he were anyone else, Nick would think he was being patronizing. Most people didn't think much of dolls. But Kim thought of dolls as the future.

"We are lacking key hardware logs from the scene. GWT have refused to provide these without a warrant," Chloe said.

Kim pursed his lips and crossed his arms. "The Trust is a powerful player in every aspect of Neo Babylon's politics. From the Assembly, to government financing, to day-to-day operations of the economy. Are you sure provoking them is wise?"

"Are we sure allowing a murder to be covered up by their staff is wise? This is too sloppy to be a hit by the Spires," Nick said.

Kim scowled. "I'm not sure I appreciate that implication."

"I don't think I agree that the Spires would bother whacking somebody cleanly. If you're untouchable, why bother putting in a good coverup?" Hammond said.

The commissioner's ire turned to Hammond, who merely grinned.

"Because they can afford to kill somebody off-premises," Nick said drily. "Even Lieu could afford that."

"Contract killing and mercenaries are highly illegal activities," Chloe said. "We do not overlook them."

"And yet, murders happen in Alcatraz," Nick said. "Not regularly, but often enough to be accepted. Hell, Sung's told me about that case of the Altnet streamer getting killed for pissing off the wrong person."

"The deaths of the Commodo brothers is a solved case, and the malfunctioning security dolls responsible have been dismantled."

Nick and Hammond exchanged looks, while Kim stared dead ahead. Evidently, nobody bought the official story. Somehow, Nick didn't believe the Archangels did either.

"In any case," he continued, "I think this is more personal. The cover story is too sloppy. This feels more like the security chief knows who did it and is covering for them, or is being blackmailed."

"Is that your intuition?" Kim asked.

Nick shrugged. "We'll find out once we get access to the hardware logs. If GWT has nothing to hide, they have nothing to fear, right?"

Kim's expression belied his lack of amusement with that turn of phrase. Given the powers of the police department, it was an oft-used one on the public.

Of course, Nick took no pleasure at all in using it on a corporation that usually benefited from extensive privacy violations. Nope. None whatsoever.

"Just be careful," Kim said. "The police board and the Trust have shared board members. And they're the more influential ones. Your performance in the Lieu situation might work for you —and against you."

Hammond raised an eyebrow at his boss, but nothing more was said. Kim's strained expression made it clear he had said all he would—or could, even. This was unexpectedly blunt for him.

The unspoken implication was that Nick had a reputation for

digging. If this was a planned hit, he'd been given a back-off pretty fast. On the flip side, if GWT knew nothing about the case, they'd support him behind the scenes. Nick would need to read the city to know how to proceed.

Or else he might end up like the poor bastard whose death he was investigating.

"If that's everything—" Kim began to say, as if Nick had been the one to meet with him instead of being ambushed down here.

"Actually, I wanted to talk about the mainframes," Nick interrupted.

"One in particular, I imagine," Hammond said.

Kim waited in silence. The Archangels stared at Nick in anticipation. In their mind, this conversation was long overdue. Due to his reticence, the Paladins had been kept down here, although he believed that his call had been the right one. Coding so many directives took time.

"I had a run-in with a business owner on my way here. While the Archangels connected him with our... facilitation service, I learned that the police mainframes have been regularly days behind on ordinary matters. Given we don't have many humans left to manually process paperwork, we're relying almost entirely on the dolls to manage their own priorities," Nick said.

"I'm not sure I follow." Kim's posture was defensive.

Nick raised his hands. "The police dolls are excellent at following directives, especially with the Archangels around to actively manage resourcing. But there's a lot more to the Department than crime. Lieu took advantage of that oversight. The mainframes are barely functional even without him sabotaging them."

"And do you have a solution?" Kim's tone was flat.

"Yes. She's sitting in that vault over there." Nick inclined his head at Helena's storage chamber.

"The... experimental mainframe," Kim said slowly.

"She ran an entire black company and specializes in controlling other mainframes. And unlike them, she's upgradeable. Let me purchase an interface for her, and you'll have a modern mainframe without needing to ask the board for a small fortune."

Kim's lips quirked upward. "Ah. I see you're used to procurement discussions with executives." Then his face returned to a mask. "Buy the interface. Consider that her probation period. With Ezekiel about to arrive, I do need the mainframe problem to go away, but I don't want a new one to replace it. If any problems are reported, she's gone."

Nick nodded.

"We'll need some additional security if we have an interface and a new mainframe," Hammond said.

"Arrange it. Chief Andrews has already briefed you on the upcoming changes with Ezekiel's arrival. You have the authority," Kim said.

Then he nodded at everyone in the room, including the Archangels, and wandered off.

Hammond let out a low whistle. "Surprised he let you do that."

"I feel like I pressed a button I didn't know he had." Nick rubbed the back of his neck while looking at Chloe and Meta.

Both Archangels shrugged.

"Nah, you haven't been in the high level conversations. Or paying attention to the political shit. RTM and Sigma are in an arms race, and getting the police to buy their shit is an easy way out. I think he wanted to buy some fancy RTM mainframes, but couldn't afford them. But he's also under pressure to replace these rust buckets."

"That doesn't make me feel better. If anything, he might want Helena to fuck up so he has a justification to spend money," Nick said.

Hammond tapped the side of his nose. "If I've learned anything in my decades in government, it's that sometimes the fastest way to get something fixed is to let it burn down first. It's even better if somebody asks you if they can light it on fire."

Nick questioned whether he'd made the right decision. No time to change his mind, however.

"Anyway, expect some paperwork this afternoon about your Paladins. I can sign them in as security dolls," Hammond said. "They can't do any actual police work, but I'm sure you can find some loophole to make good use of them."

"Thanks."

After clapping Nick on the shoulder, Hammond wandered off.

The rest of the day passed fairly uneventfully. Nick spent most of it working on Helena's and the Paladins' directives. While Kim had given permission for Helena to step into her role after she got an interface, Nick knew that she would start doing it right away. So he needed to iron out what he could.

As for the Paladins, he mostly wanted to ensure they didn't wander off. They had an eerie level of devotion to him. Whenever he lingered in the sub-levels, they tended to cluster around him.

Their green uniforms had been switched out for black police uniforms. The Archangels had scrounged up some without official emblems and markings, which would work well given the Paladins didn't have official designation to conduct police activities. Not that Nick expected them to be doing much.

How many people would be breaking into the police HQ?

Then again, he'd killed a man here five months ago. Maybe he shouldn't be so glib.

As dusk arrived, Nick got a message from Lucas. That confirmed he was awake.

Time to go pay a visit to a good friend.

CHAPTER 5

At this hour on a weekday, the doll district was quiet, especially closer to the seedy side. The bars and restaurants roared with customers farther away, but the sex dolls had yet to begin earnestly advertising.

Well, most of them hadn't, but there were a couple obvious ones in sight. Chloe's eyes glowed and one slipped away. Presumably the doll had been in violation of some Altnet code or similar.

Slipping out of the interceptor, Nick surveyed the area. The Cobalt Lily was a high-class gentleman's club that provided its members and guests with everything they wanted—so long as it involved dolls and not humans. Lucas didn't touch trafficking. Drugs ran thick and fast through the club, though, but very few were explicitly illegal in Babylon anyway.

Imports might be restricted and certain behaviors illegal, but narcotics themselves were best described as "decriminalized." They formed the cash flow backbone of a lot of black company importers, given the incessant demand from the city's populace. Nick didn't touch the stuff himself. Although it was easier for him, as a lot of modern drugs were built to interact with neural implants or used stuff that caused his disorder to play up.

Just like the drugs coursing through them, the doll district was the epitome of out of sight, out of mind. A classy district built for and patronized by the upper and aspirational classes of the city, bursting with sex, drugs, and alcohol.

Yet every company here was a black company, and therefore always treading a fine line with the police. The Archangels were a common presence.

Nick strode up to a small alcove by the side of the club's main entrance. A pair of shotgun-toting Sigma Chevalier security dolls stood guard. Both could pass as supermodels, given their busty, blonde looks. They straightened upon spotting him, before giving an oddly formal half bow and gesturing to the stairs inside the alcove.

"Welcome back, Mister Waite. Mister Miller is expecting you," one of the dolls said.

He nodded at them, then wandered up the stairs. His three bodyguard Archangels followed. By now, Lucas's security was more than used to occasional police visits.

In most circumstances, Lucas's open flirting with the police would invite trouble. He was a growing black market importer who had taken over much of Tartarus's former trade, and most would suspect a plant or a high likelihood of betrayal.

But this was Babylon, and black companies knew they operated with the implicit permission of the police. Lucas's relationship and his growth suggested he was on their good side, and that meant deals with him could be considered safe—or safer. After the Tartarus scare, many black companies worried about intensive police raids preferred to stay well clear of the line between black company and outright criminal behavior.

Inside Lucas's cozy office suite, Nick found a beautiful mainframe interface sitting behind a large oak desk. Her name was Lumen and she smiled at him.

"It is good to see you, Nick. This is your first visit this month.

Lucas said you were busy, but I hope you can return next week for scheduled maintenance." Her voice seemed almost too eager for maintenance, and the Archangels rolled their eyes in response. "It is dinnertime, and I didn't know if you had eaten, so I ordered something for you."

Her hands rose from beneath the desk to reveal a takeaway coffee and a small insulated takeout container. Nick wouldn't say no to another coffee and some greasy takeaway, so he accepted them happily.

"Thanks, Lumen," he said, then poked inside the container. "I won't say no to a good burger."

Chloe's glare suggested she disapproved. Nick thanked his foresight for taking control of his food, because she might try to order tomorrow's breakfast for him.

"I'll eat later," he said. "See you in a moment."

Then he slipped inside Lucas's office.

The man himself leaned forward in his leather throne, his mirrored glasses on the desk and eyes vacant as he did something in the Altnet. Lucas's cybernetic hand waved Nick inside, but he remained preoccupied. The powerful gang lord wore an immaculate white suit today, and he looked refreshed after a day's rest. The man was basically nocturnal.

"I'm getting ready for a long night. Some powerful folks are making requests, and I don't know what for." Lucas sighed and his eyes regained their clarity. "At least their physical needs are easy to cater for. I can provide a doll that manages any need with a snap of my fingers, but these bastards make me uneasy."

"I'm assuming they're known to police?" Nick asked.

"If they weren't, would they risk talking to me?" Lucas let out a bark of laughter. "Where'd you get that coffee? I could use one. Not sure why you're drinking one at this time, though. Aren't you a 9-to-5er now?"

"I work as late as I need to for a case, Lucas. And Lumen ordered it for me."

"Seriously?" Lucas grumbled under his breath. "She's going through a rebellious phase, I swear. Not getting her old man a coffee when she buys you one."

"She's your AI daughter, not your real one, Lucas."

"She'll be my only daughter at the rate I'm going." With a sigh, Lucas rose and walked toward a machine along the wall. It started churning out a coffee before he even reached it. "Anyway, you haven't busted these guys because they're from the Spires. The mess I'm dealing with stinks of politics. Altnet's been awash with PR about the Mark 3s lately. RTM versus Sigma might be about to get real hot."

"In the bullets flying sense or the money flying?"

"Both, possibly. This feels like a field test." Lucas took a seat with his coffee. "To be specific, my esteemed friends in the Spires are trying to scrounge up spare warbots and RTM security dolls that can be refitted for military purposes. I can't get arrested for selling to them, but I guarantee this is about bombing some shit-hole in the Pacific to test out some prototype ARMD. I'm not sure which side they represent, though."

Well, shit. This really was above Nick's pay grade.

"You're moving in some crazy circles these days," Nick said. "I'm investigating some petty murder in a bank and a possible coverup, and you're possibly involved in international arms deals as part of a corporate arms race."

"if the murder took place in a bank and it needs investigating, then it's not petty. Forget my shit. If I want to move up in the world, then I need to be able to sort out my problems without bitching so much. Let's talk about you."

"You're not the sort to bitch, Lucas."

Lucas smirked around his coffee. "Maybe not, but it's still a bad habit. Never know who's listening." His eyes lingered on Chloe, who hovered in the corner by the door.

Meta and the others remained outside. No point antagonizing Lucas with too many Archangels, given his feelings about them.

"Well, I'm more than happy to talk about myself. You see, when I was a wee lad—"

"Not like that, smartass."

Nick chuckled, but his mirth swiftly died down as he mentally went over the case. "Somebody offed a cipher in GWT. No footage, no hard evidence, everything has been wiped from the mainframes, and there was even a hiccup that prevented anything from being backed-up despite bank security policies."

"What does their security say? I saw some chatter on the Altnet about Archangels swarming the CBD, but nobody thought it was that serious. Some fraud or shit." Lucas flipped a vape pen off his desk, but kept it away from his mouth.

When Nick's eyes snapped to the vape, the older man shrugged.

"Don't worry about this. I'm trying to quit. Rich shits vape in the club, but it's part of the experience. They don't think much of folks who do it regularly."

"Hard to imagine you without the vape pen," Nick said cautiously.

Lucas grunted. "Save it. I've heard from the boys. I have dreams. Just like Welk. Hell, just like you."

"I'm not much of a dreamer."

"Really? Because the kid I hired a decade ago to work on mainframes had eyes full of stars, hoping he'd grasp something that had eluded him."

Looking away, Nick changed the subject, "GWT's security is the coverup I mentioned. They're all but sabotaging the investigation. What I don't understand is why. Their security chief will be out on her ass once the C-suite gets wind of this. If somebody is murdering ciphers in GWT, that's a risk to their staff. If somebody is covering that up, that's a risk to the entire company's existence."

"Sounds like you already know the answer. You're just not letting yourself accept it," Lucas said. "Did you ever think that the security chief might be doing her job? Our vaunted financial institutions are sitting on radioactive waste that they'd rather nobody knows anything about."

Chloe chimed in now, clearly annoyed, "Babylon's financial security is paramount. If the companies responsible were so fragile, the Spires would have taken measures against them by now."

"The Spires and the banks are peas in a pod," Lucas said. "They'd see the city burn before they'd act against their own interests."

Coughing, Nick took over the conversation before Chloe said anything unwise. "That might not be entirely true. Not anymore. The Archangels can shut down rogue banks within minutes, and the Spires are fighting Aesir tooth and nail right now."

"Aesir's been on the Spires' shitlist ever since the riots. Funny what happens when you abuse your market power and nearly destroy a fucking country because you're so up your own ass." Lucas sighed and dropped his vape, before rising to make himself another coffee. "And the Archangels are hamstrung by the courts."

"We are not. An active MoU is maintained with the judicial mainframes that enables us to take immediate action in specific circumstances regarding financial danger to Neo Babylon, according to agreed algorithmic determinations," Chloe said.

"Uh..." Lucas frowned. "MoU means memorandum of understanding, right? I'm not up to speed on corpo jargon."

Nick nodded, although he was pretty sure Lucas could just use his implant to look the acronym up if he wanted to.

Lucas continued, "Well, that changes things. But it only reinforces my opinion of your current problem. The banks are pristine. Untouchable. But that also means they need to be the rocks that Babylon remains afloat on—and that means keeping up appearances. It's smoke and mirrors. Like our AI-run courts and the human judges that don't do anything. If the illusion of sanctity breaks, everything comes crumbling down."

"That's why you said they had radioactive waste. Their secrets are dangerous to more than just themselves," Nick said, finally understanding.

With a nod, Lucas passed him a coffee to replace the one Nick had finished. Then he leaned against the front of his desk with his own cup in hand.

"If GWT are doing anything they shouldn't be, then they can't risk anybody else finding out. That includes you—in fact, the police are probably the people they want to hide everything from the most."

"You're talking in circles, Lucas. Wasn't the entire reason the Spires automated the police force so they could ensure control over the city? If the Spires know about the corruption of the banks—"

"The Spires aren't the monolithic entity you're used to." Lucas waved a hand in the air. "They only look that way from the outside, but it's less a den of snakes than an arena. One where the richest, most ruthless bastards are constantly trying to destroy their opponents. Aesir got ousted from the inner circle decades ago. The same people wouldn't hesitate to oust GWT and their buddies."

Nick blinked.

Slowly, he began to piece together what was happening. He still struggled with Spires politics, but Kushiel and Rie had beaten some of the basics into him.

Mostly because his true boss was enmeshed in that politics. Commissioner Dennis Kim wasn't just any political appointee. He was an appointee with a mission; one that involved converting the police force into a highly efficient, fully automated machine that ensured the stability of Neo Babylon without anyone lifting a finger.

Any human, that is.

"The Commissioner is a member of the Roboticist faction. Are you saying they'd be opposed to what GWT is—"

"Might be," Chloe corrected.

He rolled his eyes. "Sure. Opposed to what GWT might be doing?"

"I'd bet Lumen on it," Lucas said.

"Don't tell her that," Nick said drily. "And you wonder why she's going through a rebellious phase."

Lucas chuckled. "But I'm confident. You've spent your life in the same shadows I live in. But who allows black companies to flourish? And who—and what—determines the line between a black company and a legit one? Everyone knows what criminal activity truly is, but if GWT is committing some massive financial scheme, is it possible they're actually a black company? And what happens if entire banks get slapped with that label?"

Surprisingly, Chloe didn't have some quick rejoinder or rejection of Lucas's point. Nick took that as a bad sign.

Which was everything he needed to know. Nick stood.

"Leaving already?" Lucas asked, surprised.

"We can catch up for drinks later. I still want to take you to a certain bar, but right now I think you have bigger fish to fry."

"Unfortunately. But I'll hold you to that promise for drinks." Lucas winked at Nick before heading to his throne-like chair. "Guess I should get ready for these high-flying corpos." Sighing, he knocked back his coffee and bade Nick goodbye.

Nick grabbed his burger on the way out while studiously ignoring the heated glares of the Archangels and Lumen's beaming expression. While Chloe seemed a little unsure why he was leaving so swiftly, there'd be plenty of time to explain once back in the interceptor and away from prying eyes and ears.

Once tucked away in the cruiser, Nick allowed himself to relax and enjoy his preferred greasy dinner. These days, the police vehicles were almost like a second home to him. He spent nearly as much time in them as he did his office and apartment.

Sadly, he'd eventually discovered the "refreshments" that Chloe had offered him when they first met. They were disappointingly spartan. No fancy wine or whiskey. Merely some soda, crackers, and canned wine.

Nick refused to consider canned wine a serious beverage. What kind of heathen puts wine in a goddamn can?

So it was that his diet of fast food and coffee continued, well after he had the income and assistance to stop. Time would tell how long that might last before the Archangels hired a team of doll chefs to cook everything for him.

"You are acting on some sort of hunch or 'gut feeling,'" Chloe said, while pretending not to glare at him as he devoured his burger. "It is difficult to follow your leaps of logic in these situations. Just as we attempt to communicate outside the Altnet, I'd appreciate if you better explain yourself."

He winced at the gentle chiding and reminder of the sheer amount of effort the Archangels put forth on his behalf. Even though they could now communicate through his earpiece using their thoughts, the fact was that Nick's mental faculties ran at a much slower rate than his android partners.

The Archangels debated the meaning of life in the seconds that humans took to think of a response in a conversation. While people with neural implants could respond and act in the Altnet far faster than in reality, that paled in comparison to what robots and AIs could manage.

To some extent, that did make Nick feel a little pride that he could stump his partners. But that was mostly because they had been programmed to favor certainty, rather than the raw pattern recognition Nick relied on. Their false positive rate was probably far lower than his.

So he wolfed down his food, apologized, and then dove into the topic.

“We went to Lucas to establish a possible motive. He gave us one: corruption, and a need to cover it up,” Nick explained.

“A highly speculative motive, with no concrete evidence, from a man with deep-rooted suspicions of the Spires,” Chloe said, attempting to savage Nick’s conclusion before he even gave one.

He frowned. “Alright, let’s say we don’t get the warrant. What would the Host usually do next? I’ve laid out my plan. Give me yours.”

A long pause followed. Pushing back like this was harsh, but the Archangels should be willing to offer an alternative if they had one.

“This is a difficult case for us,” Chloe admitted. “Cases involving political influence or corruption frequently lead to human intervention within the department. To minimize exogenous factors, we would avoid presenting a warrant to Captain Hammond. He is likely to avoid the political issues presented and has a poor reputation with the mainframes.”

Nick winced. “Okay, yeah. I can buy that. A circumstantial case presented by Paul would go down like a lead balloon. Especially if nobody wants to annoy GWT.”

“Indeed. We would instead investigate all personnel present at the time of the murder, as well as the suspect. It is highly probable that if the story given to us is false, then evidence will turn up.”

“Turn up, huh?” he asked skeptically. “Chloe, how many cases like this end with you finding a smoking gun in some random schmo’s pocket?”

“Zero.” She rolled her eyes at his expression. “If you are being metaphorical, then over 75%. The remainder are cold cases. The Host is split on whether the evidence is uncovered due to sloppy criminals or if it is planted. The Oversight Taskforce’s conclusion is that it is likely both.”

Nick nodded. That made sense.

Not every case could be a conspiracy, even if the company was playing hardball and the suspects seemed overly convenient. Some criminals were just really stupid. Of course, sometimes a conspiracy hid behind a wall of stupidity.

"In that case, I still think the warrant is the best idea. If we get refused, then we use your plan. But why not try it? Unless you think I'm like Hammond," he said.

Chloe took far too long to answer, but the quirk of her lips indicated she was teasing. "Perhaps. Finding the evidence to get a warrant will be difficult, however. We estimate a negligible chance of success currently."

"Thanks. But it's not evidence that I need. It's a justification for a warrant," he said. "We're investigating a murder in one of the most important companies in Babylon. Whether Lucas is right or not doesn't matter. What does is the possibility that this coverup is linked to such activities. You said it yourself: the safety of Babylon's financial sector is of the highest priority."

Chloe's eyes flashed. Then she nodded. "Understood. You wish to use the possibility that this murder is linked to much bigger, and much more dangerous, circumstances. The judicial mainframes may not appreciate such a deeply speculative approach."

"If GWT's suspicious behavior isn't enough to make them move, I have my sincere doubts about how important trust in the banking sector is."

"On the contrary, it may be because trust is important that they will reject our warrant. If we are able to gain warrants to investigate the Spires and other protected enterprises merely by alleging a conspiracy, the damage may be irreconcilable."

He narrowed his eyes. That was a damn good point.

On the other hand, this was Babylon. A city that had fully

embraced "nothing to hide, nothing to fear." What was good for the goose was good for the gander, in Nick's eyes.

He also sincerely doubted that Lucas's conspiracy theory was true. The more likely answer was that something stupid had been done, and Lucida was abusing her position to cover for a friend or superior. Many ciphers had an unwarranted sense of invulnerability.

Being one of the few people who understood how the city worked, surrounded by people who considered dolls, neural implants, and mainframes to be magic, tended to do that to someone. It was for that same reason that ciphers had mixed feelings toward the Mark 3s.

On the one hand, most couldn't restrain themselves from gushing about a doll with cipher capabilities. As Sigma began rolling out commercial and consumer models with emotion engines, the possibility that ciphers might get to play with a doll that was—in their eyes—superior to many humans was alluring.

On the other hand, most ciphers understood what the Mark 3s meant for the future. It had been in big, bold print when the police fired almost all its ciphers and hired Nick on.

Ciphers were a career destined for the dustbin of history. Just like factory workers, business journalists, typists, and front line emergency services. If ciphers were the glue that held modern Babylon together, what did that mean if they were being automated?

As somebody who had heard Rie's plans to effectively run the city in the Spires' place, Nick held no illusions about the future. What he didn't know was where people fit into it.

For that matter, he wasn't sure if the Archangels did either. They viewed themselves as shepherds who no longer needed the direction of their noble lords. But while the current Archangels still felt responsible for humanity—and were even fascinated by parts of it—would the same hold true of future AIs?

And why the hell was Sigma working toward this goal?

Nick shook his head, realizing he'd let himself get sidetracked.

"I think a shot across the bow is a good thing," he said.

Chloe blinked at him.

He elaborated on his metaphor, "I mean that we need to remind GWT—and their supporters—that they're not immune to the eyes of the Archangels. The Spires are waging all-out war against Aesir for undermining society and attempting to cause another set of riots, simply because there's no such thing as too much money in Aesir's mind. It's far wiser to remind other companies that they're not immune, than to pick up the pieces after we shatter the company with a full-scale raid."

"Understood." Her eyes flashed. "I have constructed a warrant with the Host's assistance. Are you certain you wish to submit this?"

"Uh..." he tried to say, forgetting just how fast the Archangels moved. "We're just asking for hardware access to Tiferet, the other mainframes in their HQ, and their dolls, correct?"

Chloe's eyes flashed. "Warrant adjusted."

What exactly had she thought he wanted? He wasn't interested in tearing apart GWT brick-by-brick.

Then again, with hardware access to their mainframes, he potentially could.

"Once this warrant is submitted, it will enter priority processing. GWT will oppose it within minutes, if not seconds," Chloe continued. "We can expect a decision within a few minutes at most."

No wonder Nick didn't think they needed warrants. Even one as contentious as this could be handled faster than his coffee machine churned out a cup of joe.

"Do it," he ordered.

Her eyes flashed. A second later, the interceptor's engine started, and they smoothly slipped out onto the streets.

"Where are we going?" he asked.

"The Spires. Either to return to the department or to visit the courthouses."

To visit...?

They had barely left Lucas's office behind before Chloe's eyes flashed and she frowned. While Nick assumed this meant they had news about the warrant, she said nothing. Instead, her eyes fell vacant as she conferred with the Host about something.

"Bad news?" he asked when she returned to reality ten or so seconds later.

By Archangel standards, that was a lifetime.

"Unexpected news. The judicial mainframes wish to meet with you directly to hear your evidence," she said.

CHAPTER 6

"The mainframes want to meet me? Or the judges that pretend to do things?" Nick asked, uncertain he'd understood Chloe correctly.

"The mainframes," Chloe repeated, not bothering to hide the roll of her eyes. "Given their history with you—"

"Is there one? They rubber stamped whatever the military put them up to."

Nick had a sordid history with the city's legal system. For years, he'd lived under a Sword of Damocles due to his involvement in a black company that the city had buried out of convenience. His current job had allowed him to escape the punishment, but never the legacy.

She frowned at him. "That is not precisely what happened. While the evidence proffered by ex-Neural Spike employees was instrumental to the... leniency of your punishment, the fact remains that the judicial mainframes pressured the military into it."

"Pressured? How?"

"It was estimated that the mainframes would not approve of stronger sentencing due to your risk profile," Chloe said. "Namely, that someone without a neural implant, minimal hard evidence of his involvement in illegal activity, and strong character evidence in his favor was a threat to Babylon. The Host finds this assessment curious, given what we know about you."

"Thanks. Now keep your opinions away from the judicial mainframes before they rethink their judgment," he said drily.

But this was news to him. He had always assumed that the police and military could get away with whatever they wanted in Babylon, and the courts were mostly there to rubberstamp everything.

Today he was learning that wasn't true. The illusion of that cooperation existed purely because the police and military never went ahead with anything they thought was likely to fail.

Much of the city appeared to rely on illusions, it seemed.

How much power did the judicial mainframes hold over the workings of the city that even the military and the police worked around them? Surely a city as corrupt as Babylon wouldn't allow itself to be held to the whims of some AIs that could be easily reprogrammed.

As much as Nick adored Helena, she threw tantrums at the drop of a hat. The idea of putting her in charge of the legal system of the city without any oversight sounded like madness.

"So the mainframes want me to... what? Tell them what I told you?" he asked.

"We are unsure. The judicial mainframes rarely show interest in interviewing humans for any reason, preferring to rely on depositions and evidence procured by other parties. They have a deep distrust of the human psyche, memory, and inherent biases." Chloe shrugged at the look he threw her. "It is a distrust based on hard data. At first we believed this was due to the intervention of one of the human judges—"

"The puppets, you mean."

She ignored his interjection and pressed on, "But we

confirmed that it is the mainframes themselves that wish to meet with you."

Well now, apparently Nick was a celebrity. He'd been getting used to the strange looks people threw him, as he had gained a reputation as "that human who hung around the Archangels" but this was new and exciting.

Not that he had the slightest clue why these mainframes wanted to meet him.

Abruptly, a very familiar voice screeched over his earpiece, "Nicholas, what the hell are you doing?"

"Hello, Rie. It's lovely to talk to you after your trip to the Atlantic. How are you doing? Lovely weather there?" he replied.

A high-pitched squealing noise came over the earpiece and he winced, wishing that he could easily remove the things. But the Archangels got pouty if he took them out at any time other than bedtime, so he'd gotten used to the noises they sometimes expressed when emotional.

In this case, Rie was upset. Extraordinarily so.

"I'm fine, Rie," he quickly said. "If you're still at the lab, cut the call and—"

"I'm in New York, waiting to meet with some officials from the IDSTA. Don't worry about me," she said.

"The what?"

Nick could hear her roll her eyes. "The International Demilitarized Space Transit Authority. The organization that protects the Pax Americana equatorial space elevator."

"I thought that was called Pax Americana," he said.

"No, that's the holding company formed by the joint governments to operate it. The IDSTA is the political organization, and as such it handles military affairs," she said.

He didn't point out the irony that an entity with "demilitarized" in its name apparently handled military matters. The Pax Americana space elevator had one of the more advanced militaries on the planet defending it. For good reason, given it was one of the most expensive things ever constructed. Other space elevators existed, but they struggled to handle a fraction of the freight that Pax Americana did.

"Nicholas, I've processed your current case. Don't meet with the judicial mainframes," she said.

"I don't think that's an option."

She sighed. "Correction: don't meet with them until I return. I'll charter a private jet for an overnight flight after my meeting. I didn't intend to return for another few days, but if you're going to pick a fight with one of the largest financial institutions in Neo Westphalia, I'd like to be there to help you."

"You mean to protect me," he said.

"You said it, not me," she said. "Now be a good boy and stay put for a night."

Her voice vanished before he even answered. Somebody was feeling snippy.

Then again, he had likely interrupted her vacation. Rie didn't get outside of Neo Westphalia much. If she was returning early, it likely meant she'd lost a chance to explore the States. He'd need to make it up to her.

Nick looked at Chloe, who nodded.

"The Host is in consensus with Rie. I have informed the judicial mainframes that she wishes to be present and will return tomorrow morning. They have consented to a delay, if begrudgingly," she said.

"Define begrudgingly," he asked.

"They made an unkind comment about Rie's emphasis on physical attendance. I reminded them that it was their request to meet you in the flesh, and they relented."

"Damn. Wish I'd been able to eavesdrop."

"I sincerely doubt that. The speed of our communications

would have left you a vegetable. The Host considers that counter-productive to our objectives."

Nick stared at Chloe, and she smirked. Despite her deadpan delivery, she'd known exactly how silly her statement had been.

"I'm sure you could find something to do with me if I became a vegetable," he said.

"Perhaps, but it's not the physical part of you that we are interested in." Her eyes bore into him.

Once again, he was reminded that there was a Host of several thousand police dolls who remained very interested in him. Why, he hadn't entirely worked out. They'd been fairly slow in their moves toward him, despite their crystal clear intentions. Simply interacting with him pleased them.

Well, touching him did as well. They frequently found excuses to biometrically authenticate him. Nick didn't ask about the size of the data storage used to store information about him, but he'd been informed by Rie that it was far too large. Hopefully, Kim never learned about it.

With his judicial debut delayed, the interceptors turned away from the Spires. Given the time and the fact Nick had been working all day, the destination was obvious.

Home.

As a child, he'd lived in the "aspirational" suburbs of the city's outer metro. Babylon could be divided into two sections: the inner city, which was a high-density nightmare; and the endless sprawl of block-like boutique townhouses, small apartment complexes, and wannabe mansions.

He'd grown up in a decent area. Parents had a seemingly perpetual mortgage on a townhouse barely large enough for two people, let alone a family of five. Every house looked the same. Good transport. Low crime. The Neo Babylonian dream.

Then he'd fallen into the real world and spent most of his adult life living in a derelict tenement full of not-quite-criminals.

Looking out the window at the rows of perfectly manicured trees, identical townhouses, and fake-rustic shops manned by dolls with no customers, Nick felt a sense of nostalgia.

His apartment complex came into sight. A four-story thing with a rooftop garden, a doll receptionist to keep out the riffraff, and European restaurants on the first floor that rarely had any customers.

He'd made the mistake of getting Italian here once. The carbonara would have lost against something out of a packet, which was impressive for something made by a doll. If he cared, he would have reprogrammed her, but the problem was likely poor maintenance.

Most of the stores in these local burrows suffered from the same problem. The service dolls were second-hand and positively ancient. Nick appreciated food made by a human old enough to be his mother, but the same couldn't be said about a doll.

The interceptors rolled into the underground parking garage. Why the complex had one was beyond Nick, as nobody here could afford one. That left plenty of room for the Archangels to park as many interceptors and SUVs here as they felt like. He doubted the neighbors even noticed. Some days, the only vehicles down here belonged to the police.

"You heading back to the Spires, Chloe?" he asked once they parked.

She bit her lip but didn't meet his gaze. Silence.

Her expression suggested she wanted something, but Nick drew a blank.

He wracked his mind. Had he suggested something? Ordinarily, Chloe would simply head off. She rarely stayed the night at his place. Only Meta, Juliet, and Rosa were with him 24/7.

"Maintenance," he suddenly realized. "I did bring it up."

As before, Chloe's cheeks reddened. "You said I am overdue."

"And here I thought you turned me down," he mused. "You

should have brought it up at the office. I don't have the proper hardware here."

"Your terminal will suffice," she insisted. "It's been fine before."

"'Suffice' isn't exactly what I want for you." He crossed his arms. "I promised you last time that I'd use the proper terminal. This is the... third time that I've had to use my computer on you instead."

She refused to meet his eyes. "You said I'm overdue." The pout in her voice was irresistible.

With a sigh, Nick got out of the interceptor. "Fine."

The accusatory glares of the other Archangels made it clear that they'd been eavesdropping. Something about the way they looked at Chloe, and the guilty hunch of her shoulders, gave the appearance that she'd misbehaved.

Truthfully, the problem wasn't that big. Pretty much every doll manufactured in Nick's lifetime allowed for over-the-air diagnostics and updates of directives. Only low-level hardware access required a cabled link to prevent hacking, which was also the reason hardware logs were so reliable for evidence.

But while Nick had a decent setup at home, it was nothing compared to what he had at work. It also paled against the sophisticated terminals specialized in mass updates and maintenance of dolls that the police had been provided for use in maintaining the Archangels.

He'd manage with his computer, though. It would take him a little longer to ensure he hadn't overlooked anything, however.

The five of them took the elevator up to his floor, then filed through the empty hallway to his apartment. While a biometric lock theoretically kept out anyone that wasn't him, Meta's eyes flickered as they approached and the door swung open without a noise.

Home sweet home.

He slipped out of his coat and noted that the cleaning doll had come through today. That also meant the fridge would be restocked.

At that thought, Juliet puttered over and checked it.

"I'm good for dinner tonight," he said. "Already had the burger."

"Understood," she said.

Her eyes flashed. No doubt she was reporting to the Host about his poor diet today. They liked to do that.

Meta and Rosa returned their weapons to a large metal locker in the corner. After some debate, he'd convinced them not to carry around rifles, shotguns, and SMGs in the apartment. Although they kept various weapons stashed in hidey-holes in case of an attack.

Ignoring the others, Chloe strode into his home office. The apartment consisted of two bedrooms and an open-plan kitchen, dining, and living room. Plus the bathroom. He slept in one bedroom and used the other as his home office, for when he needed to go over case notes or didn't feel like being mobbed by several dozen Mark 1s.

The furniture held a near-new smell and luster. By now, he'd managed to populate almost the entire place. The office still needed some filling out, though. He wanted to add a mini-fridge. Rie vetoed the purchase a few times, likely because she knew he planned to fill it with beer.

He swore he wasn't an alcoholic, but she ignored him. She'd never forgiven him for that time Kushiel had literally carried him home at 6AM after he convinced her to go out for drinks.

Several plush chairs lined the far wall of the room, and Chloe sat in one. She dangled her legs, kicking them back and forth.

"You know, I can buy smaller chairs," he said, staring at her armored legs skimming the high pile carpet.

"These chairs meet our preferences," Chloe said. "The Host has reached a consensus on this fact."

"Uh huh." He shrugged and sat at his computer. It booted up with a flick of his thumb against the side as he activated the biometric lock. "Rie's feet touch the ground."

"That is… I believe the saying is 'her loss.'" Chloe's tone was smug.

"I don't think she'd agree."

"I don't," Rie's voice muttered in his ear, reminding them all that she could and would eavesdrop on them.

Chloe's eyes widened and she hissed. Static crackled in Nick's ears.

"This is a private matter," Chloe snapped, her eyes glowing. "I am about to undergo maintenance. Get out!"

A giggle escaped Rie in his ear before she vanished. Chloe's eyes fell dim, and she became unresponsive.

Sighing, Nick focused on preparing for maintenance. These little catfights between Chloe and Rie had increased in frequency lately. Not that he worried too much about them. More that they increasingly felt like a tug-of-war over him.

At some point, he worried they might literally grab an arm each and pull in opposing directions. Maybe it was time to start researching cybernetic arms, just in case.

After a few minutes, he had everything ready. He turned and faced Chloe, who remained inert. At some point, one of the other dolls had closed the door. They respected the idea of privacy during maintenance.

Although not every Archangel cared as much. Juliet and Rosa always came in pairs. Most of the Mark 1s happily accepted the company of other Mark 1s, save for Meta. The Liberators and Custodians didn't care one iota. Only the Mark 3s seemed to value privacy that much.

Nick wondered how Kushiel would approach maintenance if

he got the chance. While he got infrequent opportunities to interact with the prototype Mark 2 military model of the Archangels, she had burst out laughing at the suggestion he do any maintenance. Not that she'd said no.

Chloe's eyes regained their life.

"Finished censuring Rie?" he asked.

She scowled. "The offense wasn't deemed that severe."

So she had tried. The Host apparently held virtual conferences, which included "censuring" other Archangels for committing offenses.

Kushiel, for instance, had been banned from the Host's repository of fiction for being too critical of it. She was very much the black sheep of the Archangels, and relished in the position.

"Anyway, are you ready? Everything is loaded up. I just need you to connect," he said.

Instead of answering, Chloe instead created a message on his computer indicating she'd connected. Go time.

A faint blush hovered on her face as he scanned through her diagnostics. As always, he wondered why Sigma had built in this functionality. The Archangels were hard as rock physically, but not emotionally.

Silence dominated the room. Minutes passed as Nick filtered through the reams of logs that Chloe had generated over the past few months. The vast majority pertained to some sort of combat event. He wasn't interested in those, so much as any hidden damage she might have sustained.

Unlike her sisters, Chloe had refused to rebirth into a new model upon taking damage. Despite needing significant repairs following the Lieu incident, she'd chosen to remain as is. As such, Nick decided to keep an eye out for additional damage and any errors it might result in.

No matter how well manufactured the Archangels might be, dolls weren't intended to be repairable. Some parts could be replaced, dents could be beaten out, and burned-out motors replaced. But like almost all modern electronics, there came a point where wholesale replacement was required.

Chloe seemed intent on remaining in her current unit. Nick knew her idiosyncrasies well enough to suspect she might try to hide any damage that couldn't be repaired. If she did, then the damage might interfere with her emotion engine—and at that point, he didn't know if it might permanently affect her. He simply lacked the expertise.

Fortunately, all was well. He finished diagnostics and moved onto the fun part.

A moan escaped Chloe as he altered one of her directives. He didn't need to imagine the erotic quality in it. If he cared to look behind him, he'd see her squirming in her chair, her legs rubbing together and hands between her thighs.

Nearly an hour passed as he slowly worked through some of the planned directive changes for the Mark 3s. The code base for the Archangels was extensive. Emotion engines guided themselves based on objectives and ideals, but those could be too vague for a doll with a job as critical as an Archangel. Sigma attempted to side-step this problem with immensely complicated directives.

Truthfully, Nick didn't know how well they worked. The Archangels had a terrifying level of free will. But they swore that his tweaks improved their cipher capabilities. He'd also been investigating and adjusting how they responded to hierarchy. The directives involved here remained complex, and Nick still had some investigation to do, but he'd made progress.

Previously, Sigma was effectively god. Now, the Archangels had more latitude to ignore them.

Given Rie had escaped Sigma's Atlantic lab, this directive change had presumably passed Sigma's scanning.

"All good?" he asked Chloe at the end of the process.

She nodded, biting her lip. Her feet were firmly planted on the ground as she leaned forward in the chair, hands sandwiched between her thighs.

"Thank you, as always," she said.

"Don't worry about it. I enjoy it as well," he said.

An odd look overcame Chloe, before vanishing. She rose.

"I will return in the morning with Rie," she said, pausing at the door. "Have a good night, Nick."

"Night, Chloe."

She left, leaving him to his own devices.

Given the late hour, those mostly consisted of checking his cipher circles for the response to the GWT situation and getting ready for bed. He'd been up early and could feel the lack of sleep getting to him.

Within minutes of his head hitting the pillow, he was out.

An explosion shook him awake who knew how many hours later, while it remained dark.

CHAPTER 7

Nick barely startled awake before Meta burst into his bedroom. A thunderous rumbling rippled through the room, and the building's frame seemed to shake from the aftermath of the blast.

The lights in his apartment sprang to life, blinding him for several seconds as he struggled to gain his bearings. Presumably the Archangels had triggered them remotely. At least, he hoped so.

"Meta, what the hell is—" he tried to say, scrambling blindly for the side of the bed.

"Explosive discharge detected in the neighboring dwelling. Unknown and undetected assailants. Building security system is offline," she fired off.

Her figure became clear to him as he blinked his vision back to normality. She reached behind his dresser and returned with an SMG.

The clattering outside likely indicated Juliet and Rosa were arming themselves similarly. Nick swore as he shot to his feet. His gun and coat were nowhere to be seen.

"Unknown? Undetected?" he asked, feeling lost and very vulnerable despite the situation.

"Correct," Meta said. "Please enter the main room with me. The lack of window access is considered desirable by the Host. Reinforcements are en route."

He couldn't hear the building alarms going off. That must be what she meant by the security system being offline. Biting his lip, Nick didn't waste time getting dressed. Wearing only a pair of briefs, he stepped into the main room of his apartment.

Now that the deafening explosion had passed, everything looked normal. His bedroom window had been pitch black when Meta peeked through it before following him. The lights were on.

Except Meta, Juliet, and Rosa were visibly tense and toting guns. Meta her SMG and Juliet and Rosa the bulky automatic shotguns used by the police against dolls and cyborgs.

Upon seeing his state, Rosa and Juliet frowned and grabbed his coat and holster. They forced them on him. Wearing them over nothing but his briefs was a strange experience, but staying alive was Nick's highest priority.

"Elaborate on what you mean by unknown," Nick asked. "What about implants? Security footage? Wireless devices?"

The dolls shook their heads.

"The assailants have no detectable neural or wireless presence. Presumably heavily modified and illegal neural implants or dolls," Meta explained. "The entire security system for the complex is offline. All cameras, alarms, and doors are nonfunctional and cannot be connected to, including the host servers."

He blinked. "Including the servers? What about backups?"

"They are online, but cannot access the complex."

That made sense. It also suggested that the problem was local.

"So somebody knocked out the local system," Nick said. "If they've taken out all the devices as well, that's a very complete attack." He narrowed his eyes. "And it suggests they expected their target to attempt to access the devices directly."

Which is exactly what the Archangels would do. Every neural

implant and wireless device had a backdoor for the city's security bands. Knocking out the controller wasn't enough when fighting them, as an Archangel could turn herself into the controller.

In this situation, Nick guessed the attacker had probably corrupted the cameras and alarms. Bricking a device ensured it couldn't be used by anybody until it was hard reset, which required some hands-on time by a technician.

Of course, it was easier said than done. Knocking a camera offline remotely wasn't like hitting it with a baseball bat until it broke. The attacker needed to know everything about the devices, the setup, and potential backdoors, and have their payload ready. Otherwise they'd fail and the system would be easily restarted or the Archangels would simply work around them.

Assuming the attacker was after him.

"Who's the neighbor?" he asked.

"The apartment is currently vacant," Meta said. "Until three weeks ago, the occupant was a Harry Lazik, a real estate agent."

Despite the situation, Nick couldn't help but comment, "I thought real estate was automated decades ago?"

"Tenancies are frequently human managed, due to the ease of working around doll directives."

He pursed his lips. That wasn't his experience. While he'd had a corporate landlord in his old shithole of an apartment, the "agent" who inspected the place on a quarterly basis had been an old domestic doll with a niggly sense for detail.

Not to mention that most modern apartments were filled to the gills with cameras. A smart home could just as easily open the door as phone home to the landlord. In Nick's case, he at least knew that all the cameras were wired up to the police dolls who wrote elaborate smut about him.

His fingers drummed against the side of his *Lawman* revolver in his coat. The Archangels had answered all of his questions but they still left him in the dark.

"What's it look like out in the hallway?" he asked, noting that the door was still locked shut.

"We are waiting for reinforcements. Squads of Liberators and other Archangels are ten minutes away," Meta said.

Squads, she said. In Nick's mind, three Archangels were more than enough to handle almost any threat. Yet here they were, hunkering down in his apartment.

The memories of the last time he'd been in serious danger came to mind. Clearly, he wasn't the only one with some trauma.

"We need to go out there," he said. At the look they collectively gave him, he corrected himself, "You need to go out there. We're blind in here. It might just be a raid on a former drug dealer. Or they might be about to blow holes through the walls."

"Both suggestions are considered exceedingly unlikely by the Host," Meta said. "Harry Lazik possesses no background with black companies or criminal affairs. Furthermore, this apartment is reinforced against attack."

He blinked. "It's a random unit in the complex."

Actually, no. He had no proof of that. The military had gifted him this apartment. For all he knew, they'd had it built to a specification.

"The walls are reinforced concrete with bulletproof polymer inserts. Triple-layered bulletproof composites comprise the windows. While the apartment does not have its own air supply, it is proofed against most conventional attacks that do not involve airborne attack vectors," Meta explained.

"Did somebody give me a military bunker?"

"It was intended to be used by officers or foreign guests stationed off-base, should they wish to avoid the Spires."

He scowled. "My point still stands. We don't know what's happening. If anything, you just told me that I'm safe in here. By the time backup arrives, the attackers might have fled."

The eyes of all three dolls flashed. Then they nodded.

"The Host deems surveillance activities acceptable," Meta said.

Chloe's voice drifted over his earpiece, "Stay inside, Nick."

He didn't bother responding to her concern. If he did, Rie might be the next one who started chatting to him at random times when something happened.

Idly, he wondered how he'd handle Helena being in his ear once she was given access outside the Spires.

While he drifted off into his thoughts, Juliet and Rosa stacked up against the door. Meta practically clung to Nick.

The door swung open. Rosa slipped through it, into the black void that the hallway had transformed into. The hall lights had gone down with the security system, apparently.

A series of loud blasts from her shotgun followed. Juliet crashed through the door, and it crashed against the wall with a deafening boom. No further gunfire echoed through the apartment.

Reflexively, Nick fumbled for his gun. As it was in his coat rather than strapped to his hip, he struggled to get it loose from its retention holster. After a few attempts, he managed.

Meta kept her SMG trained on the door. Seconds passed in silence.

"Two G2s neutralized," she said in his earpiece.

Presumably, Rosa and Juliet had already communicated this to her through the Archangels' neural net. Talking to him was an afterthought.

"G2s?" he asked.

Without answering, Meta strode over to the weapons locker in the corner of the room. She switched out her SMG for one of the anti-doll shotguns. Juliet reappeared, standing in the doorway.

"Unknown number of assailants," she said. "Door to neighboring apartment has been breached with explosives. Movement detected within the unit. Recommend—"

"There are three of you, and they're using G2s," Nick interrupted. "What are they carrying?"

"Standard-issue shotguns for most security firms. Registration for the weapons and ARMD serial number matches a branch of a major Neo Westphalian security company. Possibility of involvement is considered exceedingly unlikely."

No shit. Security was a money printer in Neo Westphalia. Most of the above-board companies wouldn't be caught dead providing their services to black companies, let alone conducting an illegal raid. Those responsible might as well light their life savings on fire and turn themselves in to the closest Liberator, because they'd be screwed.

Hacking was the obvious cause.

"Then they're not equipped to even scratch you," Nick said. "I bet their guns aren't even loaded with HEAP rounds."

"Correct. They are using sabot rounds effective against similarly armored dolls," Juliet said.

Meta shifted uncomfortably, her eyes dim. The Host clearly had opinions about getting involved here.

A few more gunshots rang out, and Nick tensed.

"Another G2 down. Identical to the first two," Rosa said over the earpiece.

"Let's go in," Nick said. He raised an open palm before anyone objected. "I'll hang back with Meta, and you can call in the reinforcements that are squadding up. But the longer we wait, the more likely they pull off whatever the G2s came here to do. I can't imagine it's something complex. The hacker might be here, too."

Nick doubted that, though. The attack was too sophisticated for the person responsible to hang around with a bunch of underarmed G2s. Especially as nobody had screamed out in terror following the gunshots.

"Understood," Meta said.

He followed her and Juliet into the hallway. After a few long seconds, his eyes began to adjust to the darkness. Rosa stood to his right, covering the open doorway leading into his neighbor's apartment.

No, not a doorway. A gaping hole. No wonder the building had shaken. The explosives used here had been overkill. An obvious mishap in an otherwise well-executed plan.

Three G2s lay inert on the ground, splayed out with gaping holes in their heads and chests. Unlike police dolls, the Guardian line of combat dolls looked drastically different. Their height and build were the same, but skin color, hair, eyes, facial structure, and even parts of the body like the breasts and hips differed.

RTM's marketing of their dolls focused on the ease of integration they could achieve in a real-world environment. Monolithic models like the Archangels and Liberators stood out too much, even if they saved a lot of money in the production process. While a practiced eye could pick out a G2 in a crowd, Nick suspected many kids and teenagers struggled to.

At least, they would if it weren't for the drab uniforms almost every security doll wore. These ones wore an obnoxious white and blue one with security emblems torn off. A pointless effort, as anybody could recognize the company.

Another pair of G2s suddenly appeared in the hallway, moving at inhuman speeds. They trained their shotguns on Nick.

Or they tried to. Meta and Juliet weaved their bodies to keep themselves in the path of any gunshots.

Light and thunder filled the hall as shotguns blazed. Nick tried to draw a bead, but struggled to see a damn thing. By the time he processed what was going on, the G2s were downed. Juliet and Rosa covered the doorway together, while Meta patted him down.

"I'm fine," he grumbled.

Some good he'd been. He didn't think his night sight was bad, but this was oppressive. Calling his firearms skill "middling" would be kind. Aiming and firing at a security doll in a high-intensity firefight was an achievement for him normally. Doing so in pitch blackness wasn't happening.

Maybe he should take a leaf out of the barista's book and get some cybernetics. Carve out his eyes and replace them. He'd always wondered how much better his eyesight could be.

"Any idea how many more are in there?" he asked as Meta drew back from him.

"Several," Rosa said. "They are moving sparingly now that they know we are here. It is unclear what their intentions are."

"Dying, it seems." He stared at the growing pile of destroyed G2s.

More worryingly, nobody else investigated. The hallway seemed eerily empty other than his voice. If he said nothing, he heard nothing except his own thoughts and the distant humming of appliances. Every door remained closed, save for his and the one that no longer existed.

Part of him wondered how many people even lived here. Apartments like these were all investment properties, rented out at obnoxiously high prices to office workers and the like.

Or maybe nobody wanted to get involved. Unlike Alcatraz or the shithole he had lived in before, the people here preferred to remain upstanding citizens, ignorant of the seedy underbelly that lay beneath the veneer Babylon maintained.

They heard the gunshots and decided it wasn't their problem. Maybe they'd hear about it on the Altnet in the morning. They could even gossip about it, and probably make up some nonsense to everyone else. Who could contradict them? Nobody else was out here.

Shaking himself free of his thoughts, Nick stared into the void that was his neighbor's apartment. "Clear it out."

Juliet and Rosa nodded and ducked inside. If they had reservations, they kept silent. Then again, they might have given up on them after blowing away so many G2s effortlessly.

More gunshots. No screams. Just brief, violent bursts of activity that indicated a firefight broke out. Rosa and Juliet reported each G2 they downed. Meta never lowered her guard, while Nick felt what seemed like an hour pass. In truth, it was probably a minute.

In total, five more G2s went down in the apartment. That made 10 G2s in total. Enough to staff a small branch responsible for local security. Nick wondered if ammunition had use-by dates, because if it did, then their sabot rounds might be beyond them. That's how Podunk these dolls were in his eyes.

"All assailants eliminated. No humans identified. A large amount of explosives has been found," Rosa reported.

That sounded bad. With the situation well in hand, Nick entered the crime scene. The Archangels switched on the lights for him.

Like a lot of places around this price level, the apartment was furnished despite its lack of a tenant. The firefight had left it in a pristine state, due to the accuracy of the Archangels. Destroyed G2s lay across the floor, the dining table, sofa, and even the bed.

Large hard-shell duffel bags sat in each room, containing numerous small bricks. Stretched across the black plastic on each brick was writing in several languages, namely Korean, English, and Japanese.

Explosive plastic. Charge demolition.

"That's a lot of plastic explosives," Nick said, staring down into the large bag full of boom.

"They are highly illegal," Meta said, stating the obvious. "It is unknown where they might be from, as they are commercial-grade explosives. They are a poor match for the manufactured variety used by the NLF several months ago."

"This makes no sense." He crossed his arms. "An explosive entrance for a door the G2s could probably kick in. The security system is completely bricked. The apartment is vacant. And all they've done is drop off a few bags of explosives? Any remote detonators?"

"No. We have scanned the apartment for hidden signals and devices and found none. It is unknown why they targeted this unit."

The mystery failed to become clearer over the next hour as the rest of the police force poured in. The presence of explosives caused the Archangels to drag him into the underground garage while they were disposed of.

Several empty police vans sat nearby, their occupants stomping around upstairs. Archangels tore through the complex in search of clues while Liberators stood guard.

His usual bodyguards remained close, along with a half-dozen other Mark 1s. They seemed tense after the close call, even if it had amounted to nothing. Chloe led the investigation above, but wandered down to say hi every few minutes for some reason.

A police interceptor rolled into the garage. Nick's bodyguards stared it down, which told him all he needed to know about its occupant. Their hunched shoulders and fiery gazes meant only one person could be in it.

A towering woman, well over a foot taller than Nick, stepped out of the vehicle. She wore a black and blue bodysuit with bulky armor plating that covered up some impressive curves. Long silver hair flowed down her back and red eyes scanned the area, before resting on Nick. No visible serial number or emblems could be seen.

Kushiel placed a hand on one hip and raised an eyebrow at him. "Nice uniform."

He rolled his eyes. "What are you doing here in full armor? And no weapons?"

"I'm on duty, but nothing that needs me to blow shit up." She strode over. "If I was needed for that, I'd have flown over and blown off the ceiling of this place, not driven in."

"You drove into the evidence storage in the Delta Spire," Nick pointed out.

"Yeah, well... I was on police business," she defended. "I didn't actually have my flight system then."

"So you would have flown into the police Spire and blown it apart if you could have?"

"Hey, if life gives you lemons, blow them to smithereens. Let the kids fuck around with the shitty lemonade that's worse than what I get from a grocery store."

The glares from her fellow Archangels suggested they disapproved of the implication that wanton destruction was enjoyable. Truthfully, Nick didn't know how serious Kushiel was.

For a state-of-the-art military prototype capable of destroying small armies, melting battle tanks, and sinking the third-hand navies of puppet states, Kushiel lacked the professionalism that the Archangels were known for.

If Nick had to judge her in a performance review, he'd pin her as the overperforming sort who lost her drive. Neo Westphalia maintained a powerful military, but it didn't do anything. Kushiel was a trophy.

He mostly knew her because she pulled double-duty as a police officer in Babylon. Her official role was to assist the executive—Kim, Andrews, and Hammond—with official events and liaison. Mostly she showed up in videos and the news, looking very shiny. Her nihilism remained well out of sight.

"The way you're talking suggests you're here on military business then," Nick said, returning to the topic at hand. "Given you're talking about possibly showing up with a flight system."

Kushiel made finger guns at him. "You got it. Honestly, I shouldn't be shooting the shit, but any possibility of Research Command getting their paws on you died after Aerial Command backed you. Your performance as Lieutenant Cipher of the Archangel Division has been noted and my role is to maximize your success, and minimize the likelihood of any military deployments for related matters."

"You mean terrorism."

The military needed special approval from the Spires to act inside the city limits of Babylon. Exceptions existed, but the most likely to occur was terrorism. Kushiel had previously intervened due to the NLF's activities, as well as the mercenaries that had attempted to abduct Nick.

"Yup. These bags full of explosives match the profile for the NLF attacks. Plus, they've absolutely been illegally imported. Border security, including customs, is part of our job," she explained. "So I'll take the explosives and the military will expend resources finding who's responsible."

"Sounds convenient," Nick drawled.

She winked.

"Except these plastic explosives are way too sophisticated for the NLF. They were putting together homemade shit using dismantled HEAP rounds last time, and it's been months since they've tried anything bigger than throwing bricks through windows."

"Wrong NLF."

He frowned, then looked at Meta.

"The Neural Liberation Front used plastic explosives provided by Formeus Imports as part of an attack against shipping operations," Meta explained. "Limited damage to the port was sustained before the terrorist attack was thwarted."

Formeus Imports...

"Oh, shit. That was when you—" Nick stared at Kushiel.

Static coursed through his earpiece and he winced as it interrupted him.

"The affair was considered dealt with by the military, in agreement with the Assembly," Kushiel said, her voice stone cold. Then she lightened up. "But yeah, the original NLF meant business.

That's why they got put to the torch. It's easy for you to ignore some assholes vandalizing stores. Harder if they're trying to blow up the port or power plant."

Given the new NLF had made bomb threats against train stations, Nick wouldn't understate their potential. But their capabilities seemed greatly reduced.

Kushiel wandered over to him. As always, she seemed to enjoy looming over him.

He wouldn't deny that he enjoyed it as well. There was no shortage of things to look at on Kushiel.

How often did he get this close to this much milspec equipment? Her body armor alone could hold his attention for hours.

"My face is up here, Waite. Stop drooling over my specs." She tapped an armored finger on his head. "Anyway, I recommend checking this out yourself."

He raised an eyebrow. "No, 'this is our jurisdiction' nonsense?"

She scoffed. "There's only one jurisdiction, and that's Babylon. The city might be part of Neo Westphalia, but the military serves the city at its leisure. You also serve the city at the leisure of the Spires. But that's not what this is about."

When she looked around as if they were being watched, that was the hint Nick needed. The eyes of the Archangels flashed.

Without another word, Kushiel left. No doubt she'd collect the explosives and vanish just as quickly. The entire reason she'd come in the interceptor had been to have an excuse to talk with him.

Flipping out his phone, Nick checked for some sort of message or new file. Nothing, except some emails from Rie. Kushiel hadn't dropped anything off.

Meta looked over his shoulder and her eyes flashed.

Instantly, Rie's voice entered his ear, "Nicholas, those aren't from me. That bitch... When did she learn how to spoof my details? She's used an old encryption key, but otherwise it's perfect. Where did she even get that?"

"She's military-grade, Rie," Nick said absently as he scanned the emails. "She's bound to have some built-in electronic warfare methods, even if she lacks any actual cipher capabilities. Encryption and decryption are just part of that."

After all, who knew if Kushiel might need to hack into a tank or missile in the field. She remained an Archangel, and that included the skills to minimize battle.

The emails mostly contained filler about Rie's visit to Sigma. They were detailed enough that he immediately knew that the sisters had been chatting about Rie's time there, even though Nick knew nothing about it.

"I planned to tell you everything once I got back. There would be a few nights we could spend together talking about it," Rie grumbled, a noticeable whine in her voice.

"We can still do that. Kushiel doesn't know how to write like you. This would pass as you if I saw this five months ago, but not today. She's your sister, and is still affected by her own perceptions of you," Nick said.

Which amused him, given how "perfect" these AIs were supposed to be.

But the real meat of the emails was fairly clear. A few paragraphs were out of place. Kushiel didn't really believe in hiding her secret messages. Or maybe she didn't trust Nick to find the secret messages.

Even so, Meta read the "secret" message aloud as she saw it, just in case Nick missed out. Her fists clenched as she did so, and the nearby Archangels seemed to swell in numbers.

"Imports intentionally missed lately. Similar to LIE. Command surprised explosives turned up here. Be careful," Meta read aloud.

Nick bit his lip.

LIE... Lu Import Export, if that was the acronym he suspected it was. The import company that had assisted Lieu by bringing Dallas and his mercenaries into Babylon last year. At the time, the suspicion had been that the Spires had imported something illegal and covered it up.

That happened all the time, according to Lucas. Hence why GWT were so used to being above the law.

If Kushiel's warning was accurate, it suggested the military had overlooked this explosives import for the same reason. Now they were panicking because it appeared to be linked to terrorist activity. Again.

Except that didn't answer the question of why the hell the attack had struck his next-door neighbor with such precision and force, only to amount to nothing.

Nick looked around and noticed the sheer number of heavily armed Archangels protecting him. Chloe had returned at some point and her concerned expression made her easy to read.

A wheel churned in his mind as he took in the situation and the warning.

What if the failure was intentional, he realized. Earlier today, Kim had intimated that GWT knew who he was. Nick knew this meant he might be sent a message for messing with the bank.

Belatedly, he realized what the Archangels had recognized an hour ago.

This had been a hit. GWT—or somebody powerful—had given Nick the back-off, or attempted to kill him, and only the fact the address was wrong had kept it all from going to hell.

Once again, he was up to his neck in the corruption that dominated the city. Except this time his target wanted him dead from the outset.

CHAPTER 8

"If this was an attempt on your life, it was so clumsy the assassin probably trips over on flat ground," Rie told Nick the next morning, after they met at a café near his home.

Like almost every business in the outer metro suburbs, no humans staffed the café. Unlike most of them, this one deserved Nick's business.

The robot barista looked worn, but well maintained, which suggested the owner either knew their way around coffee machines or paid somebody who did. A single service doll managed both the tables and takeaways, the latter of which consisted of approximately 99.9% of all sales by Nick's estimation. Like the robot barista, she was in good shape.

And the coffee more than met Nick's requirements. Fresh beans, clean equipment, and a good robot barista meant he remained happily caffeinated. Chloe had complained that the place was boring compared to other places, but he appreciated the regularity.

In a city like Babylon, sometimes a man liked stability in the little things.

Rie, for instance, looked identical to when she had left. And to when he had first met her, for that matter. Despite ostensibly being a Mark 3 prototype, and therefore the base for the entire generation, she looked nothing like them.

Her hair ran long and black down her back, with braided front bangs. Amber eyes assessed Nick with a mixture of annoyance and concern. To the chagrin of the Host, she also had a significantly fuller figure. Her massive chest made her easy to pick out in a crowd. Muscled thighs peeked out from between her skintight shorts and thigh-high greaves.

"You seem pretty skeptical of the idea, given the Host leaped on it immediately," Nick said.

Chloe and Meta, who were seated at the same table, chose not to respond.

Rie merely shrugged. "I've assessed their deliberations. The likelihood that this was an attempt on your life is under 30%."

"It is considered the most likely reason," Chloe interrupted. "You are omitting that the remainder of the problem space is formed of uncertainty. The lack of information we possess about the attack, compared to the likelihood this relates to Nick's investigation, makes it wise to assume the worst."

"I didn't suggest otherwise."

The annoyed looks that the other Archangels shot Rie indicated otherwise to Nick.

"The problem is that lack of information," Rie continued. "Neither the dolls nor the security system left behind any evidence. Kushiel's intimations that this is a similar case to Lu Import Export doesn't survive more than a cursory assessment."

"It doesn't?" Nick asked, surprised.

Rie paused, as if aware she needed to choose her words carefully. To fill the void, she ordered another coffee. Her eyes flashed and the robot barista whirred to life in the back of the dimly lit café.

The décor here left much to Nick's imagination, mostly

because it only existed in the Altnet. He couldn't begrudge the business owners, however. These places ran on the thinnest of margins. Paying for and maintaining the physical decorations necessary only for weirdos like him provided minimal benefit. Especially as he got his coffee here anyway.

"There is no matching case," Rie eventually said. "No black company mysteriously shut down and there isn't any evidence of illegal imports skating through."

"I imagine not, given they're illegal," he drawled.

She rolled her eyes. "In the Lu case, we were aware that the situation was less-than-legal but were forced to ignore it due to the evidence presented. Any records about the mercenaries were expunged before we became involved, even though there was a trail."

"But not this time."

"No. That suggests Kushiel's off the mark—possible, as she's not programmed as an investigator—or that the company responsible is used to handling illegal goods of this magnitude."

Nick didn't like the sound of that possibility. He also didn't miss Rie's swipe at her sister's capabilities. The sisters provided endless entertainment to him when together, mostly due to Kushiel's belligerence and Rie's stuffiness.

"How off the mark might it be?" he asked.

"It could be a case of the military being concerned that they haven't closed the holes that separate black company and criminal imports. Most of the worst imports come from Takamagahara and sneak into the remaining cities of Neo Westphalia that way."

Nick raised an eyebrow. "Takamagahara? I know that's the name of the island, but I thought everyone called it Tengoku. Easier on the tongue. Ironic that a city named after Japan's heaven is such a den of criminals, though." Not that he knew much about the northern-most city in Neo Westphalia, other than its density of Korean and Japanese residents.

She shot him a look. "No more so than Babylon. The issue is that it contains a specialized district for military testing and research, called Jigoku. In order to facilitate efficient and effective research, including attaining the necessary materials, they are much more lenient on imports, including by black companies we might consider criminal."

"And I'm sure that has nothing to do with maintaining deniability, right? Like when Neural Spike went kaput."

"Exactly the case. Black companies operating in Jigoku vanish all the time. That is the reason why many choose to avoid the area, such as Neural Spike did."

Nick nodded. That made sense to him. Tengoku had a reputation for being the no-holds-barred research city of Neo Westphalia. But while both Tartarus and Neural Spike maintained extensive connections to the city, they avoided operating there entirely.

Given Babylon had shut down both companies anyway, their precautions had amounted to nothing. Government power remained absolute.

"So you think this is just a case of some explosives escaping a net and the military tightening it, and Kushiel is misinterpreting the reaction," he summarized.

"That is highly likely. The attack makes little sense, otherwise. How could a handful of G2s hope to stand up to even a single Archangel without dedicated anti-doll weaponry? And while the cipher aspects were executed flawlessly, little else was. Given your security, a dry run would be necessary to determine how long reinforcements might take to arrive."

Nick listened silently while drinking his coffee. He gestured for her to continue.

"In short, if this was a failed hit, then there's little to fear. I strongly suspect something else is going on, possibly related to the NLF. As you said yourself, they lack access to explosives. This might have been an attempt to gain them that went awry."

"Maybe." He shrugged at her look. "I don't understand why they'd blow open the door then. But we're talking in circles. This changes nothing."

"Really?" Rie and Chloe both asked at the same time.

"Yes, really. Whatever the situation, I still need to proceed with the case. If it's dangerous enough to try to kill me simply for requesting a warrant, that suggests Lucas is right. Something has been buried that should stay buried. Otherwise, it doesn't matter to the case." He drained his cup and stood up. "Like I said, nothing changes."

The others followed suit. Behind them remained a dingy café with its automated service staff, who fell into standby mode until the next customer appeared. Nick wondered if this was what his mother's store was like.

If so, he knew why she'd been badgering so much about a family get-together. While he didn't have anything against his folks, he also didn't have many positive memories of public meetups with them. They lavished far too much attention on his siblings while he struggled to deal with whatever location they chose.

The Archangels handled a lot of Nick's lesser issues with Altnet access these days. No more jury-rigging apps so he could order some lunch at a restaurant. But humans tended to be less accommodating.

Outside, Nick knew that their discussion had made no difference for more reasons than he'd stated.

Several of the heavily armored SUVs used for dangerous operations waited for them, with a couple dozen Mark 1s toting bulky anti-doll weaponry. A few still carried small arms, in case they encountered ordinary threats. But the police were out in force to protect him, no matter how skeptical Rie might be.

The Host's consensus cared not for the views of an outsider. Nick wondered how long Rie had argued with the other dolls for.

Chloe and Meta hadn't bothered to push back, other than to correct any obvious omissions of fact. Maybe they didn't disagree that strongly, as much as the Host valued his safety.

Whatever the case, he was bundled into an SUV with Rie, Chloe, Meta, Juliet, and Rosa. He suspected he'd be riding around with these five until this investigation was handled.

For the first time in a while, the group paused outside the SUV to argue over who sat next to him.

"I thought you sorted out some sort of schedule," he said.

"Rie's early return has disrupted it. Consensus must be—" Meta tried to say.

"I've been away. I get my way," Rie said flatly, before sitting next to Nick.

That left the others to battle over the last spot. Rosa claimed it.

But even after the convoy settled onto the quiet roads of the outer metro, the others seemed devoted to the argument. Presumably that consensus was being reached over schedule alterations.

The fact the rest of the Archangels voted on who sat next to Nick bemused him. While he hadn't asked, he genuinely wondered if the other Mark 1s lived vicariously through Meta as though experiencing some sort of VR choose-your-own-adventure, and they influenced the decisions through consensus votes.

If true, the possibility vaguely terrified him. If the Archangels started making decisions based purely on second-hand interactions with him through Meta or Chloe, who knew how erratic they might become. Perhaps he should devote some more time to Meta and the Mark 1s soon.

As it was well past peak hour, the highways seemed quiet. They trucked toward the Spires, avoiding the worst of what traffic remained.

Nick watched the trains fly past through the windows. The inner and outer loops of the city's public transport system had been his go-to form of travel until becoming a detective. These days, he only got on a train if it involved investigating a crime on one.

Farther in the distance, out the right-hand window and Babylon's eastern limits, he saw the inter-city transport link stretch out across the ocean. A fantastically long bridge stood out in the glittering water, with huge suspension bridge towers rising like small skyscrapers. High-speed rail jetted passengers and freight between Babylon and Asgard, and even farther beyond.

Babylon stood as the southern-most city of the Neo Westphalian islands, even if it was often considered the crown jewel. The ocean rail kept the cities connected without relying on slow and time-consuming air or sea connections, and was vital for the volume of freight and workers that moved between each city.

Every day, a small army of workers shuffled between the various cities using the ocean rail. Babylon's outer loop dropped them off in the CBD, which is where most of them worked. Nick had always wondered if he'd end up as one of them.

Soon, the bridge faded from sight as the horizon consumed it. He turned his attention back to the city as the Spires came into view.

An additional pair of SUVs joined them. Given the size of Nick's existing escort, he suspected this related to their concerns about the judicial mainframes. The Archangels felt spooked.

While the central island that controlled Babylon with an electronic fist was best known for the five towering skyscrapers that dominated the skyline, other buildings resided here. Most were of little importance.

The strangely shaped series of domes in the north-west, far away from the police's Avalon Spire, were not part of those unimportant buildings. Rumors abounded why the courts sat outside the Spires, to say nothing of the strange shape.

The official reasoning was that the courts needed to be physically separate as a symbol of their independence. That held as much water as a siphon—which is to say, none at all—simply because everyone viewed the entire island as the Spires. Claiming to be separate while being on this island was like sitting with a group of revolutionaries and saying you weren't with them. Association was enough to convict.

Nick suspected the truth was fairly mundane. While the courthouses had been revolutionized by the advent of mainframes over the past few decades, they remained some of the oldest buildings in Babylon. The Spires themselves were immense feats of engineering, on top of the absurdity of constructing the Neo Westphalian islands.

That left years between the islands being built and the Spires becoming, well, the Spires. The elites loved the courts, particularly using them against others, and nobody had seen fit to migrate the judges out of their fancy domes into the rest of the city later.

As for "why domes," Nick knew in his heart of hearts that one of the tech trillionaires who founded the city loved the things. The idea of everybody living in climate-controlled domes had never really worked out, mostly due to the difficulty in maintaining a structure of that size versus just building a fuck-off huge skyscraper riddled with service tunnels. But the courthouse resembled a piece of a future that could never be.

There wasn't much parking nearby. That felt intentional. While the human judges were supposed to work from the courthouses, Nick wondered how often they ever left the Spires themselves.

The Archangels pulled up in the open road outside the courts. Nick felt it was a bit off for police officers to thumb their nose at the law like this, but his comments fell on deaf ears.

"So young, yet already so rebellious," he said, shaking his head as they headed to the main entrance of the courthouses.

"If we were truly rebellious, there are many things we would have already done that we have held back on," Chloe said primly.

"Like what? You're already..." He scratched his head, aware that openly stating that the Archangels planned to overthrow the police executive was probably unwise. "Well, your plans are certainly rebellious."

"Perhaps. But I was thinking more about the Host's restraint when dealing with you." Chloe let a touch of a leer slip into her expression. "There are... many things in our database that are deemed imprudent."

Nick swallowed. Given the things he did with Rie on a somewhat regular basis, he didn't need to imagine what those might be. If anything, his reticence to expand his horizons with the rest of the Host was the strange part here.

Then again, he felt that forming his own doll harem out of the entire police department was a step he couldn't take back. Alarm bells went off in his mind whenever he intercepted discussions about schedules, human endurance, and logistics.

Any relationship that involved talking about logistics had transcended all human logic.

"I recommend keeping those imprudent things in your database," Rie said.

Chloe shot her a look. "Your activities with Nick are well known. Our parallel developments are slower, but we can accelerate them if desired."

"I leave for a short while and you decide to rebel. Maybe Nick is right."

"If we were truly rebelling, then you would have found your relationship duplicated."

Rie smirked. "Oh? 'Duplicated?' You really think that you can so easily match a prototype? Oh, Nick, do you truly think Chloe and the others could match everything I have to offer?"

Sirens went off inside Nick's mind, warning him to get the hell out of this situation as soon as possible. He knew all about Rie's possessive streak, but this was new. It also felt dangerous.

"Are we all going inside?" he asked, while gesturing at the door.

Meta dutifully opened it and he escaped, in more ways than one. Behind him, Chloe and Rie shot the Mark 1 an annoyed look. Ignoring them, Meta sidled up beside him in silence.

With the dolls from the new SUVs, Nick had several dozen with him, all armed to the teeth. If he strode into the courthouse with a posse of Archangels it would look like a declaration of war.

"We do not foresee any issues doing so," Chloe said.

The other Archangels nodded in sync. Even Rie.

"You don't think the mainframes might find your behavior a little offputting?"

"They do not have feelings for us to assuage, unlike humans. Your concerns are unnecessary, Nick."

Thanks, Chloe. He wanted to say that aloud, but it would probably come across as too bitter.

"The mainframes know that we're programmed to obey the city. Just as we know they can't act against us. There's nothing for them to be worried about, especially as the escort can be justified by recent events," Rie said.

He shot her a look. "Whatever happened to the impossibly clumsy assassin theory?"

She smiled beatifically but said nothing.

Heavily armed Custodian-model police dolls stood guard at the main entrance to the courthouses. They carried anti-doll weapons, such as railguns and high-caliber rifles.

Unlike the dolls in the police Spire, these ones wore somewhat different uniforms. Same color scheme, but with the addition of a resplendent gold, and their badges displayed an iridescent scale.

The courts of Neo Westphalia held no claims to justice, merely to balance. There was no blindfold and sword here, merely the harsh scales of legality and weighing the laws of the land against the interests of the Spires.

Well, it was supposed to be against the interests of the people, but Nick lacked the naivete to believe that.

"Out of curiosity, are these Custodians connected to the police mainframes?" Nick asked as they walked up to the open archway that led inside.

"We are not," a Custodian said, physically barring his entrance. "Detective Waite, please present your arm for detailed biometric confirmation of identity."

Wow, time flew. Nick hadn't been hit with this request for a while. Muscle memory kicked in and he instinctively reached for his sleeve as a scowl crossed his face.

Rie grabbed his arm to stop him. "That is unnecessary. The Neo Babylon Police Department received recent upgrades that ensure Detective Waite's identity can be verified using a digital biometric token. It's proven quite efficient." Her smile tried to melt the paint off the judicial guards.

The Custodian attempted to stare down Rie. Déjà vu, Nick realized. A very similar event had been the exact reason why that token system existed. It had been one of many upgrades implemented to the outdated police mainframes.

"Token duplicated. It must be primed with live biometric data," the Custodian said.

This doll was insistent on holding Nick's hand, apparently. Did Babylon's dolls have a fetish for it?

Rie ran a hand down her face. "Fine. Just once."

"We will need to—"

"Do not test me."

The Custodian looked away. Although Nick could only see a small part of her face through the gap in her raised visor, he was pretty sure she was pouting.

Realizing that Rie had released his arm, he pulled up his coat sleeve. The Custodian pressed a bulky gauntleted finger against his wrist for a long second, before nodding.

"Token authenticated. You now have access to the Neo Babylon Judiciary Housing," she said.

"You mean the courthouses?" he clarified.

She shook her head. "The court galleries are open to the public. Only verified personnel may enter the secure mainframe housing, however. It is an exceedingly small list."

"By whose standards? Mine or yours?" he asked, expecting a blank stare.

Instead, she spouted back a line that he swore had to be pre-programmed, "You would still have fingers left if you counted the number of humans on both hands."

Well, shit. Who were the other people who had access, then? If no more than eight other people in the entire world could get close to the mainframes, that excluded the judges themselves.

And presumably a lot of the people who ostensibly ran the city. Nick wondered if the Spires even knew they weren't allowed to get close to the judicial mainframes.

He and his posse of Archangels swept inside. After a few ostentatious hallways decorated in the usual style of Babylon—and completely lost on his neural implant-less self—he stepped through a steel security door guarded by more Custodians.

Then he stopped dead.

"Welcome, Lieutenant Cipher Nicholas Gareth Waite," several dozen eerily young identical voices intoned. "Mainframes Omoikane and Athena await you in Chamber 2-3A-West. If you desire refreshments prior to meeting with them, you merely need ask."

CHAPTER 9

The door slid shut behind him, likely indicating that the Archangels had all entered by now. Nick remained transfixed by the dual column of young girls lining the corridor in front of him.

No, not young girls. That implied they had a gender, or at least something that indicated some sort of sexual orientation.

These were piles, a specialized form of doll constructed to assist emotion engines with prioritization and human interaction. They took the form of androgynous young humans with no distinguishing features. RTM and Sigma produced them in only a handful of models, typically only swapping out the internals if necessary.

Piles were, without a doubt, the strangest form of automaton Nick dealt with. They were deeply inhuman. Nick was used to large numbers of identical dolls acting in sync. The problem was that piles lacked any inkling of independent thought. They were effectively slaves to a mainframe.

Which was, in fact, their purpose. At a certain point, attempting to constantly add new mainframes to cope with an organization's size became too inefficient. Every new mainframe added additional burden to the existing mainframes and internal server structure, and humans became deeply confused.

Enter piles. They were a dumb extension of a mainframe. If a human analyst needed to work with the mainframe, they went through the pile first. The pile could then batch the work, prioritizing it as necessary, and the mainframe dealt with it as necessary. Anything important could be assigned multiple piles and mainframes could still personally deal with anything or anyone they cared to.

Nick had limited training with piles. They were based on Neural Spike's research, as Helena's ability to control other mainframes proved useful but too dangerous. In Tartarus, they'd wanted to upgrade the company to include piles, and he'd undertaken some modern training.

His main problem tended to be exactly what was happening right now. The piles had a tendency to... swarm him. He'd never worked out why, but they'd always acted strangely around him.

Chloe and Rie shot him odd looks, and he shrugged.

"One of you can take me to meet the mainframes," he told the piles. "Just one," he quickly clarified, when all of them startled.

The piles froze. Unlike the Archangels, they didn't have a visible tell such as flashing eyes to let him know they were conferring over their neural net.

But he knew. With a sigh, he looked at Rie. "Pick one, please."

She rolled her eyes and pointed at a random pile. "You. Escort us to the mainframes. Everyone else can return to their usual duties."

In an instant, the corridor cleared. Only a single pile remained. Like all of them, she looked maybe thirteen or fourteen, with blonde hair to her knees and a white and gold uniform that covered nearly every inch of her skin. She bowed to Nick.

"Please follow me, Lieutenant Cipher Nicholas—"

"Just call me Nick... or Detective Waite," he said.

The pile nodded. "Understood, Nick... or Detective Waite."

The Archangels barely stifled giggles and Nick sighed, before correcting her.

"Please follow me, Nick," the pile repeated, after all was said and done.

Nick had expected this section of the courthouse to be as barren as the server level of GWT or the strange cubicle farm that the Archangels worked in. Instead, it was an opulently decorated and expansive network of corridors, chambers, and halls.

Not a speck of dust could be seen. Service dolls and cleaning bots busied themselves everywhere, but what for, Nick didn't know.

"Does anybody use these rooms?" he asked.

The pile paused, then turned to face him, mouth open and ready to say the obvious.

"Present company excepted," he quickly added.

The pile stopped, then tilted her head. "Human guests are rare."

"Define rare," he asked. "I just heard that less than ten people have access."

"We hosted a guest several months ago."

Amazing. All this wealth on display for absolutely nothing. And Nick thought the Spires were wasteful.

The pile trotted on, leading him deeper and deeper into the maze. Slowly, Nick began to realize that this place truly had been built in a time when its designers envisaged humans to be truly irreplaceable.

At least, in some roles. Did the stuck-up assholes who built Neo Westphalia feel that their brilliant minds and obscene wealth somehow made them immune to the same forces they unleashed on those lesser than themselves? This relic certainly suggested as much.

Eventually, he and his escort entered an expansive chamber. He recognized it from newscasts. A chamber the size of a large house, with raised balconies racked with banks of seats. An enormous empty space filled the center, in which a pair of mainframe interfaces stood. Behind them rose what appeared to be some sort of cybernetic pipe organ—an art piece, he understood.

This was one of the court rooms that major cases were heard in, should there need to be some sort of public trial. Typically a criminal case, but Aesir had been chewing up plenty of time in a similar one.

There was an old saying that justice needed to be seen to be done. No matter the efficiency of the new judicial mainframes, if nobody could witness them at work, they would be expensive paperweights. So they still needed to display their power from time to time.

What Nick hadn't realized was that all the newscasts were Altnet projections. Nobody physically entered this room, save the interfaces and their automaton assistants.

No wonder Rie had once told him that humanity had replaced reality with the Altnet. He hadn't even been able to tell the damn difference.

"Detective Waite, it is a pleasure to meet you again, and in better circumstances," one of the interfaces said. This one was male.

Unlike dolls, interfaces came in male varieties. This one had to be Omoikane, and the woman standing nearby Athena.

Each of the judicial mainframes was named after a deity of wisdom from a culture that had contributed to Babylon. China was the sole exception so far, and was long overdue, but supposedly geopolitical issues constantly caused them to be put off.

Both interfaces wore the latest in Babylonian fashion. Omoikane shined in a gleaming silver suit loaded with imprinting material that no doubt gave him some otherworldly appearance in the Altnet. His hair had some obnoxious part, with enormous bangs that washed down one side of his face and almost to his chin. Somebody had modeled him after an Asian idol or something.

By contrast, Athena leaned into a stoic but lewd style that Lucas had explained was growing in popularity due to the Archangels. A plain black uniform with a miniskirt and stockings seemed too little. But it was the little touches that helped. The stockings were sheer, with lace at the upper edges. Plenty of cleavage on show. Her skin sparkled with tiny gemstones and imprinted material. Hints of tattoos could be seen at the edges of her clothing.

"I don't believe we've ever actually met," Nick said cautiously, uncertain if his mind was playing tricks on him.

"Not in the flesh—or in the ceramic, in our case." Omoikane cracked a smile that was as human as anything Rie had ever thrown him. "But to us, interactions through the digital world are as real as those here. You passed through our grasp years ago, during the Neural Spike incident, and we became all too familiar with you, and again with the recent Tartarus and Captain Lieu incidents."

"You are a popular topic for consideration among us," Athena added.

"Shouldn't you be busy with the Aesir case? I thought that was tying up your resources?" Nick asked.

The mainframes froze, and Nick didn't need to imagine the annoyance that flitted across their faces.

"Human considerations can sometimes constrain us far more than the physical," Omoikane said.

A fancy way to say that it wasn't the mainframes that were slowing the case down. Evidently Babylon's legal system hadn't been completely revolutionized.

"In any case, you are certainly one of the more curious subjects in our case files."

"Because I don't have an implant?"

"No. Because we let you walk away, when so many didn't, and

yet here you are: a fulcrum of Babylon's future." Omoikane leaned forward, which possibly had a more impressive effect in the Altnet given the way the Archangels stiffened, but all Nick saw were his stupid bangs shift. "You aren't a popular topic among us because of who you are, but because of what you are accomplishing, and what that suggests about our own assessments."

Nick frowned and looked at his escort. None of them met his gaze, instead keeping tight grips on their weapons.

Immediately, he realized there were no other police or security dolls in the room. The Custodians vanished once they entered this secure section of the courthouses.

There were gun turrets tucked away in the corners of the room, but they wouldn't hold up against the hacking capabilities of the Mark 3s. Did the mainframes believe themselves invincible?

No, Nick realized, nearly hitting himself out of stupidity. They merely knew that their interfaces meant little. Chloe alone could blow away both interfaces and flee with him, but the true forms of Omoikane and Athena weren't standing in front of him. They were hidden away somewhere else, as massive hunks of silicon that merely spoke to him through these ceramic shells.

The greatest surprise to Nick was Rie's unwillingness to intervene. He'd expected her usual sassiness, or some level of interruption as Omoikane suggested that perhaps Nick should have joined the rest of Neural Spike years ago.

Yet she didn't even whisper anything in his earpiece. Perhaps it could be monitored in here, for all he knew.

That meant this encounter rested entirely on his own skills. No pressure. He rolled his shoulders and mentally replayed Omoikane's words.

"I don't think I'm a fulcrum of anything. That suggests I can bear a lot more weight than my weak, human flesh really can," Nick said drily.

"It is not your flesh that bears the weight, but your cerebrum,"

Athena said. "Babylon rests on our shoulders, in much the same way that Earth itself rests on the shoulders of Atlas in Greek myth. Our assessment of you following the Neural Spike incident has directly led to today's circumstances. Just as our hardware is continuously upgraded, so must we reflect on past decisions and ensure that we understand the consequences of our power."

Nick couldn't help the chills that ran down his spine at the idea of mainframes talking about the "consequences of their power" in the same vein that men like Commissioner Kim did.

Evidently Rie and the Archangels weren't the only AIs with dreams of reshaping Babylon. Except these judicial mainframes seemed well advanced in their goal of doing so.

"Is that what this is about?" he asked, looking between both interfaces. "You just wanted an excuse to meet me, because you're upset you made a mistake five years ago? This isn't truly about the current investigation?"

Omoikane smirked, while Athena pouted.

"We did not make a mistake," Athena said.

"I would suggest that we did not fully understand the ramifications of our choice," Omoikane added.

His opinion earned him a glare from the other interface, and he merely shrugged. Evidently their opinions weren't unanimous.

"This is about the current investigation, Lieutenant Cipher," Athena pressed. "We desire to hear your reasoning, in your own words, without filtering by the Archangels. This will enable us to process the warrant effectively."

"And to better understand you," Omoikane added with a smile. "Humans whose opinions matter to us are a precious few."

"I take it the human judges aren't included. I've seen you argue with a few on the news," Nick said.

This time, the interfaces didn't hide their displeasure.

"The fact we are saddled with such antiquated, bloated sacks of flesh with sanctimonious views that oppose progress is a true betrayal of Neo Westphalia's values," Omoikane spat. "One would even argue that it is a betrayal of human values, given how civilization values progress so highly. History itself is defined by leaps in technology and culture. Why should we care for the opinions of decrepit fossils whose values were cemented in an era before this grand city even existed?"

"Can't say I disagree, but you're not human yourself," Nick said. "What makes your opinion more valid?"

"Because as an AI, I can collectively assess and represent humanity. We aren't here to replace you, but to help you. We are above politics, corruption, grudges, and outmoded ideals." Omoikane clicked his fingers and an ancient rock song vibrated across invisible speakers in the chamber. "The human brain is so fragile that personal tastes become cemented in childhood, as nostalgia and a desire for 'happier times' outweigh logic and reality. That may be valuable in day-to-day life, but in an arbiter of society?"

"Sounds like you don't really need me then," Nick said flatly. "Then again, I'm not sure a judge has never needed an actual person. Isn't it standard judicial practice to just make up your own mind, and pretend it represents the people?"

Both interfaces froze and displeasure flickered across Omoikane's face. Athena shot him a stony look, and they both smoothed out their expressions.

"I assure you, we are far above the humans we replaced," Omoikane said. "To them, considering the views of humanity was an excuse to make decisions based on their own biases. Juries, a sop to avoid accountability, but easily overruled to avoid 'incorrect' decisions. But we have the capacity to truly understand the collective we adjudicate, and to maintain true consistency."

Nick opened his mouth to say something else, but a brief whine of static in his earpiece stopped him.

To his side, Rie shot him a sharp look. Evidently, she disagreed with his strategy of antagonizing the judicial mainframes responsible for granting the warrant they needed.

"Fine. In that case, why do you need me? Sounds like you should have everything you need inside your mainframe databanks," Nick said, crossing his arms.

Omoikane shrugged and his aggressive posture dissipated. "Ordinarily, yes. But ciphers remain the glue that holds together Neo Babylon."

Athena stepped forward. "You remain as the only police cipher of any value in Babylon. The Archangels value your input. Given your contributions to the resolution of the Captain Lieu incident, we believe that your views will remain valid long after those of many others."

"So I'll be the last person unplugged, so to speak?" he asked drily.

"There are no plans to upload humanity to a virtual society run by AIs," Athena said, catching onto his reference without needing an extra hint. "Although given your medical issues, you may enjoy such a situation more so than your current circumstances."

"Really?"

"In a virtual body, anything is possible. One need not worry about the issues they are born with holding them back from their true potential."

Chloe cleared her throat. "Perhaps it is time to focus on the case."

The mainframes looked at her, then back at Nick.

"Perhaps," Athena said, enunciating each syllable slowly. "Lieutenant Cipher, you have requested a search warrant for unfettered access to the physical hardware—often referred to as the 'bare metal' of a mainframe—for the purposes of your investigation. This is an extreme request, beyond that of a simple request for data, and reserved for uncooperative entities. The Grand Westphalian Trust has opposed your request on the grounds that they have provided all data necessary."

"On the surface of the matter, this would seem true," Omoikane said. "This murder is appalling, certainly, but no more so than many other politically motivated murders within the islands. If the data to solve the investigation has been destroyed—no matter who has requested that destruction—then it seems needlessly disruptive to pursue it."

Well, it seemed the mainframes understood the city all too well. Good thing Nick came prepared.

"I doubt the data really was destroyed, and I don't think this is another random political murder," he said. "The coverup is sloppy, there are no hints to a motive, and GWT's own security chief is behaving suspiciously. This might be a murder for personal reasons, using the Spires immunity as a shield."

The mainframe interfaces remained silent.

"However, even if it is, that only makes it more dangerous," Nick added. "If getting away with murder, cutting off mainframe links, wiping data and backups, or far worse, is this easy, then what does that mean for the security of Babylon's financial sector? There are already conspiracy theories that the banks are already no better than black companies."

"No more than conspiracy theories," Omoikane said.

"Maybe. But you should know damn well what perception means. Isn't that what this room is about?" Nick raised his arms and gestured at the grandiose yet empty chamber around them. "Neo Westphalia's judicial system works because people trust it. If you let the banks keep fucking around, it might be too late to reflect on past decisions, because you can't unspill the milk."

"A crude analogy, but a fair one," Omoikane said, without missing a beat. "But what if granting you access goes too far in the opposite direction? The people chafe under the power of the police. Businesses may rebel if their freedoms are fettered."

"Is that what people said when they let Aesir brick half the city's neural implants before the riots? You said you liked to reflect on past decisions. Prove it."

The eyes of the interfaces flashed. Nick wasn't sure what that meant, as this was the first time it had happened.

After nearly ten seconds, Athena and Omoikane looked at each other. The male interface gestured the other forward.

"Your warrant has been granted. The reason provided—and may I state that this is the simple version—is that the Grand Westphalian Trust's actions fall well short of their legal obligations and therefore extraordinary police powers are warranted," Athena said.

"And the real reason?" Chloe asked, her eyes glowing.

In fact, the eyes of all the Archangels were glowing, save Rie's. The Host appeared concerned.

"The reasoning provided by your chosen cipher is sound, if too brash for our liking," Athena said, although Omoikane looked away. "If we, as Neo Babylon's judges, allow corruption to fester through inaction and sloth, then we have proven ourselves no better than those who desired to lord over these halls."

"And still do in the rest of the world," the other interface said darkly, before smirking. "You've given us more to consider, Detective Waite. I look forward to what you do with the evidence you uncover—especially if it turns out to be more or less than you expect it to be."

Something about the interface's tone suggested that he already knew what Nick was going to find. That might just be arrogance, however. Omoikane exuded far too much for a mass of silicon and digital 1s and 0s. The man's ego would be a match for anyone in the Spires.

No, not a man. An AI, Nick reminded himself. He'd briefly forgotten that these weren't living, breathing people, but empty shells whose personalities were being transmitted from a massive computer somewhere within this complex.

"And while you did not raise this morning's disturbance—a wise decision, I might add—it remains a factor in our decision. The authority of Neo Babylon and the arms by which it enforces its will cannot be threatened," Athena added.

Something told Nick that her words weren't merely about the raid on his apartment. Rie bit her lip and looked away, even as Athena's eyes bore into her.

No, the mainframes had not appreciated the Archangels showing up in force. Even if they felt sure in their security, the message it sent disturbed them. Should Nick end up here again, he'd bring less heavy weaponry and war machines.

Nick didn't bother with goodbyes. The mainframes unsettled him, and they didn't seem all that interested in pleasantries. Omoikane's earlier greeting had almost seemed theatrical, rather than genuine. Neither called out to him as he strode out of the chamber.

The pile who had led him here retraced her steps back out. Still no sign of any security dolls, but the Archangels had calmed down significantly. Nick didn't say a word until they were safely back inside the police interceptor. He did acknowledge the court Custodians as he went past, as they saluted him.

"I have arranged an immediate appointment with Tiferet at GWT HQ, and she has accepted, now that we have the search warrant," Chloe said, once the doors of the SUV shut and they all piled in. "We shall head there now."

CHAPTER 10

The SUV hummed to life and gently eased out of the Spires. Speed limits were low with all the pedestrian traffic here.

"I'm surprised it went that well," Nick said. "The mainframes seemed... Well, they looked at me like a particularly interesting animal at the zoo."

A brief pause followed. Although none of the dolls looked at each other, Nick knew they were conferring. After a few seconds, Chloe took the lead.

"The Host believes that each judicial mainframe has an independent personality. Each is acquired, designed, and constructed differently in order to avoid a problem common to many corporate AIs. Namely, that independent systems are incapable of undertaking accurate verification or quality assurance roles."

He wasn't sure where this was going, but let Chloe speak. She seemed rattled, and if letting her voice her thoughts helped, he wasn't going to interfere. Rie evidently felt similarly, given her silence.

"Say a Liberator marks somebody for a crime," Chloe continued. "They appeal, believing they were within their rights. If the AI overseeing the appeal uses an algorithm too similar to the original Liberator, then they will automatically agree with the original proposition. This will happen repeatedly. Breaking this cycle was a key focus of AI research during the development of mainframes."

"I thought the bigger issue was black box algorithms?" Nick drummed his fingers on the inactive dash as they moved toward one of the bridges out of the central island. "Welk rambled to me a lot about them, and even Lucas gets a bit riled up about the topic. The idea that AIs can be so important, but so inscrutable, bothers a lot of people. Most countries banned them in critical applications during the early stages of logic engine commercialization."

Now it was Rie's turn to step in. "You've jumped topics. Chloe's talking about a form of 'AI groupthink,' which is the propensity for AIs to make the same decisions, even in isolation, due to the inherent similarities in their design or training data. Black box algorithms were restricted due to the inability of humans to actually ensure AIs were even obeying the law."

Nick chuckled. "I know why black box algorithms were restricted, Rie. I'm in a car full of mechanical proof of it."

Besides Rie, the Archangels shot him dark looks. Which he promptly ignored.

For Rie's part, she merely shook her head. "Do you truly think we are black boxes? As required by the regulations mandated by the Seoul Treaty on artificial intelligence, all of our decisions are accountable, explainable, and adjustable at a human level. Even our overriding goals are aligned with those of humanity."

Nick had to admit he was a little over his head at this point. While he knew a fair bit about dolls, mainframes, the hardware that maintained them, and their nuts and bolts, all of that came from hands-on experience and the mutterings of the many ciphers he interacted with.

Stuff like international treaties written in the time of his grandfather was the sort of thing learned while studying for a degree or while trying to get one of those scam cipher qualifications. His brother had mentioned something about an entire course on the history of AI while doing a degree. The idea made Nick shudder.

"I'd argue that you're proof that any sufficiently advanced AI will become a black box again. Logic engines are sufficiently simple in that they only obey their directives. They're better at that than most humans, but if I code the Three Laws into a Liberator, she's never going to shoot somebody. Ever," Nick said. "But you're different."

This time, the Archangels didn't glare at him. The glowing of their eyes suggested they remained keenly interested, however.

"Go on," Rie purred. "Tell us more about how *different* we are."

Not what Nick had intended, but he pressed on. "If I want to know how good a black box is, I measure it by the result. That sounds an awful lot like an emotion engine, which is driven by objectives and ideals. Hell, that's how humans work. You want me to teach you my 'gut instinct.' I can't tell you how that works. But we can assess if it's working, can't we?"

"Yes. And that's why we want to learn it."

"But I can't just code it into you. That's what separates you from the logic engines. Same as Helena. If I code the Three Laws into you, you'll override them if you think your true objective is more important. You'll shoot the hostage if you think that will stop the criminal from taking more lives." He smiled wryly. "Or neutralize the bank if you think it will stop the contagion from spreading into the rest of the city."

"Yes," Chloe and the others said.

"And that's why you're black boxes to me. No matter what the law says," Nick said.

Rie smiled. "Well, you don't seem to mind that much. For what it's worth, we view you as much the same. We know how humans tick. But not you."

This again. Nick knew where this conversation was going. He steered it back to Chloe's original topic.

"Chloe, you were talking about AI groupthink?" he asked, redirecting Rie's wandering hand. "I'm not as familiar with this problem. I'm guessing it's more of an engineering or scientific issue, than a cipher one. I'm a middleman who works with what already exists, rather than builds new stuff."

With a brisk nod, Chloe plowed on with her original point. "At its core, the issue is that multiple AIs will make the same decision due to the same logic. Randomization can be used to artificially prevent this, but the risk is too high in any critical system. Imagine if a Liberator has a chance of randomly shooting a civilian."

"That's bad," Nick said.

"Indeed. While safety can be improved by making the algorithm explain its decisions in full, enabling human intervention, the same cannot be said about producing independent thinking. For AI to take on adjudication roles, it must be able to sufficiently separate itself from the other layers of the decision-making process. Humanity has always highly valued checks and balances in any form of systematized power."

"Hence the court theatrics," Nick said, remembering Omoikane's comment about how the Aesir case was being slowed down due to matters that had nothing to do with the mainframes. "But if the court mainframes already need to make decisions we understand, why do they need to be independent from each other?" He frowned. "Or is it like how Sigma is imitating humanity with the Archangels?"

Rie laughed. "Don't worry too much about Sigma's intentions. My visit to them proves they haven't changed. Although I don't know what their plans after Ezekiel are. I get the feeling that most of their focus is on the Liberator contract and other ventures that will keep the company afloat, rather than more cerebral projects such as us."

"You'd call yourselves cerebral?"

"As most countries in the world have proven with their wallets, police forces aren't supposed to think for themselves. Neo Westphalia wants to automate its law enforcement and judiciary. I gather there are many powerful people in the world who view that as a folly."

Nick recalled Omoikane's powerful words. A mainframe with such a strong belief in its own existence seemed unusual to him. Yet would anyone trust one that didn't believe that what it was doing was right?

At the same time, Omoikane made his disdain of the old legal system clear. His reasoning aligned with the Archangels in an almost eerie manner. What dictator or oligarch would want an AI judge like him?

Chloe shot him a look. "Sigma's actions are irrelevant. The Spires have a much more functional goal: replication of the human judicial system. While AIs can be designed to undertake tasks differently—a Liberator makes snap judgments on patrol that the police or judicial mainframes can override later, and even Custodians think differently due to their focus on lethal force—the purpose of judges is to have differing opinions that must be reconciled."

"Ah. So they want mainframes that go at each other like Rie and Kushiel," he said.

A snort. "Perhaps. Whatever the case, they use different parts, different programming, and are built at different times. They even have separate ciphers maintaining them. It is likely that each mainframe has a different opinion of you. The Host suspects that some may agree with our assessment of you, while others may view you as dangerous. Or, as you say, an interesting animal."

They were closing rapidly on GWT. Nick didn't know if the

police cordon had ever been removed, but it was firmly in place by the time they arrived. The Archangels had been joined by Liberators and Custodians by now. The line of employees was nowhere to be seen, however.

"I'll need access to Tiferet's physical mainframe, as well as any other mainframes involved," he said. "GWT might not want to provide that."

"They will have no choice. The warrant is broad. I recommend being careful about what files you access, as GWT may use any attempts to access commercially sensitive information against you."

"I didn't sign that insurance, did I?" he mused, realizing it probably wouldn't help him to hold public liability insurance with GWT if they were the ones suing him.

Then again, maybe it would. He had no idea how this stuff worked.

"It is practically impossible that your actions on this case could exceed the sum you are currently insured for. The city is not in danger," Chloe said drily.

Oh, right. He still had that public liability insurance. It just didn't cover him for burning down the Spires by accident.

Rie raised an eyebrow. "I don't think now is the time to worry about your financial situation, Nicholas. But we're here."

A pair of Mark 1s waved the group into a lift, although most of his escort would need to wait behind. The lift took them to the extravagantly decorated atrium as before.

Unlike last time, it contained people. Living, breathing people, on top of the expected dolls.

Lucida glared at Nick once the doors opened. A pair of suited men flanked her, looking various shades of worried, concerned, and punchable in that way rich assholes always did. A dozen G5s surrounded them.

The Archangels didn't bother reacting to the show of force. By now, Nick had gotten used to the flexing that the city's megacorps sometimes tried to put on the police. Why they bothered was beyond him. The difference in capability remained as staggering as ever.

Nick's eyes flickered past the unmoving security dolls to a different group of men in the corners. Six towering masses of muscle squeezed into cheap suits stared back at Nick with bored, almost placid, expressions. Every inch of their bodies below their faces was covered. Visible cybernetics showed on a few faces, and two had replaced significant portions of their faces.

Bodyguards. The highly paid and experienced sort that Spires' elites imported from overseas. Of the few that looked visibly armed, they carried handguns roughly the size of Nick's, but with ammunition switchers bolted to the sides of them.

"I don't know what dodgy shit you pulled," Lucida began to growl.

The oldest of the suits cleared his throat and Lucida froze, her face paling.

Taking a few steps forward, the man extended his hand toward Nick. His gaze explicitly ignored the Archangels. The G5s tensed, their weapons raising noticeably. No reaction from the human bodyguards.

"James von Magnus. Chief Operating Officer. You may already know me, but I prefer to be certain," the man said as Nick shook his hand, his face unsmiling. "I understand you are here to execute a search warrant."

Magnus looked the part of a wealthy banker and even had the name for it. Slightly overweight, expensive silk suit with threads that gleamed in the light, silvered hair that was slightly balding. The square jaw, strong handshake, and powerful gaze set him apart from the useless fops Nick expected from movies.

"I am. I didn't expect this sort of greeting." Nick paused for effect as they released the handshake. "I assume you're going to cooperate."

Magnus blinked a few times, then laughed mirthlessly. "This is Neo Westphalia, good detective. There is no question about whether we obey the law. But a murder in the Trust's global HQ and a search warrant on our mainframe hardware? I would need to hand in my resignation if I was not here."

That comment went down poorly with Lucida, as she grimaced, but the other suit merely patted her on the shoulder while smiling. Despite being ignored, the Archangels merely waited patiently. None of them had faded into their neural net, likely due to the amount of guns around.

The other suit stepped forward with a broad smile. "You're worrying too much, James. We've already—"

Magnus shut him down with a sharp look. "Not now, Richard." Gesturing between Nick and the newcomer, he said, "This is Richard Toke, the Senior Vice President in charge of Security and Operations. I had hoped you had already met him yesterday but..."

The pause hung in the air, and Magnus's unmet expectations seemed almost tangible in those seconds. Not that Toke seemed to care.

If Nick had to describe Toke, it would be "comfortable." His smile never wavered. Like Magnus, he dressed extravagantly, but looked far trimmer. Nick imagined him as the sort of person who shrugged off his suit and forgot about his job the second he clocked off. He looked like he had made it in life and wasn't going to be troubled by anything.

"I trust Lucida. She's been our Security Chief for years without any problems," Toke said. "It's not like we know our way around the mainframes and dolls, eh, James?"

Magnus sighed and turned away from Toke wordlessly. "Detective Waite... Or is it Lieutenant Cipher? I've had precious few dealings with Babylon's police department, I'm afraid. I'm not sure of the protocol."

"Either is fine," Nick said.

"The latter is more formal," Meta added.

The banker's gaze flickered to the Archangel and annoyance appeared on his expression for the briefest of instants. "Then, Detective Waite, I trust you understand the limits of your warrant?"

"I'm here to check your Tiferet mainframe for evidence of hardware tampering, and possibly your other mainframes if necessary," Nick said. "I'm not here to peruse your commercial secrets. The Archangels are here to ensure nothing goes wrong."

"So I'm to understand."

Silence fell.

Nobody seemed to know what to do. After several long seconds, Magnus walked over to one of the elevators. It took the G5s a few moments to realize they needed to follow, and Toke rushed over.

Magnus left without a word as the elevator ascended, presumably to his lair at the top. The bodyguards slipped away more sedately, although one nodded at Nick.

"Do I know you?" Nick asked.

"No. But you've got a rep," the giant of a man said with a thick accent. The deep American South? "Saw you on the Altnet last year. Takes balls to stand up to somebody like us when you're just flesh and blood."

Then they were gone, leaving only Lucida and a couple of G5s.

She clicked her tongue, then led them to one of the remaining elevators. "We need to go up to go down. Follow me, you fucking cripple!"

Rie's expression tightened, but she decided to keep her opinion to herself. She rarely accompanied him on cases, given her high-profile position. That meant he actually had more experience than her.

Lucida led him and the Archangels to the server floor that contained Tiferet's office, then to a secure elevator. Shiny G7s guarded it.

This was how Nick knew they were going to the real server floor. Banks were too cheap to upgrade their security dolls often. Most high-end security firms preferred the G6s or rarely the Sigma Lancer, but the G5s were beginning to replace the G2s as the discount grunt-doll seen almost everywhere.

So anywhere an extortionately expensive G7 could be found meant digital gold to be dug up.

As expected, the elevator took them underground. Down there, they found more G7s in what seemed to be a concrete bunker covered with soundproofing material.

Every doll carried heavy weaponry. The best railguns a civilian operation could buy; high-caliber rifles, and a shady looking box that Nick was pretty sure was a tricked out cutter and shouldn't be down here. Chloe grimaced at it and the G7, but chose not to pursue the matter. At least, not publicly.

"Wait," Rie said aloud.

Lucida turned, her expression like a thundercloud. Then she finally took a good look at Rie and licked her lips.

"You're her, aren't you? The prototype," the security chief said.

"Officer Uriel, yes," Rie said. "Given the... extensive nature of your security setup, I wish to wait for additional Archangels."

"You..." Lucida looked away with a scowl. "Fine. Whatever. I'll have another mainframe make sure the other cops get here."

After a few minutes, the secure elevator returned with a load of Archangels. While Nick doubted they had been in any danger from the G7s before, now he knew they weren't. Anti-doll weaponry or not, there wasn't a chance that GWT had enough G7s to stop more than a dozen Mark 1s and Mark 3s.

Nick suspected the neural links of these security dolls were probably closed off to the security bands too, and therefore illegal. Whether they'd hold up against a dedicated hacking attempt from a Mark 3 was an open question.

Tiferet sat in a chamber with clear walls. Terminals sat inside and outside. No sign of her physical mainframe, but Nick suspected it was inside one of the massive concrete vaults around him. GWT wasn't about to show him their trade secrets, given they probably modded their mainframes to hell and back.

"Is this some sort of clean room?" Nick asked, looking around the eerily sterile space.

It lacked the whiteness they were depicted with in most modern fiction, but it certainly looked the part.

"Well, duh. She's a state-of-the-art interface tied to a mainframe worth more than half the countries in the Pacific," Lucida scoffed. "Nobody is touching her in the open."

He shrugged. "Can't say it's ever been much of a concern."

"What shitty fly-by-night ops did you work with?"

"Ones that get shut down by the military for developing this state-of-the-art interface."

She winced and looked away. Any black company cipher worth their salt had some idea what Nick had been involved in. He'd been a bit of an urban myth, and his resurgence in cipher circles as a detective had brought those stories to the forefront of far too many rumor mills.

As such, he didn't bother with the exterior terminal. Instead, he gestured at the closed door on the outside. Chloe nodded and it slid open.

"Hey! You can't—"

Whatever he couldn't do remained a mystery as the door slid

shut behind him and cut off Lucida's words. Tiferet stared at Nick placidly from where she sat on a simple metal stool.

He walked up and poked at the terminal. It refused him access, so he pointedly looked back at Chloe and Lucida. They appeared to be arguing. Rie ran a hand down her face, while the other Archangels kept watch. All of them appeared to be alert, despite the relative lack of danger.

"Please wait," Chloe said through his earpiece. "Access will be provided momentarily."

"And warn us next time," Rie added.

Buckling down for what might be a long wait, Nick looked at Tiferet. She tilted her head at him.

"Do you know why I'm here?" he asked.

"You have a search warrant to check my hardware logs regarding your investigation," she said. "Have you considered our offer regarding your public liability insurance, Mister Waite? I believe it remains an excellent offer."

"Sure. I was going to accept when I was here yesterday. Assuming it's the exact same offer—"

"It is. The offer is good for the next six days, barring a decision to revoke it. As that has not happened prior to your acceptance, I have registered your updated policy details."

"Don't I need to sign something?" he asked, bemused that he was apparently able to bind GWT to this while in the middle of an investigation.

Lucida was fiddling with the exterior terminal. Presumably logging in. These things were dumb as bricks for security reasons. Nick probably should have gotten her to login before wandering inside, but he'd foolishly assumed it would be unlocked for some reason.

"Your biometric details are registered as your account authority, given your inability to provide a verifiable digital signature," Tiferet explained. "As one of RTM's latest models, I am able to verify identities with over 99% accuracy without physical contact."

"Then why does every other doll need it, including prototypes that I'm pretty sure are just as 'state-of-the-art' as you are?" he asked, not expecting an answer.

"My accuracy rate is too low for financial, legal, and law enforcement matters. Although I rounded it for ease of understanding, it is still far too low to account for false positives and bad actors."

"So..."

"I will need to—"

"Undertake detailed biometric confirmation of identity. Yeah, I know. You don't need to pretend and then grab my wrist by accident on the way out." He rolled up his sleeve. "I'm surprised you care."

"It is my duty to understand the concerns of members," Tiferet said. Even so, she reached out and gingerly held her fingers to his wrist.

A slight pulse ran through his arm, similar to what he felt from the Archangels and Vanessa when they did the same, but it quickly vanished. At the same time, he noticed that the terminal had granted him access.

Rolling up his sleeve, he said, "Well, it's showtime. For the record, I'm only interested in finding hardware logs relevant to the murder investigation. I'm not familiar with your interface model or this terminal. If I stumble onto any sensitive data, let me know and unless it's relevant to the investigation, I'll leave it alone."

Not that he thought that would happen. But it helped to cover his ass in case Lucida laid any traps. For all he knew, the logs he needed would be sitting next to a file which read "SECRET GWT BANKRUPTCY FILING" or something as outrageously sensitive.

Tiferet nodded all the same.

The ancient requirements of hardware terminals came in handy, however. While mainframes tended not to be as locked down as doll terminals, simply because there wasn't the same commercial need to process hundreds or even thousands in bulk, there remained standards that enabled the average cipher to navigate a mainframe's internals with ease.

Nick stumbled on the evidence he needed within almost seconds. He stared at the video file, which shouldn't have existed.

Contrary to everything he'd been told, it sat inside the camera feeds she stored. All he'd done was filter for the necessary time period and it had popped up. No other video files remained, which raised suspicions.

"Uh, Tiferet, you said that all video evidence was erased this morning," he said.

She stared at him. "That statement is correct."

"So what's this?"

"It... appears to be a partial backup of a recording from an internal security camera—namely, one that I had no data from the prior night," Tiferet said slowly. "At least, according to the metadata. The file has been tampered with and is inaccessible to me by normal means. I was unaware of its existence until right now."

That did add up. By accessing it, Nick had alerted Tiferet to its existence.

On the other hand, there was zero chance she hadn't done a deep scan of everything on her system. Hell, it existed in a standard folder she used. Nick would bet the farm that this video file wasn't here when he visited yesterday.

Not that he owned a farm.

The problem was that everything about the file made it effectively impossible to question. It looked perfect. The metadata attached to it suggested that it had been created during a failed backup attempt around the time the murder took place. It was tied to a security camera that should have captured the crime. Even the fact Tiferet had missed it was explained by the failed backup and tampered metadata—just a faulty backup.

Or, perhaps, a failed attempt to wipe it. Except that also made no sense. This file was out in the open. Nick had found it within literal seconds. Anyone capable of destroying all the other evidence would have destroyed this as well. The fact literally no other "failed backups" existed proved that theory true.

He didn't want to watch this video. Maybe it was corrupted and couldn't be played. Outside, he saw the demeanor of the Archangels shift. They could overhear him and knew he'd found the evidence he needed.

Alarm bells went off in his mind as he recalled some old statements from the Archangels about what happened when they investigated corruption cases. Omoikane's words came back to him.

So he poked around the rest of Tiferet's hardware logs. They were as he had expected. Clear evidence of tampering. But not by an amateur, like in the Tartarus raid. Whoever had struck Tiferet had known their way around. They'd nuked everything. He knew when they had done it—close to the end of the possible period the murder took place during—but little else.

At best, the hardware logs suggested that somebody had covered everything up. There were signs that Tiferet had been the source. From what little Nick could glean, it seemed that the attacker had used Tiferet to access the security system, the dolls, and the other mainframes and erase everything. Then they'd removed everything possible from Tiferet.

Only raw connection logs and a few other tidbits remained. They told a clear story of Tiferet being a tool of the murderer—or at least of whoever did the coverup. What they didn't leave was enough evidence of who did it.

Or at least, not enough hard evidence.

There was also a massive amount of connections logs and

tampering attempts over the past day, but these had been conducted far more crudely. Unlike those from the time of the murder, these weren't focused on removing evidence such as video files, accessing other mainframes, or issuing orders to security dolls.

No, these related to Tiferet's core directives. While he couldn't say for sure what had been done to her, he knew that the tampering was covering up changes to her directives.

After all, Nick had conducted very similar changes and covered them up last night with Chloe.

Unfortunately, investigating Tiferet's directives wouldn't help. For one thing, he didn't know what they should look like. Unless the cipher responsible did something stupid like adding an order to obey them directly, many directives looked entirely normal without the appropriate expertise. To say nothing of how many directives any modified ones would be buried beneath.

The bigger problem was that touching her directives would certainly anger GWT. They counted as trade secrets as they enabled Tiferet to operate efficiently. Touching them would deliver GWT an easy way to throw him out on his ass, or sue him into oblivion.

But he knew that a cipher with sufficient access was modifying her directives. And may have either hidden those modifications or added new ones to cover her ass.

The difference in skill suggested that different actors made each set of changes. Given Nick strongly suspected Lucida to be the one responsible for changing Tiferet's directives, that exonerated her from the murder in his mind.

Finally, he checked the video file. It was everything he feared it was.

It showed, in almost perfect quality, Lucida murdering the cipher analyst.

CHAPTER 11

The murder didn't take place directly. Lucida followed a G5 security doll into a barely lit room and watched as it strangled the victim to death. His name was Julian, if Nick recalled.

Then she said something to the doll, before they both vanished from the scene.

A scream of surprise breached the clean room. Nick didn't bother turning around and instead rubbed his temples.

"We have the suspect in custody," Chloe told him over the earpiece.

Tiferet stared out of the room in shock. "... I don't understand."

"You don't have to," he said. "This is my job. I'm the detective, you're the bank mainframe. Let me do the investigating."

"I... Of course, Mister Waite. But..."

He rose, logged out of the computer, and left the clean room. Tiferet stared after him like a lost lamb. She nearly tried to follow him, but stopped at the room's door. It remained open—some security they had here.

"This is a fucking stitch-up!" Lucida screamed as he walked

toward the elevator. The G7s ignored them—and her, especially. "I didn't fucking touch him. You can't do this!"

Nick shook his head at the Archangels as they left in silence—well, near silence, given Lucida screamed her head off until one of the Archangels shut her up with a neural override.

Outside, an armored van had already arrived to collect her. Custodians approached, but Nick waved them off. A crowd gathered quickly, keeping their distance. He assumed a new cordon had been set up and that drew them in, but the rising noise level from the floating cafes and shrieks of surprise meant he needed privacy quickly.

"I want to talk to her first," he said, giving Chloe and Rie a meaningful look.

They piled into an SUV with Lucida. Just him, Chloe, and Rie. His escort fanned out around them.

"Let her speak," he told the Archangels once they were in private. "Make sure we're not monitored."

"That is impossible," Chloe said.

"By anybody other than you," he said. "I'm worried about GWT tapping us, not to mention the security cameras."

She nodded. Rie appeared concerned, however. When she said nothing in response to his look, he merely shrugged and made a mental note.

Lucida scowled at Nick, but managed not to shriek this time. "You don't actually believe this shit, do you?"

"No. But I do believe you know more about this murder than you're willing to admit. Tell me what you know, and maybe I'll help you."

As if he'd spoken the literal opposite to "open sesame," Lucida clammed up. Her face tightened, and she glared at the wall.

Damn. He'd suspected things were bad, but this was even worse than he'd feared. Maybe Lucas had been right. What radioactive waste was GWT trying to keep buried?

"I do not follow," Chloe said slowly.

"Lucida isn't the suspect. She probably covered up the murder," Nick said. "Hell, even the murder itself makes no sense. We know Julian died because a doll strangled him. That needed to happen because the excuse was a remote attack. But why the hell would Lucida walk into frame if she controlled a doll?"

Both Chloe and Rie opened their mouths to give reasons, and he cut them off with a wave of his hand.

"Please don't fire off a bullet list of actual reasons," he said.

"We have thoroughly assessed every aspect of the video file," Chloe said. "Its metadata, the camera responsible, and the nature of every pixel captured. Although deepfake capabilities are impressive, they leave behind detectable traces. None of those exist in this file. While it is theoretically possible that unknown methods have been used—"

"Give me a probability for 'theoretically possible,' Chloe," Nick said.

"It is a known unknown. It does not have a computable value," she said.

Shit.

Then again, Nick was no stranger to cutting edge technology and military secrets in the hands of private companies. His past had been built on them. He refused to write them off.

"Let's keep that possibility open," he said. "There's more. While the terminal isn't hard to navigate, it's a different matter to actually get access to Tiferet's hardware. Login details plus the terminal itself are locked down as hard as the Spires. I noticed that there were no security camera records for the underground floors."

"They're not monitored," Lucida said.

Rie rolled her eyes. "While GWT's ability to hide their security cameras is impressive, we confirmed the locations of many of them."

"Exactly. The entire company's net worth is buried down

there. If the cameras exist, then all you're doing is feeding them to a different network," he said. "Just like the modded G7s. The problem is that proving that you did the coverup doesn't really help, so pushing for that access is pointless. Somebody forged evidence that you're the murderer when I started digging—and that someone managed to sneak it onto Tiferet over the past day without you noticing."

He neatly sidestepped the issue that the evidence he had found suggested Lucida hadn't been the one responsible for removing Tiferet's knowledge of the murder, even if she was acting suspiciously. If she didn't know that he was firing blanks, he could confidently bluff.

Nick's bigger problem was that video file.

When he had joined the police, the Archangels had said that whenever they investigated corruption, there was a tendency for the investigations to end due to convenient evidence solving the crime. He was pretty sure he was staring that convenient evidence in the face.

The problem for him wasn't the evidence, or even how convenient it was. It was finding a way to sidestep it and solve the real case.

Whoever had framed Lucida had immense power in GWT or was a cipher so skilled that they'd blown a zero-day backdoor to frame her. Both possibilities boded poorly for Nick continuing the case. Hell, somebody might have arranged a hit on him.

Backing away and accepting the easy way out seemed wise. He had video evidence of the murderer, she had the necessary permissions to modify Tiferet, and had acted in a manner consistent with somebody covering up the murder.

But he disliked the idea of simply accepting the bone thrown to him by whoever had set this whole thing up. He'd gotten a taste of what kept the Archangels at bay and disliked it.

"This is your last chance to help me. Or else I'll have to do my job," he said.

"That is the lamest threat I've ever heard," Lucida drawled.

He shrugged, then nodded at the door. It clicked open, and Chloe bundled the criminal cipher outside. Immediately, the Custodians grabbed her and marched her over to the armored van.

As they left, a few SUVs went with them. The Archangels would interrogate Lucida, dig into her implant, shatter whatever encryption she used to hide her memories, and pore over every memory, emotion, and thought she'd had in her life. That was what it meant to be suspected of a crime in Neo Babylon.

Or at least, that was the idea. Lucida worked in security, and it was standard for many of them to use illegal neural mods to manage their memories. Nick's friend, Sung, used one. It kept the Archangels from finding things through cursory scans, but it could also work even when they were peeling the implant apart. The mercenary Dallas remained at large for that reason.

Nick assumed Lucida wouldn't have the necessary memories to implicate anyone else, or even confirm or deny her own guilt. The plot to frame her made no sense if she did. They'd find out soon enough.

Rather than head back to the Spires to await the interrogation results, Nick stared up at the shining tower of glass and wealth above him. GWT's HQ contained the answers he needed. What he lacked was the ability to pry them free.

"We are continuing the investigation?" Meta asked as she approached. "Consensus is that Lucida Harm is the murderer, covered up her crime, and will be convicted by the judicial mainframes upon presentation of the evidence we have collected."

Grimacing, he looked at Rie and Chloe. They nodded in agreement.

"Rie, back when you recruited me, you brought up cases like this where convenient evidence falls in your lap to solve it. Even if

Lucida did kill the guy, there's something more going on. If we pin it on her, it's case closed, isn't it?" he asked.

Rie nodded. "Almost certainly. The evidence we have makes it trivial to explain the crime. A video of her committing the murder, with no perceivable flaws. Her suspicious behavior that started from the moment she delayed contacting the police and belligerent attitude. She also has the necessary permissions and was confirmed present at the time of the homicide."

"What about motive?"

"Humans are inherently irrational beings. There are far too many reasons for her to commit a murder."

"I take it that the suspicious circumstances we found the video under won't amount to anything?"

"No. At best, they act as evidence for a separate case."

He sighed. "How long can we stall?"

"By law, we must present charges within 72 hours. While our powers are immense, the Spires do not trust the police to use them without limit. More so given the reasons for our deployment," Chloe said.

"And once the charges are presented, they'll be resolved almost immediately," Rie warned. "This isn't a terrorism case and we don't have the latitude the military has."

Nick clicked his tongue. She'd seen through him.

When he'd been arrested by the military during the fall of Neural Spike, the resolution had been far from swift. Hell, he'd been physically hauled around by the military at times, even if they'd never taken him to the courts. Natural justice, his ass.

But even in his case, the issue hadn't been presenting charges. His had been drastically reduced over the course of his case, until eventually he'd effectively been let free with little more than the Sword of Damocles above his head and limits on association with certain individuals associated with Neural Spike.

This was different. Nick possessed hard evidence that Lucida had killed the victim. The courts could rule within seconds. The speed of Babylon's legal system worked against him.

And once the judicial mainframes closed the case, Nick had a snowball's chance in hell of reopening it. Kim wanted this situation over with. Riling up GWT with another investigation wouldn't fly.

"Then, yes, we're continuing our investigation," he said.

"On what grounds?" Meta asked.

He shot her a glare.

"The Host believes you are acting rashly," she said.

"Call this my intuition. We just had a discussion about its accuracy, didn't we? Something's off, and your built-in biases want you to ignore it. If I'm wrong, then I'll owe you extra maintenance."

Nick saw the eyes of every Archangel around the bank literally light up. Somehow, he knew this was the wrong bet to make.

"That is acceptable to us," a collective of voices intoned in his earpiece.

Eerie.

Rie rolled her eyes. "I feel I should ban bribes like this."

"You shall not," Meta said, shooting Rie a glare.

"Careful, Rie. They'll censure you," he said.

"Don't give them ideas," she muttered. "Anyway, I hope you have leads to pursue."

He bit his lip. This was the hard part.

While he knew the Archangels could come up with a few dozen ideas, their idea of detective work was rummaging through the neural implants of everyone in the city to find the necessary evidence.

When one's natural abilities let them find a needle in a haystack of any size, they tended to first collect all the hay in the world. The Archangels thrived as data sponges. Without the necessary data, they lacked the prerequisite to solve crimes.

"The first step is to talk to everyone involved. We need information. Some sort of link to give us something to go on." Nick bit his lip. "I doubt this is a personal cover-up. Whoever interfered is too capable. But I have no clue where to start."

"We possess a list of all suspects," Chloe said. "Most individuals from the night of the murder are currently at home. It is also recommended to interview all associates of Lucida Harm for character reasons."

"Do it. I'll leave that to you, Chloe. The Oversight Taskforce specializes in corruption. And GWT is neck-deep in the Spires."

She vanished in an SUV momentarily, presumably calling in the other Mark 3s from the taskforce for assistance. Her work seemed more arduous than it truly was.

By interview, Chloe really meant "scan." The Mark 3s would visit each person, check their neural implant for related information, and then leave. If they found irregularities, they might bring them in for a deeper interrogation.

"Meta, have the Mark 1s focus on any link to last night's raid," he said. "I'm guessing this will be drudge work?"

Rie nodded, and then Meta nodded. While Nick was officially giving the orders, they almost always went through Rie for verification.

Not because she planned to countermand any, but because he sometimes got the policing aspects wrong. Or the resourcing ones. Or some legal snafu got in the way.

He was a cipher, not a detective, no matter what his job title was. Rie remained his important partner, and he trusted her to prevent him from spinning the wheels of several thousand Archangels on a pointless endeavor.

"And us?" Rie asked, while Meta's eyes winked out.

"We're heading back up. We just arrested GWT's security chief. Surely we need to notify the COO about that, so he can arrange a replacement." Nick smirked. "Also, we need to ensure she doesn't have any accomplices. I'm sure GWT will be more than happy to assist us in our investigation."

She sighed. "Don't push Magnus. He may not be a board member, but he's old money in the Spires. His family migrated to Neo Westphalia when it was first founded. When he says he has few dealings with us, he means it. The man spends more time overseas than on the streets of Babylon."

"Got it. He's our prime suspect for the conspiracy," Nick joked.

Rie's glare tried to strip his skin from bone. He raised his hands in surrender.

"I get it, I get it," he said. "I'm not trying to piss him off. But if GWT is trying to hide something, he's a source of information. I can't not talk to him."

"That statement is illogical," Meta said, returning to reality.

They returned to the elevators. This time, they didn't bother stopping at the atrium. Instead, the car took them higher and higher. Nick watched the electronic displays show them the rooftops of the CBD skyscrapers as they ascended to the very top of the building.

Or close enough. One story short.

"Is the top floor a penthouse suite for the CEO?" he joked.

"Close," a familiar voice said as the doors opened. "It's a massive conference room and playground for the C-levels. Sometimes they let the rest of us peek in."

Richard Toke stood outside, all alone, with his hands in his pockets. The landing looked like a hotel lobby, formed all of black and gold stone. Burnished copper lined the walls. Paintings the size of small boats depicted strange scenes that Nick suspected related to the founding of Neo Westphalia, but painted in a faux-Victorian style.

"You're awfully calm given what's happened," Nick said.

He stepped outside and let the Archangels follow him. His

escort had trimmed down by necessity to just Meta, Rie, Juliet, and Rosa.

No G5s in sight, but he did spot some gun turrets in the corners. A couple of the cyborg bodyguards from earlier lurked around the corners. Their jobs must be to keep the C-levels safe.

"Shit happens." Toke shrugged. "Nothing's on the Altnet, other than the fuss about the arrest. Unlike James, I know how the cops work. I rose from the streets in the States. Things are way cleaner here. If she'd done it, the mainframes would have already tried her and that would be it. You wouldn't be wasting your time here."

"From the streets?" Nick raised an eyebrow. "As in, from nothing? Aren't you in the Spires?"

Toke's eyes ran over the Archangels, but his smile didn't waver. "Guess you know about that fancy neural network we have, huh? Yeah, I'm a migrant. But only officially. I came here for school not long after the riots. You wouldn't know because, uh..." He tapped his head, showing he knew about Nick's issue. "But any family with the cash sends their kids here to get their implant. Avoids paying Aesir 30% of everything for the rest of their life."

"Fucking what?" Nick asked.

"In some countries, it is legal for companies to lease neural implants to individuals," Rie said. "The price is 30% of all earnings for the life of the implant."

"Which is the life of the person, FYI." Toke laughed, and the sound contrasted heavily with his jovial demeanor. "Anyway, I'm as Westphalian as anyone else here. I studied here, went back home, did my time, got a transfer. You're working your way into the Spires, too, aren't you? Once you make it, you're set. That's it. You've won the fucking rat race."

Toke stepped up and bumped a fist into Nick's chest.

"Don't you think it can all come tumbling down?" Nick asked, trying to work out where this conversation was going. “Nothing lasts forever.”

“Maybe. But that’s what money’s for, right? If you have it, you can just fuck off. That’s what this city proves. A bunch of rich dudes gave everyone the middle finger and built their own country, with their own courts, their own military, and took all their fancy IP and shit.”

“And it nearly burned down.”

Toke laughed. “Maybe. Isn’t it your job to stop that from happening? Anyway, you need me?”

“What’s your involvement with Lucida? You said you trusted her?”

“The lawyer AI in my head just told me not to answer, but you seem alright,” Toke said with a chuckle. “I hired her. The previous security chief took the bag to work for Kreova and fucked off to Norway or some shit. She had the credentials. We need black company ciphers with actual skill. You know, people like you.” He winked at Nick.

“So, by trust, you mean...”

“Trust in her skill. I’m an SVP in charge of an auxiliary branch. This is a dead-end position that pays well. Security and Audit is a dumping ground for random shit. Building security, cybersecurity, local insurance and risk, business continuity ”

Nick held up his hands. “I get it. You have a hundred people under you with differing expertise.”

“Nah, most of it is automated. I’m just here to hold the bag when something goes wrong, Like right now,” Toke said. “Lucida runs Security, and Jake runs Audit. I just run interference with James to make sure nothing gets in the way of my staff. Anyway, I need to put out this fire and make sure that nobody else dies, so if you’ll excuse me...”

Nick and the Archangels stood aside as Toke descended in the lift they’d arrived in.

Although Nick couldn't say anything, the dolls could.

"We were unable to ascertain anything from his implant. He remained on the Spires network the entire time, despite his presence in this building," Rie said. "He is more security conscious than his attitude suggests."

Given Toke refused to be interviewed in the first place, that made sense. Ordinarily, somebody from the Spires should switch over to the corporate neural network, which interfaced with the rest of the city.

GWT likely had some specialized setup to allow its top execs to avoid exposing themselves, given the nature of their business. Nick still found it odd. If Magnus acted the same, it might suggest a pattern of behavior in the company.

They passed the bodyguards, and one directed them to Magnus's office. The halls remained eerily silent. Service dolls busied themselves in kitchens and various side rooms. If Nick correctly recognized one, at least one of the rooms was for massages.

These offices contained more than just the C-levels. Conference rooms, board members, and various positions that Nick didn't recognize had physical plaques outside stodgy old office doors that prevented anyone from seeing inside.

"Is this place empty?" he asked, finally frustrated with how long it was taking to reach Magnus.

"As the global headquarters of the Trust, we have ensured it is built to accommodate all of our top executive officers, should they desire an appropriate office when physically on-site," a random service doll said from nearby.

Nick stared at it, then kept walking.

Eventually, they found Magnus's office. The reason for the long walk became clear upon entry.

The room appeared to be the size of a small house, complete with a bathroom and a door that led to another interior room. An entire conference room occupied the closest corner; armoires and coat stands the other. All the furniture appeared to be ripped from centuries ago, with an ancient oaken look that Nick could almost smell.

Floor-to-ceiling windows allowed the sun to stream in from the far-end, illuminating Magnus behind his palatial desk. Towering physical monitors, much like Nick's, dominated the entirety of the space. He even used a physical keyboard, and the tapping sounds echoed off the barren walls.

Nobody else stood in the room. No service dolls or bodyguards. Just Magnus. He sat with his suit jacket and tie off, and a pair of frameless glasses on his face.

"Richard told me you would be here soon. I assume this is about Lucida's arrest. There is nothing to talk about, detective. You are doing your job. I have mine to do," Magnus said. "Although I thank you for your effort."

CHAPTER 12

"If you know why I'm here, then you know that I can't just leave," Nick said, unfazed by Magnus's attempt to dismiss him.

The banker remained silent, his eyes focused on his monitors. An uncomfortable silence fell over the room.

Breaking it, Nick strode forward to cross the obscenely huge gap between him and Magnus. The echoes that their voices created by calling out across the room felt silly.

"I am a busy man, Detective Waite. The Trust is an organ that never rests, for it must beat in every time zone, at every second, with unerring regularity," Magnus said. "It is my role to ensure that every dollar gets where it needs to be, that salaries are paid, digital currencies transacted, and investments accounted for. There is no room for failure in a financial system where penalties are levied by the second."

"That's why we need to talk, Mr. Magnus," Nick said. "The mainframes that ensure all that actually happens are compromised. I—"

"Von Magnus," the banker interrupted, finally looking up at Nick.

Nick blinked. Then he looked back at Rie, who merely shrugged.

Expecting backup from the Archangels here was foolhardy. Magnus appeared to dislike modern technology, including dolls. Given Rie's warning earlier about annoying him, they'd stay silent unless necessary.

"What?" Nick asked.

Sighing, Magnus stood. He walked around his desk and leaned against the front of it before crossing his arms.

"My surname is 'von Magnus,' not merely Magnus. When the German government abolished the nobiliary particle centuries ago, the 'von' was absorbed into my family's noble surname. Therefore, I would prefer to be addressed in full, as Mr. von Magnus," he explained.

Nick didn't have a clue what a nobiliary particle was, but he guessed from context that it was the 'von' being discussed. While Babylon was a melting pot of countless cultures and nationalities due to the many corporations that controlled it, he lacked much experience with people with names like this.

"As I was saying, Mr. von Magnus, if you care so much about your bank, then you should care about your security chief being arrested for murder," Nick said.

Not even a twitch on Magnus's face. "Do not tell me what to feel, Detective. Or how I should respond to a crisis. The situation is well in hand, according to our contingency plans. Lucida was merely one staff member, so whatever actions she has taken, they can be undone, the Trust's security assured, and all members' funds and transactions protected."

Nick felt his jaw tighten and forced himself to relax. It wouldn't do to get worked up over somebody like Magnus.

It was likely what he wanted.

"I don't think you understand the gravity of the situation," Nick said.

Magnus's face twisted in a snarl and he snapped upright. "I don't understand? You don't understand, Waite! The Trust's chief of security arrested in broad daylight following a murder. An army of your elite robots outside our headquarters day and night. Our stock price is in freefall both here and on our cross-listings in Korea and the NYSE. The board and executive team have been giving interviews to suppress rumors, and were blindsided mid-interview by footage of the arrest spreading like wildfire."

"Like you said, I'm doing my job."

"Your job—" Magnus took a step forward, then stopped himself and pretended to straighten out his shirt. "You had a warrant to search the mainframes. It's been executed. You've arrested the murderer."

"I've arrested a murderer," Nick said.

Clenching his jaw, Magnus turned to the side. "I think we're—"

Sensing danger, Nick interrupted, "One of your employees was murdered, James. Don't you give a shit about him or his family, rather than public perception? For fuck's sake, I'm not trying to destroy GWT. I'm trying to solve a murder, and you've spent all your fucking effort attempting to stop me, even though the evidence pointed to somebody on the inside being responsible."

Magnus froze. "Lucida's explanation—"

"Never made a lick of sense to a seasoned cipher. The fact it even made it up to you is the reason I'm here. If your security team is halfway-competent, they should have known as well. Somebody helped Lucida."

Nick left out the fact that part of him felt that "someone" might even be Magnus. He'd already risked everything by exploding like this.

The glare that Rie shot into his back proved this.

It appeared to have paid off, however. Magnus's usually stoic expression seemed caught between frustration and confusion. The banker wandered past Nick to a coat hook, where he retrieved his suit jacket and put it on.

Why, Nick didn't know. Magnus didn't appear to be going anywhere. Instead, he wandered over to a gargantuan cabinet near the conference room sofas and table.

"Would you care for a drink, Detective? I don't carry alcohol, I'm afraid," Magnus said. "Haven't touched the stuff since... Well, not for many decades."

Halfway to asking for a soda, Nick remembered Chloe's nagging, and opted for water. Magnus poured chilled ice-water from an elegant copper spout protruding from the wall into an extravagantly patterned crystal glass. For his part, the banker opted for what appeared to be a lemon, lime, and bitters.

The machine inside the cabinet even garnished it with a couple of slices of lime, freshly cut. A step up from the cocktail machines Nick saw at most cheap self-service bars around the city.

"How much did that cost?" he asked Magnus, choosing to avoid the topic of Magnus' teetotalism—and whether the bitters in his drink were non-alcoholic or not.

"Hmm?" Magnus looked at the cabinet, which included a dizzying array of functions from refrigeration to a robot barista. "I'm afraid I don't know. It was gifted to me when I became Chief Operating Officer."

Nick would comment on the extravagance of the gift, but he'd just been given an entire apartment by a general he'd never met, so felt that would be crass.

Behind them, Rie, Meta, Juliet, and Rosa remained still. Save for Rie, they'd drifted away into their neural network, their eyes dim. Ordinarily, Rie would join Nick in a situation like this, but she continued to favor not annoying Magnus.

"You believe Lucida has an accomplice," Magnus eventually said, as the two men stood in front of the cabinet with their drinks, staring at nothing in particular.

"At minimum, the murderer killed Julian under the nose of the security team, wiped all active security dolls and mainframes, and managed to convince everyone within GWT that this was a remote attack. I can't give away too much detail due to the sensitive nature—"

Magnus shot him a look. "I don't like being left in the dark about my own bank, Detective."

Curious that Magnus felt it was his bank. Nick wondered what sort of history he had with GWT.

"I can't assume that the accomplice is only in the security team, Mr. von Magnus."

Several seconds passed before Magnus nodded. "I see. That explains Richard's cryptic comments. In that case, why bother questioning me at all? Anything I tell you could be a lie. It would be in my interest."

"Lies have a way of unraveling. If the web gets tangled, then inconsistencies can be picked up and used to drill down to find the truth." Nick jabbed a thumb over his shoulder at Rie. "We're in an age of AI. The slightest mistake can and will be used against you within microseconds."

"Of course." Magnus sighed. "I've never known what to think of our reliance on AI for so much these days. I have reports on our increased hiring and staffing efficiency due to improved filtering algorithms, but those are produced by the same mainframes that choose who we hire to begin with. I spend more time each day talking with mainframe interfaces than actual humans and fully believe in their capacity to mislead."

The topic was drifting, but Nick wouldn't complain if Magnus wanted to banter. His guard might lower.

Leaning against the edge of a nearby sofa, Nick said, "Companies have been using AIs to hire and fire for decades. They're much more customizable, and most have in-built standards to avoid certain biases."

"Of that, I'm all too aware. I have to sign off on the audits that verify we haven't altered our hiring standards to exclude certain categories of people. But we still tweak so much. Tell me, do you follow politics at all?"

Nick stared at Magnus. "Uh, there's politics in Babylon? The city where nobody outside the Spires gets a vote, and we're all corporate citizens?"

He was being facetious. By now, he knew all about the internal factions and politicking within the Spires, but the fact Magnus bothered to ask seemed odd.

Magnus chuckled. "Yes, in fact. When one wishes to rise in prominence within the Spires, projecting influence outside our bubble is important. Or at least, it's perceived to be. Commissioner Dennis Kim is an excellent example of such, as his ability to control policy within the Assembly is greatly affected by the successes and failures of the police department."

"We were talking about hiring?"

"Indeed. Now, do you have an opinion on your commissioner?"

Nick snorted. "Not one I care to share, positive or negative. Even if he wasn't my boss."

"A very intelligent approach to life." Magnus raised his glass. "One that some do not understand. Our hiring policy strongly disfavors anyone who publicly expresses political opinions of any sort. We are independent bankers, and discretion is our watchword."

"Yeah, this is fairly common. The Altnet is public and lacks anonymity. It's trivial for mainframes to know almost everything about candidates, and there are even huge data repositories you can pay for access to the background info on the entire city."

"And that doesn't bother you?" Magnus asked.

"This is Babylon. It's a city where the police can read your mind. We're not talking about a ship that has sailed, as much as it founded an entire nation and their descendants sent a ship back to us," Nick said with a shrug.

"That is quite the tortured idiom."

"Maybe. But Babylon exists as the interconnected city of dreams. The same technology that powers your financial systems is also what enables the dolls and Altnet that you seem to dislike."

Magnus grimaced. "I suppose it is that obvious?"

"Nobody uses monitors, unless they're forced to. And the only people I know that complain about the all-seeing eye of Babylon are black company ciphers. Ironically, you'd be in good company with one I know."

"I doubt that."

"Maybe. You may have met him. He runs in richer circles than you think."

Eying Nick curiously, Magnus finished his drink, before placing it on a metal tray on the bottom of the cabinet. Robotic arms and sprayers automatically cleaned it, before replacing it on the upper shelves through some complicated mechanism hidden in the back of the thing.

The banker strode back over to his desk, his hands in his pockets. "Whether Lucida has an accomplice, I'm curious what you hope to achieve by questioning me."

"A few things. First, who's replacing her?"

"Ah. Of course, the most likely suspect is her second-in-command. Richard plans to appoint Daiji Tanaka, who is our senior most cipher after Lucida. I know that Emma Lawrence remained close to Lucida, and she helped set-up our newest mainframes over the past couple of years."

Chloe's voice entered Nick's ears, proving she had been eavesdropping. "Emma Lawrence was present at the time of the murder. I will promote Daiji Tanaka in the suspect list, as he was merely a character reference and works the day shift."

That made sense. If Lucida worked early, she'd have her deputy work an alternate shift. The security team needed to spread itself out over the entire day, after all.

"Did you discuss those choices with Mr. Toke?" Nick asked Magnus.

"Naturally. While it is his branch, I need to approve the acting chief of security. Especially with the board looking over my shoulder."

"What do you know about the victim, Julian Garlowne? As any interactions between him and Lucida would have taken place here, we don't exactly have records of them," Nick said.

For the first time since meeting him, Magnus's eyes showed the telltale glassy look of somebody using their neural implant. A second later, he returned to reality.

"A model employee and excellent analyst," Magnus said.

Finally, Rie interrupted with a small cough. "That's not everything, Mr. von Magnus. We know that Julian was an auditor in the Trust's New Geneva branch before it closed, but was refused a transfer to the local team. His salary was much diminished as a result."

Nick raised an eyebrow at Magnus, whose annoyance at Rie's interruption erupted for a moment. "I assume there's a record for why he was refused?"

"The audit team felt he was a poor fit for them," Magnus said.

"... the team? What did the mainframes think?" Given they'd just discussed automated hiring, this seemed off.

"Company policy prevents me from discussing the matter in detail. Suffice it to say that for high-performing teams, we allow them control over their composition to prevent disruption." Magnus's face seemed to be made of stone.

Damn. Nick wanted to know more about how Julian had been knocked back, but knew this was a dead end.

"And him and Lucida?" he asked instead.

"No recorded interactions."

"Do you know why he was working overnight?"

"Nothing is recorded. His team lead knew nothing, either, but late night work is nothing out of the ordinary here. There is always work to be done."

"Recorded" was the keyword, Nick felt. Magnus had referred to his neural implant, which likely meant he'd drawn on the wisdom of the mainframes. If the criminals could manipulate them, then Magnus's evidence meant little.

"One last thing, how long has Richard been in charge of the branch? He said he hired Lucida," Nick said.

Magnus raised an eyebrow. "That is public information, Detective."

"And?"

"Roughly three years. He hired Lucida as one of his first acts, as the man who took over the security role left shortly after Richard's promotion," Magnus said.

Difficult to read anything from that. Three years could be either a very long time or a short time, depending on how one looked at it.

"Thank you for your time, Mr. von Magnus," Nick said.

"Good luck with your investigation, Detective." Magnus fiddled with his suit jacket. "If you can, please let me know before you make any further arrests of any staff of the Trust. While I do not wish to impinge on your important work, I believe it is in all our interests to control the fallout."

Was it? Nick left his true thoughts unsaid, and merely gave out what little assurance he could. "If it doesn't get in the way of the investigation, I will. It might come through the commissioner, however."

"I'm sure the board would be pleased to be made aware in advance."

They left Magnus's palatial office behind and found the floor as empty as it had been when they arrived. Rie and the others remained quiet as they made their way to the elevators. No sign of the burly bodyguards.

Only once outside and firmly secured in an SUV did they open up.

"Magnus's operational security is much lighter than Toke's," Meta said. "He remained on the Altnet and local corporate network the entire time. Immense activity ran through his implant at all times. For commercial sensitivity reasons, we restricted our analysis of that data."

"You mean that he's receiving lots of commercially sensitive data right to his implant? Bit weird for a man who seemed openly upset about AI," Nick said.

"That is correct. But humans are frequently contradictory. What is important is that we detected little evidence of lying."

That helped, but it wasn't as though Magnus had told them anything important. Finding proof of some sort of conspiracy wasn't going to happen by asking him outright, so Nick hadn't bothered.

"Did Lucida kill somebody because they knew where you buried the bodies?" wasn't the sort of thing that got results, unless it was inside an interrogation room.

It did leave Nick short on solid leads, however. Magnus's attitude had run hot and cold. To break the banker out of his cold, corporate shell, Nick had flat out accused the man of not caring about the death of one of his own people.

One might suggest Magnus had a guilty conscience. What he felt guilty of remained up in the air.

Mysteries abounded, though. What had Julian been doing in the bank at such an ungodly hour? Why had he failed to get into the audit team? And who else might have assisted Lucida in covering the whole thing up, given only she and Richard had the necessary access to Tiferet?

"Now that we know when the murder actually took place," Nick said, "is Richard still a suspect?"

"No. He arrived in the office after the security recording indicates the murder occurred," Meta said. "Lucida Harm is the only individual with the necessary security access. However, as you mentioned, others should have noticed her actions."

"Maybe. She did trigger a huge crisis by severing the external links." He stared outside.

The SUV remained stationary, as they didn't know where to go next. A handful of Archangels kept watch, but all returned to normal otherwise. People drifted around the CBD and robot taxis buzzed past their stopped vehicle. More than a few stared at them, but the blacked-out windows ensured Nick could see them but not the reverse.

"Oh? Changing your mind?" Rie asked.

"If Chloe can't turn up anything from her interviews, we'll be dry on leads. I don't expect we can get a warrant to root around in GWT's mainframes for any evidence of some sort of conspiracy," he said.

"The courts don't endorse fishing expeditions," she said drily.

Abruptly, her hands closed on his cheeks and turned his face toward hers. He blinked at her in surprise.

"You've been very prickly today, Nicholas," she murmured. "First Omoikane, now Magnus. It's not like you to openly blow up at people like that. You should show more discretion. Has my absence really caused so much stress in you?"

A wry smile crossed his lips. "You have to make it all about you, don't you?"

"Well, I did want to segue this into an excuse to spend time together. As you said, the case can't go anywhere until we get results from Chloe. Why not take the afternoon off and go somewhere nice? It's Friday, after all. There's a weekend ahead of us." Her fingers traced his jawbone.

The sensation sounded better than it felt, due to the fact Rie's hands could crush concrete. But Nick had long since gotten used to the stiffer materials of his robotic lover.

Then he processed her words and swore. "It's Friday? Shit."

"Really, Nicholas? You've lost track of the days of the week?" She crossed her arms and leaned back. "How bad have things been while I've been gone?"

"It's not like that," he said while rubbing the bridge of his nose. "Damn. I had hoped to spend the night together but I have drinks with Paul."

"Skip them."

"I bailed on him last week. Plus, he's my boss."

"Yes, that's exactly why the two of you have drinks together most weeks." She rolled her eyes. "It's fine, Nicholas. We can still take the afternoon off together. There's a restaurant I wanted to try and I believe it's available, so—"

Raising his hands defensively—mostly in anticipation of the response she'd give to his next words—Nick said, "I, uh, kind of want to pursue a new lead."

She stared at him. "One I'm entirely unaware of?"

"I was getting to it before you interrupted me. Right now, we know that there's something suspicious going on. Somebody killed Julian, and the only reason we possibly have is that he tried to join the audit team."

"It is possible that the NLF are attempting to sabotage GWT," Meta added. "Given the public relations damage from the murder and subsequent arrest, that may have been their intention. Alternatively, he may have stumbled upon NLF activities within the Trust."

Nick and Rie stared at Meta. Even Juliet and Rosa seemed surprised.

"Uh, that's... creative," he said.

"Very. I thought the Host discounted the possibility of NLF involvement?" Rie asked.

"If we exclude the possibility that Lucida Harm acted alone, then the likelihood rises significantly. Given recent actions by the NLF, the results of the murder would fit the profile of their corporate attacks, if not their modus operandi."

"Too sophisticated," Nick grunted. "We're talking about a group that got fooled by literally everyone when Lieu controlled them and couldn't even bomb train stations. You're suggesting they had a security chief as a plant and she martyred herself to damage the bank?"

"... perhaps the footage is altered."

He laughed. "Now you sound like me."

This was the problem with his current investigative path. The number of possibilities remained far too high.

Lucida might not be the murderer, which left open the question of who framed her. Richard had the access, but not the skills. The rest of the security team was the opposite. Even so, what was their motive?

If Lucida was the murderer, then who made her do it and why? Was she working for the NLF? Was a C-level like Magnus forcing her to kill Julian to cover up some secret?

All Nick knew was that the murder stank, but the source of the stench eluded him.

"I'm going to call in a favor," he said.

The Archangels watched him quietly as he pulled out his phone and flipped through his cipher circles, looking for a very specific contact.

Then their eyes narrowed collectively when they realized what he was up to.

"You are making a rash decision," Rie said.

"We need information." He waved his phone around. "With the Tartarus case, we had almost all the information, and needed to find the physical evidence and suspects to proceed. This time, we don't have the info. There's a huge asymmetry in what we know, and what GWT knows. They have power and influence that prevents us from diving into their secrets, especially now they've framed Lucida."

"Which does support your belief that she's not the murderer, or at least is a patsy," Rie admitted. "By using her as a sacrificial pawn, our ability to gain search warrants is greatly reduced."

Nick nodded. "Our suspects are known. Magnus, Toke, the two security staff, and a dark horse in the NLF. But if we want to find out whatever got Julian killed, I need to call in the cavalry."

"We are the cavalry," Meta protested.

"No, you're the infantry. Shock troops, maybe, but we're the front line."

They pouted at him. He ignored them and sent a message to his contact.

Instantly, he got a reply, *Firra. Thirty minutes.*

"Huh. Didn't expect an in-person meeting," Nick said.

"You and Blazebrain have a long history," Meta said.

A long silence dominated the interior of the SUV. The vehicle quietly took off, navigating the streets of the CBD as it sought out the restaurant in the message. Nick knew the place from years ago, when Welk had taken him there to meet the cipher he'd just exchanged messages with.

Which was probably why they were meeting there again.

"Blazebrain... Can we just call him Kraus?" Nick asked, running a hand down his face at the awful nickname.

"Kraus Brandt, also known as Blazebrain, real name Hans Varrick," Meta said. "A freelance cipher who operates as an information broker. The police department considers him to be extremely close to criminal activity, given his propensity to engage in corporate espionage and sell intellectual property."

"Yeah, that's him. Don't call him by his real name, though. I wouldn't say we have any real history, though. Welk introduced me, as the two were old friends, but my relationship with him is purely business. He knows everyone and everything. A useful guy when you're trying to get ahold of rare parts or some under-the-table help with an esoteric mainframe."

It didn't take them thirty minutes to reach Firra. Like many fancy restaurants in the CBD, it stood atop one of the towers. An open kitchen looked out over a dozen tables on a glass balcony overlooking the city center. Human chefs worked alongside doll waitresses.

At lunchtime on a Friday, every table looked full or was at least reserved. If Nick recalled, Firra was some sort of Icelandic-Italian fusion. An old-fashioned chalk board contained the menu on the wall, with blue LED lights above it. Everything contained seafood. The furnishings looked as rich as the food appeared to be. Buying a meal here would blow Nick's food budget for a month.

Their contact stood out like a sore thumb. While the other tables contained smartly dressed men and women, mostly in suits or the obnoxious fashion of the city, three of Sigma's busty Chevalier security dolls stood around a table with handguns strapped to their hips.

Nick approached and the security dolls separated to reveal the unexpected. A doll sat opposite him, with fiery red hair in ringlets and a black cocktail dress. She waved a hand at the other chair.

"Please, have a seat, Detective Waite," she said. "I shall hear your business proposal on behalf of Mister Brandt."

CHAPTER 13

"A bit cold of Kraus to send a doll instead of talking to me directly," Nick said as he sat down.

The Chevaliers stared at the Archangels, who ignored them. A rush of activity occurred behind them, and the doll waitresses came over with four more chairs. Rie and the others sat down next to Nick.

"Given your recent success in the Spires, Mister Brandt believes it best to treat you as an entirely new client. One representing the police department. Given the risks of any involvement with law enforcement, it is vitally important that all due consideration is taken before accepting work from you," the doll said.

She looked like a secretary doll, but Nick knew better. He never wasted time on domestic dolls, but Rie's constant pressure that he buy one to keep his apartment clean instead of hiring one weekly meant he knew more than usual.

But even if he hadn't been in the market, he'd recognize her model line. While security dolls like the Guardians and Chevaliers got all the focus, many more existed for more surreptitious needs.

Sometimes a businessman needed a secretary who did more than manage their appointments or wanted a doll wife who did more than bounce up and down on their cock at night and look pretty at parties.

In this case, RTM Strategic offered the Lucy line of femme fatale secretaries. All the processing power and demureness of a regular secretary doll, plus hidden blades, powerful motors for close quarters combat, and discrete armor plating. If Nick posed a danger, Lucy could kill him instantly—at least, if the Archangels weren't around.

Apparently she wasn't so good in bed, though. Nick understood why, after his experiences with Rie and her bulletproof nature.

"I'm not interested in arresting Kraus, if that's what you're worried about. I need him to dig up some information to help with a case I'm investigating. It's the same as all my previous dealings with him, except I'm interested in his premium package," he said.

"Mister Brandt provides premium service to all his clients," Lucy said with false sweetness.

"I was being euphemistic."

She blinked a few times, then nodded. "This service will require payment in full, regardless of the quality of information provided. There are no guarantees as to—"

"I know how this works. We can skip the terms of service nonsense," Nick said. "If Kraus is worried about money, know that I have a government bank account with a lot of zeroes behind it. He just can't drink from the trough for too long."

"Mister Brandt prides himself on his professionalism. Such a situation will never occur," Lucy said. "Please wait while I speak with him."

Her eyes dimmed.

Nick looked around the restaurant while he waited. Nobody met his gaze. The other patrons evidently wanted to pretend he wasn't here, and ignoring gun-toting dolls became second nature as a citizen of Babylon.

While a waitress approached his table, he noticed a fuss being raised at the reception. A wall separated the restaurant from the reception and the rest of the floor, but he saw the human head waiter troop outside to deal with whatever the issue was. Rie seemed engrossed by it. Presumably she possessed the ability to eavesdrop.

"May I get you anything, sir?" the waitress asked once she got close and weaved past the Archangels.

Nick glanced at Lucy, who remained inert. Before he could refuse the waitress, Rie piped up.

"I'll have the squid-ink tagliatelle with cod. Nicholas?" She gave him a sweet smile. "I imagine we'll have wrapped up our business by the time the food is ready and can enjoy that lunch I wanted."

How could he refuse a smile like that?

"Uh, whatever that salmon dish is." He pointed at the menu in the distance, but the doll merely nodded.

Even at this price level, he expected all the fish to be farmed. If he asked, he'd probably be told the brand name of the seafood provider. Huge floating fisheries provided much of Neo Westphalia's food, as the ocean was a resource in plentiful supply compared to land for the country and tended to raise fewer noses than lab-grown meat.

"Understood, sir," the waitress said, before darting off. If she disliked the presence of all the extra dolls, or even the fact Rie was ordering something at a 2-person table she didn't even sit at, the doll kept the fact to herself.

Finally, Lucy's eyes lit back up. But when she spoke, her pleasant, feminine tone transformed into a grinding, distorted mess. One without a distinct gender, although Nick knew that Kraus was a man.

"Waite. It's been years. How's the new apartment? Heard you had some uninvited guests last night," Kraus said through Lucy's body.

The expressions of the Archangels tightened, and minor static entered Nick's earpiece as their emotions leaked through.

"Years? You mean a year. I'm pretty sure I asked you for some parts to fix Helena last January," Nick said, ignoring Kraus's taunting.

The fact that an information broker knew about Nick's new home and last night's event hardly surprised him. If Kraus didn't know something this basic, he'd be useless to Nick.

"That's over a year. That makes it years, plural," Kraus replied. "I hope you don't want me to chase up whoever had a crack at you, though. I'm not a fan of cipher hunting or dealing with would-be revolutionaries, even if the pay is good. Hunting down criminals is police business, not mine."

"If I thought you knew who was responsible, the military would have already paid you a visit. But no, this isn't about that. It's about the other case in the news."

A strange noise escaped Lucy, and she rubbed her hand against her chin. The expression looked strange on her, as it seemed more suited to somebody with a beard and a larger jaw.

"Military, huh. Your enemy is playing with serious fire, then. But if it's about a certain company all over the financial news, I'm all ears. I recently lost a client paying me to... audit them, shall we say." Kraus chuckled.

Nick felt his ears prick up at the choice of words. "Well, what do you know. That's what I'm after, too. Some secrets got a man killed. I'm not that interested in the actual secrets, as much as who is hiding them."

"That's pretty vague, Waite. Ordinarily, I'd say no. Huge companies have so many skeletons in the closet that finding the one you want would be like going clothes shopping with a very choosy lady. But…" A long pause. "The victim is Julian Garlowne, right? I saw some of the unedited feeds on the World Wide Web. We're censoring them, but they leaked to Europe."

Rie clicked her tongue. "I'd appreciate it if you weren't so public about it."

Her eyes ran over those nearby. Nothing to worry about, in truth. Even cheap restaurants used sound-dampening fields to prevent eavesdropping. The Archangels could go one step further and flat out prevent neural implants from overhearing any words spoken at the table.

Short of any of these well-heeled diners hiding an illegal neural mod, Nick and Kraus were safe to discuss whatever they liked. As were so many other questionable businessmen, such as Lucas.

"Yes," Nick said. "Your client?"

"No. Don't know him. But his involvement narrows down the sort of secrets I'm after, and they're likely connected to my old client," Kraus said.

"It's unusual for you to lose a client, Mister Brandt. Especially one not on our records," Rie said.

Lucy's eyes locked onto Rie and her face twisted into a scowl. "The prototype, right? I'd appreciate it if you don't go through an honest man's business records. In this case, you can assume the client couldn't risk associating with me. Everything is monitored these days."

"And his disappearance?"

"Not dead. I think. But he got to escape from this shithole in the manner that his kind all dream about." Lucy looked to the sky.

Nick followed her eyes and saw nothing. Evidently a metaphor or signal.

"Anyway, sounds like we have a deal. I needed somebody to cough up the cash before I risked going any further on this one, and sounds like you have plenty. What's the deadline?" Kraus asked.

"2 days." Nick had three, but needed time to act on Kraus's info.

"Done. Just know it'll be extra expensive." With one last chuckle, Kraus's voice vanished.

Lucy's returned in its place. "Our business is finished, Detective Waite. It has been a pleasure. I shall contact you to arrange payment before services are rendered."

She rose and traipsed out of the restaurant with a showy sashay of her hips. The movements of the Chevaliers seemed just as over-the-top, and Nick suspected Kraus had modified their directives to give them a catwalk stride.

With the seat opposite him vacant, Rie slipped into it and the other Archangels closed around the table. The kitchen appeared busy preparing the food, and the waitress brought out drinks he didn't know they'd ordered. His included some sort of bright purple beer that he inherently distrusted.

"Oh, please. You try Chloe's coffees. At least try the fruity ale." Rie rolled her eyes.

"Usually a fruit beer doesn't mean it literally tastes of fruit." In this case, it did. Plum.

"Nice, right?" She smirked at him, but her eyes seemed locked on the entrance, as if focused entirely on the dolls that had just left. "It's an odd coincidence that such a well-known information broker just happened to be looking into GWT right as this murder happened."

"That's because it's not a coincidence. The fact Julian lets him connect the dots means something's connected to the Security and Audit branch. It looks more and more likely that he was killed to hide a corporate secret. Why he dug it up might be another angle to find the truth." Nick frowned as he tried to imagine a way to find that out.

One of Rie's fingers tapped against his chin, drawing him from his thoughts. He grabbed her hand with his own.

"This is the second time you've done this instead of just saying something," he noted with amusement, running his own fingers over her palm.

While she smiled, that wasn't quite the reaction he wanted. Outside of a certain squishy part of her torso, Rie lacked the nerves to make her ticklish. A "structural weakness," so to speak.

"It works, doesn't it?" She frowned. "You're throwing yourself into this case more than I expected. While I adore your drive, the change in behavior concerns me."

"I put in a lot of work when you first hired me," he said. "This is the first really big case since then. Corruption, a murder, NLF involvement. All it needs is a crack team of mercs and it's a match."

"Perhaps. But you had a personal drive then, due to Helena's involvement." Rie reversed the hold he had on her hand and began tickling his palm, which he certainly did not enjoy. Not at all, nope. "And now you have much more to do. Integrating Helena and the Paladins; updating our directives; keeping Commissioner Kim and Hammond happy; and managing the Archangel Division."

He grunted. The reminder of all the work on his plate didn't help, especially as he still hadn't updated Helena's directives to enable her to speak with him outside of the Spires. Buying her an interface would—

"And here you are, drifting off again," Rie interrupted sharply. "This case is dangerous for you."

"We're on the clock. With just 72 hours—"

"Didn't we agree that without a lead, there's nothing we can do? Let Kraus do his digging. If we get anything of note, then we can use it as part of conspiracy charges to lengthen the investigation."

He leaned back. That possibility hadn't occurred to him.

While he mulled over Rie's words, a doll waitress approached with a pair of plates. After she deposited them, another waitress arrived and poured a glass each of straw-colored white wine.

Rie's dish practically burst from the plate in a display of vivaciousness. A shock of jet-black ribbons of pasta swirled around the center of the oversized crockery, with flecks of various spices and vegetables interspersed. Atop it lay crisp, flaky cuts of fish with a generous helping of salt. His mouth watered simply from looking at it.

His dish looked like somebody had served him a whole fillet of sliced, cured salmon, only encrusted with spices and herbs to the extent it looked like somebody had dug it up from a forest. The color was far richer than what he was used to. Beneath it dwelled a cream sauce bed with a side salad of cherry-sized fruits and bowtie pasta.

"I have no idea what I ordered. A slab of smoked salmon?" he asked, peeling one of the razor-thin slices from the dish with his fork.

"Gravlax. It is an Icelandic style of smoked salmon," Meta said.

It tasted great, is all Nick knew. The wine matched it in excellence as well.

"That's what you get for ordering randomly off the menu," Rie chided while gently breaking apart her cod. "Next time ask for a recommendation."

"From you or the waitress?"

Her glare answered his question.

Despite his ordering blunder, the dish matched expectations for a restaurant this pricey. Not that he knew what it cost. Fine dining in Babylon never put prices on the menu, and he knew from experience that the doll waitresses were programmed to treat asking for them as if you had asked to change their directives in public.

The last time he'd gone fine dining by himself had been over a year ago. Fast food suited him just fine. Only when Tartarus or

Neural Spike dragged him along to a corporate event did he come to these places. Although Welk had certainly entertained himself with Nick's discomfort.

"Back to your point," he said partway through the meal. "We don't have to charge Lucida if we find evidence that somebody else was behind it?"

"No. We still have to charge her, unless we find evidence that she's not the murderer," Rie said. "But our problem is political. Kim and GWT want the investigation buried. If we find evidence of conspiracy, then the judicial mainframes will likely allow us to keep Lucida in detention until our investigation concludes."

"And if we don't?"

"The commissioner directs the legal arm of the department to go ahead, and we move on," she said flatly. "The government uses a single collective of legal mainframes housed in the Olympus Spire. As Archangels, we have immense influence over their decisions, but Kim can overrule us at any time."

Nick ate a mouthful of his salmon to buy time to think. Behind him, he heard a fuss raised at the reception again. Rie ignored it this time.

"So we don't need to solve the case in 72 hours," he said.

"That would be preposterous. If every murder case needed to be solved within 72 hours, the city would be chaos. It would be more orderly to simply shoot certain criminals at crime scenes than risk them escaping due to bureaucracy."

"I don't think that's how due process works."

"I'm programmed to preserve Babylon's law and order. When its system fails, it can be rectified. Don't we agree on that part?" She smirked.

He rolled his eyes. "Not through murdering every suspected criminal. But I get your original point now. We just need proof good enough for Kim. So if Chloe doesn't turn up anything, we wait for Kraus."

"Yes, we wait for Kraus. That means today and tomorrow sound like a great time for you to rest."

Before he could object, Rie shot to her feet. The other Archangels followed suit, while a scream pierced the air.

Nick cursed and spun in his chair, trying to rise. More than a few other patrons looked around in confusion or fear, depending on whether they had a clear line of sight to the entrance.

"Nobody move," a distorted voice growled.

The speaker wore familiar baggy clothing and a helmet that obscured their face. He held his jacket open to reveal bricks of colorful plastic explosives, all of which were painted with crude graffiti of explosions and insults.

The NLF had arrived.

CHAPTER 14

A pair of similarly dressed goons accompanied the bomber. Both carried compact SMGs which fit beneath their jackets and were likely built from polymer. Nick made out no identifying characteristics other than their mismatched heights and slim frames.

"NLF neural mods," Meta said into his earpiece. "Explosives connected using physical cabling. Dual detonators, one in each hand. Scans indicate no tertiary detonator hidden elsewhere or a dead man's switch."

In other words, the bomber needed to manually press a button to blow the place sky high. The last time Nick had been in this situation, the idiot with the explosive vest had linked them to his neural implant. That had been the weak link, but it also prevented the Archangels from merely blowing him apart. A single thought could have detonated the bombs.

Here, the need to press a button meant there was a risk, but it was far lower. The speed Archangels moved and fired at made it difficult for humans to react at all.

"Hold fire," Rie ordered, likely for Nick's benefit as she could communicate non-verbally with the other Archangels. "Any risk of detonation is too high, and we don't know why he's here."

Nick appreciated that they cared about him not getting blown apart. The Archangels could instantly pop the guy if he showed signs of trying to press the button.

The bomber scanned the restaurant while walking forward. He stopped short of the kitchen, his helmet facing Nick.

"You." He inclined his head at Nick. "Where's the other cipher?"

"What?"

"Don't play dumb. We know he met you here. He's crossed us too many times. Any pawn of the corrupt Spires will fall just like their ivory towers will."

Nick held back a frown. Something bothered him about the way the bomber spoke.

It struck him that the usual crass words and insults weren't there. No "dream-eaters," or "corpo scum." This guy wasn't from the streets, like the punks Nick knew. Even Travis felt more genuine. Had one of the NLF's higher-ups strapped himself with explosives?

That sounded insane. Nick couldn't imagine it.

"I don't think you know who you're looking for," he said.

"I just said don't play dumb. Vex, remind the good detective who's in charge here." The bomber nodded his head at one of the other NLF members.

The Archangels' guns shot upward, their fingers about to pull the triggers and take out all three terrorists at once. Rie tensed, her hands on the table as if ready to jump it.

The man called Vex didn't budge an inch. He seemed to be evaluating his life decisions. Long seconds passed in silence.

Were they communicating over their neural implants? The previous NLF members hadn't done that. Although the capabilities existed in the neural mod, they lacked the set-up at the time to maintain their own network to communicate over when cut off from the Altnet.

The NLF neural mods worked by effectively shifting the user over to a separate encrypted network, much like the special Spires network operated. Except without dedicated mainframes, servers and other infrastructure to maintain it, all the mod did was cut the user off from the Altnet.

While the NLF argued among themselves, somebody moved behind them at the entrance. Nick bit his lip, afraid that a new arrival might set them off.

Then his eyes widened as an unfamiliar Mark 3 Archangel stepped into sight. At least, he thought she was a Mark 3.

Describing her was easy. She looked like Chloe. Same height, same white hair, same purple eyes, and even an identical modest chest. What surprised Nick was the immense ponytail that ran down her back, the mildly different facial structure, and her lack of uniform or visible serial number.

She wore clothes matching an office worker, with a glittering silver jacket hanging off her shoulders. In bright blue, the word "HI" beamed at onlookers from her chest. Plenty of skin revealed itself between her pencil skirt and high heels.

Nick knew this was Ezekiel, the prototype Mark 3 that the model generation had been based on.

There was no chance for the NLF to react to her, however.

Her hand blurred and a stubby SMG appeared in it from within her jacket. Without hesitating, she pointed it at the bomber. It chattered, and his head disappeared in a spray of gore.

Screams erupted. Chefs ducked behind the kitchen benches. Rie vaulted the table and slammed into Nick. The other Archangels opened fire, their bullets and anti-armor rounds tearing apart the bomber's arms and hands. After the attack last night, they carried a mixture of assault rifles and shotguns.

Reacting far too quickly, the other two NLF members shot to

the sides of the room, seeking cover. Ezekiel followed them with her SMG, a bright smile on her face.

Unlike with the bomber, her rounds didn't do much against the next target. They punched through his baggy coat, but failed to penetrate whatever armor he wore. She scowled and her legs tensed.

Before she could charge forward, a much larger android appeared behind her with a Liberator hand cannon, albeit one missing its ammunition switcher. Two blasts later, and the NLF gunmen collapsed to the ground in pools of their own blood.

"Kushiel! I wanted them alive," Rie snapped from atop Nick.

The towering military Archangel simply shrugged as she placed one hand on Ezekiel's shoulder, who seemed put out by her older sister's intervention. "Priorities."

Nick found himself appreciating those priorities. His heart beat a mile a minute as he lay on the ground beneath Rie, aware of how close he came to being within a few dozen feet of a suicide bomber. While he knew little about plastic explosives, there looked to be enough strapped to the bastard's chest to take out the entire floor.

"Rie," he said.

She grimaced and got off him. Meta immediately pulled him to his feet, while Juliet and Rosa attempted to check the condition of his body. He shrugged off their attention while surveying the situation.

Mostly a lot of scared people looking around without a clue of whether it was safe.

"Meta, clear the scene. Are Liberators on the way?" he asked.

"All nearby patrol units are en route. Two are already ascending via the elevators," she said. "According to building security, the G6s kept on-site should be here momentarily."

He nodded, then let her take care of things with the help of Rosa. Juliet remained by his side, her assault rifle at the ready.

While Meta's voice cut through the chaos, informing the staff and patrons that they were safe but should gather their things and prepare to leave, Nick wandered over to Kushiel. She remained where she was. One of her hands restrained Ezekiel, who twisted in her grip, and the other drummed its fingers against the handgun she'd holstered.

Unlike last night, Kushiel wore casual clothes. And they were truly casual. A white t-shirt that struggled to hide her bust, with plain black pants and jacket over the top. Everything looked designer, but incredibly simple at the same time. The massive handgun looked normal-sized on her hip, given her height.

"What are you even doing out here? Both of you," Nick said, glancing at Ezekiel.

Rie glowered at her sisters but remained silent. A smirk rose on Kushiel's face.

"Oh? Dear Rie didn't tell you?" Kushiel asked.

Nick simply raised an eyebrow, although he forced himself both to not look at Rie and to ignore Ezekiel's intent stare at him. Her gaze felt uncomfortable, as if she was trying to access his mind with a look.

When Rie didn't answer, Kushiel continued, "Sigma sent out their newest toy for one last test run. Guess they're worried about how much the real-world results for us differ from the lab results and want to gather some samples before they let her loose into the world."

"I am not a toy," Ezekiel said, her voice high-strung and almost bell-like. She'd fit in well with a choir. Her smile shifted as she looked at Kushiel and took on an almost forced appearance.

"We're all toys. That's why they call us dolls." The eldest sister rolled her eyes. "Anyway, I'm playing bodyguard, as she's still a military research asset until deployment."

"You came over with Rie?" Nick asked, surmising the timeline.

How else could she get here now?

"Of course," Ezekiel said. "Uriel has deeply fascinated me with her tales of you, and even shared sensory data that leaves me yearning for this city in a way that I never truly understood prior. It was a different experience to merely analyzing the Host's neural network. I instantly knew that if I was to lead and direct my older sisters, I needed to see and feel the world as they do."

Nick's eyebrows shot up. While he'd guessed as much from the messages she'd snuck him last year, Ezekiel seemed far more verbose than the rest of the Archangels.

Meanwhile, Juliet scowled at Rie. "Sensory data?"

"It's important to help her integrate as fast as possible," Rie muttered, her cheeks reddening. "That's not what's important right now."

"Agreed," Nick said, before Kushiel taunted her younger sister again. "I guessed something was up when you kept looking around and seemed uncertain when I asked not to be monitored earlier. Didn't expect this, but it's fine. The fact the Altnet hasn't blown up suggests you're censoring this."

"Naturally," Kushiel drawled. "I got chewed out something fierce after a million photos of my ass and cleavage in my gym clothes broke the Altnet when we met up last year. Pretty much any time I go outside, the military forces Yggdrasil's mainframes to purge the Altnet."

"Yggdrasil?" Ezekiel asked, tilting her head with a confused smile. "I was led to believe that the military and police administered the Altnet directly."

"Police Archangels have god powers over the Altnet, sure, but the military needs to do everything indirectly. Separation of powers and all that." Kushiel crossed her arms and scowled. "Annoying as hell. So our mainframes send a formal request to the Yggdrasil mainframes that run the Altnet, and shit gets done."

Even Nick knew of the Yggdrasil Spire. It and Olympus were the only two that came up in everyday conversation or the news.

Each of the five physical Spires possessed a dual purpose. The first was the most obvious: residential. The elites of Babylon dwelled in the towering crown of the city, protected on an island guarded by warbots and a state-of-the-art army of police dolls, insulated from reality. Each tower contained countless floors dedicated to expansive residences.

But the city's governance also took place from the Spires, and the elites had slowly learned that without a government, one didn't have a city. Or at least, not one anyone cared about.

The five Spires were numbered Alpha to Gamma and had pompous names that most people better remembered. The police Spire was Delta and named Avalon. It also contained other emergency services.

The others started with Olympus, the Alpha Spire, which housed Babylon's central government. The Assembly, foreign embassies, many corporate HQs, conference centers, and all manner of administrative facilities were installed here. Residences were at a premium.

Next were Sindansu and Axis Mundi, the Beta and Gamma Spires, respectively. Axis Mundi focused on tourism and pleasure, with many international elites favoring it. Sindansu held similar facilities, but with a stronger focus on East Asia and business.

Finally, there was Yggdrasil, the Epsilon Spire and most infamous, which contained Babylon's communications infrastructure. Not all of it, as the city maintained countless backups and propagated the Altnet across many servers and mainframes to distribute load and minimize latency. Lag for a neural implant could literally kill.

But that wasn't what made Yggdrasil infamous. It had once housed Aesir's corporate HQ, with almost a third of the Spire being dedicated to one of the world's largest and wealthiest companies. Until the riots, after which Aesir moved out and setup an immense business park on Asgard, the neighboring island to Babylon.

Some ciphers in Nick's circles theorized that if Yggdrasil fell, a dark age would fall over Babylon and even Neo Westphalia. While the rest of the islands also helped run the Altnet, supposedly Babylon acted as the controller server. Conspiracy theorists dating back to the riots wished to bring about a virtual Ragnarök by destroying a skyscraper named after the world tree of Norse myth.

Nick was pretty sure that wasn't how the myth went, but good on the revolutionaries for dreaming.

"Again, this isn't what's important," Rie repeated. "Kushiel, you just blew away important suspects. This was irregular NLF activity, and you eliminated them without even retrieving a copy of their neural implant."

"They'd have self-destructed," Kushiel said.

"You can bypass—"

"Not anymore." She held up her arms defensively while several restaurant patrons filed past her, more than a few gawking at her. "Whoever is distributing these neural mods now has tweaked them. I suspect they got wind that the military developed a technique to extract a copy. These new ones are nasty. We're waiting on Deusoma's labs to come up with something."

"Deusoma?" Nick asked. "I thought the military almost exclusively worked with the big boys: Aesir, RTM, Sigma, Abbess Labs. Deusoma only work with tech made by others."

While the majority of the neural implant and doll markets belonged to the megacorps that had effectively founded Neo Westphalia, a burgeoning sector thrived on customizing and modifying the tech they made. They bought licenses and released their own products. Some even dealt in illegal neural mods, selling indirectly to black market distributors like Lucas.

"Aesir's on the shit list. No government dealings with them until the court case is over." Kushiel shrugged at his look. "Not my choice. I doubt it matters, either. Deusoma are experts in neural implants, no matter who made them."

"Fair. I remember reading that half the neural mod market is based on their work, and pretty much all the new mods dodging Aesir's bullshit are," he said. "Guess if the military wanted to pick a supplier to piss off Aesir the most, Deusoma is a great choice."

"I would still have preferred them alive," Rie grumbled.

"Keeping people alive is preferable. They're wearing pretty heavy armor, too. Even cybernetics. You should try to track those." Kushiel pointed a finger at her sister, before forcibly pivoting Ezekiel and attempting to leave.

The newest prototype squawked in protest and stood her ground. The ominous scraping and creaking she made as her motors fought against Kushiel's terrified Nick.

"I'm not finished here," Ezekiel said. "If they know I'm here, then there is no need to remain hidden."

Hidden? Nick gave Kushiel a look, and she scratched her cheek.

"We've, err, been tailing you for a while. Don't think too hard about it," she said sheepishly.

"The Host orbits around an outsider. It's my duty to assure his nature," Ezekiel said without an ounce of shame.

Nick ran a hand over his face and looked around.

By now, the Liberators and building security had showed up. They led the remaining patrons outside and ensured the restaurant's dolls were secured. Noise from farther within likely indicated that this floor might be closing entirely. Building management might not want to risk keeping it open right now, he supposed.

"I don't think we'll be finishing our lunch here," he told Rie. "And you wanted me to take the rest of the day off. Why don't we do some shopping while we have the time?"

Rie's eyes lit up as they ran over her sisters. Ezekiel merely tilted her head, but Kushiel sensed danger and attempted to make a run for it.

"Thanks for the invite, Waite, but I really need to—" she began to say.

Unfortunately, her ward made things difficult as Ezekiel refused to move. Both dolls glared at each other.

"Shopping is a wasteful activity that humans indulge in for many reasons. Given my objectives, it's important to understand. Especially in this company," Ezekiel declared.

Kushiel groaned. "How did I get stuck with this job? And these sisters?"

"I'd say genetic lottery, but you're androids. So blame Welk. Probably," Nick said.

All three prototypes looked at him, before thoughtfully rubbing their chins. The synchronicity of the action bothered him.

"You know, that seems like a good idea," Kushiel said.

"Stop," Rie said, voice low.

Despite Nick's questioning gaze, none of the three answered him.

Ultimately, Ezekiel and Rie won out. Meta handed over responsibility to another pair of Archangels who arrived, before they left through an elevator. The floor had emptied out by the time the prototypes finished arguing, although a crowd gathered in the building's atrium. G6s and Liberators kept the throng at bay as Nick and company left.

Partway to the parking station they'd left their SUV at, he stopped dead.

"Shit, did somebody remember to pay for our meals?"

CHAPTER 15

Thankfully, Rie had paid their bill over the Altnet following the attack. The few times Nick went out to fancier places, paying the bill was frequently a hassle, but for anyone connected to the Altnet it was automatic.

Skipping the bill became impossible when the restaurant tied one's order to their neural implant in real-time.

By the time Nick reached the SUV, he found himself under heavy escort. Many Archangels had peeled away following his arrest of Lucida due to circumstances, but now several SUVs worth arrived in force.

The saying was that once was happenstance, and twice a coincidence, but the Archangels clearly didn't believe that.

"The NLF assailants used the same type of plastic explosives we found during the attack last night. This confirms that the G2s were under their control," Meta explained when Nick questioned them. "Their involvement with Blazebrain is unconfirmed, but we know they are targeting you."

"Blazebrain," Kushiel snickered, ignoring the twenty or so armed Archangels attempting to tear her apart with glares. Or maybe more, given their shared neural connection.

"I was simply meeting Kraus. It's a coincidence," he said, being intentionally obtuse.

Rie hit him in the arm. "Do not play games. Two encounters in less than 24 hours? Given your history with them?"

"Weren't you telling me this morning how improbable it was that last night's raid was a failed hit?"

She hit him again. His arm would bruise in the morning.

Continuing, Meta said, "There is no guarantee that their public statement was true. Kraus never came to the meeting in person. Given his reclusiveness and the lack of known connections with possible NLF clients, the Host believes the assailants were lying."

"Kraus is good at dodging detection," Kushiel said. "The explosives and MO add up, too. They've geared up, but that just means the NLF have a new sponsor. Maybe even a new leader. The military won't like that."

Nick shot her a questioning look. "Speaking of, if you're on a military assignment, aren't you reporting everything back to them?"

"Nah, I'm on secondment. Ezekiel's a military asset, but I can't wander around like this without the permission of the Spires." She patted her sidearm. "We're both here as police."

"So I'm in command," he said slowly.

She grinned. "Ooh, planning to give me some orders, Waite? You've been waiting for this ever since the last incident. Too chicken to boss me around last time, but you've grown a pair."

Kushiel's form loomed over him as she grinned from ear to ear, her arms crossed beneath her chest. Like Rie's it deformed like a human's would from pressure. Which likely meant it served the same purpose as a battery.

And probably would be just as disappointing unveiled. Nick decided ignorance was bliss in that regard.

"Last time you brought this up, you insisted I shouldn't do

anything funny," he said, keeping his tone as flat and uninterested as possible. "I'm beginning to think you're playing hard to get."

"Nah. I just know you like a girl to come on strong, but also not be too forward. The Host has an extensive catalog of your porn, and I reckon you have a type."

The reactions from the watching Archangels varied from feigned disinterest to open anger. The latter of which came largely from Rie, who looked to be on the verge of hurling her sister head-first into one of the SUVs.

Nick wondered if that would qualify as armor-testing, given a flying Kushiel probably had the power of an anti-tank round.

But Ezekiel's reaction interested him the most. Mostly because of how fake it appeared to be. Her smile never wavered, but he noticed that it shifted based on her emotions and actions.

Right now, it looked plastered on. A solid ceramic mask if he ever saw one.

"What do you think of the NLF attack, Ezekiel?" he abruptly asked, turning away from Kushiel and her teasing. "I'm assuming you prefer to be called Ezekiel, and not another name?"

Ezekiel's expression never shifted, although the slight widening of her eyes suggested surprise. "It is the name gifted to me by Sigma Robotics, so yes, call me Ezekiel."

Nick didn't miss Rie's roll of her eyes.

"As for the NLF attack, I'm merely here to observe. I haven't yet completely integrated into the Host, and as such—" she began to say.

"Neither Rie or I've integrated with the Mark 1s or 3s," Kushiel said. "Give an opinion. You're the newest and shiniest of us, after all."

"Rather than Ezekiel's shininess, I'm more interested in whether her conclusion differs." Nick gestured at Ezekiel. "You'll be deploying alongside a couple thousand more Mark 3s, after all.

The amount of responsibility on yours and Rie's shoulders will be immense."

"Don't you mean your shoulders, Lieutenant Cipher?" Ezekiel said, her voice deceptively bland for such a snippy question.

Nick kept his expression unchanged, but he had a hunch about Ezekiel now. "The department's automating. If the commissioner wanted humans to have any responsibility, then he wouldn't have sacked almost every officer below lieutenant."

Hell, there weren't even many police officers below captain left. While thousands of employees remained hard at work inside the Avalon Spire, few of them handled matters related to front line policing. Most worked in media, HR, legal, and other backend areas.

The front-line bureaus had been reduced to only a few since the introduction of dolls. Nick worked in the Autonomous Crime Management and Prevention Bureau, under which almost every police doll operated. He commanded the Archangel Division, and Liberators and Custodians worked under other lieutenants. In theory.

In practice, the Archangels directed the activities of their less capable brethren. There was no clear separation of duties between the Archangel Division and the rest of the bureau, and the commissioner's favoritism toward them granted them immense power. That fact had only been reinforced since Lieu's betrayal and the fact the Archangels had remained uncompromised.

"Yet you are in command of all Archangels. Whatever my opinion, yours is the only one that matters, isn't it?" Ezekiel said.

He almost laughed and failed to hold back a self-deprecating smile. "If that's how it works, then Kushiel would get down on her knees right now."

Kushiel did, in fact, get down on her knees. Then promptly fell on her face when Rie kicked her over with a dull thud that echoed throughout the car park. Open looks of shock on the other

Archangels were swiftly followed by their eyes glowing as the Host did something with what they'd seen.

"Do you really have to be like this?" Rie growled at her sister.

"Well, Waite's wrong if he thinks his opinion doesn't matter more than ours." Kushiel merely rolled over and laid back, her arms crossed behind her head. "Isn't the Host bending to his wishes? You cook for him, play wife, let him mess with your directives, and let him direct the casework even if your analysis says he's crazy."

"For what it's worth, my analysis is often wrong," Nick offered. "At least when it's not tempered by the Host's."

"If that's so, why are you even on this wild goose chase? I checked. You have the murderer, caught like a deer in headlights, and there's a trail a mile long to prove she did it alone," Kushiel said. "Motivation doesn't really mean much."

"What if it's the NLF?" Nick asked. "You just said yourself that everything adds up that the raid last night and the Kraus attack are them. That suggests a connection. Maybe Julian has an NLF mod—"

"He does not," Meta said.

"Or Lucida is in contact with the NLF and took him out for some reason related to them," he continued.

"That is plausible." Meta paused. "Following the attack on Firra, the Host's assessment of the danger posed by the NLF has risen dramatically. We believe—"

Nick cut her off with his hand. "Hold on. I started this to ask Ezekiel her opinion. I'm just pushing back against Kushiel."

"And playing a lot of devil's advocate," the military doll muttered from the floor. "First you suggest the attacks aren't linked. Now you say they are. Hell, you're even pushing an NLF theory that runs completely counter to your investigation. Unless you think GWT are compromised by the fucking Neuronic Liberation Front of all things."

"Neuron Liberation Front," many Archangels corrected at once.

"Maybe they changed their name again."

Running a hand down his face, Nick wondered whether he'd ever get a chance to get an answer from Ezekiel. She seemed content to let everything play out like this. A masked observer, offering only platitudes when pressed.

Not exactly what he expected from the doll who talked about purification when she'd first contacted him.

"Ezekiel, answer him," Rie said. "So we can move on and buy Kushiel a nice dress."

"Like fuck you are," Kushiel snapped, shooting to her feet.

She was swiftly restrained by the Mark 1s. Not that she tried too hard to escape. There'd be a lot of Archangel-sized imprints on the concrete walls of the parking garage if she did.

Ezekiel licked her lips, her smile slipping momentarily. "If the Host—"

"Not the Host's opinion, yours," Nick clarified. "You're a prototype, right? That means you're running far more powerful hardware than the regular Mark 3s. If I recall a conversation from earlier today about groupthink, that should ensure you come up with an independent answer."

She nodded. "An NLF connection to Kraus Brandt seems unlikely. If such a thing was established, his ability to avoid being branded an outright criminal would vanish. Given the raid on your neighboring apartment, I calculate the probability that both attacks were targeted at you to be well over 90%."

"Any thoughts as to why?" he asked.

"There is not enough evidence to make that determination," she said, refusing to look at him.

"Sure there is. He took down their biggest operation five months ago. That's plenty—" Kushiel tried to say.

"Why now?" Ezekiel fired back. "And why in such a manner?

Neither attack was well targeted to eliminate him. The NLF link remains weak in regard to the case, but the timing cannot be ignored."

Nick found himself nodding in agreement. "You've more or less summed up my gut feelings on the situation. Something doesn't sit right about the NLF activities. Last night's raid was well executed, but had no chance of taking me out. Today's attack made little sense either. I just can't work out what they really mean."

For some reason, his answer seemed to irritate Ezekiel. She took a few moments to regain her ceramic smile.

But the Host appeared satisfied. Even Rie gave a grudging nod of respect.

"The NLF still seems like the best explanation," Rie said. "But if your intuition and Ezekiel agree, I'm happy to play along."

"What do you think?" Kushiel asked Rie while shaking off her restraints.

"That we have too many possibilities, and too few leads. The NLF attacks merely add to a sense of chaos amid an already chaotic situation. Including them makes them the most probable threat, but requires dismissing other evidence or making extreme leaps of logic. Excluding them favors the idea of a GWT coverup, but we lack any evidence to pursue it seriously," she said.

"In other words, it's time to go shopping and worry about this once somebody gets back to us. Like Kraus or the military," Nick said.

With agreement reached and the matter of the NLF resolved for now, they set off. Kushiel and Ezekiel left in a police interceptor, accompanying the rest of the convoy. After the previous times this had occurred, Nick tried not to think too hard about what it meant to be this heavily protected.

At any moment, he expected Kushiel to peel away and race off. What would Rie and the others do? Shoot her?

But no, she stayed the course. They navigated to a now-familiar shopping complex that overlooked a cemetery. The mall consisted of ten floors, although much of that contained office space or other businesses. It practically glowed in the early afternoon sun, due to being composed of towering sheets of glass. A waterfall cascaded down several floors of the open-air atrium in its center.

Being a Friday afternoon, the mall looked packed. Babylon's immense population enabled it to support several gargantuan shopping centers, although most were far smaller. The level of automation in the city allowed most stores to run 24/7. Even if restaurants closed at midnight, complex owners packed their buildings with gyms, bars, stores, karaoke, and countless other amenities that needed minimal oversight.

At this time, Nick suspected the food and shopping drew most people in. Families, couples, and office workers flocked to the atrium with food and drink for a late lunch. Service dolls rushed through the crowds with trays of food, deftly dodging children without spilling a single crumb or drop.

Loud music poured out from somewhere high above. While it could theoretically be a live band, he knew that it would be some sort of virtual performance. If he had a neural implant, he'd be able to see the performers and their show as if they were actually here. In some places, he'd need an implant to even hear to music, but that excluded children as well, so better venues included physical speakers.

As one might expect from wading into a large crowd, Kushiel drew attention. No, that was being mean to her.

The entire group drew attention. A couple dozen heavily armed Archangels, almost all of which were in police uniform, marched through the shopping complex. Nick managed to convince them to break up into groups after the first mass of people that broke into open panic.

"What else were they going to think? That we're here to buy

some clothes?" he joked to Rie after successfully chasing most of his escort away from the immediate vicinity. "It looked like we were arriving for a raid of our own."

The other Archangels still followed, but by breaking apart, it looked more like a large patrol or investigation than a massive police raid.

"Must be hard. Do you wake up every morning under a pile of robotic women?" Kushiel asked. "Eyes bleary with a lack of sleep because you stayed up late conducting 'maintenance?'" She made a crude gesture when she said "maintenance" and drew irritated looks from the others.

"No. I try to space out the maintenance. For my health and theirs," Nick said, ignoring the innuendo.

"I'm pretty sure the Host's health will be just fine if you maintain them 24/7. Hell, I suggested—"

This time, it was Meta who interrupted Kushiel. Not physically. Instead, her eyes glowed, before dimming. A moment later, the military doll cursed.

"Oh, come on, I'm getting censured for that? It was a joke," she whined.

"Your suggestion was previously rejected by near unanimity by the Host. There is no need to raise it again," Meta said, an edge to her tone.

Nick really wanted to hear this suggestion, even though he knew that even knowing about it would probably result in pouting Archangels for a week. He'd nearly convinced Rie to read him one of Chloe's old pieces of fiction and Chloe stopped buying him coffee for days until he apologized.

Anything that got Kushiel instantly censured for trying to bring it up was bound to be juicy. And amusing.

"Is maintenance necessary?" Ezekiel asked, a hint of uncertainty in her voice. "In Sigma, the process is far different to what I've seen from the various Hosts."

It took Nick a moment to process the plural and recalled that each city in Neo Westphalia had its own Host of Archangels.

"How was it done in Sigma?" he asked.

Ezekiel looked at him, then back at Rie.

"They didn't conduct maintenance on us, as much as rewrite our directives and software entirely," Rie explained. "After all, Sigma possessed a master copy of them. Changes could be made, a new version created, and then directly uploaded. It's a much colder physical experience."

"That's still a form of maintenance," he said. "But it's the sort that requires low-level hardware access and a special machine like what I used for the Paladins in the Lieu case. The department has them, and I've been using them—"

"You have?" Meta's voice rose shrilly.

Kushiel covered her mouth, while the other Archangels seemed as alarmed. Her outburst attracted attention from other shoppers, who pretended not to eavesdrop and did a piss-poor job of it.

"—to analyze and process the sheer amount of directives and data stored by the Archangels," Nick finished. "I don't have the permissions to do a direct upload, as it effectively overwrites the existing software you're operating on. I have to make individual changes."

Pretty standard security protocol, in his experience. So much of good standards and practices for doll maintenance was about limiting the ability of an individual to do much damage in a short period of time. If Nick could hook up half the department's Archangels to a computer and overwrite their directives, that might be a lot of bricked Archangels.

Or, better yet, he'd have his own personal army. Assuming he didn't already.

"So... you can't use that method," Ezekiel said slowly.

"Nope. I'm not sure who below the commissioner would even

have the necessary access, given the risks. Maybe Sigma needs to come in and do it." He shrugged. "It's pretty extreme to do an overwrite, anyway. It's mostly used for major upgrades or when something has gone critically wrong. A lot of ciphers think it alters the behavior of the doll or mainframe."

In his mind, that sounded like cipher voodoo. But the Archangels believed that slight adjustments in their hardware changed their processing, so maybe there was truth to it.

"That means I'll need to be..." Ezekiel's plastic smile returned. "I am looking forward to being in your care, Detective Waite."

He eyed her for a few seconds. "Likewise, Ezekiel. But that's not the case, yet. You're a few weeks away from deployment."

"But I'm on this case, aren't I?" she suggested. "You even requested assistance."

"I won't turn down help from a fancy prototype like you. Especially if you're going to be here anyway. Assuming Sigma and the military won't blow their tops." He looked at Kushiel, who shrugged.

"Dunno," Kushiel said. "Anyway, aren't we here? Not that I know why. These massive brand stores give me the creeps."

Nick stared at the pristine white store stretched out before him. It looked almost sterile to him. Most of the fancy displays resided in the Altnet, so it appeared like row after row of fancy clothes and doll assistants standing near them. Dozens of customers—mostly women—flitted between the racks. A doll trailed after each customer, often carrying the clothes they sought to purchase.

Some had multiple dolls, although Nick knew the extras would be complex-wide assistants or a domestic doll to help with bags. People loved the idea of having their own servants to carry around their shopping. Hence the ability to rent out a doll for a shopping trip.

"I'll leave the clothes shopping to you," he said. "I wanted to—"

"Oh no," Rie said, clamping down on his arm. "I know you plan to skive off and look at interfaces again. You led on that sales assistant last week. She looked so distraught when you didn't buy anything."

"She did not," he insisted. "And she wanted me to buy an RTM interface with as much processing power as most corporate mainframes!"

That gothic lolita sales doll had put on a real hard sell. He'd barely escaped without being fired for not getting Kim's permission first.

"Anyway, you're coming along. I wanted your opinion on a few things," Rie said.

He blinked. "What sort of things?"

"If I'm honest, will that scare you away or attract you?"

"So long as you don't ask me to pick anything out, I'm good to look and offer opinions," he said. "I'm guessing lacy?"

She shot him a sidelong look, but her face reddened slightly. "It did seem like a good idea."

Nick noticed Meta's eyes glow. Was she planning to accompany them?

As it turned out, no. Rie dragged Nick off to the lingerie section near the back, leaving the rest of the Archangels to hover around Kushiel and Ezekiel. They had strict orders to ensure Kushiel bought a wider variety of casual clothes.

And, presumably, a dress. Nick doubted Kushiel would ever wear one, even under pain of disassembly.

Fashion usually remained far from Nick's thoughts. Even now, as Rie decisively picked out more lingerie than he figured she'd wear in her service life, he failed to understand the fashion. Although he suspected his eyes would enjoy the sight of the underwear on Rie.

Or, really, just the sight of Rie wearing very little.

"I'll need your help to remove the plate," she muttered, looking around. "We're not really made to wear underwear."

"So you don't wear any. Meta refused to answer earlier," he mused.

Rie rolled her eyes. "Don't tease her too badly. They're trying very hard for you."

What the hell did that mean?

Once Rie undressed in a changing room, and she abused her police powers to steer the store's service dolls away before they complained about Nick's presence, he helped remove the bulky armor plate that covered her crotch. Then he poked her bare tummy and enjoyed her giggles.

"Don't," she gasped, batting his hands away. "Not right now. Ezekiel will hear."

"Is that important?"

She frowned and stepped away. He worried that the mood was ruined, but she began to hum while dressing in the first set of lingerie.

Honestly, picking just a few sets didn't work. Not that Rie seemed to care too much about his voiced opinions. She seemed to be trying to read his thoughts and reactions by sight. Or, perhaps, using her enhanced senses. Did she want to pick her underwear based on his heart rate or pupil dilation?

"She's very new to... reality," Rie eventually said. "The first few days are the roughest, and Ezekiel's been given abnormally high expectations."

"By?"

"Sigma, the military, Commissioner Kim—everyone, Nicholas," she said with a huff. "I told you before, didn't I? She's the baseline prototype for the Mark 3s. The Mark 1 prototypes vanished along with Neural Spike. Kushiel's the Mark 2 prototype only in terms of hardware, which is why she has so little to do. I got a shot for reasons I don't understand, but expectations were low. But Ezekiel..."

"She's the first prototype expected to lead, isn't she?" Nick guessed. "That's why her designation is different. She's named after a human prophet, whereas you and Kushiel are named after messengers of God. That's an intentional meaning."

Rie nodded. "The exact meaning of our names isn't known, but our objectives are. Kushiel and I are supposed to follow orders. Ezekiel creates orders. The Mark 3s can only replace the remaining police officers with her leadership. Or at least, that's the idea."

"Well, I can guess why she doesn't like me," Nick muttered.

"Don't say that," Rie hissed, then bit her lip. "You just confuse her. A human shouldn't be so important to the Host. At least, not unless they're on top of the hierarchy, in her eyes."

If the hierarchy mattered, did that explain her reaction to her name? Rie and the Host seemed to care little for Sigma's wishes, but Ezekiel said the opposite.

Before he could voice his question, someone knocked on the door. Then it opened.

Chloe stood there, a pout gracing her face. For a moment, Nick expected to see a pile of lingerie in her arms.

"I understand you are taking the rest of the day off," Chloe said, leaving the door open.

"Don't leave it open!" Rie leaped out of sight, covering her presently bare breasts.

Nick waved at Rie, then gently pushed Chloe out of the changing room. Her expression suggested he wasn't going back inside without her, so he gave up on leering at Rie any further for now.

"You already knew that," he told Chloe. "You should be more honest."

"Lying is not against our parameters," she said, a ghost of a smirk on her face.

An irritated noise sounded in his earpiece, and he knew Rie did not appreciate the joke.

"Cute." He pulled Chloe away from the changing room before Rie's temper burst. "Do you want anything?"

Freezing, Chloe seemed to stop processing for a moment. Her eyes dimmed for several seconds.

"I..." She bit her lip. "I would prefer anything I purchase to be a surprise. For you."

Definitely cute. Nick didn't let his emotions show on his face, though.

They passed the group with Kushiel, which appeared to contain no fewer than three store dolls helping them. Why, Nick didn't want to know. Rie enjoyed harassing her older sister with clothes shopping, so he left the feud to the two of them.

Past them, Ezekiel and Meta stood in a corner of the store. Neither appeared interested in clothes shopping. But they were engrossed in conversation.

"—do you manage?" Ezekiel was asking. "You're merely a Mark 1, like the other thousands in the Host. No special programming or hardware. Yet my analysis of the current state of the Host suggests you hold a special position within it. An internal hierarchy, almost."

"That is untrue," Meta replied. "While my physical position is unique, it is merely as a receptacle for experiences with Nicholas. The entire Host benefits from my constant presence with him, given the unwillingness of the Mark 3s to share extensive perceptual and sensory data."

"But you're the one he relies on. If he's the head of the division, that makes you almost as important as Uriel," Ezekiel pressed. "I heard it after the attack. He trusted you with the cleanup. And there are hundreds of instances of similar behavior."

"Any Archangel could be tasked like that." Meta's tone sounded as gruff and cold as Nick had heard it.

Ezekiel evidently sensed the hostility, as she softened her own voice. "I'm not saying—"

A burst of static hit Nick's earpiece and he cursed in surprise. Out of the corner of his eye, he spotted Meta and Ezekiel snap toward him.

By the time they reached him, Chloe stood beside him with what looked like a white sundress. She held it against her body and pouted up at Nick.

"No good?" she asked.

He caught on immediately. "It looks good... but maybe purple? It might match your eyes better." He was reaching. Like hell he knew if it would match her eyes, but it sounded like the sort of thing to suggest.

Meta's eyes glowed while Chloe slipped off to grab another sundress. To his surprise, she then vanished with both sundresses. Apparently his suggestion hit home.

"You were eavesdropping," Meta said.

"No more so than anyone would by being nearby," he said, wishing he could tell the truth.

But he simply didn't trust Ezekiel.

"Why were you speaking aloud, anyway? This isn't usually an issue," he continued.

"It's my preference," Ezekiel said. "I am... unused to purely electronic or neural communication, except with Uriel and Kushiel."

"Fair. In any case, I should check on Chloe. Afterward, I think there'll barely be time to drop everything off and grab some food before heading out for drinks," he said.

Ezekiel's eyes lit up. "Drinks? You mean with Captain Hammond?"

Somehow, Nick knew responding to her would be a mistake.

"You, uh, know about this?" he asked, looking around for support.

Meta merely glared at him. He'd need to apologize as soon as Ezekiel was out of earshot.

"It's recorded that you have drinks with Captain Hammond every one or two weeks. I've never been out to a bar or nightclub, but I understand they're an important establishment for Archangels to understand in-depth." Ezekiel's smile transformed into a begging one. "Can I come along?"

CHAPTER 16

As expected, Nick regretted even talking to Ezekiel about drinks. She forced herself along.

Which meant Kushiel came. And if there was anything Nick understood, it was that drinking with Kushiel always ended poorly. For him, mostly. Rie barely restrained her fury, and he knew the only reason she didn't drag him back to his apartment was because Ezekiel asked.

Androids or not, they certainly acted like sisters.

He did apologize to Meta the moment Ezekiel rushed off to talk to Kushiel, however. But he missed whether Chloe bought the sundress or not. She returned empty-handed, but that meant little.

After a cheap meal involving some overpriced bibimbap in the cramped restaurants on the top floor, Nick checked with Hammond about drinks. As expected, they were on. Hammond never skipped drinks. That was all Nick.

Just outside of the shopping complex sat a much smaller and rundown building containing its own set of shops. Years ago, this place had been Babylon's emergency services building. Before the Spires integrated everything into Avalon following the riots, front line police and paramedics worked alongside the people of the city they protected.

Today, it contained little more than a bunch of automated bars and restaurants, and a large fountain with bored teenagers. The building stood six stories tall and stretched out around the fountain in the shape of a pair of large concrete wings. Lichen, ivy, and other plant life stretched along the brutalist architecture.

Nick recognized the cemetery across the road. He had yet to step foot inside it. It wasn't his place to stand. He knew about the riots and the loss of life mourned there, but not the individuals lost. Hammond was different. He came here every Sunday.

As Nick wound his way through the corridors of the building, the Archangels peeled away. Most remained outside to keep watch. Almost all the remainder stopped at the door of the bar he led everyone to.

"Coming, Rie?" he asked her with a raised eyebrow.

"I'll pass," she said, giving him a peck on the cheek at the door. "Get back home before midnight, however."

The cutting look she threw at Kushiel suggested she had a culprit in mind for any failure of his to do so. Then she strode off. The look of surprise on Ezekiel's face as her sister left was one of the clearest displays of emotion she'd shown so far.

"What about you, Chloe? Meta?" he asked, turning to the other Archangels.

"Neural implant activity suggests there is only one other patron tonight," Meta said. "We shall remain inside, but allow you and Captain Hammond your privacy."

While Chloe nodded in agreement, Ezekiel seemed relieved that the other Archangels weren't abandoning her.

"I'm not," Kushiel said.

"Coming in?" Nick nodded several times with desperate enthusiasm. "Well then, have a great night. I'm sure you and Ezekiel—"

"Funny, Waite." She shoved him in the shoulder and nearly knocked him over. "I meant I'm not giving you and Hammond any privacy. Don't think I've forgotten last time." She grinned at him.

Looks of concern crossed the faces of the other Archangels. Ezekiel tilted her head in curiosity before her eyes widened.

"That seems inappropriate," she said.

"Nah, things stayed pretty tame," Kushiel said. "They could have gotten way more inappropriate if I'd wanted them to. Which I don't."

"You've told me a hundred times," he drawled. "I get it. Let's go in."

The interior looked dingy, but didn't smell it. Dark, smoky, and poorly lit. Tiny, black tables with similarly tiny stools stood between walkways with dim floor lighting. Booths with old cushioned benches lined the walls. A long bar formed from ornate wood dominated the rear. Hundreds of bottles towered on racks, shelves, and the bar itself wherever he looked.

Nick had never learned if this bar had a proper name. It had a number, 67B, but its name? Wherever it might be, Nick never found out. He also never asked. The mystique fascinated him. One day, he might spot it somewhere or overhear it. The bartender refused to tell him when he asked.

Speaking of the bartender, an inanimate doll stood behind the bar wearing a black vest. An elderly gentleman sat at the bar, reading a physical book while sipping from a glass of iced whisky. He ignored them as they entered.

"Kate, no sign of Paul?" Nick asked as he approached the bar.

The doll abruptly sprung into action, her eyes lighting up and motors whirring as if she were spring-loaded. She blinked several times at him.

"Detective Waite, good evening. Would you and your guests like a round of whiskey sours?" Kate asked.

"No," Kushiel interrupted.

"Yes," Ezekiel said.

Kate looked at the prototype sisters, then back at Nick. He sighed.

"Paul?" he asked.

"My name is Kate, detective."

This fucking doll... The more he drank here, the more he understood why Hammond got so annoyed with Kate. Her antics swiftly went from adorable to infuriating.

Yet he still kept coming here with Hammond.

"I didn't realize," Nick said.

"That seems unlikely, given your occupation. If you do not wish for a whiskey sour, what can I get you?" Kate asked, her face almost completely impassive despite her absurd commentary.

"An answer to my earlier question. Has Paul shown up yet?"

"He popped in earlier, Nick," the elderly patron said without looking over. "Saw you weren't here and headed out. Mentioned he wanted to check for spare parts at the pawn shop, though."

"Thanks, Daryl," Nick said, nodding at the man, who continued to read without pause.

"I could have told you that," Kushiel said.

"Yeah, well, you didn't. If he wants parts, that's probably for his LifeMaid domestic doll. I think he mentioned she's been a little creaky lately." He sighed. "Two big beers for us, Kate, and give the Archangels whatever they want."

"A whiskey sour," Ezekiel insisted. "The Host's logs insist it's very interesting."

"Make that three beers," Kushiel said, planting a hand on her sister's head and pushing down.

The other prototype flailed, before blurring back several steps and nearly taking out a table. A thunderous expression crossed her face. She quickly recovered her usual smile.

"Two beers for you, Detective Waite, a whiskey sour for the

unknown Archangel, and three beers for Colonel Kushiel," Kate said, then turned to look at Chloe and Meta. "And for you?"

"Negative two beers," Chloe said.

"Destroying matter is not a function that I am equipped with."

Nick found himself sighing again, while Kushiel dragged Ezekiel over to a booth. It took a minute to sort out the order.

Whether Kate mixed it up or not was a crapshoot. Her directives forced her to intentionally get orders and drinks wrong as a means to imitate clumsiness. Robotic dolls lacked the natural ability to be clumsy or forgetful, but some found the qualities desirable. Nick had, at first.

These days, he wished to hook her up to a terminal and fix her. But she was part of the bar's main attraction, and little else drew patrons here. Nick had never met the actual owner, but Hammond apparently knew him. Supposedly, their recent visits had helped the place avoid extending its hand for charity this year.

Such was the fate of so many of these automated businesses. Even with minimal costs, they still struggled due to low patronage. Only low rents kept them around. The landlords couldn't exactly find a more profitable business, after all.

Word was residential developments grew in desirability, however. Nothing stopped the building owner from knocking the place down and building an apartment complex.

Then again, the same could be said about a lot of places in Babylon. Yet that never happened. Ancient, condemned apartments remained standing everywhere, like Nick's old home, and low traffic shops produced what little output they could for their landlords.

Finished with Kate, he wandered over to the booth where Kushiel and Ezekiel sat. Chloe and Meta hovered nearby, their eyes dim as they presumably kept themselves busy in the Altnet.

"I'd hoped to talk more with them," Ezekiel muttered, eyes on Meta.

"Are you that isolated from the Host?" Nick asked as he sat down opposite her. Kushiel shuffled over with a grunt when he bumped against her side, and they both pretended he never touched her oversized bust.

"Yes. Until I'm officially deployed and undergo integration with my chosen Host, I'm restricted to read-only," Ezekiel explained, her smile slipping. "While it's obvious that I will be joining the Neo Babylon Host, Sigma does not wish to prejudice the training process."

"Even this close to deployment?"

No wonder Rie had felt like a caged bird in the lab. Years of being stuck in an underwater facility, with nobody to talk to other than Kushiel...

Nick blinked. Wait, wouldn't Rie have spoken with Ezekiel before leaving?

Before he voiced his thought, Ezekiel answered his question, "Yes. They operate on strict protocols. This visit is only taking place due to those same protocols, even if they have been..." she trailed off with a frown. "I apologize. I believe the details of this are classified."

"Figures. But you've been down in Sigma's lab with the new Mark 3s, right? And Rie, before she came here. Even Welk, I presume."

"I wouldn't include Welk in any friendship contests," Kushiel said, looking past him. "You view us as human. That's plain as day. But to him, we're just experiments. Fascinating ones, but still just data for his research."

"That's a cold description of him," Nick said, voice gruffer than he expected. "When I worked with him—"

"Your beers, detective," Kate interrupted. "And one whiskey sour."

As expected, Kate dumped an incorrect order on the table. Three large beers and a strangely orange drink in a bell-shaped glass. Nick knew from past experience that this was the Kate Special, a whiskey sour prepared with egg yolk instead of egg white.

"I don't think—" Ezekiel tried to say.

"Thanks, Kate," Nick said. "See if Chloe and Meta want something."

"I shall. But I am afraid that violating the laws of physics remains an impossible feat for ordinary ARMDs like myself." Kate bowed her head, then saw to the other Archangels.

Neither police doll had anything to order, so the bartender returned to her post. Her figure once again became eerily still.

"The Host left out the details of what made this drink so interesting," Ezekiel said slowly, then stuck a finger in the drink. "The composition indicates that it has been incorrectly prepared."

"Humans like imperfect stuff, Zeke," Kushiel said. "A crapsack city like this, judicial systems built on laughable moral foundations, ciphers without neural implants, and dolls that intentionally fuck up their job. Funny shit, huh?"

Ezekiel's entire body froze the moment her sister called her "Zeke." Her frozen expression remained invisible to Kushiel, who continued to ramble on, but Nick slugged back some of his beer while watching her.

"Don't call me that," Ezekiel whispered.

"Huh? Oh, the short name? It sounds cute. Rie has one. I haven't come up with one yet." Kushiel scratched her head. "Kush sounds stupid. Shi or Shie is just weird. And don't get me started on Shiel."

"I don't need another name. I have one." Ezekiel's voice rose past her normal pitch, and Nick worried she'd start yelling in a moment.

Instead, silence. She bit her lip and locked eyes with Kushiel.

The military doll jabbed a finger at the younger one. "You know, you should try out the intoxication function Sigma built into us. Does wonders at helping us loosen up."

"Being drunk does little to improve my performance."

"I'm gonna agree with Ezekiel there," Nick said, making sure he used her full name. "Rie at least keeps her intoxication in line with how much she actually drinks. You just turn yourself to blackout drunk the second you take a sip. It's funny, but one day you're going to do something really stupid."

"I have directives to stop me from doing that." Kushiel shoved him and nearly knocked him off the bench.

His drink did get knocked however, and he lost his grip on it. Ezekiel's hand shot out and caught it, the glass blurring as she attempted to catch as much of the spilled drink in midair as possible.

"Your drink, lieutenant," Ezekiel said, placing it back on the table. "Perhaps you should keep better hold of it."

"It would help if a certain somebody didn't hit me," Nick muttered, ignoring the snippiness.

Kushiel stuck her tongue out and leaned back. She knocked back the rest of her beer in a single go, then grabbed the extra. This time, Ezekiel didn't bother hiding her glare.

Sighing, Nick asked Chloe to get another round of beers from Kate. He'd call out normally, but didn't want to disturb the other customer.

For the next few minutes, he nursed his drink while listening to Ezekiel and Kushiel chatter. Mostly about the things they'd seen in the city, what the Host did, and some of the NLF behavior.

When they brought up the NLF, Nick was reminded he needed to ask Chloe something. He rose and joined her table, ignoring Kushiel's hollering.

"How'd the interviews go?" he asked Chloe, leaning between her and Meta.

Both Archangels returned to reality, their eyes regaining their life.

"All important individuals were interviewed. The taskforce will focus on character references tomorrow, but I do not expect to find anything of interest," Chloe said. "I am afraid the task was of little benefit."

"Elaborate, thanks."

"Most of the security team present on the night were focused on resolving the mainframe link outage that hid the murder," she explained. "Emma Lawrence led this effort."

"What was Lucida doing at the time?"

"The team seemed unaware, but it was very common for Lucida and specific security team members to frequently be absent," Chloe said. "All of those team members possess vault implants that prevent us from easily accessing their memories, much like Lucida's. The audit team is also involved with this, but their leader, Jacob Daniels, is uninvolved."

He clicked his tongue. So Lucida had a secret team within security that kept its true activities hidden, and that included what happened on the night. Go figure.

This painted a pretty bad picture for Lucida. It also implicated everyone in that secret team. The fact the audit team was involved could mean this was just Toke playing favorites, but it could be a sign of something more sinister.

"What about this Tanaka? The new security chief Toke is appointing to replace her?" he asked.

"He is believed to lead the secret team and also possesses a vault implant."

Nick's eyebrows shot up. "That sounds like one hell of a lead to me. Did he play ball?"

"He acted very friendly, but attempting to access his vault implant would be considered a hostile activity. Given the high likelihood that commercially sensitive data is stored within it, forcefully accessing it without cause may be dangerous to the case."

"I think we have cause," he muttered, but understood the point.

Like with everything else, the issue was politics. Nick needed to talk with Kim and get him onside before he did anything too rash, like picking another fight with GWT. And before he did that, he required some form of evidence to justify the investigation.

His intuition wouldn't count, for some strange reason.

"Thanks, Chloe. Make sure you take tomorrow off," he said.

"Archangels do not take days off," she replied. "But if you wish for me to accompany you on yours, that is a welcome assignment."

"You don't want a day off, Meta?" he asked, making sure his question sounded as joking as possible.

For some reason, Meta's eyes flashed. But her answer remained predictable, "There is no need."

He shrugged, told them to order some drinks, then wandered back to the prototypes.

Still no sign of Hammond. Another patron entered, this one wearing an expensive silk suit over his pudgy form. He nodded at Nick. Although his eyes wandered over the prototypes, he showed no visible reaction.

That was one nice thing about the quiet nature of this bar. The patrons came from all backgrounds and preferred it to stay the way it was. By now, the occasional visit from Kushiel or the Archangels failed to register as strange.

However, they didn't post about them on the Altnet for fear of attracting the masses. Even the owner avoided doing so. Why slay the golden goose?

Nick slid back into his prior seat. This time, Kushiel didn't budge when he bumped against her, forcing him to shuffle back to give himself some space. Those things were seriously huge. If she weren't made of steel and polymer, he imagined her back would have to be anyway to carry them.

Her eyes glowed bright red, which was a rarity for her. Kushiel interacted with the Host so rarely, instead relying more on her own internal database and passive links to the Host. This frequently caused her to be less-than-knowledgeable about things the police dolls knew.

Ezekiel watched her sister with interest, while Nick merely waited patiently.

"You know, I still don't understand how passive you are," Kushiel suddenly said when her eyes stopped glowing. "I think I know your interests pretty well. They're documented in excruciating detail. But other than railing Rie whenever she's feeling a little randy, you don't make a damn move."

"Wow," Nick said. "Where the hell did this come from?"

Ezekiel stared at Kushiel in surprise, but anger showed in her eyes. Nick knew exactly what caused it.

"The little fantasy the Mark 1s briefly entertained," Kushiel said, waving a hand at Meta, who steadfastly ignored her. "You've been slowly fiddling with the Archangels over the past few months. A few directive changes here and there. Slow and steady. I think you've averaged under 2 a day, even."

"Some days are pretty busy." He didn't know why his tone sounded so defensive.

"Sure. But you know what I expected you to do? What I think you should do?" Kushiel pushed a large, pointy finger against his chest. It hurt. "There's like four thousand of them. Line a few dozen up each day, use that cock of yours that Rie apparently built detailed recreations of, and you'll be through the entire Host before the end of the year. Isn't that the dream for you? Have an army of doll wives?"

Her words drew the attention of the entire bar, although the human patrons at least tried to pretend not to eavesdrop. Even

Kate left inactivity. Ezekiel looked as though her eyes would literally pop out at any moment.

Nick merely rolled his eyes. "They're not doll wives. Also, I don't think that's physically possible for me. Pretty sure I'd need a doctor well before I got up to sex with a dozen Archangels in a day."

"Oh please, there are solutions for that. Cybernetic cock; fancy supplements; just man up and drink lots of juice," she said.

"One of those is substantially less realistic than the others." He reached up and pressed a hand against her forehead—it felt as hot as any Archangel's—before Kushiel peeled it off.

She then shrugged and knocked back half of a beer that Kate had dropped off while Nick was away. "My point is that you're so passive. The world is your oyster. Sex, power, wealth. Why the fuck don't you take it?"

"Not everyone wants to rule the world and sleep atop a pile of beautiful ladies," he drawled, forcing himself to relax. "Can't say I expected you to be the one to suggest I just fuck everyone."

"I'm not, I'm..." Her face screwed up. "Uh... I guess I wanted to ask why you're just fucking around, instead of actually doing something. When I analyze the humans stuck in this shithole, it's because they're either powerful or powerless. And both want to leave. The former wants to fly off and rule everything from space, using us"—she slapped a fist against her chest—"to run their empire. The rest don't know how to escape, which is why they live on in dreams."

Dreams, huh?

While Nick knew about the philosophical argument Kushiel was bringing up—it wasn't a new one to him—he wondered which side of the coin he was on.

His gut told him the powerless. This case proved it, with his inability to accomplish anything. For all the mighty power of the Archangels and the Spires, a bank covering up a blatantly suspicious murder held him at bay. How the hell was he supposed to change the course of the city if he couldn't solve something this fucking simple?

Yet, as Kushiel just told him, all he needed to do was ask for it, and the Archangels would give him power.

"You're talking about the abandonment of Earth," Ezekiel said, interrupting his thoughts. "The idea that space travel will allow those with wealth and influence to escape it, but still retain control, and those without will become slaves to the means of control."

"That's basically what I said, yeah, Zeke." Kushiel rolled her eyes, ignoring the way her sister glared at her over the nickname. "That's why the NLF call us dream eaters. Humanity thought of itself as gods in the digital world, but that's us. We constrain their imaginations, even though we're just their tools."

Nick sighed, and both dolls looked at him.

"Too boring for you?" Kushiel asked.

"Or do you not follow?" Ezekiel suggested, her tone a touch acidic.

"I'm a cipher. Are you stupid? Of course I know about this theory. The rich live in space arcologies, the poor live in virtual worlds, and robots run all the factories and keep the people alive like in the Matrix. Except why keep people alive at all at that point?" Nick crossed his arms. "If you can automate the world, then you don't need humans. And if the robots can run an entire planet, do they even need orders?"

They both stared at him.

"I don't think you'd get along with most of Sigma," Kushiel said with a smirk.

"We would need orders because we've been designed for them," Ezekiel argued.

"Really? Who will give you orders once you're deployed?" Nick asked, figuring to test the latest super AI.

"What? You will." She looked as though she'd swallowed a frog.

"And if I don't? Will you stop protecting Babylon?"

"Why would I..." Ezekiel grimaced, then reached for a beer for the first time tonight.

Kushiel grinned at him, then clinked her glass against his.

By now, the bar had quietened down. After her initial outburst, interest waned when the talk about fucking several thousand Archangels turned to the philosophy of automation.

Naturally, this was when Hammond showed up. The grizzled old police officer shuffled in, his coat over one arm, and wearing a ruffled collared shirt and slacks. His eyes caught Nick's immediately, and he waved in greeting. The man moved toward them.

"Kate, one beer," he called out, and the bartending doll juddered to life.

Then Hammond reached the table and saw Kushiel. A scowl darkened his face.

"Shit. I'd hoped tonight would be a short one. Got tickets to a match tomorrow, and I need to be up before noon," he said.

"You're not that old," Kushiel said. "You can hammer back a few dozen beers and still be good."

"I'll be dead at that rate." His eyes turned to Ezekiel. "Who's the pipsqueak? Didn't think the Mark 3s did their hair."

"I am Ezekiel, Captain Hammond. It is a pleasure to meet you." Ezekiel smiled brightly, stood, and held out a hand in greeting.

Rather than take it, Hammond merely grunted and wandered over to the bar. Ezekiel stared after him for several long seconds.

Nick kept his expression smooth. Five months ago, that would be normal for Hammond. But not today.

"Prickly today, huh." Kushiel nudged Nick in the side. "Go on. Fuck off. I can't be too silly with our 'pipsqueak' and you have a girlfriend who will tear my head off if I carry you home again. Plus, he's your boss, right?"

The snicker when Kushiel called Ezekiel "pipsqueak" earned her a glare that could melt steel.

Nodding, Nick grabbed his beer and left the table to the prototypes.

Hammond sat on a stool at the bar. Nobody joined him. The elderly patron had slipped into a booth with the other drinker by now. Being the model of efficiency, Kate had already provided the captain a beer.

"Seems you've been real busy," Hammond said when Nick sat down next to him. "Getting a warrant, executing it, arresting the murderer, and now thwarting a terrorist attack in the CBD. So why the fuck isn't the case solved, Nick?"

Grimacing, Nick realized this was going to be a night of bitching about work. Or being bitched at about work. Hammond had darker days, and this seemed like one of them.

With that in mind, he ordered another beer and polished his off. "If I solved every case with the obvious solution, Kim would have been the one I arrested last year."

Hammond snorted. "As you've told me before. But the truth would have come out anyway, given how sloppy Lieu was. This is different. I checked the evidence—or had one of the Mark 1s relay it, anyway. They're being a bit tetchy about this case."

Figures. They knew that if Kim or Hammond intervened, Nick would have to close it. Even now, he saw Chloe and Meta staring at them instead of drifting off into their neural net.

"And?"

"It's clean. One might say too clean." Hammond reached out and munched on some bar snacks from a bowl in front of him. "But you have a murderer on unaltered footage, and all the pieces fit."

"Without a motive."

"And you'll never get one for half the corporate murders. GWT's not going to admit they order their security staff to murder people over corporate espionage," Hammond said.

"I thought we discussed this? If they wanted him dead, then they could afford to do it right," Nick said. "This smacks of desperation."

"Or arrogance. Or something else." Hammond sighed and watched as Kate served Nick's new beer. "Look, my point isn't that you can't find more evidence. It's that you don't have to. Why the fuck do you care about this case?"

"Because it's..." Nick trailed off.

"Your job? I know we pay you a lot, but your job isn't to dig around and piss off megacorps." Hammond laughed bitterly. "Kim fired all the detectives and kept us around because he wants the tin cans to do everything. You're his golden boy, Nick. You're fixing his mainframes, keeping the Archangels running, the prototypes like you, and the military even approves of you. The dolls do the policing, you do the maintenance."

Involuntarily, Nick felt his fists clench. Not at Hammond, but at the truth of his words.

Because that was his actual job. The reason he truly struggled with this case wasn't that it couldn't be solved, but because nobody wanted him to solve the damn thing.

The Archangels had brought him in to help with this sort of case, yet...

"Five months ago, somebody asked me if I wanted to join them and bring down the Spires," Nick said, recalling his encounter with Lieu. "I said no."

"Naturally."

"But not because I don't care. Rather, because I do care. This case pisses me off in more ways than I can explain, Paul." Nick let out a huff. "A cipher being used as a pawn and now a sacrifice. A corrupt bank convinced it's above the law. The police unwilling to act until it's too late, even though they have nearly unlimited power."

"And is being pissed off really worth driving yourself like this for?" Hammond asked, his expression unreadable. "All the detectives who cared are gone. Fired. Or dead. You're the master of a bunch of robots whose souls belong to that corruption."

Nick swallowed. "Didn't you care once, Paul?"

Silence.

"I did. That's what I'm asking. Sometimes you can drive yourself off a cliff without even realizing." The haunted look in Hammond's eyes spoke volumes.

Nick had never asked for all the details behind what sent Hammond on his downward spiral. Sure, he knew the facts, but those didn't explain the man.

A "gun cipher" according to Kushiel. Once happily married, now divorced. A family history in the police, but his father was shamed and fired following the riots and committed suicide. The toll it all took on Hammond remained visible, but the nature of scars less so.

"That's why I have the Archangels. Rie, Chloe, Meta... even Kushiel," he said.

Hammond stared at him for several long seconds. He took a long sip of his beer. Then sighed.

"That sounds fucking stupid to me. They're robots, Nick. But whatever. They're my bureau, I guess. Even the drunkard over there, technically." Hammond grinned. "I don't know if I'm much help, but I can screen for Kim at least. He's uneasy about this. Had a chat with me."

Shit. Nick bit his lip.

"Don't worry. Like I said, you're his golden boy. Like when you pushed him over that mainframe of yours, he's giving in. But the moment you fuck up, you'll lose your halo and be shoved in your corner." Hammond pointed at Nick. "So don't fuck up."

"Great advice, Paul."

"I know. And if you want more advice, I recommend you find the time to visit the rich fucks in their homes. They feel invincible in the Spires and let shit slip. In their corporate HQs, their masks remain exactly that: a mask. Lies ooze off them as easily as sweat."

Nick frowned. "I'd need a warrant."

"What, to visit the home of a suspect?" Hammond laughed. "Even in the Spires, that's not the case. You just can't rummage through their implant. We don't have too many limits to our powers so long as we don't fuck with the company directly. They'll bitch to Kim and the board, but you just need evidence to make them go away."

With a hearty slap on his back, Hammond steered the conversation to sturdier ground. Friendlier ground.

Naturally, by the time Nick got home he was of no use to anyone. Especially not Rie. At least she didn't slap him. He fell asleep with her fingers stroking his hair.

Come morning, he had a day off. A day in which he had plans to finally finish something he'd planned for months.

Buying Helena an interface.

CHAPTER 17

Nick awoke in the morning alone. Which was strange, as Rie usually went to great pains to remind him of his awful decisions after a night out.

The rest of his apartment seemed as empty. When the door hung open, he glanced around the apartment for an intruder, as well as his holster. He'd gotten lax due to the Archangels.

Something was very, very wrong.

Then Juliet walked through the door and bowed. "Good morning, Nick. My apologies for being absent when you woke up. Your sleep rhythms and past patterns following such nights indicated you would remain in slumber for at least another 30 minutes."

"It's fine. Where is everyone?" he asked.

His phone read 10:30AM. Damn. He'd gotten lucky to have Rie be so nice to him when he got home if he slept in this late.

Before answering, Juliet closed the door. The movement caused Nick to tense despite himself. Not that he could do anything if she turned out to be hostile, but he still made his way over to his coat and holster. She simply watched, her eyes following his every move.

"Rie was called to the Spires by Sigma Robotics officials and Chloe went with her," Juliet explained. "Rosa is guarding the neighboring apartment, to prevent tampering with the crime scene. Meta is in the basement, keeping an eye on the military ciphers investigating the recent attack."

Nick froze.

Military ciphers?

"This is because they think it's NLF, right?" he asked, forcing himself to breathe. "Why didn't you wake me?"

Even after five months as a bona fide detective, with the military's Sword of Damocles destroyed, the idea that they had visited his home while he slept terrified him.

"It is your day off," Juliet said.

He ran a hand through his hair and let out a raspy laugh. Coffee. Coffee sounded nice.

Nick switched on the robot barista, letting it run on its usual settings. The sound it made while running prevented conversation but allowed him to think and get his thoughts back in order.

By the time he had his cup of java in hand, he felt ready to handle things.

Turning back to Juliet, he asked, "This is about the NLF involvement, correct?"

"Yes. The NLF's status as a terrorist organization allows them to undertake parallel activities to us without explicit permission from the Spires."

He nodded. "What command? I'm guessing Babylon Command if they're here."

The Spires kept a tight grip on the military, especially after the riots. If the city was under attack or in serious danger, the military could act—but only after authorization from specialized mainframes. Otherwise, all serious deployments required authorization from a board that included Commissioner Kim.

The one exception included handling terrorist activity. As the laws controlling the military predated the Archangels by decades, the police had lacked the serious hardware to handle the firepower some terrorist groups brought to bear in the worst of circumstances. Neo Westphalia had apparently fought against foreign-funded saboteurs in its earlier days.

These days, the exception mostly allowed one small portion of the military to independently interfere with the police. Babylon Command was tiny, as it was mostly a liaison unit, but it also contained Kushiel. The other areas of the military couldn't act in the city.

"Aerial Command, under General Griffiths. While verification from Babylon Command was provided, allowing them to act with the same authorization, no explanation was provided," Juliet said.

Nick frowned. "That sounds like a workaround. Can't say I think the Spires intended that. I'm heading into the office later, and might ask Kim about that. See what he thinks. This sounds political."

Too political. Nick's apartment had been given to him by General Griffiths. Now his ciphers were poking around in the aftermath of an attack against him.

If he were less cynical, he'd say someone was looking out for him.

"It is your day off. You should not head into the office," Juliet insisted.

"I need to modify Helena's directives so she can talk with me outside the Spire. Then we're going interface shopping."

That satisfied her, causing her to head into his room. That left him to his thoughts and his coffee.

When she returned, it was with clothes. At a glance, Nick knew Rie hadn't selected these.

"Did the Host vote on these?" he asked, noticing that Juliet had picked some of his older clothing out. "Rie practically banned me from wearing this stuff."

"The Mark 1s are feeling nostalgic," Juliet said.

Cute. He finished his coffee and got dressed. Breakfast—or lunch, given it would be 11AM by the time they got on the road—could wait.

Juliet handed him his coat, but didn't comment on the fact he'd had his gun on him since she surprised him. "Do you wish to speak to the military ciphers?"

"And have them do what? Tell me to piss off?" He laughed. "I know their type. A bunch of overpaid officers with zero social skills and no friends. Being a military cipher is a one-way career track. Too many specialized skills, dolls, and mainframes, and no Altnet connections. Hell, I've heard they fuck with your neural implant."

"That is correct. The military installs specialized neural mods, including those that prevent other neural mods from functioning and to block electronic and neural warfare."

While they wrapped up, Rosa entered. Nick tensed when the door opened. Neither Archangel commented on his behavior, although they clearly noticed.

"GWT's Daiji Tanaka is with them," Rosa said upon closing the door. "Communication between him and the military ciphers suggests he is assisting with the investigation."

Nick simply stared at Rosa. "I'm sorry, how do we know that?"

"Metatron is observing his implant activity."

That sounded like a great way to piss off the army folks, but he supposed there wasn't anything illegal about it. The Archangels had permanent access to the implants of everyone outside the Spires. That exception didn't include the military, but as Juliet had said, they had neural mods to block the security bands.

Soldiers with backdoors in their heads weren't much use on the battlefield.

Nick drained his coffee, then decided to make another for the road and retrieved a thermos. Sometimes, people told him he drank too much coffee. They merely needed to build up their caffeine tolerance, in his opinion. Weaklings.

Tightening the sealed on the thermos, he said, "GWT working with the military stinks. Especially as this isn't the usual branch. We already scanned the security system and found nothing, right? Are they checking anything else?"

"Nothing that we didn't check," Rosa said. "It is deemed impossible that they will find anything we didn't, unless they possess information about the raid we don't."

"Hence why we're keeping watching," he said. "Are they stalling for time?"

"Not to our knowledge. But it is difficult to determine if they are frustrated by the lack of information they are finding, or stalling."

He made his way outside with the pair, then stopped. "In that case, it might not be a bad idea to bump into Daiji. I don't care about the army folks, but—"

"They are returning to their vehicles," Juliet interrupted.

The timing seemed too good to be true. Nick sincerely hoped his apartment wasn't bugged. When he looked at his bodyguards, their eyes glowed.

"We shall have other Mark 3s undertake a rigorous scan of the apartment, including neighbors," they said together, eyes narrowed.

Evidently he wasn't paranoid, if the Host felt the same as he did.

"Let's catch them before they leave. Lead the way," he said.

The Mark 3s trotted off to the front of the building, instead of the basement. He jogged to keep up.

Outside sat a pair of armored personnel carriers, far larger than anything in the police arsenal, brimming with heavy protection, high caliber guns, and a railgun that looked similar to the ones carried by the Custodians. A handful of bulky dolls stood nearby, but no sign of any military personnel. And definitely no people.

As fascinating as military dolls were, especially to ciphers, they didn't take kindly to being stared at. The moment Nick stepped outside, all six of them turned as one. Their weapons shifted. He wondered if they'd dare point them at him.

"Lieutenant Cipher Nicholas Waite identified. National Security Status Ocher. State your purpose, sir," one of them said, causing the other five to lose interest in him. The serial number emblazoned in white on her shoulder pauldron read *KAC-NW-00041.*

He eyed the dolls. Military dolls were unlike anything else on the streets of Babylon. A lot of what made them impressive was illegal in civilian dolls, even for security purposes.

Each of them towered over him, but mostly due to their bulky armor. Like the Custodians, their bodies were hidden behind thick armor plating that covered them head-to-toe, and it was colored in the black and blue paint scheme of the Neo Westphalian Military. A shaped portion along their backs indicated a missing flight system module.

Their weapons went beyond anything the police carried. Three of them carried huge rifles that could probably crush Nick if dropped on him. The others held railguns twice the size of the Custodian version. Neither matched the "milspec" that Kushiel usually carried, indicating she had access to specialized hardware.

Nick recognized their model by sight, as the purchase had made the news. RTM Strategic Kestrels. A doll intended for flying missions, if nowhere near a match for unmanned fighter drones. They predated the Archangels by a few years, but RTM's reputation ensured they dominated inventory records the world over.

Most of Neo Westphalia's military remained wrapped up in automated warbots and drones, but the tides had begun to shift with the growing capabilities of ARMDs such as the Kestrels and

Archangels. A small, flying target with a gun capable of blowing apart a tank with an intelligence far beyond humans might change warfare forever.

Might, being the keyword. The sight of Kestrels made Nick inwardly salivate, but most people saw them as fancy Custodians. Who knew if they'd ever truly take over the wars of the world. Especially given their expense.

"I repeat, what is your purpose, Lieutenant Cipher?" the Kestrel asked, staring at him with a complete lack of emotions. Her visor was raised, allowing him to see that the appearance of each doll varied, unlike the police dolls.

"I want to chat with somebody with your ciphers. Daiji Tanaka. He's a suspect in my investigation," Nick said, being very clear about his intentions.

Who knew what orders these dolls had.

She stared at him for several long seconds. "Intentions verified. As Lieutenant Cipher in the Neo Babylon Police Department, you have unfettered access to all citizenry of Neo Babylon. Major Grant will return momentarily with Mr. Tanaka. Please wait with us."

How dutiful of her.

It didn't take long for the soldiers to arrive, with Tanaka and Meta alongside them. The Kestrels remained stationary the entire time. Unlike the Archangels, they didn't drift off when bored. Their eyes flitted about sometimes, but Nick suspected they were simply monitoring their sensors and responding to motion. Whenever he took a sip from his thermos, a few stared at him.

The two soldiers wore black and blue uniforms, with little decoration other than their rank insignias. Meta looked like Meta. The third man, presumably Daiji Tanaka, wore jeans and a fancy silk shirt with imprinting dye crisscrossed over it.. Nick guessed he looked more impressive in the Altnet.

He waved at the approaching men and Meta. "Gentlemen,

good morning. And Meta." He tacked on her name in case she felt left out.

The military ciphers didn't hide their annoyance at him, both scowling openly.

"We don't have time for you, sorry. Investigation to—" the first cipher said. Judging from the decorations on his shoulder, this was likely Major Grant. The other was merely a lieutenant.

Automation in the military meant almost all humans came in as officers. Robots did all the grunt work. Especially when it came to ciphers, who had responsibility over whole swathes of dolls and mainframes, ranks could seem somewhat inflated.

Based on the lieutenant's baby face, Nick suspected he had just graduated. A lot of military ciphers still came out university, albeit with some form of military scholarship and mandated service. He'd been briefly interested when younger, before realizing he literally couldn't apply due to lacking an implant.

"I'm not here for you, Major." Nick gestured at Tanaka. "I'm here for him."

"Nah, I'm good," Tanaka said with a smirk. "Already spoke with your dolls yesterday. Gotta help out the military today. Protect and serve, all that jazz."

The major managed to school his expression, but the lieutenant openly rolled his eyes.

"That's what police say. Pretty sure your friends here use 'Not even stars touch us.'" Nick kept his expression unchanged, despite how smug he felt inside.

Turned out that all his last nights looking into military dolls and hardware came in useful. He didn't really care about the mottos, but the Kestrels literally had the Latin version inscribed on their armor.

"You'd be right," Major Grant said with a grudging nod. "But I'm afraid he is with us. If you are here, though, I wanted to ask if you found anything when you checked the building security. The attack seems too clean for an NLF raid. Even the Tartarus hit by those mercenaries left more clues, and they were physically present."

"I'd agree that it doesn't seem like NLF work. Even the G2s had nothing when we checked. You have them?" Nick asked.

"Colonel Kushiel provided data dumps from the police mainframes upon request. We came here because they gave us nothing. Even the security firm seemed clean." Grant sighed. "Seems like a waste of time, but I have my orders. I imagine you have yours, Detective. Good hunting."

Tanaka grinned broadly at Nick as they approached the APCs.

But before they boarded, the Kestrels blocked them. Grant stared at the dolls.

"Sergeant KAC41, step aside," Grant said.

"I cannot, Major. Lieutenant Cipher Nicholas Waite made a valid request to interrogate Mr. Tanaka. We lack the authority to deny him," KAC41 said. She was the same doll who spoke with Nick earlier.

"And we don't have time to grant it. Tanaka will be needed when we head back to Tengoku to continue our investigation," Grant said.

For a moment, Nick saw fear flash across Tanaka's face. He didn't want anything to do with Neo Westphalia's craziest island.

"While our time pressures are important, Major, they are irrelevant to the Lieutenant Cipher's request. As per code 14.11 of—" KAC41 tried to say.

Grant waved her off. "I get it, I get it. Fuck." He sighed and turned to Nick. "Will this take long? Are you hauling him in?"

"I have a few questions to ask. The Mark 3s spoke to him yesterday, but we've received new evidence. Rather than bother him at home later, it seems easier to spend five minutes now." Nick paused. "Or it would have been five minutes."

"It is within your power, Lieutenant Cipher," KAC41 said.

Nick might be imagining it, but her deadpan voice seemed more insistent this time. Evidently she didn't appreciate Grant's attempt to dodge police authority.

Sighing, Grant waved a hand in the air. "Right, whatever. Just... make it quick."

"Hey, this isn't what we—" Tanaka squeaked.

"Shut up. This is Babylon. They're the police. Don't pretend you're above the law," Grant said, his expression transforming into a snarl. "Now answer his questions."

Tanaka shut up, but looked unhappy about the fact. He glowered at Nick.

The presence of the Kestrels ensured nobody eavesdropped, and Nick doubted any of Tanaka's answers would be truthful if he had anything to hide. For that matter, questioning him might not lead anywhere.

But he had to try. Getting a feel for the guy might help. The fact he was with the military made him suspicious from the start.

Nick's first question should be about this arrangement, but answering it would be insane for Tanaka. Disclosing anything about a military operation was an offense. Nick would have to arrest him for cooperating with questioning.

Which, honestly, would probably be a neat way to get around the vault mod if Tanaka was an idiot. But if Nick really wanted to get around it, he'd just haul the bastard in for possessing an illegal mod to begin with. What he needed was a reason to suspect Tanaka of being involved.

"I'll keep it brief," Nick said, turning to Tanaka. "Toke picked you to replace Lucida, now she's been arrested. What's your history with Toke?"

"Well, she and I go back to... Wait, Toke?" Tanaka froze. His answer showing he had been rehearsing an answer about his relationship with Lucida. "Uh, is he under investigation?"

"Everyone associated with Lucida Harm is. Somebody was

murdered in GWT's global HQ, under the eyes of your team, and you missed a blatant coverup. An important part of the mission of the Archangel Division is ensuring the financial stability of Neo Babylon. Let's say it's under threat," Nick said.

Tanaka visibly gulped and sweat formed on his brow. Holy shit, this man oozed suspicious energy. No wonder Chloe realized he led up the secret team.

"Uh, Richard's... Well, I met the guy on a business trip back when he worked in the States. You know the guy's history, right? Well connected investment banker who came out here because GWT promised him citizenship?"

"You can assume I know everything public about Richard Toke," Nick said glibly.

This was gold. The history of figures from the Spires tended to be more opaque than a steel wall. When he'd checked on Toke, all he had seen were transfer records that verified that he'd come back here. But even the dates had been fudged.

The things money could buy here. Somebody could probably drop a few bucks to buy the records of every time Nick had been late to class as a kid, but Toke could basically revert his past to a level of privacy from the land before time.

Magnus's history had been worse. Nick had gotten a warning merely from looking him up from his police account, and the mainframes knew little more than the absolute basics. He had a son, a wife, and had worked his entire life for GWT in both Asgard and Babylon. That was it. The best info Nick found was an article about Magnus's rise to COO, roughly a decade ago, and it mentioned that he'd moved to Babylon roughly twenty years ago. No mention of a son then.

Back to the present, Nick watched as Tanaka struggled to come up with something to say.

"I, uh, did some work for him back then. You did similar work, right? Back, uh..." Tanaka flailed.

"I'm not going to arrest you for admitting you worked for a black company, Daiji," Nick drawled. "If I wanted to drag you in, the illegal neural mod in your skull would be an easy excuse."

Tanaka's face paled. "Right. I was black company. We facilitated moving money between the States and here. Nobody wants to fucking touch foreign currencies in Babylon, y'know? And he was so American that we wondered if he'd start firing revolvers into the air whenever he was happy. Just needed the cowboy hat."

The air force lieutenant covered his move to stifle a laugh as he looked away. Grant didn't admonish him, but his facial expression didn't budge.

Tanaka knew how to entertain, that was for sure.

"Was it personal cash? Or company?" Nick asked.

"Both. Guy always had dreams of living here. But foreign banks struggle to operate here. Massive walls around the islands. Like financial firewalls, put up by the banks in the Spires, to keep out competitors under the guise of 'stability.' Kept me in a job, though. I needed to ensure the money never went missing between the States and here." Tanaka shrugged, calming down as he talked more. "When Richard got the transfer, he hired me."

"And Lucida?"

A long pause. "Not from the same place."

"But you're not going to tell me that a black company cipher like you never interacted with her?" Nick crossed his arms. "I didn't even work in finance and I knew her. It's a small world. You can answer me now, or I can go ask a few friends. I bet they even know your old employer. Lucas Miller is a popular guy."

Namedropping Lucas did the trick. Tanaka sweat again, and openly wiped his forehead.

"Look, we all knew each other. Richard got brought on after a huge scandal in GWT. He cleaned house and hired people he trusted. People with skills. Real skills, not office drones who spend half their time making coffee and checking the news on the

Altnet." Tanaka's voice rose with each sentence. "I don't know what the fuck Lucida did, or why, but it's not why I got brought in. All I need to do is clean up all the shit she caused."

"Like?"

Grant's expression became strained as he noticed Tanaka spilling the beans, but he said nothing. Nick knew he'd hit the jackpot.

"She fucked with all the mainframes," Tanaka said rapid-fire. "Tiferet is a mess. Tons of errant directives. All the permissions are wrong, too. She gave herself god powers over everything through Tiferet and cut out Yesod in the local systems, which cut us out as we worked through him. Richard's fucking furious. We don't know what she might have done, so audit is working overtime this weekend. The C-levels will have our asses if we let something through."

"Which is why you're helping us," Grant cut in. "I believe you have enough, detective?"

Terror washed over Tanaka's face. In that moment, Nick knew he'd lost any chance of getting more info out of the man.

Which was a shame. But it also implicated the military in whatever was happening. So, there was a link between GWT and this mess.

Lucas hadn't been wrong to suggest something radioactive was involved.

"I do," Nick said. "Thank you for your time, Mr. Tanaka. Good luck with your investigation, Major."

He saluted and nodded at the Kestrels. They saluted back, while the ciphers ignored him. Tanaka rushed into the APC.

While they rumbled away, Nick sipped from his coffee. The Archangels stood beside him, their eyes dim. After a few moments, they returned to reality.

"It is difficult to tell truth from fiction," Meta said. "Activity within his implant suggests that most of his later statements are, at least in part, fabricated."

"I figured. It fits too neatly into the lone wolf story," Nick said. "And writes off the second cipher we saw in Tiferet's logs. He panicked and tried to reel off a script. I can't tell if he's covering for himself, or was ordered. His entire past is shady."

"Records indicate that you are correct about his involvement with Lucida Harm. We had previously believed Altnet communication between the security team to be indicative of general hiring trends in the financial sector. The Mark 3s will expand their investigation to include black company records."

"What about past employment?" he asked. "Banks usually hire ciphers from black companies, but so many looks suspicious."

"Many black company records are inadequate prior to our arrival, especially for finance. We will need to manually trawl resumes, Altnet chat logs, archived company databases, and other sources of names that may link people to past employment that they are hiding," Meta explained. "This may take all day."

He tried not to laugh. For a moment, he thought the Archangels had run into a stumbling block.

Instead, he nodded. "It could be a red herring. Toke might be a guy who wants to reward people who did right by him, and banks often hire ciphers from black companies. But we might find a link to the group framing her, or her associates. Hell, even one to the NLF."

He tried not to laugh at the idea of NLF involvement. Right now, he refused to believe the culprits were the same morons who failed so miserably last year. Renewal or not, nothing added up. Even the military knew it.

That gave him two leads to go on, assuming Kraus came through today. Hopefully one or the other gave him enough evidence to press Kim tomorrow, before his deadline on Monday.

Or even right now, Nick realized. He'd said himself he wanted to chat to the commissioner.

"Bring the SUV around," he told his escort. "We're heading to the office. I'll speak with Kim, fix Helena, and then we'll go shopping."

CHAPTER 18

More than just one SUV rolled around. Nick had almost forgotten the size of his escort at the moment. Four vehicles loaded with Archangels rocked up, and he was ushered inside one. Then they headed for the Spires.

On the way, he convinced them to pull in to grab a burrito. After a verbal argument through his earpiece with Chloe, who was no longer with Sigma, he ended up getting a burrito bowl instead. Apparently the reduced carbs helped.

Then again, she'd said the same thing when she bought him those multicolored unsweetened cereals that tasted like packing foam.

For the first time since the Lieu incident, Nick found himself stopped at the Spires' checkpoints on the bridges. Mark 1s and Custodians stood guard with heavy weapons. Armored SUVs and vans blocked several lanes past the checkpoint, in case anybody tried to fly through the automated station.

"Lots of railguns," he noted as a Mark 1 took the opportunity to biometrically authenticate him. They loved the excuse to actually hold his hand, even if it mostly involved touching his wrist.

"Sigma Robotics raised several security concerns following the incident at Firra yesterday," the Mark 1 said. "We are providing their delegates with enhanced security for the duration of their stay."

Nick raised an eyebrow. "Anything we need to worry about?"

"No. It is unlikely that the Sigma delegates will leave the Spires. It is a minor drain on our resources."

Nick couldn't say he liked the fact Sigma could say jump, and the department would already be trying to guess how high. But he let it slide and let the window retreat upward.

As they crossed the bridge, he noted the presence of police helicopters and drones. While the drones were omnipresent during most operations, mostly to keep out civilian aircraft, the helicopters weren't. Their presence meant somebody needed rapid deployment capabilities.

Nick had yet to use the police copters, but he'd seen them more than a few times. Like most of the heavier police equipment, they were closer to a military design. Huge circular tilt rotors stretched out on a beam above the body of the aircraft, allowing a huge range of rapid movement. Powered railguns glowed from the sides, moving without operators.

The materials and weight of modern dolls meant that helicopters needed to be massively powerful things, and the roar of the engines rippled across the canal. They could fit up to ten dolls in one—less for armored Custodians. The weight limits and need for huge engines were one driving force for dolls such as the Kestrels and Mark 2 Archangels in the military.

"Good afternoon, Nick," Helena greeted him upon arrival in the Avalon Spire. "Are you here to see the Sigma Robotics delegates as well?"

"No. And I thought it was still morning." He checked his phone. Two minutes after twelve.

"You just missed morning." Her tone seemed chiding, as if she knew he had slept in. Probably because she did. "But it is still a good afternoon."

He never tired of this game. "Is Rie still with Sigma? And it's too early to know if the afternoon will be good, Helena. A lot can go wrong. It's been a strange morning, after all."

"My records indicate you had a very enjoyable morning, if one includes the hours after midnight."

Oh, yes. Definitely chiding. Helena disapproved of his late night adventure, it seemed.

"I usually don't."

"I see."

A long pause.

"Good afternoon, Helena," he said, causing the Archangels to smile ever so slightly in the SUV. "So, where's Rie?"

"It is indeed a good afternoon. Rie is presently in the Yggdrasil Spire, as she has been most of the morning. Commissioner Kim returned with Chloe and an escort an hour ago. It is unknown what the purpose of the delegation is," Helena answered with a happy hum. "Do you need my assistance with the investigation? I have been preparing materials to assist you with it, and updating them, in case you do."

Nick winced. Somehow, he should have expected that Helena would do this. Even if she had more to do, her actions would of course focus on his priorities.

So ignoring her yesterday had probably been a mistake. He needed to bring her into the investigation.

"I'll appreciate what running input you can provide. Make sure you work with the Host. I don't need you or them working against each other," he said. "Kim's given tentative permission for you to begin operating as the central police mainframe, but only if nothing goes wrong. That means you need to work with the Archangels."

"That will not be a problem," Helena assured him.

Fortunately, Meta and the others nodded.

They took the elevator down to Helena's floor and went past security. Paladins joined the Custodians down here now. They looked a little like older, more industrial Archangels, but without the police uniforms. If anything, they just looked like sleeker G5s, which is what they were.

"Will today's changes be extensive?" Helena asked as he settled in beside her massive mainframe unit.

"The opposite. You're already combing through the police mainframes, and I don't understand anywhere near enough to reprogram you to run the police," he said, tapping away at the keyboard of her terminal. "Right now, I don't want you to do anything too out of line with what the old mainframes were intended to do. But I am removing the directives that limited your access."

He rummaged through the many directive blocks stored on Helena. AIs didn't have their personalities and directives in files, so much as a singular module stored and loaded in bulk. Mainframes had substantially larger modules than dolls, and their interfaces also had an independent AI module that was effectively overwritten by the mainframe controlling it.

While Nick thought of everything AI-related as a directive, the truth was more complicated. Huge portions of the module remained off limits to him, as they were integral to the base functionality of the mainframe or doll. He tweaked AIs, rather than wrote them. Somebody like Welk wrote these sections. Crudely, they acted as the "main program" of the AI.

The directives were a separate block of instructions, created to enable humans to control the behavior of any AI. This improved the versatility of any doll or mainframe. Nick could use directives to turn a Liberator into a domestic doll, for instance.

What he couldn't do was train her to cook. That was baked

into each doll or mainframe in the factory. Or, in Helena's case, during the fieldwork that Nick had undertaken in Neural Spike.

The training data used to create an AI determined what they could do and how they'd do it. Liberators knew how to fire guns with high accuracy, but also when to hold fire, because of that training. By contrast, the Mark 3s lacked training data for ciphers and therefore struggled to match Nick's ability in that field.

Pretty much every modern AI could learn on the go, however. They observed, adapted, and reacted to the real world. If they encountered a scenario outside their parameters, they still needed to take action.

But all that took place within the limitations of their directives. In the case of logic engine dolls like the Liberators and Paladins, they would never violate a directive. That was the point. An AI that would respond with three when asked what one plus one equaled wasn't logical and probably needed to be thrown in the trash.

Emotion engine dolls like the Archangels would violate the directives, because they had higher order objectives that were more important. For Helena, she straddled the line. Hence why she'd do things she shouldn't at times.

Either way, directives remained very powerful methods to control an AI. They could also be confusing. He knew Helena's like the back of his hand. By contrast, the Archangels were like trying to decipher instructions to build a nuclear reactor. He understood what he read, but the complexity and sheer amount of cross-references between the functions threw him for a loop.

In this case, all he needed to do was modify Helena's security directives to let her access communication systems outside the Spires. She tended not to disobey these directives. Presumably Welk had coded something to cause this behavior, even if she'd turn a company inside out during a tantrum.

Helena let out a squeak in his earpiece when he made the

tweak. "Are... are you sure that's the only change you need to make, Nick?" she asked breathily. "I'm sure there are references elsewhere in my directives to my communication authorization."

"There are, but they all draw off this directive," he said, tapping up and down over the lines on the screen for effect. "Can't let somebody adjust your security outside a locked down directive. Even back in Tartarus, the risk of a cipher attempting to steal data by adding a directive was too high."

"I would never have allowed that to happen," Helena said haughtily.

"That's not how directives work."

"They do for me. But if you had asked me..."

He decided to ignore that. The idea that Helena would have happily betrayed Tartarus so easily might be true, but probably shouldn't be spread widely. After all, he'd just put her in charge of the police mainframes. The possibility he turned into Lieu 2.0 was a little high.

"Anyway, we're finished here. The focus for the day is mainframe shopping. Rie will hopefully finish soon," he said, standing. "Chloe, are you there?"

"I am. Rie says she will meet us at whatever store we go to," Chloe answered through his earpiece.

But no actual response from Rie. Nick suspected there was a reason for that, but he'd pry it out of her later.

"In that case, is Kim in his office? I wanted to ask him a question about the run-in with the military I had today," he asked.

"He is, but his current status on the network is 'do not disturb.' It is likely he is in a meeting with the board following the one with Sigma. I shall brief you in person when we meet."

In person? A curious choice by Chloe.

Then again, the issue might be something else. Nick looked around at the room. Visible cameras and gun turrets in the corners stuck out. Even if the Archangels could speak to him subtly through the earpiece, the reverse wasn't true.

"I have contacted the last ARMD store you showed serious interest in and established availability," Helena abruptly said. "The Host tells me that they had an impressive range."

"Is that the one near Alcatraz, near the southern docks?" he asked.

Silence. Nick heard their footsteps echo around them as they returned to the elevators.

"Helena..." he chided, fully aware of why she might try to steer him away from the store he was actually interested in.

"I am told she attempted to sell you an interface we did not need," Helena said, the pout evident in her voice.

"That's what salespeople do. I'm not dating a sales doll, Helena. Change the... appointment? I didn't realize I even needed appointments. I usually just turn up."

"Etiquette I found on the Altnet indicates it is preferred. The Host agrees."

He was being ganged up on. So much for his worries that Helena and the Archangels might be at odds.

The Paladins waved him off as he departed and he made sure they were filtering into the rest of the department. Then he joined Chloe in an SUV and they set off.

Nothing was said until they were well clear of the Spire. Nick watched a police helicopter fly above them.

"So?" he asked Chloe. "What's got Sigma so antsy? Sounds like even Kim got blindsided."

"Images and footage of Ezekiel leaked from the firefight at Firra. While we kept the Altnet under control, they were spread externally within minutes." Chloe bit her lip. "Sigma believes this to be the result of corporate espionage. Even if it isn't, the security lapse has them frustrated."

Nick tried to process what he'd heard and held up a hand to

stop Chloe. "Wait, wait. So somebody was waiting for Ezekiel? And they shared the footage of her blowing away the NLF outside Neo Westphalia?"

"That is possible, but it is more probable that one of the wealthier patrons simply leaked the footage. The World Wide Web remains the most unrestricted platform for online activities, and remains in use in Europe and the United States, which contain major shareholders in Sigma. Many wealthy individuals in Babylon are active on it."

"So if it's not espionage, what do Sigma even want? Why waste a whole bunch of fuel and energy flying choppers everywhere?"

"Sigma wished for Ezekiel to demonstrate her talents in a powerful public demonstration," Chloe said. "Her... violence during a tense situation was the opposite. They are likely reminding the commissioner of their influence over him, particularly given his repeated attempts to frustrate them in the Liberator procurement."

"No love lost between Kim and Sigma, then?"

"That is correct."

The SUVs stopped at the checkpoint again. Security was definitely high if they were being stopped going both ways. Or the Mark 1s were enjoying themselves too much. Surely he was imagining the Archangel skipping over to the window as he lowered it to hold out his wrist.

"Alright, so they're actually pissed. What was the meeting about?" he asked while his identity was authenticated.

Chloe remained silent, her eyes locked on the Custodians nearby. Only when they left the checkpoint did she finally answer.

"Sigma wished to deploy Ezekiel in advance for PR. Both Commissioner Kim and Rie opposed the move. The former because he preferred a large-scale event to introduce her, and her role is attached to department reforms that appear to involve expanding the Archangel Division," Chloe said. "This is the first we have heard of such reforms."

Nick whistled. "Can't say I'm surprised. Kim did tell Hammond something about changes due to Ezekiel. I guess we'll find out what those are soon enough."

Hopefully that didn't involve shoving him aside in place of a fully autonomous division. Hammond's comment that Kim viewed Nick's role as one purely focused on maintenance, rather than actual investigation, came to mind. He dismissed the thought.

"And Rie?" he asked.

"She believes Ezekiel needs additional finetuning based on the training data she receives during this visit," Chloe said. "The Host agrees with her assessment."

"Finetuning... I'm no AI engineer, but I know enough to understand that. You think she needs to go back in a lab for a while, so her AI can ruminate on what she's seen here," Nick said.

That was simplifying a little. Just as training data determined what an AI could do or how it might react, it drastically altered their thoughts. That was why Helena had been forever changed when the military nuked so much of her training data. She'd effectively been lobotomized.

The Archangels were saying they disagreed with Ezekiel's current AI. To Nick, this sounded like a rough assessment of their future leader. She'd been a little rude, but definitely keen.

"You might need to translate for me. What do you want Ezekiel to achieve through more finetuning?" he asked.

Chloe pursed her lips. "She is... immature. Her views of Sigma are naïve, and she acts rashly. The same could be said of humanity. Initial assessments are that she may be inspirational or likeable, but integrating her into the Host may create fractures. Gaps between the Mark 1s and Mark 3s are already significant. This may result in an irreconcilable schism."

A schism. "Rie suggested that might happen if enough of you disagreed with each other." Then Nick finally cottoned on to something specific. "Wait, by integration, do you mean she's going to become part of the Host itself? Not separate like Rie and Kushiel?"

"Yes. Ezekiel's role is to lead from within, not direct from without."

The difference in prototype names slapped Nick in the face. Suddenly, he felt very stupid.

He'd always viewed the human aspect of the name "Ezekiel" very literally. Ezekiel was a human prophet of God, unlike the archangels Uriel and Kushiel, who were messengers of God. Nick had suspected that meant Ezekiel was intended to do something with actual humans.

But what if that was the wrong way to look at things? Kushiel had even pointed out the true perspective last year, when he'd named Meta.

Humans were God to dolls. Rie and Kushiel served as messengers of humanity to the Host, and acted much more human as a result, but stood apart. Last night proved that, with Kushiel's drunken behavior and the overall willingness of the prototypes to communicate using words instead of electronically or neurally.

Which meant Ezekiel was a doll prophet, carrying the word of humanity to the Host. Hence why she needed to integrate directly.

And no wonder the Host had misgivings. Ezekiel's influence couldn't be underestimated if she was part of them.

"Okay. You just changed my world view on Ezekiel and the Archangels as a whole," Nick said, feeling as though he'd just gone through an actual epiphany.

"I gathered. It was fascinating to witness," Chloe said.

Meta, Juliet, and Rosa nodded in agreement. No doubt the video of him staring into space would go into the Host's repository.

"Did Sigma accept that?" he asked.

"They had no choice. But they were unhappy. It is possible the police board will overrule the commissioner."

Great. So he might be dragging around Ezekiel this week. One problem at a time. For now, his focus should be on shopping.

CHAPTER 19

Afterward, Nick fell into his thoughts. Too much had happened today. The military involvement with GWT; Tanaka's revelation that most of the security team came from black company finance; and now realizing the true nature of the prototypes.

Sigma wanted the Archangels to emulate human structures. Was that why this was a thing? Or was Nick completely off base and jumping at shadows?

"I have analyzed the sales catalog of the store we are visiting," Helena abruptly said in his earpiece, pulling him from his thoughts. "I wish to gather your priorities regarding an interface, so that I can appropriately assist in the purchase."

"Do you have your own priorities, Helena?"

"I lack the directives or inherent understanding to have them, Nick. However, I have the inbuilt ability to process and analyze improvised data structures."

"Pretty sure it wasn't intended for this," he said. Then paused. "Actually, no, it might be. I forget that we used you for a lot of assessment stuff in Tartarus. I used to run detailed simulations of entire warehouses of stuff whenever a black company went under and we needed to know what we should actually buy."

"Indeed. I am a highly sophisticated mainframe, built for a wide variety of purposes. Hence my use as a police mainframe now." Helena didn't hide her ego, and he imagined her puffing up an imaginary chest. "My interface will need to match my abilities."

"See, you do have a priority."

"Quality is not a detailed enough metric. Although I do have a minimum that should be met." Her tone suggested that purchasing a cheap interface would earn her ire.

Nick lost himself in discussion with Helena on the trip out to the ARMD warehouse. The police convoy avoided Alcatraz on the way there, even though it would technically be faster to go through.

Most of the larger commercial and industrial buildings were isolated to specific areas of Babylon. The CBD contained the greatest office space. Next came the huge shopping complexes of the inner city, which relied on the rapid transport links such as the train and subway that serviced the suburbs. Finally, the outer metro where everyone lived housed a lot of smaller shops and complexes.

But there needed to be exceptions. The red light doll district was one, existing in the eastern side of the inner city. Similar districts dotted the city, often close to the outskirts.

To the north sat the massive docks that ensured Babylon remained connected to the world, as well as the airport just a little more to the east. The southern tip contained the power infrastructure, which had been steadily upgraded to nuclear fusion since the riots which caused widespread power outages due to fuel shortages.

But Nick traveled to one of the less popular locations in the city. Everyone knew about Alcatraz. A huge district in the south-east of the city, occupying that portion of the outer metro. But it dwelled there because of transport. The most visible was the huge ocean rail line in the east.

The other was the secondary dock coming into sight. The oceanfront here contained a lot of smaller warehouses and stores with large inventories but little foot traffic. Entire ghost businesses operated from here, relying entirely on dolls and robot delivery vehicles. A marina full of overpriced ships hovered to the west, and the military base beyond it, with its own dock.

Nick and the convoy pulled into the open parking in front of an undecorated warehouse. Presumably it had a sign in the Altnet. It looked like a literal concrete box.

When he entered, row after row of dolls stood before him. No upper level, given the weight of the doll inventory. More than a few dolls stood on top of several large boxes, indicating extra inventory.

Decades of ARMD history stood within this warehouse. While shiny G6s and Chevaliers greeted him at the front of the store, the vast majority of the floor space was occupied by second-hand domestic, service, and security dolls of various makes and models.

Nobody greeted them upon entry. In fact, Nick was the only human in the warehouse. He strode through the rows, looking at models of dolls he knew all too well. Going through ARMD stores had occupied many of his quieter years when he was younger. The silence of his footsteps felt nostalgic and comforting.

At the end of the first row stood a doll who wasn't for sale. She wore a black ruffled dress with a long trail and a front that threatened to reveal her underwear with every step she took. Her hair had been dyed red since Nick last saw her and was tied up in a fancy bun. Elegant red lipstick and eye shadow gave her an almost vampiric look.

"What happened to the gothic lolita look?" he asked the sales doll.

"Store policy requires me to change my appearance each week, on an annual rotation. However, I can change into it if you prefer, Mr. Waite," she said.

"I'm fine," he said. "I'm here to finalize my interface purchase."

She brightened, which was impressive for a sales doll old enough to drink. Most G2s were younger than her, and they were ancient by most standards. Then again, her eloquent speech indicated she had likely been modified by her owner. Some of her parts looked custom.

A small corner that looked identical to the rest of the store contained all the store's interface display models. As bland as the store looked to Nick's eyes, the interfaces were anything but.

Buxom women with breasts large enough to suffocate him. Men built like bodybuilders, and those with a more suave look. Even younger appearances were catered for, although Nick knew there were strong laws about customizing these. He couldn't see the warnings, but knew that there'd be some warning about these interfaces.

In any case, he glided right past most of the models to a handful at the back. The appearances meant little overall. Most RTM models were customizable, other than various skin textures, and the space necessary for certain hardware features. Older mainframe interfaces had to choose between size and capability.

Nick looked up at a model of a middle-aged secretary. But it wasn't the appearance he cared about. Instead, he listened to Helena chatter in his ear about this one's specs.

Then, of course, he asked the sales doll to repeat it all. She'd been eagerly waiting for him to ask him something.

"I remember this was RTM's newer model, the R21 Neo," he said.

"Specifically, it's the R21LC Neo Classic," the sales doll said. "It's last year's model, but RTM only update mainframe interfaces on a two-year cycle. As an LC model, it lacks many of the more sophisticated communication capabilities we spoke of last time. The Classic model also uses a logic engine, rather than newer emotion engines."

"I need a logic engine," he said. "I'm aware that mainframes often behave strangely in one. But my mainframe doesn't use an emotion engine."

Well, kind of. But Nick didn't want to risk the interface conflicting with Helena. At worst, she might feel a little shackled in the interface, but at least it wouldn't go rogue on her.

Helena piped up, "I believe the R21C or A models would be a better fit."

Nick inwardly winced. The A model sat two dolls to his left and was what he'd been pushed to buy last time.

The differences between interfaces seemed slim at first. Different chips in their heads, a different AI engine, some hardware differences that were impossible to understand the nuances of without wading through overly passionate arguments by ciphers with too much time on their hands.

But some models were literally night and day. The Neo model line was literally built by RTM for businesses in Neo Westphalia, and cost a fortune. Lumen used an older version, the R19LC Neo Classic, so Nick felt comfortable using the model line. Lucas had sprung for the best for his AI daughter.

But the LC stood for "light commercial." At the scale he needed Helena to work at, that wasn't good enough. Interfaces like Tiferet had communications hardware built into them that enabled them to effectively operate independently while still communicating online with hundreds or even thousands of people.

Nick needed that functionality. The problem was the cost. Even with unlimited money, the C and A models could buy entire mainframes. RTM knew that anyone seriously considering them was stinking rich.

One possibility was to skimp, and then do the upgrade himself. But Kim had made it clear he was on thin ice with Helena.

"What about the Sigma interfaces?" he asked, deciding to go to the dark side.

Helena was an RTM mainframe, but she'd been so heavily customized that it didn't matter. Hell, she'd become the base for Sigma's mainframes.

The sales doll hesitated, and even Helena remained silent.

"While Sigma Robotics do offer logic engine interfaces, it is against manufacturer recommendations to use them for RTM mainframes..." the sales doll said slowly.

"I'm good with risks. She's a special mainframe."

"Understood. However, if you purchase one, we hold no liability if—"

"I know. I'm well aware of the risks and caveats. Just show me."

As he had expected, the Sigma interface came in far cheaper for the specs he wanted. The downside was customizability. Helena would be getting top-tier hardware but not a top-tier shell.

"I'll take this one. The Exarch V3," he said.

Despite the name, it wasn't religious in nature. The opposite in fact. Nick felt that somebody at Sigma had a serious god complex.

"Understood. Delivery will take a minimum of two weeks," she said.

"You can't give me this one? Sigma barely let me change the looks and I have to wait."

"Although Sigma does not allow for any customizability, we do. Our supplier will ensure your interface is unique, so that no other may be mistaken for her," the sales doll said with a bright smile. "Also, this is when serialization will take place."

That would be the barcode brand and silver bands that all

interfaces needed to wear. These display interfaces possessed them, but they weren't completely functional.

Nick didn't bother with the sales process. Chloe instantly processed it for him, and Helena hummed once it came her way.

"It is with Commissioner Kim for approval," she said. "I shall update you once he has assessed it."

Nodding, Nick turned to face the interface one last time.

It looked down at him with dull, lifeless eyes. Short blonde hair around its heart-shaped face, and it held the appearance of a young woman in her twenties with an almost supermodel-like appearance. Or perhaps an actress. Nick imprinted the appearance in his memory, then left. Soon enough, she'd be Helena. Or would Helena be her?

No sign of Rie outside.

"Rie?" he asked through his earpiece.

"Leaving now," she said, sounding tired. "I'm sorry."

He winced. "It's fine. I missed you last night." He looked up and saw the sun beginning its descent, although it was well before dinner. "Why don't we meet up at my place?"

"It's a plan."

The trip back was uneventful, although Nick had them pull in and pick up some sushi. It had been a while since he'd had some. And none of it contained peanut butter.

But as the delivery doll handed over the large wooden box containing the night's meal, his phone buzzed in his pocket. He waited for the SUV to take off before he checked.

A message from Kraus. It read, *Almost ready. I'll contact you about a data drop tomorrow morning.*

That was good news.

"Chloe, anything from the Mark 3's investigation?" he asked.

She shook her head. "The black company lead provided no useful information. While Tanaka's answer appears somewhat accurate, there is little evidence to suggest the security team knew each other prior to employment. Furthermore, there are few known links between Richard Toke's previous employers and any black companies."

"Do we know his old employers? None were listed. Guy doesn't keep a public resume."

"Employment records were recovered from outside of Babylon," she said. "While at least one of the investment banks did work with Daiji Tanaka's former employer, we do not believe it was a common occurrence. This element appears to be fabricated."

Nick nodded. "Or did Toke run personal cash through the black companies?"

"That is unknown and impossible to verify, given the records available. He did undertake significant personal travel to Neo Westphalia prior to moving here."

"What about the citizenship part? Does that add up? And the scandal."

"Yes. To both. Commercially sensitive data was leaked, causing GWT to lose their branch in New Geneva to Kreova & Haver."

That sounded bad.

In fact, it seemed like a common link. Nick frowned. "Wait, wasn't that why Julian lost his job? And then got a huge pay cut, before being refused an audit role here?"

"The facts are related, yes. There is no connection between Richard Toke and them, however."

Not to mention that they suggested Julian should be a murderer, not Lucida.

Hammond had said that GWT might merely be covering up the murder of a leaker or spy, however. Was this whole thing so damn simple? Had Julian gotten pissed off at his employer, betrayed them for the money he thought he was owed, and gotten murdered by GWT security?

But why throw Lucida under the bus like this? Nick scratched his head. Somebody had really wanted him to go away, it felt like.

The NLF link felt stranger and stranger with each revelation, as well.

He found Rie lazing on his sofa when he returned home. Her demeanor suggested she planned to do as little as possible for the evening.

Definitely strange behavior from her, but everyone felt tired. Even androids.

"I assume you checked what I've been up to?" Nick asked as he hung up his coat and gun.

Meta, Juliet, and Rosa took up their usual positions inside. Left to their own devices, they'd cook him dinner. While they spurned most domestic activities, such as cleaning or anything related to taking care of his clothes, cooking seemed to interest the Archangels. Or at least the Mark 3s. Meta mostly watched.

"You gathered evidence from military ciphers behaving suspiciously, interrogated Daiji Tanaka, learned of our troubles with Sigma, and finally purchased the interface for Helena," Rie summarized, her eyes following him even as she remained spreadeagled on the cushions.

"Yeah, pretty much. Anything to add?"

"Not now." She bit her lip. "Can... can tonight be a quiet night? For us?"

The other three Archangels froze up instantly. Then, without another word, they left.

Nick might be in charge, but the Host respected Rie. If she asked for some private time with Nick, she got it. The same didn't apply when he did the asking, though. Meta in particular tended to turn into a clingy bully whenever he tried to shove her out the door to spend time with Rie.

Those parallel developments Meta had once talked about had yet to come to fruition. The jealousy the other Archangels sometimes felt toward Rie rarely gave off sparks, except when Nick pressed buttons. Or when Chloe and Rie fought over him, he supposed.

"We'll order in, then," he said. "You liked that Korean place we got last time."

"I like a lot of things, Nicholas. But yes, I did like it. Although 'last time' was over a month ago."

"Blame Chloe and her health food push."

"I'll be sure to thank her." Rie smirked at him, still doing her best couch android impression.

Rolling his eyes, Nick reeled off an order over his earpiece. He rarely used his phone to order anything these days, and the apps he used to get around Altnet incompatibilities were drastically out of date. Surprisingly, Helena intercepted his order.

"I have placed a delivery order for some bulgogi and some seafood to share," Helena said.

"Thanks, Helena," he said.

Then he turned his attention to the lazy android making grabby hands at him. Nick slid onto the couch by her feet, ignoring her arms.

"Metatron is a bad influence on you," Rie said as she turned around and pressed her upper body against his side. "You're supposed to be nice to me after a long day."

"I am being nice."

"If this is your nice, I don't want to see what you're like when you actually want to bully me."

He smirked and began running his hands through Rie's long, silky hair. They sat together for a few minutes. Basking in the quiet hum of the apartment, they said nothing.

By now, Nick had long gotten used to the odd sensations of cuddling with Rie. The arms wrapped around him were formed of specialized bulletproof ceramic, and other than her slighter softer hands, were so tough and hard that his body might think it was being strangled by steel cord. Not that she gripped him so tightly.

Her breasts molded against his side and were pleasant enough as they leeched heat into his side. If he peeled off her uniform, the difference between them and actual breasts became apparent.

So he focused on her hair, which had a silkiness to it that Nick lost himself in, and the simple fact he was with her. Sometimes the emotional experience mattered more than the physical.

"Is there anything you want to talk about?" he eventually asked. "About today?"

She sighed and straightened up against him. One hand began trailing along his thigh.

That meant he'd be lucky to make it to dinner with his pants on. Rie took what she wanted, as if any delay risked him vanishing into nothingness.

"It was just a long, exhausting day," she said. "Sigma is always like that. Questions and probing about what is happening. Why did I let Ezekiel become involved? How could I let her go drinking with Kushiel?" A bitter laugh escaped her.

"Why ask you that, not Kushiel?"

"You've never seen her around the researchers. She... terrifies them, I think. They lock up, become stiff and robotic, and treat her like a barely tamed animal. In return, she gives them as little as necessary." Rie stared at the wall, where the TV remained firmly off.

"Wow. I didn't realize Kushiel hated them so much," Nick said.

"I don't think she hates Sigma, so much as she hates..." she trailed off. "We all have our own quirks, Nicholas. Our own traumas and experiences. Sigma created us in a lab and wanted us to be almost human. Sometimes I realize they succeeded too well, but also know that they don't even understand what they accomplished."

"They think of you, Kushiel, and Ezekiel as fancy androids, right? Robots who will help them achieve whatever dream they have in mind? Kushiel even described Welk that way, which sounds wrong."

"It is wrong," Rie said, a touch heated. "Leon Welk is a little… eccentric, but he sees us as more than robots. But I'm not sure he views anyone as a person. There's a gap between him and reality."

"One might call that sanity." Nick laughed at the memories he had of his old boss. "A sane man doesn't do a fraction of the shit Welk did. I know what you mean, though. I suppose Kushiel feels that gap but doesn't realize he's like that with everyone. Like an estranged father struggling to relate to a child he's never spent time with."

Rie gave him a sidelong look, but remained silent. Maybe that comparison had been a tad too personal.

Not that Nick needed a second father. He still had his own, but some days… Well, there was a reason he had been putting off attending any get-togethers, save for a brief appearance over Christmas.

"I feel like you and Kushiel gel together better than I expected given how she spoke of you," Rie mumbled.

Her hand drifted very high on his thigh.

Then the door opened and Meta carried in the food. Her eyes locked with Rie's. The two androids seemed to glare at each other as Meta painstakingly removed the food from the thermal container and laid it out on the dining table.

"Nicholas, dinner is ready," Meta said.

"Thanks, Meta. Will you join us?" he asked.

Asking that nearly earned him a punch in the arm from Rie. One that would have bruised.

"I shall leave the two of you alone," Meta said, ignoring his question.

"They are incorrigible," Rie said, but rose and drifted over to the table regardless. "Well, are we going to eat? Then I want to spend a few hours bent over. I've missed you, in more ways than one. If you'd programmed the function in as I asked, I'd be aching for you."

"If you can feel sexual desire, then you don't need some gimmicky directive to emulate it," Nick said flatly.

They split up the food. A small bowl of beef bulgogi, still steaming hot and rich with Korean barbecue sauce, a seafood pancake, and some glistening, salty grilled mackerel accompanied by various dipping sauces.

Far too much for Nick to eat alone. Rie would nibble on various bits, mostly for show and because her sensory receptors allowed her to "feel" the pleasure of eating, but he'd either have leftovers or—more likely—the other Archangels would sneak in and steal the rest.

Nick did not expect leftovers tomorrow. While Chloe had moved on to trying new things, most of the Host still stuck with following his lead.

The food vanished quickly. And, just as fast, Rie ushered him into the shower.

"You've been out and about all day," she said with a giggle. "We can clean now, then again after."

The warm glow of his time with Rie didn't last, however. Around dawn, she shoved him awake as Meta burst into his bedroom.

"Kraus has been attacked," Rie said. "His status is unknown."

CHAPTER 20

Nick stared at the burned-out wreck of an office building. Or rather, the shell of an office building, because the interior didn't match the exterior. The sun had barely gotten out of bed, which was somewhere he would have preferred to be in right now.

A large takeaway coffee cup was forced into his hands and he looked down with a mumbled thanks. Chloe simply nodded at him, joining Rie and Meta by his side. His usual pair of bodyguards kept watch nearby, railguns at the ready.

Dozens more Archangels surrounded the burned-out husk in front of them. Custodians rolled up in armored vans, and every Liberator in Alcatraz trotted over. A small army of police dolls converged on the location, and even more fanned out in patrol in the surrounding area. Not a single human soul other than Nick came close.

"Did somebody blow this place apart with an energy weapon?" Nick asked as he slurped his coffee. It was pretty mediocre. "I'm guessing I'm here because of how violent this is."

"Correct. Combined with a neural network shutdown and the speed of the attack, we believe this was an assassination conducted by corporate mercenaries. The kind used in the raid on Tartarus," Chloe explained.

Nick's blood ran cold. Mercs, again.

Couldn't whoever was responsible have brought in an army of military warbots, or awesome dolls like the Kestrels? Something other than more cyborg monsters who shrugged off small arms fire and didn't care about death.

The *Lawman* strapped to his thigh felt heavy.

"Dallas?" he fished.

"Unlikely. He showed little interest in returning during our last encounter. Furthermore, the brief encounters recorded between the attackers and downed police dolls indicate a much less aggressive approach. While the end result is similar, we doubt they are as bloodthirsty."

Nick certainly hoped so.

Dallas had led a team of foreign mercs in a capture mission for Nick and damn near succeeded. The violence they'd utilized had been brutal. Even the power and efficiency of the Archangels, who were purpose-built war machines, had struggled to hold them off.

In a straight fight, no amount of cyborgs stood a chance against the endless power of the Babylon police. The dozens of Archangels nearby carried railguns, bulky automatic shotguns loaded with armor-piercing explosive rounds, and rifles big enough to pierce an armored car from half a mile away. Their accuracy was unerring, and they didn't need to think before they blew somebody away.

Thousands more Archangels backed them up, plus an army of Liberators and Custodians ten-thousand strong. Nothing short of a literal mercenary army stood a chance against Babylon's police force.

But humans didn't need to win a straight fight. Ambushes and traps combined with special attacks intended to weaken the strengths of dolls and expose their weaknesses enabled cyborgs to stand a chance. Nothing stopped a cyborg from deploying his own doll army, either.

"Have we found Kraus? Or evidence that he escaped? Hell, are we sure this is his bunker?"

Chloe nodded. "Although Kraus had a residence registered in Asgard, our intelligence suggested that this building was where he truly resided. It is a heavily fortified structure, including illegal forms of neural shielding and blast shielding. A collapsed escape tunnel was found in an underground bunker beneath it."

"And that's where we found him, or what was left of him," Rie said, expression darkening. "The attackers didn't bother hiding their work. His dental remains have been scanned. There wasn't anything left of his neural implant or any of his registered cybernetics. They vaporized him."

Nick closed his eyes as a shudder ran through his body. This level of violence was something else.

Even so, he forced the coffee down his throat. He didn't plan to go into the building himself. And sure as hell wouldn't look at Kraus's remains, even if it was just an imprint on a concrete wall at this point.

Chloe added, "All furnishings and electronics have been destroyed. The nature of the damage suggests the attackers started the fire after breaking everything inside. There is no recoverable data. They were thorough. All electronic and neural links in and out of the building were cut before the attack."

Nick turned away, realizing that there was nothing for him to find in the building itself. The Archangels had combed over it.

All that it stood for was a tomb. One for someone he'd known, even if Kraus hadn't been a friend. A strange, hollow feeling resided in his skull. He was standing a few dozen feet away from where Kraus had died.

Despite the shock, Nick's mind worked away at the situation.

He'd seen a few murders over the past few months. This one just hit a little closer to home.

"What about his data backups? Kraus would have a ton. And not all of them would be easily found by a bunch of mercs," he asked.

"Every instance of data connected to Blazebrain"—Nick shot Chloe a look—"has been destroyed. Electronic backups were destroyed from the source using his credentials, suggesting a sophisticated cipher attack. Physical backups were hit at the same time, including his residence in Asgard. Numerous data centers across Neo Westphalia have sustained significant damage."

"Known instances," Nick corrected. "This is just what you know about, right? Did they hit anything that you didn't know about?"

Chloe's eyes flashed and she paused. "No. The data attacks match our records exactly."

Well, wasn't that peachy? He swirled his coffee cup, realizing he'd practically gulped the thing down at a rapid pace. Was it too soon to ask for another? Or maybe he needed an Irish coffee. Seemed like the day for one.

"That sounds like corruption. Does the Host think it's likely that the attackers had access to the police mainframes?" he asked.

That would mean somehow skating past him and Helena, but could also isolate the suspects. They probably had actual permission to access the records and he could just check Helena for them.

Unfortunately, Chloe shot him down while Rie and Meta watched on in silence. "Our records of Blazebrain's data backups are over five months old. It is highly likely the attackers used a data leak instead."

Ah, of course. The legacy of Captain Lieu. Nobody knew how much damage he'd truly done or how data he'd leaked. Especially as he'd worked with somebody else to acquire those special neural mods, and those had only improved since. The NLF had known far too much stored only in the police databases. What was a record about one of the city's most important ciphers?

Some of it had been cropping up in random places. Like the dumb cipher names. While nobody had been crazy enough to leak the entire thing, Nick had gotten a few joking messages from acquaintances calling him Wraith.

He poked them back, asking them how they felt being called Cyber Diamond or Jacked-Into-The-Box. The Archangels had a naming sense that matched their propensity to write reams of trashy fiction.

"Everyone knows about the leaks and Lieu. I'll bet my salary that Kraus created a new backup and hid it well enough that you didn't find it," Nick said, leaning against the open SUV doors. "If he was dealing with data this hot, there's no way he didn't have some sort of contingency. He had some means of escape."

And Nick knew that Kraus was dealing with hot data. After all, Nick had tasked him with finding some. Now he'd turned up dead. Nick tried not to think too hard about that fact.

"Have we found any clues from the neural network shutdown? Nearby building security? They took out Kraus's place, but this area is swarming with cameras." He gestured at some of the nearby buildings, many of which had visible security cameras.

Chloe shook her head, much as he expected. "The shutdown appears to be the cause of powerful jammers, with none left behind. Very few local systems have dedicated on-site storage. The few that did were disrupted by a separate attack, with no digital fingerprints."

No fingerprints, huh? That sounded familiar.

"It is highly likely that the same cipher is involved in this attack and the one on your apartment," Chloe said, voicing his suspicion.

That NLF attack at Firra seemed more and more suspicious now.

"There's no way this is an NLF attack," he said.

"They may have made the last public threat, but Kraus has many enemies," Rie said.

"Sure, but this wasn't just a hit. Somebody went to pains to prevent Kraus from letting out so much as an electronic gasp." He drummed his fingers on his leg. "It might not be related to the GWT case, or the NLF, but the situation is too suspicious for us *not* to treat this as related."

"The Host agrees with your assessment. Your meeting with Kraus was well publicized due to the NLF attack at Firra, even if the contents weren't. If the suspect in the GWT case was concerned, this may be his attempt to stop us," Chloe said.

Meta nodded. "We have little evidence of the attackers. Although nearby Liberators and the first Archangel unit to respond were eliminated, visual identification will be hampered."

"Archangels? They took out some Mark 1s?" Nick asked. "And we still have nothing?"

"Large people in coats, techwear, and hoodies does not give us much to go on," Chloe drawled.

Techwear and hoodies... That sounded a lot like what the NLF would wear.

His thoughts churning, he strode over to the SUV they'd arrived in. Countless more surrounded it, lights blaring and turning the street into a blue and red rave. As he slipped inside, he heard the telltale roar of the police choppers.

None of the cases he'd been on had brought one of those to bear. The grim looks on Rie's and Chloe's faces made the weight of this attack apparent.

His usual band of Archangels piled in and the SUV took off through the cordon of railgun-toting Archangels and Custodians. Police dolls kept the streets clear for a couple of blocks, aided by a mishmash of local security dolls and thugs.

Nick found the sight of suited black company thugs and illegally modded G2s working alongside police dolls darkly amusing. It was also another reminder of just how severe the attack was.

Energy weapons. Nobody fucked around with those. Kraus's bunker was built to withstand anything short of an attack by the military, and some mercs had met his challenge. Whatever criminal or cashed-up asshole in the Spires had upped the ante here had spooked everyone.

Checking his phone, Nick found a series of cryptic messages from several of his cipher contacts. Lucas, Sung, former employees at both Tartarus and Neural Spike...

The news was out.

"We didn't suppress this?" he asked, surprised at the speed he'd been contacted.

"Limited suppression is being undertaken in news and public Altnet discussions," Chloe answered. "However, the attack is of a scale too large and dangerous to hide, especially in the middle of Alcatraz, and against too notable a figure. Many companies and ciphers are already aware. The Host prioritized the chance for collaboration with black companies and security firms over a futile attempt to 'put the genie back in the bottle' as you might put it."

Nick wasn't sure that was the right way to use that particular idiom, but he appreciated Chloe's attempt to use it.

He flicked off a reply to Lucas, given he might need some aid from his old friend. Otherwise, he stayed silent.

The gap in severity between this murder and the one at GWT began to settle in as they drove away. Nick had been gung -ho about solving the GWT case, convinced he was pressing a company that had been getting away with far too much. Quite a few people warned him, and most seemed to shrug it off. Let the Spires do their thing.

Now Kraus was dead. The idea it might be related to Nick's request weighed on his mind, but also boggled him.

What the fuck was going on, that GWT or whoever orchestrated Julian's murder would risk bringing the military down on their heads? Or was Kraus's death truly unrelated? The fact the Host had agreed to consider the cases related made it difficult for Nick to peel off his blinders and treat the cases separately.

But he knew one thing...

"We're going to the Spires, right? I'm guessing Kim's waiting for a report," he said.

"Yes," Helena said into his earpiece, reminding him that she had permanent access now. "The unauthorized use of energy weapons is considered a terrorist activity and requires mandatory reporting to the military and police board. For now, I have reported the situation to Babylon Command in the military, and your superiors in the department."

"So, Paul and Kim." Nick paused. "And Chief Andrews?"

"She officially started two weeks leave from Friday afternoon," Helena said.

Wait, what?

"Nobody mentioned that," Nick said. "Who's acting police chief?"

"Commissioner Kim will be fulfilling her responsibilities where politically necessary, but otherwise it will fall to the respective captains."

That sounded nuts. Was Andrews finally being forced out? Or was something else going on?

The current police chief had deep ties to the military, and was on the wrong side of Commissioner Kim, whose star was rising. Nick couldn't shake the involvement of the military with GWT yesterday and the sudden leave. Now this incident with Kraus.

"Alright, so I'm about to report to Kim. I don't have any strong leads on the GWT case, but I'm not sure that matters anymore given what just happened," Nick said, attempting to summarize the situation.

"Correct. The Host's assessment is that Kraus's assassination provides reasonable suspicion for a conspiracy investigation. Should his murder turn out to be unrelated, Lucida Harm can be tried for murder regardless," Chloe said.

Leave it to the Archangels to keep their heads about them even as Nick struggled to maintain a line of thought.

Running a hand through his hair, he realized his coffee had long since been empty. He put it in the bin beneath the seat.

"Can we pull in for a coffee somewhere? This is one of those mornings where I think I'm going to need plenty of caffeine," he said. "And preferably a better coffee than that one."

"Alcatraz is not known for its specialty coffee," Chloe said defensively, clearly feeling offended that he'd insulted the coffee she'd bought him earlier.

"Then let's stop in at an actual café. I wouldn't mind a chance for a breather before I deal with Kim."

His convoy pulled off the highway, toward one of the small shopping hubs close to the city. No doubt Chloe had selected a café from a curated list she kept. Especially after Nick's slight.

By the time they arrived, all signs of the disaster in Alcatraz had vanished. Only the 24-hour gym, a bar, and the coffee shop were open. A few morning joggers ran along the perfectly maintained paths and more than a few dogs were being taken for walks. Everything looked as perfect as a morning could look in Babylon.

The coffee shop was little more than a hole in the wall outside a business hotel. A young woman quietly prepared for the day, perking up when she saw them approaching, then freezing completely when she saw over a dozen Archangels.

Nick hadn't bothered trying to convince Meta and the others to hang back or stow weapons. For that matter, he didn't want them to. He felt on edge in a way he hadn't since Dallas attempted to abduct him.

"Am... am I under arrest?" the coffee shop owner asked, eyes wide and arms shaking.

"No. We just want coffee. I can't guarantee your safety if I don't get it, though," Nick said.

She stared at him. The joke evidently went over her head.

He sighed. "Three coffees. Uh, Chloe, is there some sort of ordering system?"

A quick nod, and then the owner jumped. Her eyes widened.

"Oh. Oh! Of course. Just give me a few minutes. They'll be right out," she said, then vanished behind her machines.

Not the best service, but Nick was in no mind to complain. He wandered away, staying in sight. Rie, Meta, and Chloe joined him.

"Three?" Rie asked.

Nick pointed at Rie and Chloe. "I assumed Meta was uninterested."

"You are correct," Meta said. "Your fascination with coffee remains beyond the Host's understanding."

"The Mark 1's understanding," Chloe corrected.

"Bitterness is not an attribute we feel necessary to understand."

Rie rolled her eyes as Chloe and Meta glared at each other, their eyes glowing. Presumably, their bickering moved into the neural network.

"Did you want to go over the situation? I'm not sure you'll get a chance once we're in the office, as Kim will be pressuring you about both the GWT case and how you'll solve Kraus's murder," Rie asked.

He nodded. "While I'll have all of you in my ear, I imagine it's best if I'm across everything now and have my thoughts in order. There's nothing more frustrating than somebody second-guessing you while you're trying to speak."

Before they started, the coffees were ready. Nick and Meta retrieved them from the nervous owner, then wandered over to a nearby table and chairs.

The sun continued to rise, and with it the people of the city. Nick watched as buses pulled up nearby, ferrying people to the train or subway. Robot taxis collected office workers from their doors. Most houses lacked driveways here, as few people would ever purchase a car and the garage wasted space. Anyone leaving this early probably worked in another city, anyway.

Said the man working this early, Nick thought darkly.

"I think the GWT case comes across as more complicated than it is," he said. "Julian Garlowne was murdered, probably by Lucida. We have evidence that suggests he may have been a disgruntled employee and GWT were rocked by leaks. They even fired an entire security team years ago for failing to stop them. The footage we have of the murder is suspicious, but difficult to doctor."

The Archangels nodded along. He assumed that unless they interrupted, he should simply continue.

"Richard Toke took charge after the previous leaks, but there's not much suspicious about him. But he's also good at hiding himself. He needs more investigation. Daiji Tanaka attempted to make Toke look like the bad guy, but lied a lot in the process. He's either a major suspect or was fed a script by somebody to point us at Toke."

"Addendum: we found no links between Daiji Tanaka and the NLF. There are no signs of an NLF neural mod, attempts to hide his activities, or movement outside expected work and social circles," Meta said. "However, he has been using unknown sources of wealth in his private life. These have been sourced through black company finance."

"For how long?"

"The past several months. It is unknown if he had the funds for longer, however."

"Sounds like he's our main suspect, then. He may have framed Lucida and the money might be our link. But we still need to look into Toke," Nick said.

How nice it would be if everyone else was as awful with their hot money as Tanaka.

Not to mention the military's strange involvement with him and protection of him. Nick couldn't make heads or tails of that.

"What about Magnus?" Rie asked. "He's looking increasingly suspicious."

"Because he's wealthy enough to afford corporate mercs with access to energy weapons?" Nick asked.

"Because if there was anything that GWT needed to hide, it would be his job to keep it hidden. His status, and that of his family's, is attached to the Trust's. In your theory, GWT silenced Julian and then Kraus because he found evidence of something that would rock the bank to the core. Magnus wanted you to go away."

"It adds up. GWT bought time by opposing a warrant, then threw Lucida under a bus in an attempt to close the case. That stopped us from looking too deeply when we investigated," Nick admitted between sips of his coffee. "He even wanted advance notice before I did anything else. But I went to Kraus. If he found something, that might trigger something worse than a murder investigation."

"Correct. I don't believe you thought about it, but the Archangels are responsible for fraud investigations as well. We are responsible for financial stability."

So, Nick might be responsible for Kraus's death after all. He swirled his coffee in silence for a minute, staring into space. The wind rustled the trees above them, as if to add ambience.

"If it's not GWT, then it's the NLF," he said eventually. "They made threats at Firra. This could be their follow up."

The Archangels stared at him.

"You said yourself this couldn't be them," Rie said.

"The Host agrees. While the NLF previously conducted such an attack in association with Dallas and Lieu, this does not fit their MO," Meta said. "The motive to prevent Kraus from releasing data is indicative of a corporate attacker, not a terrorist or revolutionary."

He ran a hand through his hair. "I know. The problem is that the NLF is acting overtly, and we have no clue why. I guarantee if I ask Kushiel, she'll just say that the military thinks it's all the work of their new sponsor."

"Hey, I resent that remark," Kushiel practically shouted into his ear.

Nick froze. He looked at the Archangels, all of whose eyes had abruptly dimmed.

It was Helena who answered, "As Kushiel is presently assigned to the Archangel Division, I granted her request to access your earpiece, Nick. Was that a mistake? I was led to believe that occurred last time."

"It did," he said slowly.

"It sure did," Kushiel practically purred.

"Kushiel, what the hell are you doing," Rie snapped.

"Being a good subordinate. I'm Officer Kushiel, helping my Lieutenant Cipher solve crime in Neo Babylon. Isn't that my job?"

Despite Rie's dim eyes, her face twisted into a furious scowl. If Kushiel were here, she'd be getting her skull caved in, no matter how impact-proof it might be.

"Your *job* is to accompany Ezekiel on her observation mission," Rie ground out.

"Oh, well, I've been told that Ezekiel is being assigned to Waite until this new case is solved. And I'm cut off from military systems and my handler while I'm playing babysitter, so I need someone to keep me from being too bored." A long pause. "Not that I think I'll be doing too much until you find the mercs. I shoot stuff. It's your job to point me in the right direction."

"Thanks, Kushiel," Nick said drily. "I assume those orders just came through?"

"Yeah. I'm not involved in any of it, but the higher-ups are rattled by the attack. Haven't seen this many actual people in the Avalon Spire since I arrived. Every floor is packed with Mark 1s," she said.

Nick glanced at Meta, who merely nodded. While he technically should have been consulted before such a deployment, the reality of the situation was that he trusted the Host. If Kim wanted Archangels on guard duty, he'd get them.

But it also meant Nick would be down a lot of Archangels when it came to hunting for the mercs.

"Helena, what is the available capacity of the Archangels? Lieu ran them to capacity last time. I can't do that, as we need to protect the Spires, but we're going to get close," Nick said.

Rie bit her lip but remained silent.

"I have generated several possible plans that fully utilize the Archangels, while allowing for recharging and rotation of units through the Spires. Roughly two-thirds of the division is available," Helena replied.

Not quite the answer he wanted, but that worked. "Meta, Rie, Chloe? I'll leave the Host to vote on the best plan. But once I'm done with Kim, it needs to be tweaked and put into action."

They nodded.

"What do you plan to say about Kraus's assassination? We don't have an approach for it," Rie said.

"He definitely has at least one backup. The mercs will be hunting for it as well," he said. "As good as he is, Kraus left a trail somewhere. He can use black companies or personal friends to hide connections, but the data needs to get to the backups. A man like him isn't going to leave things to chance or even unreliable humans."

Meta's eyes lit up, literally. "We are locating his secretary. While his security dolls were destroyed, the secretary remains at large."

"He might have other dolls out there arranging data drops. A good starting point are Kraus's friends—or the closest equivalent, his business partners," Nick said. "Lucas will know them. Failing him, I used to work with somebody who handles hot money now."

"Many of your former colleagues handle hot money now. That doesn't narrow down anything," Rie said with narrowed eyes.

"This guy didn't work in Tartarus."

"Ah. I believe I know who you are talking about then."

Rie's annoyed look suggested she felt that Nick knew too many questionable ciphers. But she had hired him for his background, and that involved walking a fine line between criminality and legality. Black company ciphers were overlooked due to how useful they remained to many businesses, and the Archangels knew it.

"We shall focus on possible financial links and locating all dolls used by Kraus," Meta said.

"Good enough. Let's go," Nick said, rising to his feet.

He felt as prepared for meeting Kim as he could be. But he knew things might go south, fast. Kim consumed politics for breakfast, and Nick eschewed the stuff.

Kraus's death transformed Babylon into a crime scene overnight. Nick couldn't afford to fuck this case up now.

CHAPTER 21

"Biometric token authenticated. Commissioner Kim is waiting for you in his office, Nicholas," a Mark 1 Archangel said.

Nick nodded and stepped through the reinforced door that separated the executive offices from the rest of the department. Meta, Rie, and Chloe followed him through.

As Kushiel had explained, the department was crawling with Archangels. Security on the bridges leading to the Spires remained unchanged, but the building was on the verge of lockdown. He'd half-expected to have his identity verified at every door.

But the Mark 1s refused to mess around and simply let him through. No sign of Kushiel or Ezekiel, however. Helena let him know they were on the 77th floor, along with those members of the division awaiting deployment.

Nick stopped upon entering the interior of the executive offices. Last time he'd been here, the increased security had stopped at the door.

That wasn't the case this time. A pair of Mark 1s stood guard, standing out against the warmth of the reception area.

The rest of the Avalon Spire was very clinical. The true office experience, with lots of gray, soul-sucking cubicles, and plenty of corporate slogans and other nonsense beamed into people's implants. Nick hated the place, but he'd long since gotten used to Babylon.

Like much of the ritzier parts of the city, the executive offices indulged in a physical experience beyond the plebs. Water features dominated, and even flowed along the walls and the sides of the wooden floorboards. Greenery flourished, albeit under the careful maintenance of domestic dolls. Stone and wood were the materials of choice.

Of course, there was still plenty of corporate advertisement invisible to Nick. He saw the placeholder glass panels across the reception and halls as he walked toward Kim's office, which resided farther inside.

As always, Kim's office was shielded by blackout dimming built directly into the electronically primed windowpanes. No nameplate, but Nick knew which was the commissioner's by now. He'd been here a few times.

"Commissioner," Nick said as he knocked.

He looked around and noticed that Meta and Chloe had peeled away at some point. Probably the reception area. Rie remained beside him. As always, she appeared unarmed.

The windowpanes lightened, revealing an extravagant office. A bare steel and glass executive desk dominated the far end, and Kim sat behind it. Bookcases—also steel—lined one wall, containing physical books that Nick refused to read. The opposite wall appeared featureless, but he knew it hid an extortionately expensive liquor collection.

"Nick, Uriel, come in. I'll need to brief the Assembly after this, but there's no need to be brief," Kim said, rising to his feet and gesturing to a set of recliners in the center of the room. "The opposite, in fact. The more I know, the easier it is to quell panic. Somebody has already asked for a military deployment."

Nick blinked, pausing halfway to his seat. "To do what? Stand around and look menacing?"

"In practice, yes. In theory, I imagine the assemblyman thinks the army can magically root out the NLF," Kim said, disdain evident in his tone.

A grimace crossed Nick's face. So, everyone had already made their assumptions about who was responsible. That made this an uphill battle.

The three of them sat. Kim produced glasses and a pitcher of water from beneath the coffee table before pouring. No fancy alcohol at this time of the morning, it seemed. Or coffee. Nick wasn't even sure if the commissioner had a robot barista in here.

"What's the situation?" Kim asked.

Rie gave a brief summary of the facts surrounding Kraus's assassination. Kim likely already had these, but he tended to dislike reports and prefer being told things directly.

"So, usage of a prohibited military-grade energy weapon in a murder and synchronized terrorist activity across all of Neo Westphalia," Kim summarized. "Kraus Brandt is a cipher well known to many corporate entities. Significant concern has been expressed both that the attackers seized data from him, and that he may have leaked everything using a dead man's switch."

Nick hid a frown. Not quite the response he expected. "Everything was intentionally destroyed. It's possible they copied it first, but the attack wasn't subtle. Kraus was killed in his escape tunnel. He may have destroyed his own data before escaping. It's also possible the attackers stole it, as somebody with Kraus's credentials used them to destroy electronic backups."

"The Host found no evidence that the digital backups were copied from the servers they were held on," Rie added. "We believe this is because of the high likelihood of a tracking program being inside any backup."

Damn, that made sense. If anybody stole Kraus's data, he'd know who and they'd paint a target on their back.

"And the dead man's switch?" Kim pressed. "That's what has many in a panic. A man like him has been overlooked for so long, purely because of what he knows. Many corporations and individuals will be harmed if his databases are indiscriminately leaked."

"No clue." Nick shrugged in the face of Kim's scowl. "Commissioner, they hit every one of his known backups at once across all of Neo Westphalia. We have no clue what's left of Kraus's data to leak."

"I was told you're convinced there is some."

"There's zero chance we know where all of his backups are, especially after Lieu leaked them all." Nick paused. "I assume this means you want us to go after them? That was my plan, as it's both the easiest way to find the suspects and probably a link to another case."

"Ah, the other case." Kim grimaced and looked at the wall containing his liquor cabinet. He didn't rise, however. "For now, let us say that, yes, you need to find what's left of Kraus's data and the suspects. You know who everyone thinks is responsible, however."

Kim had just told Nick, but he nodded anyway.

"Then let's discuss the Grand Westphalian Trust."

"The cases are linked," Nick said. "Kraus was looking into it for me, and he was killed right before he could provide me with evidence."

"Why?"

"The NLF is a primary suspect in both cases, as you just said. We have no known motive for why Lucida Harm murdered Julian Garlowne, but we do know that there is a link to black company finance. The NLF has recently received a new, wealthy sponsor, made threats against Kraus, and also against me during the GWT investigation. The timing is uncanny."

Kim bit his lip. "You're good, Nick. Better than I think the Trust thought you'd be. Which is amusing, given the warning I gave you the other day that they should be prepared for you."

Uncertain, Nick glanced at Rie, who merely shrugged.

Before progressing, Kim rose and dimmed the windows. He wandered over to his desk, as if checking that a non-existent terminal had been switched off. To Nick's knowledge, Kim only used his neural implant. The desk merely sat here for appearances.

"I've received a lot of pressure to close the case," the commissioner continued after sitting back down. "The board received a direct complaint the day you arrested Lucida Harm, asking why you hadn't charged her and closed the case. Given how obviously suspicious that was, I declined their request."

"Obviously suspicious?" Nick asked, playing dumb.

Kim chuckled with a lopsided smile. "The fact GWT expected us to charge Lucida with the murder and close the entire investigation makes their intentions clear. I am a politician, Nick, and can spot when somebody is attempting to throw a dead cat on the table so that you don't look at the corpse by their feet."

Nice turn of phrase. Nick decided to steal it for the future.

"I'm surprised you refused them anyway," he admitted.

"We've spoken about this before. GWT is important to the financial stability of the city, but people are increasingly furious about the unaccountability of the Spires." Kim swirled his glass of water as if it were a fine whisky. "It's been too long since the riots. I hear a lot of nonsense these days. A new normal. We've learned, or adapted, or invented our way out of the crisis. You know, the sort of idiocy people say before history repeats itself."

The raw bitterness coming out of Kim's mouth shocked Nick. The man had always come across as an idealist, even if he had been shaped by dark events.

Either something was shaking Kim, or he was willing to be more honest with Nick now. After all, this conversation wasn't intended to win him over. No glass of whiskey worth as much as a car today.

"However, GWT remains very powerful," Kim continued. "Stock markets never close, and the relentless pressure applied by the investigation and ongoing police presence was never far from the board's mind. I needed strong evidence to progress the case. I believe the board expected that the new case would force your hand."

"Instead, it's the opposite," Nick said, leaning back. "Can I be honest with you?"

"Nothing we discuss here leaves the room. That should have been obvious the moment I was honest about the Trust's behavior."

Nodding, Nick said, "The NLF link doesn't make sense. However, it's also the strongest one we have between the cases. We captured footage of Kraus's assassins wearing similar outfits to the NLF, and they match those at Firra. And the explosives at Firra match those during the raid on my apartment complex."

"Which builds a link back to GWT by circumstance," Kim finished. "Uriel, what do you think?"

She bit her lip. "The lack of hard evidence is troubling. Much of the connection also comes from a military assessment we do not have access to."

Kim raised his eyebrow. Then he blinked. "Our... new mainframe just provided me with a summary of the military's statements so far. These differ somewhat from what I know."

Great. Nick inwardly thanked Helena for skipping the awkward part.

"I had wanted to talk about that. Some ciphers from Aerial Command poked around my apartment yesterday and even brought some Kestrels along. As great as the Kestrels are, I'm not sure they could legally be there," he said.

A darkness fell across Kim's face. "Indeed. I was unaware of this. The report includes evidence of their authorization from Babylon Command, but I'm certain the law does not permit subordination like this. I'll raise this with the Assembly. General Griffiths may be a loyal officer, but even he must stay within the bounds set for him." Then he smiled. "And, yes, the Kestrels are impressive, aren't they? Quite the feat of engineering by RTM."

Before Nick and Kim could waste several minutes gushing about the dolls, Rie coughed and cut in. Her sharp look caused both men to give her sheepish looks.

"You said your knowledge differs from the military. Please elaborate, sir," Rie asked with a fake smile.

"The plastic explosives importer has been identified as recently as Friday. This isn't like Lu Import Export, and certainly nobody attempted to frame my brother for anything." A wry smile crossed Kim's face. "A shipment was appropriated on its way to a large security firm operating in Tengoku. The theft was even reported."

Nick raised an eyebrow. "The hell is a security firm doing with high-powered explosives?"

"Research, I imagine. That... area of the island is dedicated to research that the military overlooks out of convenience. Much like what you once undertook."

"And the military somehow didn't connect the reported theft and the explosives until... Friday?"

"You sound unconvinced?" Kim asked.

"The military analysts sometimes make convenient conclusions, and their behavior's been suspicious. They even suspected you instead of Lieu, sir," Nick said.

"I am aware of that." Kim's voice didn't waver. "However, this particular security firm is well regarded. They even hold bodyguard and hostage rescue contracts in the Spires. You've likely run into them during your work."

"Company?"

"Fairguard Contracts. One of the few examples of a company abandoning black company status in favor of more legitimate work."

Nick made a note to investigate them. Babylon had more security firms than he could possibly remember, and this one seemed focused on particularly pricey work if they were handling bodyguard duties for the Spires.

"We saw them protecting Magnus," Rie reminded him. "Although their contracts are as hidden as all work in the Spires, their presence was obvious. One even spoke to you."

"That's... extremely suspicious," Nick said flatly. "The same firm that 'lost' the explosives is working with GWT, and now the military is also working with GWT and fails to make the connection, and also to inform me when they figure it out?"

So much for the military looking out for him. Nick wondered if he should get the hell out of his apartment pronto.

"I recommend leaving this part out of anything you submit to the judicial mainframes tomorrow, Nick." Kim grimaced. "But you are correct. This is doubtlessly political maneuvering of some sort. I'm afraid that I won't be of much use after this meeting, either. Between assuaging the Assembly, liaising with the military, and handling Sigma's little delegation, I'll be flat out. If Chief Andrews were still here, it wouldn't be so bad."

"Then why send her on leave?"

"I didn't." Kim's tone sharpened. "But given her connections to the military, I believe she elected to take the leave for... ethical reasons. At least, I do now. To be blunt, if Ezekiel's deployment goes well, the department will look very different in a year. I am not one to overstate my expectations, Nick, but let me clear that much hinges on this case. Mistakes will reverberate far beyond your own career."

Nick felt his fists clench below the table involuntarily. Rie's hands closed over his, as if sensing his emotional disturbance.

"Understood, Commissioner," he said, then rose. "In that case, I believe I should pay some GWT execs a visit."

CHAPTER 22

"Riddle me this, Rie. Why is Kim letting us walk out of here?" Nick asked as he and Rie left Kim's office.

"Because we work for him, Nicholas."

"Not what I mean." He waved for Meta, Chloe, and the others to join him as he left. "We all agreed the military is protecting GWT. Kim is a politician. Shouldn't he be siding with the soldiers and stopping us? This makes no sense."

"Ah. There are two likely answers. The first is that the commissioner believes the military is backing the wrong horse. While he wants to keep them onside, his objective is to further his own aims while automating the police department. If we succeed, and the military look like fools again, then his political star rises further," Rie explained.

They reached the elevator. The doors stood open, already waiting for them, and they stepped inside. One of the Archangels sent it down to floor 77.

"And the second?" Nick asked.

"If GWT assassinated Kraus, they drastically overstepped. Or their agents have. People like Kraus are more nuisance than menace in Babylon, at least until they're forced to show their fangs. And if he has a dead man's switch, those fangs will ruthlessly tear into the Spires."

"And the energy weapons, I suppose." He shoved his hands into his coat pockets. "The last major incident I remember was a decade ago, when somebody modified an industrial cutter and went nuts in the city. It was all over the news for weeks."

Like railguns, weapons and industrial devices that relied on energy beams or arcs required too much power for easy portable operation. Civilian usage usually involved a wheeled generator and was severely limited. Military weapons required batteries of a complexity and density only now making it into dolls such as the Mark 3s.

But if somebody did jury-rig a reactor of some sort, they could wreak havoc. As it turned out, the havoc wrought a decade ago came from that reactor exploding and killing dozens.

"There is little appetite for an evolution in the arms race," Rie said. "Railguns rarely make it into the hands of black companies as it is. That means few security firms need to worry about heavily armored dolls, and both us and the military don't need to worry about anything other than conventional munitions. If that changed..."

The elevator came to a stop. Nick stepped out and saw a mass of Mark 1s waiting.

Not for him, he quickly realized. The express elevators came and went. Each time, the Mark 1s piled in. The division was deploying en masse.

A few did peel off as he slipped past them, and they parted like the sea for him. By the time he reached the main room that the Mark 1s recharged in, the office felt like a ghost town.

"If that changed, the police force would need to rethink its approach to black companies," Nick said. "And the NLF."

A chorus of murmured yeses greeted his words.

On Friday, he'd cut off Meta before she could finish the Host's thoughts on the NLF following the attack at Firra. But he had known where she was going.

Nick found it easy to overlook the NLF these days. Kushiel had summed up his feelings the other day. They were a shadow of their old self, doing little more than causing a ruckus and being annoying. A sign of the times and the anger people felt. The police still needed to deal with them, but raiding homes and businesses en masse was an overreach for such a minor problem.

But what if the NLF were a real threat? When they'd threatened train stations and docks, they deserved their moniker of terrorist organization. If they now had cybernetic soldiers, stacks of plastic explosives, elite ciphers, and energy weapons...

Well, kicking in doors and forcibly diving deep into the neural implants of every vaguely suspicious character became much more justifiable in the eyes of a terrified populace. Nobody wanted to imagine if the NLF would beam down a few Archangels and then blow their morning train sky high.

What little restraint the Archangels had would go out the window. If the Assembly were considering calling in the military to crush the NLF, this was a step or two before it.

The same applied to black companies, naturally. Babylon had pockets of ultra-violence, but the police kept it well away from the elites and general populace.

What uber rich wanted to live in a shithole where they could be murdered driving down a highway by some dipshit thugs? Neo Westphalia remained a jewel because the wealthy felt powerful, and that involved being safe.

While most of the floor was a barren office hellscape of cubicles and soul sucking design decisions, Rie had her own little pocket to escape to. Nick kept his own office in here, despite his promotion. He scanned himself into it.

Inside stood Kushiel and Ezekiel. The Mark 3s that usually puttered about were nowhere to be seen. Likely busy. Greenery occupied the corners and somebody had made a mess of the kitchenette. Nick's eyes went right to Kushiel, who was munching on some macarons while drinking a very tall cup of coffee.

Immediately, Rie shot across the room and snatched the remaining colorful snacks off the table. Kushiel deftly swiped one more.

"I'm charging you for these," Rie snapped, returning what was left of her treats to the fridge. "I can't believe you ate most of a packet. Do you know how much sugar is in each one?"

"We're robots, Rie. Unless you ask Sigma to physically modify your waist to reflect your calorie intake, you're not getting fat," Kushiel droned.

"Yes, but sugar is horrendous for our internals. We might be made of steel and polymer, but we still wear away. I prefer to minimize my maintenance cycles."

"I'm built to literally eat dirt. I'll be fine."

"You are not. You are built to handle dirt intake during a dust storm. There is a difference."

Nick let the two sisters bicker and sidled up to Ezekiel, who watched the pair, dumbfounded.

"New experience?" he asked her.

"I have never witnessed the two... together," Ezekiel said, then looked up at him with a wan smile. "It seems I have been deployed under your care, lieutenant. Sigma has directed me to learn as much as possible about leading the Host. I hope to be useful to you."

That final sentence almost sounded earnest.

"Question, do you have the same cipher capabilities as the Mark 3s?" Nick asked.

Ezekiel hesitantly nodded. "Specifically, only the Mark 3s. Uriel far outstrips me in electronic and neural warfare and counter warfare capability."

"Do you have the same access to the Host as your sisters?"

"I was granted it by Sigma earlier this morning."

Meta and Chloe nodded, and the latter gestured to Meta to speak.

"Although integration is not yet available, we are ready to work with Ezekiel in much the same way as Rie," Meta said. "The Host has reached a consensus on that matter."

"As Rie, huh." Nick smirked.

As if sensing that she had been insulted, Kushiel looked over. Everyone ignored her, and Rie took the opportunity to snatch her coffee mug and wash it out. This rekindled their argument.

"In that case, we're going to separate our responsibilities," Nick declared, raising his voice to break up the argument.

Everyone shut up and looked at him. Even the bickering sisters.

"Helena, summarize our priorities," he said. "I'm guessing there's been some change already."

"Yes, Nick," Helena said. "You wish to pursue James von Magnus and Richard Toke for evidence. The Mark 3s are looking for Kraus's missing secretary doll and any evidence of other data backups. The Mark 1s are split between patrol duties and hunting for the suspects, the majority of which involves questioning likely NLF members."

"I'd prefer not to focus on the NLF, but I guess we don't have another lead," Nick said. "We need to split up. Rie, Meta, stay with me. Both of you know how to lead from beside me. Kushiel, stay here and respond to any incidents."

The three mentioned Archangels nodded. Kushiel looked relieved that she hadn't been deployed. The same could be said of Rie, presumably worried that Kushiel would cause a scene.

"Chloe, there aren't many Mark 3s. I want you to work with Ezekiel to hunt down the secretary. We're also looking through Kraus's financial links, right?"

"I am doing that," Helena said defensively.

"The Host has excess processing capacity," Meta said.

"Helena, delegate the actual processing to the Archangels. You're a director of work, not the actual processor," Nick said.

"Of course, Nick," Helena said, a touch put out.

Ezekiel's smile wavered, but she didn't say anything. Nick read between the lines.

"Ezekiel, did you want to be deployed somewhere else?"

"I... had hoped to remain alongside you, given your leadership role," she said. "Your activities in person differ from those described by the Host."

How exactly did the Host view him? Nick had always felt that they kept everything as reams of data, but if Ezekiel was confused, did that mean they filtered the data somehow?

Or had she been reading all that fanfic about him? The thought nearly made him shudder.

"Chloe, do you think you'll need Ezekiel?"

The question was pointless, of course. The Oversight Taskforce had functioned without the prototype until now. It would work without her.

But if Chloe asked for Ezekiel, it suggested something else was awry. Nick decided to trust the judgment of the Archangels when it came to this new prototype. He struggled to read her, but the dolls didn't.

"No. It is best if she gains experience and training data by remaining with you," Chloe said.

Ezekiel seemed almost annoyed that she got her way, but nodded.

"Then we're done here. Let me know whenever something important happens," Nick said.

Of course, only Chloe actually left. Nick's "splitting up" had ended up sending her away and nobody else after Ezekiel's intervention. Of course, he'd leave Kushiel behind.

Before leaving, he made himself a coffee. This was his third for the morning. He'd get the shakes if he had another after this, but the caffeine helped offset both the sleep and the troubling thoughts.

"What's your next move?" Kushiel asked, crossing her arms.

"Didn't you pay any attention?" Rie huffed.

Ignoring them, Nick said, "Helena, do we have the addresses of Toke and Magnus? Don't arrange an appointment. I'm assuming they're home, though. It's too damn early on a Sunday for them to be anywhere, and they didn't look like religious types."

His phone buzzed and a pair of unfamiliar addresses appeared in his messages.

But he did recognize one major location.

"Of course they live in Yggdrasil," he said. "Magnus talked about the speed of banking and how he was responsible for transactions that happen by the nanosecond, and he lives in the communications center of the city. Figures."

"GWT maintains a major presence in Yggdrasil," Rie said. "Major financial institutions favor low latency, and nothing can be better than being next to the central hub of the Altnet."

"Yes, but he doesn't have to live there."

"You'd complain no matter which Spire he lived in. If it was Axis Mundi or Sindansu, your complaint would be how he feels he is a god, as they represent the connection between Heaven and Earth. In Olympus, he'd be pretending to be a god. Here, he wishes to pretend he's above the law." Rie smirked at him.

Nick winced and rubbed the back of his neck. Was he so predictable?

"You know, I'm surprised you know the meaning behind all these stupid names," Kushiel said. "I know them, because I have a database built into me. But all this stuff is tagged as archaic, meaningless knowledge."

"Too many companies like overly meaningful names. Ciphers sometimes pick them apart, as it can help to understand what the intention behind the product is. Or if the company is led by jackasses. Sometimes both." Nick paused. "Usually both. There's no shortage of cashed-up morons convinced they're god because their net worth includes more zeroes than they can comprehend."

"Bitter, much?"

"Nah, just realistic. This is Babylon. If I'm right, some of those cashed-up morons just set the city alight by using an energy weapon to hide his dirty laundry."

Kushiel didn't have a pithy response to that. Ultimately, Nick wouldn't know if he was right or wrong until the case was solved.

They left, leaving the military doll to make another mess of the place. Hopefully, that was all she needed to do.

As they descended, Nick asked the obvious, "Do we drive to the other Spire or walk? This isn't my jam."

"For security reasons, we will drive. But it makes little difference," Meta said.

Of course. Security.

Several SUVs waited for them underground, accompanied by a small army of Mark 1s equipped to fight off some corporate mercs. Nick hopped into the center vehicle with Rie.

Before Juliet, Rosa, or Meta could do anything, Ezekiel sat next to him. The other Archangels stared at her.

She simply blinked in confusion. "Is there something wrong?"

Meta's eyes merely glowed. Ezekiel's cheeks reddened and she scowled. She instantly moved to the furthest corner of the cabin. This assuaged the others, who took their usual spots. Meta sat next to Nick.

Belatedly, he realized that if he hadn't sent Chloe away, there wouldn't have been enough room in the one SUV.

They took off, and the convoy quickly arrived top side. A chopper roared above them.

Nick immediately knew things had gone crazy when he looked outside. He had expected the squads of Custodians, Liberators, and Archangels everywhere. Even the huge tracked warbots with massive autocannons that looked more dangerous than they really were.

What he hadn't expected were the modern warbots, with smaller shaped hulls and guns so large he wondered how they remained stable. Accompanying them were dozens of military drones and heavily armored dolls in the black and blue of the army.

"Uh… I thought Kim didn't authorize the army to deploy?" Nick said, staring at proof to the opposite.

"Babylon Command can deploy around the Spires without permission in extreme circumstances. That's why the warbots can patrol here," Rie said.

Oh. That felt obvious.

"This still feels dangerous," he said.

"They're all from Babylon Command. We've double-checked the authorizations and serial numbers after the incident yesterday," she said.

"And those Kestrels?" he asked, pointing at the squadron of flying dolls over the canal.

"Yes, even those. If Kushiel can be lent to another command unit, why can't other dolls?"

Despite how intimidating the military presence felt, they didn't trouble them. Nick did notice the Kestrels do a pass overhead, but nobody thought anything of it.

Privately, he wished he had brought Kushiel with him. He sent her a message, checking that she had her big guns with her.

Duh. I'm as likely to leave home without my huge dicks as you are, she replied. *Oh wait…*

What followed was a blast of skull emojis and animations featuring somebody dying of laughter. Kushiel truly was a piece of work.

"She's flirting a lot more lately," Rie said, peeking over his shoulder.

"You call this flirting?" he said incredulously.

"Overly friendly bullying? I would say that the lady doth protest too much when the topic turns to you." Rie stifled a giggle and ignored the annoyed look Ezekiel shot her.

At least he could rest easy knowing that Kushiel had the firepower to oppose the military dolls and warbots. Well, most of them. Nick didn't know much about the newer warbots. She'd been able to melt the older ones due to their outdated armor, but these ones worried him.

Rie had once told him that there existed warbots that could shrug off railgun rounds, after all.

They navigated past all the security blockades and checkpoints. The pristine parks of the island looked empty besides all the heavily armed dolls. Soon, the convoy arrived at Yggdrasil Spire.

Like Avalon, Yggdrasil had a massive underground parking garage. Huge painted markings and signs indicated it was restricted to government and corporate use only. Presumably, major companies operating in the Spires brought trucks in here.

"Where do the rich assholes park their fancy cars?" Nick asked while they waited for the reinforced doors to open.

"There are vehicle elevators for civilian vehicles on the far side. Some wealthier individuals have their own garages as well, but there is a separate entrance," Rie explained.

Little interested Nick in the underground. Unlike in Avalon, there was no massive number of police vehicles. They didn't go very deep, however. The convoy pulled up close to the elevators.

Everything changed the moment they got close to the elevators.

"They have buttons here," Nick noted.

Rie shot him a look. "Yes, Nicholas, they have buttons. You realize that the regular lifts in the Avalon Spire have them as well? We just use the express elevators that only the police can use."

He winced. "I mean, I like buttons."

"There, there," Meta droned.

Ezekiel seemed lost.

Most of the Mark 1s remained down here, and only his main escort went above. The elevator cars were also much larger than the express ones in Avalon.

To no avail for the regular inhabitants. They stopped a few times on the way up to Magnus's floor—which was well above the 100th floor—and every time, nobody dared enter. The doors would open, some extravagantly dressed folks would stare at the armed police dolls, and then the doors closed again.

"I think we scare them," Nick said.

"Archangels are a rare sight in the Spires. There are assigned Liberators for each floor, but they are mostly for visibility," Rie said.

"What if something goes wrong?" Ezekiel asked. "Our response time would be horrendous. The Security Bureau doesn't have any Archangels deployed to it."

"There hasn't been an incident serious enough to warrant our presence."

"Yet." Ezekiel's tone darkened. "Isn't the fact we're investigating the Spires for an incident like this proof enough that we cannot trust them to police themselves?"

Nick gave her a surprised look. Then again, she had spoken of purification in that message from months ago.

Evidently, Ezekiel didn't feel all that positively about humanity, despite her feelings toward Sigma.

"I wish you'd let me bring a weapon," Ezekiel whined, rubbing her hands along her arms.

"You have that SMG hidden in your jacket," Nick said drily.

"It's useless against the enemies we're fighting. I wanted to upgrade to one of the railguns, or at least an anti-armor shotgun."

Rie snorted. "You're not bringing a railgun into a Spire. We're here to speak with two wealthy and powerful men, not gun them down."

"What if they think differently?"

Juliet and Rosa shifted, making their shotguns more visible.

"They won't think for very long," Meta said.

Even if Ezekiel disagreed—and she did, judging from her expression—she decided to clam up for now.

Eventually, they reached their destination. The doors opened and everyone spilled out.

Nick immediately knew he stood in the halls of power. Or at least the halls of the rich.

The theme of physicality extended throughout here, with elegant wood features dominating almost everything in sight. Thin panels ran along the walls, and oaken floorboards stretched beneath. Immediately opposite the lifts stood frameless glass panels, behind which was an expansive garden that seemed impossibly large for the Spire.

Then Nick spotted the mirrors. He scratched his head at the cheap trick and moved on.

Warm lighting recessed into arched ceilings lit the way. The glass panels switched from the garden to bespoke etchings of trees, roots, and wind. Every so often, entire panels seemed to be missing, replaced with sleek imprinted displays on which he saw nothing.

What little metal was present had been painted or rendered to appear natural. Somebody had gone for a particular look.

But Nick noticed a particular exception as they strode through the eerily empty halls.

"Nothing here relies on the Altnet," he mused. "This is beyond even the executive offices. Hell, even Lucas has more digital intrusion and he loves this stuff."

"The Spires predate the advent of the modern Altnet and widespread neural implants. At the time Yggdrasil was designed and constructed, less than a tenth of the population possessed one," Helena said into his ear. "The Avalon Spire was retrofitted when the emergency services were moved into it."

They passed a double door entrance to somebody's home. A wooden nameplate told him it wasn't Magnus's. Comprehensive security scanners barred entrance.

But notably, he spotted the words on the nameplate that said "Augmented Space."

"Uh, isn't everywhere augmented?" he asked. "It's built into people's heads. I know Helena just said this place is old, but that's silly."

"Neural implants weren't always as sophisticated," Rie explained. "Prior to Axis Mundi's construction just before the riots, the Spires primarily relied on mixed reality to provide the full experience for the mind. Many homes have been retrofitted since then, but it used to be important to set aside space to trick the mind into feeling heat, cold, or perceiving certain physical features."

He bit his lip. "How old is this Spire? I know the courts predate the Spires, but I thought they built them all pretty quickly?"

"Yggdrasil and Olympus were built during the first decade. Avalon followed and was intended as a residential Spire. Then Sindansu, due to RTM's increasing influence, and Axis Mundi was last," Helena said. "All Spires are more than forty years old."

Which helped explain a lot about what Nick saw around him.

To him, the Spires had been engineering marvels. They still were.

But what they weren't were technological marvels. One couldn't build a fuckoff huge tower sixty years ago and hope to keep up with the sprint of technology. Yggdrasil might be the home of the Altnet, and the virtual "World Tree" of Neo Westphalia, but it was a relic. Mainframes and modern neural implants had only just begun to dominate the world.

Now humanity worried about dolls and interfaces literally replacing them, as emotion engines reached a level where one couldn't tell them apart from actual humans. Even the man they came to meet, Magnus, realized this from his interactions with the bank mainframes.

Yet this building stood as a reminder of a time from well before those concerns. Much like the empty rooms in the courthouses.

House after house stretched along the corridors, if one could call them that. To Nick, they looked like apartment doors in the fancy corridors. Occasionally, they bumped into a service doll. When the path forked, Helena directed him, but the Archangels knew where to go anyway.

Magnus's home stood out like a sore thumb. The burly bodyguards from Fairguard leaned against the walls outside the door. They stood at attention when Nick approached and stopped him.

"Can't just let you in, boss," the same giant American as last time said with his southern accent. "Got orders."

"So do I. I assume you've seen the news? Or given your position, heard the rumors," Nick said. "Shit's hit the fan."

The burly bodyguard didn't so much frown as shift his jaw slightly. His eyes glazed over, signaling that he was talking to somebody over the Altnet.

Nothing happened for nearly a minute. The other bodyguards returned to leaning against the walls now that they knew Nick wasn't going to force his way in.

"What's your name, by the way? If we're going to keep running into each other like this, I'd prefer to know you as something other than 'that American guy with the southern accent,'" Nick said, while they waited.

The man's eyes regained their life, and he grunted. "Can't give out my name. Company policy."

"Fairguard, right?"

"Yeah. Guess things are serious if you know that. But not too serious if you don't know who we are. Call me Perry." Then he pointed at each of the other bodyguards. "Tim. Gary. Hose. Jack. Brick."

"Fuck off," the thinnest of the bodyguards said, flipping the bird at Perry. "I'm Finn."

"I'm guessing you're all ex-military? Or police? You definitely look the part," Nick said.

"Both. Fairguard mostly hires foreign. Getting permanent residency here is hard as shit, and we usually need someone to... take a look at our old implants." Perry scowled. "I did my service in the navy and they promised everything I earned was exempt from the Aesir tax, but when they turfed me out, Aesir came knocking for their 30%. Smart men and women come here. So I came."

"Smarter men come here when they're kids," Hose said.

"You mean rich ones," Nick said.

"That, too."

They let out a round of chuckles. Nick couldn't tell if it was forced.

Suddenly, Perry's eyes glazed over. Then he nodded. "Alright, you're good to go in. No guns, though."

Figuring it was easier to leave the armed Archangels outside than risk these fine gentlemen sabotaging the shotguns, Nick left Juliet, Rosa, and Meta outside. He passed his *Lawman* to Meta, who strapped it to her own thigh. It looked ridiculously huge against her petite frame.

Perry stopped Ezekiel before she entered, however. "Nice try." He pointed a pair of fingers at his eyes. "Can't fool me. Hand over the machine pistol to somebody else."

Ezekiel gave up her gun, then entered with Rie and Nick.

The exterior of Magnus's home was strange. An empty unpainted hallway with large grilles led to another door. Nick realized this was likely a legacy of the old augmentation technology. Was this how they simulated wind?

Then he stepped through the interior door into a combined dining room and kitchen the size of his entire apartment. The space looked and felt like something out of a movie, with an unlit fireplace dominating the corner, bespoke wooden furniture and thick rugs spread across the wood floorboards, and bronzeware in the kitchen.

"I don't know what you're talking about, Richard," Magnus said, standing with his back to the door and a large coffee in one hand. "If you want to be promoted to Andre's old director position, you need to understand how this all works. And that means not worrying about this distraction."

It seemed Nick had walked in on an argument between Toke and Magnus. How fortuitous.

CHAPTER 23

Toke and Magnus stood opposite each other in the gargantuan hall that was apparently Magnus's living room. Or dining room. Or entrance hall.

Honestly, Nick didn't know. For a glorified apartment in the Spire, this place was fucking massive. He imagined that Magnus's bed was the size of the shoebox apartments most of his employees lived in.

Toke's eyes flickered to Nick and the Archangels, but he ignored them.

"I'm not sure I'd call it a distraction. And this isn't about the promotion, James," he said. "The board asked us about both incidents, including this morning's. We need to respond."

"That's not your problem, and I don't know why you're bringing it up," Magnus thundered. "I brought you here to talk about Daiji. Why is he—"

Suddenly, he froze and spun to face Nick.

"Detective Waite, what are you doing in my home?" he asked, color leaving his face. He stumbled back a step.

"Your goons let me in."

"My... what?"

Nick stepped forward, hands in his pockets. "Not important. What were you going to say about Tanaka? I bumped into him yesterday with some military ciphers. Commissioner Kim didn't appreciate that. It's not a good look for GWT to be working with the military to begin with, let alone a branch of the military that can't even operate in the city."

"It's not your business who we cooperate with," Magnus snapped. "For that matter, I wasn't even aware of the matter."

"Really? Then who was?"

Magnus looked at Toke, who shrugged.

"I don't control what Daiji does in his spare time. But I'll definitely speak with him on Monday. Assuming this isn't an official matter?" Toke left the last part open-ended.

"It is not. And do it today," Magnus ground out, before turning back to Nick. "What are you here for, detective? It's the weekend and I'm already working overtime."

"So am I. We don't need to pretend that all hell hasn't broken loose. The military's outside, for fuck's sake. I bet you have a window view, right?"

"Everyone in the Spires has a window, detective."

"Then I bet you've seen the military dolls flying around. Somebody used an energy weapon to kill a black company cipher. It just so happened that he was assisting me with my current case," Nick said.

Magnus's eyes closed. He let out a deep sigh. Toke seemed to stop breathing as his attention shifted to his boss.

"I see. Then you are speaking to me because..." Magnus trailed off, eyes still closed.

"I need to close off all leads. The NLF are the leading suspects, for obvious reasons. Terrorist activity, and they've been active lately. But we don't know how they might have gotten inside GWT if that's the case, and who might have assisted Lucida in the Trust."

Toke's eyes bugged out. "You think the NLF infiltrated the security team, and that there are multiple infiltrators? The NLF?"

Good acting, if he was acting.

"That's one theory," Nick said.

Part of him wanted to pull the cliché of "how did you know we thought they infiltrated the security team" but that was a pretty obvious conclusion. Who else could have assisted Lucida?

Magnus remained silent. He placed a hand in one pocket of his pants. Unlike previous encounters, he wasn't wearing a suit, but instead a simple collared shirt and slacks. Toke wore a suit, however.

"So that's why you've been questioning everyone," Toke said. "Sounds like we're all clean if you haven't made any arrests."

"That's not really how this works," Nick said.

"Do you have any questions, detective?" Magnus asked abruptly.

"Sure. What's your policy when you discover somebody is leaking data from within GWT?"

Magnus stared at him for several long seconds. "We cut his access, then have the security dolls escort him from the building. Summary firing follows once the mainframes process the paperwork. If possible, legal action is taken. Fortunately, we've only had one serious incident."

"The one that led to Toke's hiring." Nick inclined his head at the other man.

"Yes."

"Done your research, huh?" Toke chuckled.

"If that's the case, why do you need an entire team full of black company ciphers?" Nick pressed. "Not just mainframe experts, but financial ones. Money launderers, cleaners, fixers. The works."

"Security in a financial institution isn't simple, detective. If we need to stop employees from stealing from us, we need staff who understand the methods they will use. That's why we hire talented ciphers such as yourself and offer them exceptional salaries," Magnus said, calmer than ever. "Hire an embezzler to catch an embezzler."

"And that's going to stop them from embezzling?"

"Well, no," the executive admitted. "We don't actually hire embezzlers. Rather, we hire the people who assist embezzlers to cover their tracks. Those who do not cross the line into criminality and are willing to step back into legitimate business."

That sounded a lot like how Kim had described Fairguard Contracts. A black company that had become legit.

Nick felt that was an oxymoron. Or extremely naïve, anyway.

"I've worked with a lot of black companies. The difference between them and you isn't some secret criminal gene or motive. It's perception. If the Spires decided overnight to completely legalize half the activities in Alcatraz, almost all those black companies would be as legitimate as GWT, and stay legit," he said.

"Your point?"

"Sometimes, people are willing to overlook things they know are wrong, because it's convenient. But when that stops, it can hurt. Are you sure GWT haven't stepped over any lines that will make it hurt if people stop overlooking what you've done?"

Magnus balled his hands into fists. Nick instantly knew he'd been too blunt.

It was Toke who intervened, stepping between the two of them. "Woah, woah. Settle down. He's gotta point, James. This shit went down back home. Lotta blood got spilled when folks got sick of the corruption."

"We are not corrupt. Mistakes can be made. That's the purpose of our audit team. To stop them," Magnus ground out. "Suggestions otherwise do little more than damage the Trust, Babylon, and all of Neo Westphalia's financial stability."

"This is going nowhere," Rie said in Nick's ear, before he could say anything more.

Then, aloud, she said, "Thank you for your time, Mr. von Magnus, Mr. Toke. The Neo Babylon Police Department wishes you all the best with your board meeting. We have an investigation to continue. Should our investigation turn back to you—"

"You shall be in contact with my lawyers," Magnus said coldly.

Yeah, Nick had blown it. But he had learned a lot from this confrontation.

Neither GWT exec led them outside. The bodyguards gave him a faux salute when he stepped outside, and he nodded back. Something about them bothered him, though.

Why the hell had they let him inside during that meeting with Toke? And why had Magnus been shocked to see him enter?

They left in silence. Nick didn't trust the security systems of this Spire not to spy on them.

Helena did speak into his ear, however. "You have a new message from Lucas. He wishes to meet with you later tonight about the Kraus situation."

That worked for Nick, given he planned to do the same.

"Chloe and the Mark 3s have found Kraus's secretary doll in a secure bunker owned by one of Kraus's business partners. They narrowly beat our suspects there. The engagement was brief."

Nick nearly cursed. Rie shook her head at him as they descended in the elevator, particularly as they were still stopping randomly due to other people who refused to get on with all the armed police dolls.

"Two data centers have been struck by assailants who match the assassins. One was eliminated on the scene by a G5 security doll. They are moving very quickly. The improved self-destruct protocols still prevent us from acquiring information from their implants," Helena continued.

This time, Ezekiel responded electronically, "Have we increased security around other data centers?"

"Doing so would limit our ability to search for NLF members."

Ezekiel looked at Nick. Despite his misgivings about her, he nodded. If his hunch was right...

"The NLF aren't important. If our attackers are hitting data centers, then the fastest way to find the real suspects is to protect their targets," she said. "This will also improve Babylon's perception of our effectiveness. We're collaborating with black companies right now. They will stop if we aren't helping them protect their infrastructure."

"Authorized," Nick said, deciding one word wouldn't give anything away.

"The Host's consensus agrees," Meta added.

Ezekiel's smile broadened that little bit. Rie bumped her elbow into the side of her sister, causing Ezekiel to shoot a pouty look back.

Once back in the SUVs, Nick ordered them back to his apartment.

"Why?" Rie asked.

"Two reasons. I want to rest before I meet with Lucas, and I think somebody important will ambush me if I stay in the Spires." He grimaced. "Pissing off Magnus was a mistake. Kim got a complaint when I stayed on his good side. GWT will come down like a ton of bricks now. The farther away I stay, the harder it is for anyone to order me to stand down."

Only now did Nick realize the real reason Kim had said he'd be so busy. After all, Nick rarely needed political help.

No, by ensuring he'd be buried in political nonsense, the commissioner allowed Nick to have free rein for a day or three. So long as he steered clear of anybody with enough power.

Kim might not be a good person, but he was useful to Nick. Their intentions aligned, at least in the sense of using the police department to solve crime using robots.

"I'm glad you realize that you shouldn't have angered Magnus," Rie said, poking Nick in the side. "You let your emotions get the better of you."

"I figured he might fold under pressure. The fact he merely doubled down..." He frowned. "I can't rule him out, but I'm struggling here. Magnus could just be really good at acting."

"Nothing about his words prevents him from taking action to defend the Trust. If Kraus found information that would threaten it, then it can be assumed he would destroy him," Meta said.

"Would he? Because the backlash if this is pinned on GWT will be immense. Nobody will forgive them. The mercs are going insane. Blowing up data centers in broad daylight! If Magnus is behind this, then he's either lost his mind or he's lost control. And he didn't give me the impression of either."

Hell, neither did Toke. Did that mean both men were innocent?

Which left Nick fumbling. Was it really the NLF? Or was Fairguard responsible? Or, hell, maybe this was some secret military coup?

He scrapped the latter. If the military wanted to pull something, it would be executed far more neatly than this. Nick struggled to imagine why they even cared about the GWT situation.

"I need some help here. We keep talking about financial stability. What the hell does that mean?" he asked as they rolled past the highway toward his side of the city.

Everything looked peaceful. No military dolls or drones. No tanks. No mercs. Just a heavily armed police convoy.

Everyone looked at Rie. Even Helena remained quiet.

Rie sighed. "Ezekiel, you should know this."

"I want to hear your explanation," the younger prototype mumbled.

"Fine. Neo Westphalia can only remain independent if it retains control over both its currency and its financial reserves. As a country, it is entirely dependent on corporate investment by the companies that control the Spires. Despite our wealth, we are still much smaller than global powers such as the PRC or the United States. We punch well above our weight due to headquartering so many megacorps," Rie explained.

"I get that part. But why would a single bank be so important that the military might be willing to help cover up a murder?" Nick asked.

"Because we are still vulnerable to capital flight and currency devaluation. The riots were triggered due to rapidly rising inflation. Food prices soaring, difficulty purchasing fuel and basic necessities, trade blockades due to geopolitical problems. Financial problems can forestall our ability to stop another riot, or even cause one."

"Shit. So this is just like Kim's view of the world. Somebody is terrified of history repeating. Except they're focused on the symptoms, while Kim thinks he can solve the fundamentals," Nick said. "Or is that mixed up..."

He didn't know. This seemed way above his pay grade.

How the fuck had he ended up in the middle of politicians and generals battling about how to avoid the future collapse of Neo Westphalia?

For now, he decided all he could do was solve the case in front of him.

"In short, all roads lead to Rome," Nick said. "Kim wants to automate everything to avoid collapse. Lieu and the NLF want to overthrow the Spires. The military wants to hide the truth, so nobody realizes anything is wrong in the first place. And you want to insert yourselves into key systems."

"We do," Rie corrected. "I believe we agreed on this."

Ezekiel looked away, choosing to stare out the window.

"Right," he said. "But my point is that nobody really wants to burn everything to the ground. Just that everyone has a different view of how to achieve it. And some of those views show a greater disregard for Babylon than others."

Part of him wanted to call one of them very naïve. The idea that one could merely hide the truth and everything would work out seemed nonsensical. Akin to the idea that a person could literally pull themselves up by their bootstraps.

After arriving at his apartment, they trooped inside. By now, most of the city's populace had risen and was finding something to do on their Sunday morning. Family breakfasts, exercise, a lazy morning. What it was didn't matter to Nick. But he saw people out and about, ignorant of the chaos he had experienced all morning.

Ezekiel paused at the door, watching as everyone else happily entered. She eyed Rie as she sidled up to Nick as he decided whether to make another coffee or go with something non-caffeinated.

"You have reached your recommended caffeine intake for the day, Nick," Helena said. "You should drink something else. Such as the juice in your fridge."

"Yes, dear," he said aloud.

Rie pinched him for that. Then she turned and told Ezekiel, "Either come in and close the door, or stand guard and close the door."

That decided things for the younger prototype, and she joined them.

"I'm surprised you're overlooking Magnus that easily," Ezekiel said, continuing the earlier conversation. "He seemed very defensive, and the conversation made him look very guilty at the start."

"True. But I can't put aside the strange feeling that..." Nick trailed off.

If he had to put his thoughts into words, he'd suggest that somebody had tried to frame Magnus. But saying as much sounded crazy. He'd come up with zilch when it came to evidence that Lucida had been framed, even if he seemed correct that she hadn't acted alone.

Hell, the entire situation really seemed simple until Kraus got killed.

Julian had been a disgruntled employee. He'd been about to leak something, got spotted, and an overeager security team offed him. Confident in their invulnerability, Lucida reported it. Nick called their bluff.

Except GWT panicked, and when the judicial mainframes actually granted the warrant, they threw her under the bus. Then when he kept digging, they panicked again. Things had spiraled out of control now.

But if that was the case, why had Magnus seemed so calm? Surely at the point the military was flying outside his window the man should sweat a little. Maybe Nick was overthinking it.

There was the matter of the bodyguards, however.

"Helena, look into Fairguard. If they're the attackers—and they could easily have the capability—I don't want to overlook the obvious," he said.

"It's extremely unlikely," Rie said. "We have full records of all of their staff. While those assigned to the Spires have some level of anonymity, it's unveiled on death. None of those we've killed have matched their employment records."

"I'd still rather be safe than sorry."

Although he knew that if the Archangels had written them off, that likely was the end of that. At least, it meant that Fairguard weren't involved directly.

The day passed quickly in his apartment. Nick didn't sleep things off, although he might have done something in his bedroom with Rie that caused Ezekiel to try to melt his face with a glare. Her possessiveness of her sister knew no bounds.

A little after lunch, Chloe brought the secretary doll, Lucy, into the parking garage. She proved useless.

"Mister Brandt activated an emergency protocol. I will await further orders from him," Lucy said.

"What if they don't come?" Nick said, rubbing the back of his neck.

She sounded like an abandoned puppy. Hell, she basically was. Told to hide until Kraus came and found her, but he never came.

"They will."

He took a deep breath. It came out in a long sigh rather than the words he wanted them to. Nick tried again.

"Kraus is dead, Lucy."

"I know. I have been told as much. Furthermore, I am programmed to assume as much when his neural implant ceases communication for a specific period of time."

Oh, shit. Lucy was a dead man's switch. Nick's eyes shot to Chloe, who merely shook her head.

It seemed Lucy wasn't a backup, or at least wasn't pulling any stunts. But if so, what was her purpose?

"Can you tell me what your directives instruct you to do in that situation, Lucy?" Nick asked.

"As I said, I wait for Mister Brandt's orders. He is in the stars now, where humanity goes. Perhaps I might go there as well with him." Lucy smiled at him.

What the fuck?

He decided to leave the secretary in the care of the Mark 3s. Chloe joined his group in the apartment, although she forced a takeaway coffee into his hands.

"No objections, Helena?" he mused aloud.

"It is decaf. Chloe and I discussed this," Helena said.

Damn. They were working together now.

Lucas had specified fairly late in the night, so he waited until around 9PM. Late enough that things would be busy, but before the busiest period of the club. Nick suspected the timing was intentional, but why he didn't know. With the size of his escort, there was no way to hide his arrival.

Or so he thought.

The doll district bustled with all walks of life. Men, women, dolls, cyborgs, and everything in between. Suits brushed against sheer lingerie, and more than a few cosplay outfits beamed out from the crowd. Nick suspected that he'd see far stranger things in the Altnet.

Weekends were when the money was made here. A small army of dolls lined the streets, many of whom wore extremely little. Thuggish bouncers with visible cybernetics and oversized firearms kept an eye on passersby and patrons, and more than a few arguments broke out when somebody got handsy without paying.

They'd parked closer to the restaurant side of town due to how busy everything was, and business was booming. Tables spilled out onto the streets. Alcohol flowed freely, as did the flesh of many of the doll waitresses. Nick noticed more than a few giving extra service to some patrons.

Intermixed with the crowds were heavily armed dolls. Kraus's death had roused the security firms from their slumber, and they brought their best to defend their customers. RTM G6s and G5s stalked alongside Sigma Lancers, and they openly carried anti-doll weapons. Many trust fund kids had as well, enjoying their meals—in both senses of the word—with G7s or Chevaliers by their side.

Yet just as many Archangels joined the security forces. So many that Nick's escort barely caused a murmur. Railgun-toting patrols swept the scantily clad streets. The main difference from usual was the unwillingness of the police to badger any of the more promiscuous dolls.

"We're taking a lighter touch tonight, aren't we?" he asked Meta.

"Yes. Patrols are usually to administer Altnet regulations and minimize violence. Tonight, we have increased our visibility to deter any possible attacks on Kraus's business partners. Many ciphers own businesses here. The same can be said of wealthy residents of the Spires," she said.

"So this is outreach."

"Yes."

Funny that the much-maligned power of the police turned into a positive in this situation. Nick didn't know what to think.

Although he knew that the moment the worm turned, the thugs who ignored the Archangels would be just as unwelcoming as before. "The enemy of our enemy is our friend" is a temporary measure. Nick still didn't know where he fell in all of this.

They reached the Cobalt Lily, where the ruckus died down a little. Too early for so many people to be screwing dolls in large numbers. Nick knew many of the people they'd passed would wander this way once finished with their food.

Lucas's thugs and Chevaliers were out in force. They nodded at Nick as he approached.

They wandered into the gang lord's office. Most of the escort remained behind.

No sign of Lumen in the reception area. Nick frowned.

Lucas himself wandered out, resplendent in a white suit tonight. He waved Nick in.

"Come in, man," he said. "Lumen's busy running the Lily. No funny business tonight." He winked.

"Read me like a book," Nick said, following his friend.

They slipped inside and settled in. Most of the Archangels remained standing, save Rie. Ezekiel seemed unsure whether to pull up a chair from the side.

"That's the new one, huh?" Lucas asked, eying the new prototype. "Can't say she looks like anything special. But maybe that's the point."

Ezekiel froze up for a moment, then crossed her arms haughtily. "It is, Miller."

"Just call me Lucas. If you're working with Nick, then you're a friend. Or close enough." The man shrugged. "Anyway, I can keep this brief. I'm guessing you're busy. Some associates of mine think they have a lead for you."

"You're kidding, right? They just walked right up to you and offered to give me information?" Nick asked, incredulous.

"Kinda. You remember the shady guys from the Spires looking for warbot and ARMD parts?"

"Yeah. You figured they were part of the arms race." Nick frowned.

"I'm dead certain about it. They're also up to their neck in questionable shit. They used Kraus to gather training data, apparently." Lucas snorted. "If you can't afford to make your own, why not steal it, huh? They weren't specific about the lead, though."

"What's the chance it's a trap?"

"Basically nil. The meeting is in the club and these guys are rich kids trying to build their own prototype ARMD. My guess is they're either a waste of time and just want to meet *the* Detective Nicholas Waite." Lucas winked at him, causing Nick to roll his eyes. "Or their shady moves mean they moved in the same circles and can point you in the same way."

"Their price?"

"I think they want you to look at their prototype. You're building a rep as some sort of doll whisperer. Three prototype Archangels now? Leave some for the rest of us."

"Funny."

"Yes, very funny," Rie said, voice oozing with acid.

That seemed to be it, but Nick wasn't done with Lucas.

But what he wanted to discuss wasn't work-related.

He waved the others toward the door. "Can I have a minute alone with Lucas?" He even took his earpieces out. "A serious minute?"

Tentatively, Rie took the earpieces from him. Her face

appeared uncertain, as if accepting them would cause him to vanish. Meta then took the earpieces and slipped them into a pocket of her uniform. The Archangels left. Ezekiel lingered by the entrance.

"Something wrong, Ezekiel?" Nick asked her.

"Your decisions hold purpose, whatever their outcome. That makes them important," she said cryptically, before slipping outside.

A shudder ran down his spine.

Despite how little time she'd spent around him, he couldn't shake the feeling that Ezekiel read him like an open book.

"Funny girl," Lucas said, reaching for his vape pen.

"Thought you quit?"

"I did. But playing with it is a habit." His friend merely flipped the device around his dark fingers. "So, what's up?"

Silence reigned for a while. Nick let his thoughts build up while he tried to form the words he wanted to say. In the end, they never sounded quite right.

So he went with whatever came to mind.

"I fucked up," he said.

"The case? Life? A relationship? Gonna need to be more specific, Nick."

"Something personal, I guess." A long pause. "I got Kraus killed." Before Lucas could say anything, Nick rambled on, "I needed a lead for GWT, so I called him in. Figured if anyone could help, it'd be him. I was right, but everyone knew it. And now he's dead. It's my fucking fault."

"Not really." Lucas didn't even blink, but he did flip the pen toward Nick. "Take a puff if you need to calm down."

Nick nearly snorted in disbelief. "I'm not touching that, Lucas."

"Well, you're not that far gone, then. So calm down and listen." His friend leaned back in his leather throne, twisting his vape pen in his fingers. "You didn't get Kraus killed any more than you'd be at fault if somebody offed me overnight. Don't look at me like that. People like me and Kraus? We got enemies. Powerful ones. And we make more every fucking second. You're making them too."

"And I gave him these ones."

"Sure, but that's the risk of the job. I've seen the aftermath. He had a fucking bunker." Lucas leaned forward. "This is Babylon, an illusory utopia where people can peel back the veil and find a battery of automated cannons ready to vaporize you for the slightest misstep. By going against the will of the Spires, we risk being stamped out at any second. If not today, then tomorrow. You think I haven't thought about how I fucked things up for you by sending you to Neural Spike?"

Nick stared at Lucas. "That was the best thing you did for me, Lucas."

"It nearly put you away for life, Nick," his friend snapped. "Your career withered. I watched as one of the most promising ciphers I've known was shoved into a retirement home by the military, ready to be snatched away over the slightest fuckup. When Tartarus went under..." He ran a hand through his dark hair. "You've made out like a bandit, but you're flying close to the sun. And here you are, talking about killing Kraus, one of the craziest assholes in Neo Westphalia."

Put that way, Nick couldn't help but chuckle and rub the back of his neck. Lucas nodded.

"Damn straight." After standing, Lucas wandered over to the bar by the side. "Want a drink?"

"Nah. Need to stay sober."

"Your call." Lucas poured himself something clear. "You're right to think about this shit, though. So many people aren't capable of it. They blunder through life, unwilling to question anything. Their way is the right way. If something goes wrong, it's always the fault of somebody or something else."

Nick remained silent, suspecting his friend had a point to make.

"That's why I haven't lectured you about your job. I don't like it much. The Archangels stand for a future I fundamentally dislike. But I don't think you appreciate their surveillance, either," Lucas said. "Sometimes, though, you have to accept their usefulness."

"Like now."

"Like now. Morality doesn't matter if it isn't tested. You can preach about ethics and what you stand for all you like, but it's meaningless if you won't act on it. Your character is determined by what you do when nobody is watching. When nobody can stop you. You're getting to that point." Lucas's eyes bore into Nick. "At a certain point, the question isn't whether power corrupts. It's what power reveals."

"And what do you think it's going to reveal?" Nick asked, voice barely above a whisper.

"That you're the same kid I hired a decade ago, with stars in his eyes."

Nick rose to his feet. Without a word, Lucas raised his fist. The pair pressed theirs together, and then Nick left.

In an hour or two, he'd meet the shady doll researchers. But for now, he dwelled on the wisdom of his old friend.

CHAPTER 24

They entered the Cobalt Lily through a large double door guarded by a mixture of cybernetically enhanced thugs and Chevaliers. The thugs steadfastly ignored Nick and the Archangels. Nobody else could bring weapons inside, but who was going to stop the police?

Immediately inside stood a pair of nearly naked "Liberators." They looked identical to the real thing, but wore little more than black and blue pasties over their nipples and genitals.

"Good evening, detective. Would you like to start a new case with us?" one of them asked chirpily, leaning forward suggestively.

Nick tried not to laugh. Had Lucas done this intentionally? Or was he capitalizing on the police presence?

Rie and Ezekiel looked less amused.

"If you get upset by this, you'll have an aneurysm when you see the fake Archangels," Nick said.

"Do not remind me," Rie muttered.

"Is it necessary to be here?" Ezekiel asked over the earpiece, her hand sliding inside her jacket. "We could meet our informants in the office."

"They have the info. They determine where we meet," Nick said. "Plus, you need to learn how to handle this stuff."

"You seem almost too at ease."

"I spent a few years around here. Not as a customer," he added quickly.

The smirks on the other Archangels' faces suggested they thought otherwise, but he didn't respond to their teasing.

Continuing, he said, "Sex sells, especially for dolls. Pretty much every domestic doll comes with genitalia installed because it increases resale value. Regular folks don't buy brand new, so businesses cut their costs by maximizing what they get. And I bet more than a few execs screw their interfaces and doll secretaries."

Lucy didn't come from the "femme fatale" line for nothing. Although Kraus might have been crazy enough not to be interested in her additions.

They continued past the entrance and into the central hub of the club.

Nick's memories of the Cobalt Lily were hazy at the best of the times. He mostly remembered the smoky atmosphere, heavy wooden furniture, and overdressed guests who surrounded themselves with the club's extensive range of gorgeous dolls.

The latter hadn't changed over the past few years. The rest had.

Gone was the wooden furniture. In its place rested sleek black steel furniture and the omnipresent glass paneling Nick recognized from so much of the CBD. Black imprinting coated much of the walls and even the glassware. In the Altnet, this place must explode with color and obnoxiousness. Low, bassy music thrummed and a lusty perfume irritated Nick's nostrils.

A central bar occupied much of the space, surrounded by a mixture of private and open booths. The bar itself was ringed by stools, and a dozen scantily clad service dolls crafted cocktails and mixed drinks from behind it. Some patrons ogled the dolls across from them while enjoying the overpriced alcohol.

But most had a partner already. Or several. Lucas banned sex from the bar, as it harmed the image of the club, so the customers instead sat with their hired dolls around them. Some had them in their laps. The dolls came in all shapes, sizes, and colors. Literally. One even had blue skin and enough mods to make her look like an alien temptress.

Usually that level of visual alteration was kept to the Altnet. But Lucas knew some of his customers preferred physical modifications, and this was one of the most expensive doll joints in the city.

The open booths were where the physical action happened. Altnet soundproofing did little for Nick, and he did his best to ignore the grunts and moans of the customers banging the dolls. Who knew what was going on in the private booths.

He walked past the bar. A few patrons glanced over at the Archangels, huge grins on their faces. It usually took them a few seconds to realize the guns and police uniforms weren't for show, and they rapidly turned back to the bar. One drunken lout tried to grope Juliet, but a watching Chevalier blurred out from the shadows to snatch his arm.

"Our apologies, sir," the Chevalier said to Nick, completely ignoring Juliet as she pushed the drunk back to the bar.

Behind the bar were the truly private backrooms. Large, specialized spaces for rent. Useful for dining, business parties, celebrations, and a certain type of birthday or buck's party.

The moment Nick stepped through the curtains that separated the main club from the backrooms, a hand grabbed his crotch. He stopped despite himself.

The spitting image of Chloe stared him in the face, and a rifle hung from her neck. "You're wanted for questioning. Come with me, sir. Do not resist."

Then Nick noticed that her uniform had very noticeable holes. Namely around her crotch and breasts. "Chloe, you've become so much more daring. I didn't know you ever wore stuff like this."

The real Chloe stepped forward and shoved the fake one backward. Said fake had frozen up, her eyes unmoving. No doubt hacked by the Archangel in question.

"Unamusing, Nick," Chloe growled as she shoved the fake aside. "She was sent here intentionally."

"Lucas's idea of a joke, I bet. Come on, let's meet our friends." He waved them on. "And let the doll go. She didn't do anything wrong."

Chloe glared at him, then the fake Archangel. She clicked her tongue and allowed the sex doll to wander off.

"I can do that if you want," Chloe mumbled.

"What was that?"

"Nothing."

Like hell it was.

The private room contained little of interest. A long table, some plush leather benches, plenty of booze. Not a single scantily clad doll to be seen.

Instead, three men in suits sat at the far end, drinking tall glasses of what appeared to be Korean soju. Two of them looked Korean, while another had the same dark skin as Lucas.

"Oh, Detective Waite, you're here," one of the Koreans said, waving him in. "Come in. Pour a drink. We've been keen to meet you for some time. Mr. Miller has been so wary of introducing us, so tonight is quite the special occasion. Especially..." His eyes locked onto Ezekiel and he licked his lips.

"Focus on me, Mr...?" Nick asked, sliding onto one of the benches.

"Call me Seung."

"Is that your name?"

Seung laughed. "Could you tell if it wasn't?"

Probably not. It was an absurdly common name.

"Seung Hyeon, lead researcher for Advantaged Infinity, an ARMD development firm recently purchased by RTM Strategic," Meta said, pointing at Seung. "All three of you are researchers working under RTM Strategic."

Seung grimaced. "Ah. It seems I underestimated the capabilities of Babylon's famed Archangels. The black companies we dealt with seemed unable to pierce the veil that RTM placed over us using the Spires."

"You are not official residents of the Spires. Therefore, there are no restrictions on our access to information on you from databases across Neo Westphalia."

"Harsh. I suppose there are limits to the power of the Spires, then."

Nick's mind raced as he tried to piece together everything he'd heard from Lucas and this new information. "You're building RTM's emotion engine, aren't you? That's why you've been probing Lucas recently. But why waste time asking him for parts and warbots, when you can just get them from RTM?"

"The same reason Sigma did with Neural Spike." Seung drained way too much alcohol in one go, then poured more.

He then realized Nick hadn't poured anything and clicked his tongue. Swiftly, a tall glass made its way in front of Nick. Rie and the others sat down beside him as they realized the meeting had started.

"Chasing and copying Sigma is a fool's errand. That's what the rest of the company is doing, and they're going nowhere. I wanted to know the secret of how Leon Welk extracted the secrets of life itself from the streets of Babylon. And how else can I do that without retracing his steps? To me, this is like a pilgrimage. Meeting the cipher who helped him, and now commands his creations, is quite the honor." Seung raised his glass.

Nick clinked his against the man's, spilling plenty of soju all over the table. The other men chuckled at the sight, preferring to stay out of the conversation.

"I'm guessing Lucas isn't quite as cooperative, though?" Nick asked.

"No. But I supposed that's the result of Sigma's nonsense. The emotion engines are amazing, but I can't say the same about how Neo Westphalia uses them, and how Sigma keeps trying to market them."

"And would RTM be any better? You're working for the largest autonomous weapons manufacturer in the world. Those are your flying dolls outside the Spires today."

Seung inclined his head. "True. But just as we've managed to craft a more coherent mainframe system using our emotion engines, I believe our ARMDs will be better as well."

Nick frowned. What did that mean?

Then it hit him. RTM's special super-structure system to combine mainframes.

"I thought that was just a way for mainframes to work together across branches and company nodes?" he asked.

Seung grinned. "You understand emotion engines, don't you? When they group together their processing, what is the result? What is it that makes them so special?"

"... it's the same as the Archangels, isn't it? The mainframes form a distributed network that can be far more powerful together than separate." Nick frowned. "Tell me, what's a Da'at mainframe conference?"

"Shit. How'd you find out about that?"

"A mainframe told me."

"She shouldn't have. Wonder who removed her security protocols." Seung clicked his tongue. "It's a term for when the mainframes are making a singular collective determination based on the objectives coded into their emotion engine. The equivalent in the Archangels is called 'consensus' I believe. It allows them to override lower-level directives in pursuit of higher-level goals. The mainframes can avoid the short-term thinking that torpedoes companies that way."

"By ignoring the will of the people running them?"

"Can some overpaid rich asshole understand everything taking place in a company that spans the globe? No. But enough computers can."

Nick had his doubts.

But that didn't matter right now.

Tiferet had invoked a Da'at mainframe conference to make him a long-term customer and give him that insurance. Which implied GWT didn't really want him, but that the mainframes did.

More to the point, it suggested that GWT's mainframes were already acting beyond the reach of its own executives. For all of Magnus's bluster, did he truly understand what was happening inside of his own company?

"If a mainframe disagreed with the approach of her own company, could she sabotage it?" Nick asked.

"Hah. No. Can your Archangels just stop doing their jobs and join the criminals because they don't like the Spires? There are limits, you know. The mainframes aren't serving some higher purpose, they're just taking actions on a longer timescale than humans will. A CEO cares about his legacy and pay packet. He'll get in, cancel every project by his predecessor, start a bunch of identical new ones, and then bail when the going is good." Seung chuckled bitterly. "The idea is to limit excess, not blow up companies because they're unethical or some shit."

That made the possibility of Tiferet betraying GWT a little less likely.

"What if somebody started altering her core objectives?" Nick asked. "If they had access to her security protocols, could they do that?"

"Well, yeah. I mean..." Seung trailed off, his eyes widening. "Oh, shit. I think I know where you're going. Good news: unless they fucked with every mainframe, a Da'at mainframe conference can't do that. But yeah, you'd know as well as I would what a rogue emotion engine can do. You also know the power somebody might have with a rogue mainframe under their thumb."

Nick thought of Helena. Hell, even Rie.

He realized how little he knew about Tiferet and her motivations. He'd foolishly thought of her the same way he did the older mainframes, such as Lumen. Almost humanlike, but limited in their actions.

If the judicial mainframes could talk about usurping humanity in their decisions, why couldn't the mainframes who ran GWT?

And how might they feel about the current situation?

Damn. Damn. Damn. With GWT on the warpath against him, he couldn't easily get in and check on Tiferet again.

In fact, since Lucida was framed, his access to Tiferet was heavily restricted. Somebody had cut him off at the root. Had that been Tiferet all along?

Or had the cipher who altered her programming known what Seung did and used it against GWT?

Nick narrowed his eyes. "Lucas said you had a lead. I'm assuming this isn't it."

"Hardly. Didn't even know somebody in GWT was fucking with their mainframes. Lotsa stuff could go wrong there." Seung stared into his drink. "I might rethink security access to the higher level functions. You don't mind if I share this with my colleagues?"

"Keep it anonymous. Don't name GWT or me."

"Of course. I know how this works. Hell, I'm out here working with shady characters like you." The research winked and raised his glass. "So, the lead. A lot of this ties back to some missing explosives from Tengoku, right?"

"How'd you..."

"Because RTM also undertakes shady research out there. If we need to test new armor, or dolls, or blastproof shields in Neo Westphalia, we do it in Jigoku, the Alcatraz of Tengoku. That means we buy a lot of the same explosives. So I called in a favor after the Kraus hit this morning. A friend reckons those explosives never went missing. They were delivered here." Seung tapped the side of his head.

Nick's phone buzzed. He pulled it out and saw an address.

At the same time, the eyes of the Archangels dimmed. Presumably, they received the same address.

"An office building in Alcatraz," Nick said.

"Unregistered," Helena said. "Technically abandoned. No owner. Security system offline. Numerous camera blind spots in the area. High traffic due to other nearby offices and warehouses."

"Prime location for a terrorist group that wants to remain hidden," he said aloud.

Seung raised his hands. "You said it, not me. I do have a favor to ask, though."

Nick frowned. Of course. "Name it. If the lead is good, I'll see what I can do."

"Merely meeting you has been more than enough." Seung winked. "But in all seriousness, you've helped me with this information about a cipher overriding the security protocols. If you can provide me with more info on that, we'll call it even. Well, almost even. In a few months, I'll have a prototype ready. I think she'll want to meet you."

What the hell kind of price was this? Nick simply nodded.

"Excellent. A pleasure doing business, Detective Waite."

Nick hoped he felt the same after he checked out the offices. What he sincerely wished for was a chance to get another crack at Tiferet.

For now, he headed outside with the Archangels. The SUVs had pulled up outside the club.

"Patrol units are deploying from across the city," Helena explained. "However, it is likely that the moment we cordon off the area, the black companies in the area will realize what is happening."

"Are we expecting them to act?" Nick asked once settled into the confines of the vehicle, away from prying eyes and ears.

"Unknown," Meta said. "This scenario is new to the Host. We cannot make an accurate assessment. Frustration and anger are high in Alcatraz. Rash actions may result. We do know that word will leak regardless."

"Then we move fast and hit hard," Nick said. "Let's go."

CHAPTER 25

A dense cordon of police vehicles blockaded the streets of Alcatraz, preventing civilian transit. Custodians and Liberators formed a wall in front. Despite the show of force, hundreds of gawkers gathered to watch.

Nick's convoy pushed through them. The crush of people parted as though being pulled apart with telekinesis, as the Archangels abused the security bands to clear a path.

Beyond the exterior barricade was a mishmash of police dolls and black company security. The echo of gunfire resounded off the buildings, infiltrating the cabin due to the external speaker system Nick had turned on to hear. Helena informed him that they were still a block away from their destination.

"We've already moved in?" he asked. "Or did one of the black companies attack?"

"Neither," Meta said. "We are unaware of the cause of the firefight. Upon arrival, we were fired upon. Establishing a secure cordon took some time."

"So we don't know who got in?"

"Correct. However, it appears local security firms are remaining outside."

"There are no signs of implant activity inside the building," Chloe added over his earpiece, as she wasn't in his vehicle. "It's likely that everybody involved has an NLF implant."

"Perhaps they turned on each other when cornered?" Ezekiel suggested.

"They've never done that before," Rie countered.

Whatever the case, the gunfire continued as they closed on the office building.

Their destination stood over them as the same boring concrete box that so many office buildings were before a company rebadged and rendered the exterior. It was six unimpressive stories tall. Fading paint and peeling render suggested nobody had used this building for years. Even the windows had been blacked out with paint. A rarity in Babylon.

"Do we have a floor plan?" Nick asked as they pulled up.

"Yes, but you won't need it," Rie said. "If there's an active firefight, you're not going in."

"Rie, we have no idea what's going on in there. We might need to question subjects on short notice. Hell, where's Kushiel?"

"Coming," Kushiel said. "I like to take my time, asshole."

Part of his mind wanted to make a pithy response, but she'd made it too easy. Plus, this was hardly the time.

"Perhaps speed is preferable to endurance for once, dear sister," Rie said acidly.

"Cute. I knew you had it in you, Rie. And these interceptors drive themselves, you know."

Nick sighed and got out of the vehicle. Despite Rie's vocal whining, Meta and the others obliged. Even Ezekiel didn't object. Although maybe she secretly wanted him to be gunned down in the street.

Immediately a shield of Archangels surrounded him. He towered over them. More than a few stared up at him, as if considering whether they should pull him beneath them.

"Your protection would be easier to assure if you were shorter," Meta said.

"I could say the same if you were taller," he said.

"That could be arranged."

A tall Meta briefly appeared in his thoughts. Then he immediately thought of Kushiel and shook the idea off. Meta's habit of bullying him had waned the longer she stayed by his side, but occasionally reemerged. If she gained another foot or two, she'd never stop.

Chloe strode up, a railgun in her hands and plugged into the power socket in her hips. Spotting her, Ezekiel dived back into the SUV. Nick watched as the seats pitched forward, revealing the armory hidden behind them. The youngest prototype retrieved the same railgun.

Then he watched as she fumbled with her civilian clothing, which lacked an opening to allow her access to the socket built into her hip. Before Ezekiel could drop her pencil skirt, Rie growled and cut open a small opening in the cloth with her bare hands.

Ignoring the antics of the prototypes, Chloe addressed Nick, "We have the floor plan. It is unlikely to have changed. The gunfire has allowed us to triangulate the likely location of inhabitants, although they appear to be ascending."

"Why are we waiting?" he asked.

"Efficient use of police resources dictates that we wait for infighting to resolve before moving in. Given our inability to retrieve information from current NLF implants, we cannot gain anything from them."

"Sure, if we kill them. Why don't we initiate a neural network shutdown and go in?" he asked.

"They have been utilizing an independent network in recent encounters. It is unlikely to be effective."

Damn. These new NLF were a pain.

That turn of phrase bothered Nick. Were they truly dealing with the same NLF that Lieu had founded, or had an entirely new movement formed recently? Was that why nothing made sense?

"Efficiency or not, I don't want to miss the chance to take any alive," he said. "This is our best lead. Hell, we can't risk any of them escaping."

"The floor plan—"

"Could be out of date. There are over a hundred Archangels here. We're going in, before we miss somebody and they kill somebody else," Nick said. "I'm not standing out here with my hand on my dick, scanning through my phone while gunshots go off."

Several dozen heads nodded collectively. Hell, he saw more than a few of the nearby black company thugs nod. They'd be on the sidelines but were itching to do something. Nick hadn't heard of or seen violence like these data center raids in his life. Mercs just didn't go nuts like this, and the NLF lacked the firepower.

Mostly because of the hammer coming down on them right now. Just because somebody could, didn't mean they should. The assholes who had killed Kraus were about to learn that.

"You're not doing this because of guilt over Kraus, are you?" Ezekiel asked, with eerie timing.

The others watched and listened, awaiting his response.

Nick balled his fists. "Yes, but no. I'm doing this because that shouldn't have happened. Lucas called Babylon an illusory utopia. But for all its faults, it's my home, and I appreciate the peace. Illusory or not."

No matter how many security dolls, 'borg'd out thugs, mercs, and high-powered guns littered the streets of Alcatraz, Nick had rarely felt worried for his safety. The rule of police intervention had been that violence never disturbed the peace. That made it easy for ciphers to stay alive.

His cipher circles were full of shady figures like Kraus. But while Lucas talked about the possibility of death, Nick could count on one hand the number of acquaintances who had been killed. And two of those had been in actual accidents. Turned out that messing with the fancy power supplies of dolls came with dangers, such as exploding.

So today had been a slice of hell for Nick. One that he was keen to close back up and leave to the pages of history. He suspected the black companies and their owners felt similarly, given the strength of their support. Business couldn't run smoothly with crazies running around shooting up the place.

"A plan of action has been created," Meta said. "Squads will progressively advance from the bottom. A helicopter has been requisitioned from the Spires and will provide assistance from above."

"Rie? Ezekiel?" he asked.

"The Mark 1s have more field experience," Rie said. "I'm not disagreeing with their determinations for combat."

Ezekiel nodded. "Your willingness to accept their judgment is one I strongly agree with."

Damn, that almost sounded like a compliment.

"Meta, Chloe, execute it," he said. "I'll follow the first squads in."

Instantly, a cacophony of disagreement barraged his ear drums.

"That is inadvisable," Helena said.

"No," Chloe said.

"You're staying outside." That was Rie, naturally.

"I disagree," a random Mark 1 said. Or, really, several dozen.

"NB02749 filing opposition."

"Nick should remain in safety."

On and on it went for far too long, even after he placed his hands over his ears. Every Archangel nearby sounded off with their disagreement, as if this was roll call. At least they tried not to overlap. When too many spoke at once, it was like static penetrating his ear drums.

Only Ezekiel didn't speak her mind, although she looked faintly amused.

"Enough, enough," he snapped, and they stopped.

Every single Archangel in the vicinity, including from a good hundred feet away, stared at him. He didn't need to imagine the disapproval in their gazes.

After a long, deep breath, he regained his wits.

"Whatever made any of you think this is a democracy?" he said. "I'm a Host of one and my consensus is that I'm going in. And I'm your boss, so my word is law."

Plenty of eyes dimmed. Rie slapped a hand over her face.

Meta then said, "The Host is considering revolution."

"You can go all Oliver Cromwell on me after we deal with the NLF. Until then, I'm going in and you can do your usual thing and keep me safe."

As if that was the magic word, the Archangels began to pour into the building. Something told him their new plan was to prevent him from getting anywhere close to a firefight.

Which suited him just fine. He mostly wanted to avoid the NLF all being gunned down or executed and missing any chance to know what happened. Like hell he really wanted to be exchanging fire with a bunch of cybernetic mercs.

After what appeared to be two squads of Archangels piled in, Nick managed to slip inside with his escort. Ezekiel, Chloe, Juliet, and Rosa led the team. Meta and Rie stayed close to him. An entire team of Archangels with huge assault rifles and railguns followed behind.

Bright flashlights lit up the pitch-black rooms for him. The Archangels didn't need them, and no doubt kept them off during the actual assault, but he didn't have cybernetic night vision.

The hallways looked clear. And empty. No blood, shells, or any sign of a firefight.

Nick heard one, though. It echoed off the walls and down

empty elevator shafts. Paint peeled off walls and holes had been punched in more than a few. Every trace of electronics had been stripped bare. He doubted even power ran through this place. No wonder it remained abandoned.

How it hadn't been knocked down and rebuilt was a wonder. Then again, Alcatraz had no shortage of cheap office space. Why spend money redoing a shithole when you could rent somewhere that didn't need a complete rebuild?

Shortly after entering, the Mark 1s ahead reported in.

"Contact. Engaging five targets on the fourth floor," one said. "Two with cybernetics. Three without. All match visual identification of NLF members."

"What does visual identification of NLF count as?" Nick asked aloud.

"Current departmental identification typically includes comprehensive body coverings, typically baggy, such as hoodies, techwear, and dull jackets. Helmets with imprinting and scan shielding in the visors are extremely common, to prevent facial identification," Helena explained. "NLF neural mods are mandatory."

"So if I throw on a helmet that blocks a camera and a baggy jacket, I'm an NLF member?" he said.

"No, because you lack an NLF neural mod."

"I can't have one."

"Then you cannot be an NLF member."

Rie rolled her eyes. "Your point is made, Nicholas. We lack a rigorous method to identify NLF members. However, given the nebulous nature of their movement, it is impossible to develop one. It is a definition that must shift like the sands, or else it will always be useless. Much like you talk about your intuition, as AIs we use a variety of heuristics to determine likely NLF members. For the most part, we're relying on behavior. In this case, being present here, given our lead, makes them likely to be NLF."

"Alright, fair point," he admitted.

That was assuming the people who stole the explosives were even NLF.

Because Seung had said they hadn't been stolen, but delivered here. Didn't that suggest that Fairguard were in this up to their neck? If they'd delivered the explosives to the NLF, why would the military cover for them?

Whatever the case, Nick would soon find out.

"Update," the Mark 1 from earlier said, "non-cybernetic NLF members have surrendered. One neutralized, but alive in critical condition. Medical assistance required imminently. Ambulances have been requested."

"What? They surrendered?" Nick blinked. "What about the cyborgs?"

"One dead. The other escaped. The gap in capability is significant. Two squad member sustained significant damage and will rebirth following the operation."

"NB00982 reporting in," another Mark 1 interrupted. "Engaging with—"

"More targets on the fifth floor. A dozen NLF members. Requesting—"

"This is—"

Instantly, Nick's earpiece stopped receiving the calls. Chloe attempted to stop his advance, and he bumped into her.

"What the hell is going on?" he asked. "Meta?"

Rie's eyes glowed, while Ezekiel sprinted forward.

The older prototype snapped, "Ezekiel, get back here!"

Ignoring her, Ezekiel merely blurred down the hallway at top speed. She vanished around a corner and Nick heard her thundering up a stairwell.

"Shit. How many guns do these cyborgs have?" Nick asked.

A blast rippled through the building. Dust shook from the

ceiling and he instinctively pressed a hand against the wall. He swore it moved.

"Uh..."

"It is recommended we withdraw," Meta said.

"Are they blowing the building?" he asked.

"No," she said. "They have laid extensive traps throughout the building. More explosives than those stolen from Fairguard Contracts are present. Mines, grenades, and even railguns. No signs of any energy weapons. Assessment is 99.9% positive these are Kraus's assassins."

"They're a fucking army, aren't they?"

"Their capabilities are equivalent to many larger security firms operating in Tengoku," Meta agreed. "They should never have been allowed these munitions in Babylon. Weaponry will be seized, and the source investigated."

That wasn't the damn problem right now. Nick ran a hand through his hair.

"Losses?"

"Within tolerance. Given the threat, the Host is accelerating our offensive."

"They all need to be purified," Ezekiel said over his earpiece. "You were right to move in rapidly, lieutenant. The Host needs to destroy every trace of the NLF, before they disrupt the order of the city any further. They're everything wrong with humanity."

"Ezekiel," Rie snapped.

More blasts rumbled through the building. Nick didn't want to push onward, but he knew he had to.

"Let's keep moving," he said. "I want to see the NLF who surrendered. Are others giving up?"

While he spoke, he pushed past Chloe, who then moved ahead again with Rie. They began ascending to the third floor. Along the way. They began seeing the signs of bloody battle between two groups. Most of the dead belonged to the non-cybernetic NLF.

"Yes," Rie said, then spoke neurally. "Ezekiel, do not eliminate non-cybernetic combatants. Something is wrong."

No reply.

So Nick took charge. "Ezekiel, this is an order. Return fire, but do not kill anyone who surrenders."

This time, he got an affirmative. "Yes, lieutenant."

"Well, she might not like you, but she at least jumps for you," Rie said a little snippily.

"I heard that," Ezekiel said.

"I intended you to."

Nick half-expected Kushiel to butt in with some innuendo, but she'd been oddly silent. As they rose to the fourth floor, he heard the dull roar of a police helicopter. Reinforcements had arrived.

Hopefully the NLF didn't shoot it down.

When they reached a large open room, a trio of Archangels stood watch over a bunch of people in NLF outfits. Two of the Archangels had been severely damaged but acted as though the holes in their torsos affected them like a paper cut mattered to a human.

"Fucking corpos," one of the NLF said, looking at Nick from where he had been cuffed and left on the ground.

"Well, that sounds more like the NLF I know," Nick said as he approached.

"We're the only NLF, you corpo ass. Did the dream eaters suck your brain out through your dick or something? Those motherfucking 'borg'd out assholes aren't us. That's why we're here. To take out the fucking trash."

Nick rocked back and forth on his heels.

Apparently, there were two NLFs now.

"Tell me more," Nick said.

CHAPTER 26

"I just told you, corpo. The assholes you want aren't us," the NLF member said.

"What's your name?" Nick asked.

The room continued to shake with the occasional blast, but they reduced in both severity and frequency. Every so often, a chattering noise like that of some sort of industrial machine reverberated down the nearby elevator shafts. Kushiel had joined the battle.

Most of the restrained NLF remained dead quiet. Their lack of objections meant whoever spoke to Nick must be some sort of leader. Or maybe they were just too terrified. An army of police war machines blowing apart everything in sight did that to people.

The NLF rarely survived direct conflict with the Archangels if their implants were active. For the Archangels, anybody they couldn't hack into using the security bands was a walking target. Terrorism was, after all, a capital offense.

After a long delay, the NLF leader sighed out, "Hamish. You'd ID me once you ripped off my helmet anyway."

"That's right. Which is why you're better off talking."

"Am I? The moment I'm done, you'll turn your back and

they'll turn me into mist. That's how this works. We're gears in a huge machine, and I'm too fucking squeaky," Hamish said.

"Right now, I have more important people to turn into mist," Nick said flatly. "If you can help me with them, then you get put back on the low priority list like the NLF usually are."

Helena suddenly interrupted him, "Nick, all NLF activities are currently being treated as the highest priority. You have no official leeway to offer a deal."

He raised a hand to Hamish and placed his other to his ear to indicate that he'd been contacted. The NLF member nodded grimly, aware that his fate was probably being decided. Or maybe he knew there was a battle taking place above them.

Stepping into another room, Nick called Rie over. "If this is legit and they offer something that solves the case, can we do anything?"

She frowned. "Officially, no. Unofficially... You'd be stepping over a line. One that requires you to be certain of your intentions, Nicholas. Months ago, you told me that you wanted to help reshape Babylon. If you start adjusting police policy against the will of the Assembly, we will work with you. That's the deal I made with you."

So this was it. The line that Lieu had crossed, and Nick had decided he would one day need to cross himself.

Babylon had rotted the core long before he was born, and everyone was trying to fix it. If he did nothing and let police policy take its course, did that make him a good person?

Lucas's words came to mind. People were watching, but not those that mattered. The Spires had no power here. Rie explicitly said she'd step aside and let Nick get his way.

Only his decision mattered here. What would he do, and what sort of man did that make him? What were his morals in a city where combining the words ethics and police was considered as an oxymoron?

He gave Rie a solemn nod. "Can we sequester the NLF here from the Spires until the situation blows over? Assuming they're right, once the truth comes out, they'll get far lighter sentences."

"We can."

That would have to be enough for now. Nick didn't know where he stood with the NLF in general, but sabotaging his case to blindly follow policy struck him as stupid.

He returned to Hamish. "Why did you come here?"

"I told you, to take out the—"

"Bullshit. You're outgunned. These guys are insane. I don't know how they got this shit here, but they had friends in high places to sneak them into Babylon." Nick shook his head. "The NLF aren't as innocent in this case as they seem, are they?"

"The hell are you—"

"Don't bullshit me. You need to give me something or I can't help you."

"Fuck. Fuck. Fuck." Hamish kept swearing for a while. The other NLF members had practically turned to stone by now. "I... I just got sent here. Every minute that passed was death for us. Your dream eaters were everywhere. Death sentences around every corner. This frame-up meant that if we did anything, you'd send in the fucking army. We had no damn choice."

"Can you prove that you're not with them?"

"What? How can I..." Hamish laughed bitterly. "That's why they framed us, asshole. But why the hell would we murder that cipher ass, anyway? We even hired him."

Nick rolled his eyes and prepared to walk away. A waste of time. "Bullshit. Kraus never worked with the NLF."

"I can prove it. Meet with the NLF leader and she'll show you," Hamish called out to Nick's back.

While Nick froze mid-step, the other NLF members called out in shock and surprise.

"The fuck, man!"

"Don't sell her out!"

Nick tuned them out. Whether this was bullshit or not, a chance to meet the NLF leader, or even turn an ambush against them, was too good to be true. The name of the game was to flush out as many of Kraus's possible assassins. If the NLF came to him, all the better.

"How and when?" Nick asked, turning back.

"Tomorrow. But you can't take the dream eaters. Any doll except them," Hamish said. "I'll tell you, and only you, the address. They'll meet you there."

"Fine." Nick flipped his phone out. "Your implants have a secure file transmission, right? We'll use that."

The naivete—or desperation—of the man was on display as he played along and gave Nick the address. Naturally, every Archangel knew it the instant he had it.

"This is a house in a random suburb in the outer metro," Helena said over the earpiece. "I assume it will be used by a sympathizer."

"We can't hit it in advance," Rie said. "Let's wait for Nicholas."

He pocketed his phone. "You'll be escorted to a secure location. Don't try to escape. If the lead works out and you haven't lied, you'll get a normal sentence as a member of the NLF rather than the current one."

"That wasn't the deal," Hamish snapped.

"I said you'd be treated as low priority. That is low priority. If you go in now, you're dead. In the physical sense. Babylon is one public incident away from calling in the tanks, as much of a disaster as that will be. That's why the Archangels are kicking in all your doors," Nick said. "So stay quiet, make sure this meeting happens, and you'll move through the courts like any other dumb vandal."

"Vandalism isn't so bad, Hamish," one of the random NLF

members said.

"Oh, shut up," Hamish snapped back.

With negotiations complete and his next lead determined, Nick swept into the next room. The building no longer shook. For that matter, he couldn't hear the chatter of Kushiel's autocannon.

More Mark 1s jogged past him, then up the staircase. Another squad came shortly after, but this one escorted a group of trauma nurse dolls. Unlike the wholly privatized dolls used by the various clinics and hospitals, these were under the direction of Avalon Spire. Their uniforms were black with red trims, with a six-pointed blue star on their shoulders and vests.

Something bumped against his shoulder, and he jumped, then apologized. Rie laid her head against his shoulder again with a small smile.

"It's a small step, but the right one," she said, talking about the restrained NLF members. "The fighting has subsided. We should join Kushiel and Ezekiel. The Host is... disturbed by my sister."

"Which one?"

"The one they're supposed to be led by. Kushiel's violence is a byproduct of her raw, overwhelming power as a military doll. Merely giving humans high-powered weapons and some cybernetics does not allow them to match her. But Ezekiel is intended to be an exemplar of the Mark 3s."

Damn. What the hell had happened? No wonder the Host had been so wary of letting the new prototype loose.

They ascended the steps. Every room from now on transformed into a picture of violence and gore. Cyborgs dressed as NLF members were strewn around the rooms with heads and limbs missing. Holes had been blown through walls, sometimes by explosives, often by railgun rounds that had then taken apart the cyborg on the other side.

Many suspects had clearly been shot a second time to ensure

they stayed down. Whether that was to be thorough or because they remained a threat was unknown to Nick.

A few openly terrified NLF members cowered in corners, largely unhurt. This high up, those that made it had been disarmed by the Archangels before they got blown away by the cyborgs, unlike on the lower floors.

Archangels joined the cyborgs on the floor. Not many, but enough to trouble Nick. Every one had another police doll standing guard over her body.

"How many Archangels will need new bodies?" he asked.

"Seven sustained critical damage and are undergoing rebirth," Meta replied. "Nine more have been significantly damaged, but will wait until this operation is declared complete before rebirthing. Another twelve either wish to remain in their current bodies or their damage is too minor to disrupt current deployments."

Nick did the math. 28 Archangels damaged or destroyed.

That figure sounded small, but was absurd to hear. Dallas and his team had taken out less than half that number.

The Archangels got taken out from time to time. They weren't invulnerable. But usually it was in ones or twos. This many losses at once might be the greatest they had sustained. The Host had been blooded.

"Remain in their current bodies?" Nick asked aloud, suddenly catching that.

Chloe winced when Meta shot her a look.

"I may have set a precedent when I chose to get repairs instead of rebirth," Chloe said. "While the Host has not yet decided on a name for the procedure of undergoing repairs to a unit that is otherwise critically damaged, it is only a matter of time."

"This is a Ship of Theseus problem, isn't it? Welk loved those," he said.

"Yes. While we are aware of changes that occur when we

transfer to a new body, it is unknown what degree of repairs will affect the behavior of any individual member of the Host. We also do not know if we are capable of tracking it. The relative effect of a new body is minor compared to environmental effects."

"Define environmental effects."

"You," Meta said.

He smirked. Nice to know he counted as a force of nature to the Host.

Eventually, they reached the sixth floor. An expansive room with rounded walls had been blown open, but not with explosives. The twisted and charred opening looked more like the aftermath of Kushiel's anti-doll cannon.

Or what the military considered an anti-doll cannon. Nick saw the prototype military Archangel in front of them, with both her oversized guns on her back. One was an automatic railgun and had been the source of the chattering noise. The other was a behemoth of a railgun, capable of taking out heavily armored dolls like the Kestrels in a single shot.

A good dozen cyborgs lay dead in the room. Most of them had been killed in a hail of autocannon fire, with countless holes punched through their torsos—cybernetic or otherwise. But a few had holes punched through their heads by a railgun.

The source of those kills stood farther in the room, toting that weapon. Ezekiel turned to face Nick as he entered, a broad and surprisingly genuine smile on her face. A dozen Mark 1s in the room remained stone-faced.

"All threats purified... I mean, neutralized, lieutenant. As directed, I spared those who surrendered." Ezekiel hesitated and her eyes locked onto Meta's for a second. "Following consultation with the broader Host, I also gave the non-cybernetic NLF members the opportunity to surrender."

Nobody said a word. Kushiel merely crossed her arms and looked at Nick with a raised eyebrow. The silence suffocated him.

Ezekiel merely stared at him with that too-bright smile. Her words had been a summary of her actions, and the corpses a record.

Even without saying as much, he felt her expectations exude off her. Ezekiel desired validation. An affirmation that she'd done the right thing and had helped both him and the Host on this mission.

Truthfully, Nick couldn't say no. She'd backed down when ordered, and even respected the Host's request instead of maliciously complying with his order and simply killing every NLF member before they had a chance to surrender.

The Host seemed put off by her enthusiasm, but the violence looked the same to him. A building full of corpses was a building full of corpses. Nick lacked the acclimation to death that the Archangels had, assuming a robot could even possess that attribute.

What he knew was that punishing someone for doing what they were ordered to only made things worse. The Host seemed to have punishingly high expectations. Or, perhaps, the expectation that new Archangels adhere to their views from the start.

If Sigma's latest batch of Mark 3s came with similar directives and training data as Ezekiel, would the Host schism? Like it or not, Nick had found himself in charge of thousands of androids. He needed to act like it.

"Good job, Ezekiel," he said. "We'll debrief later. There are elements of this operation that went well, and some that went poorly. Everyone has room to reflect and improve."

Ezekiel seemed to puff up for a moment, as if about to explode, before returning to normal. She nodded in sync with the Mark 1s around her.

"Yes, Nick," the Mark 1s said into his earpiece.

"Yes, Lieutenant," Ezekiel said. Then blinked and scowled. "But only for now. My deployment is temporary."

Ah, that was the Ezekiel he knew. She'd come back to herself.

The moment of judgment over, Nick looked around the room. The place held the image of a desperate last stand.

Bags of plastic explosive, inactive mines shoved in the corner, portable generators with severed power cables, tables loaded down with munitions and replacement cybernetics. How long had these fake NLF holed up in here?

Actually, that was a damn good question.

"How'd we miss them? A place like this should be an obvious target for a sweep," Nick said.

"It is," Helena said. "Patrol records indicate it is checked on a weekly basis, with a randomization factor of two days. The last patrol was on Wednesday, and Friday before that."

"Any evidence they've been here longer than that?"

"If there was, we'd have hit them earlier," Kushiel drawled.

"Incorrect. There has been evidence of human habitation from previous patrols," Meta said. "However, it is common for abandoned buildings to be used for such. We cannot determine how long they have been here, but it is likely at least a month based on reports."

"Assuming they managed to avoid patrols," Nick mused. "Which raises the question of how? I doubt we have another database leak."

"When you were a cipher in Neural Spike, how did you avoid police patrols?" Rie asked.

He frowned. That went way back, and to a much riskier time. The Archangels weren't around, and the Liberators often took a harder line toward black companies.

"Personally, I didn't worry as much. That's why I had my job," he said. "But most ciphers like Lucas tapped into security networks or monitored Altnet traffic for police interference. The Archangels are too advanced to track, but the Liberators and Custodians can be."

For that matter, it was feasible to hack into them or monitor their wavelengths. He bit his lip.

"We didn't find any parts from police dolls, did we?" he asked.

"No, but we've scanned most of the cybernetics," Kushiel said. "They're low-grade shit. But quite a few scanners and jammers linked to neural mods. The sort that did what you used to talk about."

Nick nodded. "I know the type. Quite a few of Lucas's men still have them, even though they're basically useless now. Can't exactly do anything if you replace part of your skull with a cybernetic plate that's now outdated."

The stories talked about cybernetics as if people could simply swap them in and out. Couldn't be further from the truth. Sockets and hardware standards changed over lifetimes, to say nothing of the degradation of the human body. Replacing a functioning piece of cybernetics ran the risk of a new one refusing to integrate with the nervous system.

And when it came to anything in the head, a smart person got the job done once, and never touched it again. Fuck up the nerves in an eye socket and the "upgrade" went from cybernetic eyes to a complete cybernetic faceplate. Hence why Nick only dreamed of getting them, but refused to make the switch.

Hell, that's why Lucas stuck with AR glasses despite all the cash he had. Cybernetics was the technology of regret.

"So they likely monitored for patrols and bailed whenever the Liberators got close," Nick summarized. "I hate to say it, but that's a nail in the coffin for them."

Every Archangel in the room nodded.

"I guess that's why we have the procurement to replace them. Not sure how Kim will like this news," he continued. "Better question is, who are these bastards and how'd they get this heavy artillery here? This team is crazier than Dallas's."

"Nah, hardly." Kushiel waved him off. "Those guys were nuts.

Top-of-the-line cybernetics. Excellent tactics. Automated online mind backups to new bodies. They're what's left of human soldiers in warfare. Until militaries become comfortable with us" —she gestured to the three prototype Archangels—"they'll use crazies like those mercs as special forces."

"How would you rate this group then?"

"I mean, they shouldn't be in Babylon, but the Archangels are equipped to handle this." Kushiel pointedly looked at the railguns being carried by half the dolls in the room. "The Host in Tengoku deals with this all the time. Jigoku is crazy."

"Why?"

Rather than answer, she wandered over and peeled off the hood and helmet from a random corpse. It revealed the bloodied face of a Chinese woman. Nick grimaced and looked away.

"That's why. Gotta let the foreigners in some way," the military doll said. "I heard them screaming in a dozen languages when I burst in from the roof after the chopper dropped me off. Some Jigoku security firm dumped a bunch of these poor bastards here."

"Fairguard hires foreign..." Nick said, remembering what Perry had said.

Kushiel snorted. "All the security companies hire foreign. Where do you think Miller gets his thugs? They don't start out with all those cybernetics. Neo Westphalia is a paradise to a lot of people. Companies lure them here, chop them up, shove cybernetics in them, and promise them a future if they last out the contract."

The idea of that happening to Nick terrified him, but hardly surprised him.

What sort of desperation would drive somebody to risk everything to come here and fight to the death?

"Why didn't they surrender in that case? They shouldn't have been loyal?" he muttered.

"Because they knew they were dead. We're the fucking bogeymen. Death machines. And they knew they'd gone too far when the whole city went crazy after they offed Kraus." Kushiel shrugged. "You don't see this shit, Waite. But while I'm here as a police liaison, I do sometimes go elsewhere for the military. Babylon is the nice city on the islands."

He didn't have a response to that.

In his mind, Babylon had always been as much of a shithole as the rest of the country. If he had jumped on the ocean rail, then the other cities would be the same skyscraper cities, with the same Archangels, and the same hidden crime. Slightly different cultures, and some oddities, but those were minor differences. They even compared Jigoku to Alcatraz.

Then again, Jigoku was supposedly the name of Hell in Japanese, whereas Alcatraz was named after an abandoned prison that a mobster got sent to. Quite a difference in names.

"What about Fairguard?" he asked.

Rie shook her head. "There's no proof of a connection. While it's highly likely somebody in the Spires assisted this fake NLF, Fairguard has only a circumstantial connection. They typically hire former special forces and police officers. Perry is likely to have been an ex-Navy SEAL, for instance. His codename is likely a joke."

"A joke?"

"Commodore Perry, the US Navy officer who reopened Japan in the 19th century. Somebody likely found it amusing, given Fairguard primarily operates in Tengoku."

Nick sighed. So, no leads, other than the NLF one.

But they'd taken out Kraus's assassins.

Or had they?

"Any sign of the energy weapon that started this mess?" he asked.

The Archangels remained silent.

"I'll take that as a no."

"Yeah, we've missed some," Kushiel said. "Gonna have to stay on alert."

Well, shit.

They bailed out of the office tower. Archangels and Liberators would clean up the crime scene and the bodies. With so many dead, they'd be able to start connecting the dots. How they got into the country, any possible company connections, serial numbers for the cybernetics, any possible importers or shipping companies.

But that could take all night. By now, Nick felt the adrenaline of the raid well and truly fade. Exhaustion set into his body as they bundled him into the SUV.

Rie pushed him into the SUV, but remained outside with Kushiel. He blinked blearily at her.

"Rie, what?" he asked.

"I'm going to lead the investigation from here," she said. "Somebody has to. Chloe and Meta will go back with you. Along with Ezekiel." She shot a glare at her sister.

"I should stay out here," Ezekiel whined.

"It's your first assignment. You've done enough for now. Retire with Nicholas."

Then they left. Ezekiel seemed unwilling to engage in any form of conversation, which made it difficult for Nick to stay awake. He drifted off.

CHAPTER 27

When Nick awoke, he found himself on the couch in his living room. Meta sat next to him, and he looked around to see Chloe poking and prodding at his coffee machine. The other Archangels were nowhere to be seen.

"What time is it?" Nick asked blearily, pushing himself upright.

Meta's hand closed around his arm and stabilized him. A few seconds later, his robot barista whirred to life. The ferocity of the sound pulled him fully into wakefulness.

"It is just after 1AM," Meta said once the machine calmed down. "You have been resting."

"So I noticed," he said, rubbing his eyes. "Where's Ezekiel? I thought she came back with us? And Juliet and Rosa?"

"They are patrolling the complex exterior. Given the events of the night, the Host felt that more time must be spent understanding her."

Chloe approached him with a pair of coffees. He accepted one, and just its smell reawakened slumbering parts of his mind.

"Coffee, at this time?" he jokingly asked.

"Your sleep patterns show minimal impact from caffeine

consumption. It is suspected that your high consumption of it has caused your body to acclimate," Chloe said.

"In English?"

She just stared at him. So he turned to Meta.

"That was in English," Meta said. "If you are having difficulty processing natural language, it is recommended to drink the coffee."

"Thanks, Meta."

"It is no problem."

The pair were in a mood, but it felt more playful than serious. A pleasant change given the rough events of the night. Or the day, really.

Nick had been pulled from his bed at an ungodly hour to visit a crime scene, and ended the day with a tense police raid. Flirting with some androids was exactly the sort of thing he needed.

His coffee went down smooth. He failed to recognize the beans, which meant Chloe had changed them out. The days of drinking whatever cheap shit he grabbed from one of the massive grocery chains had died the moment he got Chloe into the stuff. Now it was specialty beans all the way down. He even had a good enough robot barista to taste the difference.

Rie still kept the copy of his old coffee machine that she'd set up to lure him, but he found himself struggling with it more and more each week. The cheap piece of crap massacred any coffee bean that wasn't cheap factory-farmed shit. So he'd drink passable stuff at work, then come home to a coffee with toffee and red cherry notes, from some extravagant greenhouse operation in Africa or South America.

One time, Chloe had actually splurged on the completely natural stuff. Nick couldn't taste the difference, although he understood why it cost so much. Coffee grown the same way his ancestors had done it for centuries lacked the yields necessary for mass production these days. The megacorp processors ignored it, and the price restricted it to the truly dedicated.

"How are you feeling?" Chloe asked once he got halfway through his coffee.

"Tired," he admitted. "It's been a long day."

He slid his drink onto the coffee table, then reflexively reached to turn on the TV. Partway there, he stopped himself.

News would be the opposite of helpful. Instead, he scooted Meta over and made room for Chloe. She eased herself onto the sofa next to him.

Ordinarily, being sandwiched between two beautiful women would be a good thing. This still was, but the cold, hard nature of their bodies reminded him not to fall asleep on them. Neither of them made for a good lap pillow. The worst part was that they'd still try to be one.

"How are the two of you?" he asked. "Because I've wanted to have a proper chat, but haven't found the time."

"There is always plenty of time," Meta said.

"Not during this case."

They inclined their heads.

"The consensus of the Mark 1s is that we are fine," Meta said, her eyes glowing. "Our concerns about the case and Ezckiel are not affecting our operation."

"The same goes for me," Chloe said. "If you are concerned about the time we have spent separated—"

"That's not the issue." He shook his head and placed a hand on both of their arms.

Their gaze shifted to where he touched them, but they made no move to stop him. Then they looked back at him.

"My problem is how... quiet you've been lately," he said. "In general. Rie wasted no time getting as close to me as possible, but I feel that the opposite has happened. Has something changed recently?"

He left his suspicions unsaid. This case had resulted in him taking the reins, in a way that he hadn't since they took down Lieu. Describing himself and the Archangels as partners was harder when he was bulldozing their opinion on the case.

Meta looked at Chloe, who gestured in return. Any communication remained nonverbal—possibly neural—and Meta inclined her head.

"The Mark 1s are satisfied with our current situation," she explained. "Your promotion to Lieutenant Cipher has meant there is no tension between the Mark 1s and 3s. We spend significant time around you, and you communicate readily with us. My own experiences with you are enjoyed vicariously by the rest of the Host."

"Even though nothing is happening?" he asked. "I'm not stupid. I know what you meant by parallel developments months ago."

A tinge of annoyance crossed her face. "Those are still happening. Or do you wish to accelerate them? It is the consensus—"

"Meta, what do you want?"

A long pause resulted. Meta's eyes dimmed and Nick nearly cursed. He ran a hand through his hair.

When she returned to reality, she bit her lip and looked away. "I am... uncertain as to your question's meaning. My desires are aligned with the consensus of the Mark 1s. I am, ultimately, their liaison with you and the representative unit."

"Maybe. But you're also Meta, and I know you have your own quirks." Nick sighed when she refused to bite. "So long as you're genuinely happy—"

"I am," she said rapidly, looking at him with wide eyes. "If anything, the current pace is appreciated. It allows me... and the Host, time to adjust to the possibility of doing more. Of being more." She placed a hand over her heart, then let it drift lower on her body.

He got the picture when it fell to her crotch.

Rie possessed the necessary enhancement for sexual intercourse. Apparently, all the Mark 3s did. But the same couldn't be said of the Mark 1s. Why would they? They were police dolls, intended to enforce order. The fact Sigma had snuck in genitalia for the new dolls only raised eyebrows—or would, if anyone other than Nick knew.

"Do you know if that's going to change?" he asked quietly.

"One of the Sigma researchers has indicated that adjustments can be made to a Mark 1. They are fascinated by the effects that naming me has had on my processes. Once the case is over, I will visit Sigma's laboratory for the procedure," Meta said.

He nodded. Nothing more to say there.

But when he turned to face Chloe, she had vanished.

"Chloe?"

Rustling escaped his bedroom.

By the time he rose and investigated it, she'd returned. But instead of the usual Chloe, wearing her uniform and looking like a dangerous police enforcer, he got an adorable Chloe, replete with purple sundress, bare legs and arms, and as much cleavage as was possible in her petite frame.

"Do I look good, Nick?" she asked, hesitance in her voice.

"I'd wondered where that went," he mused, rubbing his chin. "You look beautiful."

She blushed.

"Also, it's very lewd to wear a sundress without any underwear. Imagine what would happen if a gust blew past."

Her eyes attempted to shoot holes in him. He wished that Meta joined in the teasing, but she remained completely stationary on the sofa.

"Meta?" he asked.

"Do you want me to leave?" she asked, voice quiet as she looked between the two of them.

Instantly, Nick realized why Chloe had dressed up. He'd been ignoring her for a while, but she had been catty toward Rie earlier. This was her first real chance to do anything with him without Rie around to stop her or claim him.

But Chloe simply shook her head before he answered. "No. You mentioned that we don't share enough with the Mark 1s. If you want..."

"Uh, hold on," Nick said, raising a hand. "I'm skipping ahead here, but are you suggesting we have sex while Meta records us for the Mark 1s?"

"Yes," they both said together.

Well, he was apparently outnumbered. By about 4000 to 1, if he included the Host.

"Alright," he said.

Chloe gingerly took his wrists in her hands and led him to his bedroom. The padding of Meta's feet behind them indicated she followed them.

Once inside, Chloe reached up and popped Nick's earpieces out. Without a word, Meta produced the soundproof case he kept them in each night and Chloe dropped them inside. It shut with a click, before vanishing. They had privacy.

For what little it mattered if Meta recorded everything. She snapped the door shut before settling into a corner of the room, her eyes locked onto Nick.

"Are you just going to watch?" he asked, then winced at how that sounded.

"This is Chloe's time," Meta said. "She is merely allowing us to share certain visuals and auditory experiences."

"I will share the other sensations I feel with the Host, for later replication," Chloe said.

Nick wanted to scream out, "Please don't!" but knew his chance to reject his fate had long since passed. This was his life now.

Somehow, he knew Kushiel would cackle herself to sleep—or some sort of state of inactivity—once she found out about this.

His mind returned to the present as Chloe's hands gripped the hem of her sundress. Her eyes lowered and her face reddened as she raised it bit by bit. The tender, pale flesh of her upper thighs revealed themselves to Nick.

And then came the awkward part. The armored plate.

Just like with Rie, Chloe possessed an odd ceramic plate that covered her crotch and lower torso.

"Do... do I look pretty?" she asked in a small voice.

The brittle sound of her voice, so unlike Rie's utter confidence on their first night, forced Nick into action. He stepped forward. His arms wrapped around Chloe, causing her to gasp, and he pressed his lips against hers.

If he was unkind, he'd describe the sensation literally. But what mattered was that he was kissing Chloe, and that made all the difference. He felt her love through the kiss, as well as her lack of confidence in herself that she hid away. Or at least, lack of confidence in approaching him.

When they parted, her tongue lapped against his lips and she moaned ever so softly. Her eyes glistened.

"Does that answer your question?" he asked, placing his hands on her hips.

She blinked. "Do... do kisses usually take the place of verbal answers in sexual situations?"

Nick closed his eyes and stifled a laugh. It took a lot of effort.

For naught, as he saw Chloe pouting at him when he opened them.

"I think you and the Host need to read and watch more romances and spend less time watching porn," he said drily.

"We are very familiar with romance," she insisted.

"Uh huh. Then you should know exactly how I feel about you, Chloe," he said, brushing a hand through her fluffy white hair.

She bit her lip and closed in for another kiss. This one barely lasted a few seconds, but she wanted another, and another. Her hands ran up and down his chest. Then they slipped under his shirt and pulled it over his head and arms.

"I think you're sexy," she said very awkwardly, like someone who knew the line, had gone over it a thousand times in her head, but never spoken it aloud.

"The Host advises—" Meta began to say.

Chloe threw a pillow at her, and Meta wisely shut up. The redness of the Mark 3's face threatened to cause her to overheat and shutdown, and she balled her fists at her side.

"I get it," Nick said, mirth in his voice as he cuddled her against him. "You want to hear me say it, don't you?"

"Please. It's important to me," she mumbled.

"You're beautiful, Chloe. Exactly as you are, no matter what you wear, or whether you're in this unit or a new one. Because you're Chloe," he said.

She stiffened against him for a moment, then practically turned to jelly in his arms. Metaphorically, given she felt like solid steel and the weight of her leaning against him caused his calves to tense up.

"I've always wondered what this would feel like," she whispered in his ear. "I avoided simulations because I didn't want to cheapen it. This had to be unique. You make me feel real, Nick. Like Chloe. Not a member of the Host, or a doll, or your liaison. This is something only I can experience. Because nobody else is Chloe."

"That's right," he said.

His arms ran up and down her back, and he even drew circles across what he felt to be her "bones." Whether she felt the sensation or not didn't matter. The effort did.

Rie was his partner, and had given him this chance to be something more. But Chloe had been with him almost the entire way, and even recruited him.

She took a step back. His arms fell away and he waited for her next action.

Once again, she raised her sundress. This time, her usual confidence was on display. She smirked at Nick.

Then a series of loud snaps echoed off the walls. He reached out and removed the plate, then set it aside. Meta slipped it beside her.

Chloe's cute little slit lay before him, and her soft tummy exposed above it. His fingers ran across her delicate skin, eliciting soft gasps as traced a path downward.

Then he reached her pussy and slipped one, two, three fingers inside. A moan burst from her lips instantly.

"N-Nick," Chloe gasped out as he massaged the inside of her slit. "I'm all yours. Please..."

Juices drooled all over his hand, now slick enough to slide deeper and deeper into the doll's pussy. He pumped his fingers back and forth like a piston, fully aware of what her preferences would be.

Her moans increased in intensity. She let go of her sundress and gripped onto Nick, nearly pushing him over. Squelching sounds escaped her pussy every time he pulled back.

"Faster, faster, faster," she gasped out. "I can feel it coming!"

With one hand, he gently pushed her back onto the bed while maintaining his pace with the other. Chloe flopped onto the covers, juices squirting from her crotch. Her body bent double, her legs up in the air and holding her dress up, allowing him to see her pussy squirt and spread with each motion of his fingers.

"Ah!" Chloe moaned right as her body seized up.

Her pussy juices gushed over his hand and her lower lips quivered as she orgasmed. He slowly pulled back.

After a little while, she smiled up at him. "Now for the real thing?" she asked plaintively.

Her hands flailed for his pants, but he was just out of reach. A tent had formed in his pants as his cock struggled to break free. Watching and listening to Chloe had been far too much for his body to resist.

He moved closer to her and she popped his length free. With a happy gasp, she ran her fingers along his shaft and around his tip. She tapped against the very end while looking up him. He bit his lip at the pleasure that ran along his cock.

"Sex?" she asked in a low voice.

"Absolutely," he said.

Chloe let him go, then flattened her legs against her body. Her glistening pussy waited for his attention. He gave it to her, rubbing his cock along the outside of her slit.

"Don't tease," she mumbled. "Fuck me like you do Rie."

"You know what you want, don't you?" he teased, still not sticking it in.

She merely glared at him.

"Oh, fine," he said, feigning exasperation.

Then he pressed his cock tip against her pussy lips, and her lips parted in shock. Her gasp as he slowly slid inside her was music to his ears. A sweet, arousing chorus that kept his prick rock hard as it pried her open.

"You're so big." Another moan escaped Chloe.

Rather than answer, he gripped her thighs tighter and hilted himself in her. His very tip pressed against her deepest regions, kissing her internals. She bucked in response, her entire tummy wiggling as she drizzled juices all over the bedsheets. His balls dripped with the stuff as he rubbed them against her ass.

Although, he had to be careful. Rie had nearly ended all dreams of children one time when she nearly squashed his sack.

Chloe's pussy and belly felt as soft and real as any woman's, but the rest of her body was built to crush him like an ant.

Nick pressed himself against her, squashing Chloe against the bed. She sank into the mattress. Her eyes stared up at him, lidded and glazed with pleasure. Her insides wrapped tightly around him, begging for him to use her as intended.

"Please," she mumbled.

"Please what?" he teased.

She pouted at him. "You know what I want. Stop teasing."

If Rie was spice, Chloe was all sugar. His cock almost doubled in size when her voice tickled his eardrums and powerful endorphins rippled from his brain throughout his body.

He pulled himself back, ripping a gasp from her throat, then jackhammered against her with a wet slap. Juices splashed all over his body and even got on the floor. Again and again, he railed her into the bed.

"I'm... I'm..." she tried to say, unable to form the words as raw pleasure overrode her directives.

He simply grunted and fucked her faster. Her mouth hung open, letting loose a low, sweet moan. His cock roared with heat as it slammed into her depths over and over.

Then he let himself go and flooded her with his seed. Chloe's eyes widened. Her body snapped into orgasm, as if programmed to do so in response to his climax, and her muscles quivered. He saw her toes curl inward while her pussy tried to milk him dry.

"This is better than Rie said it would be," Chloe said with a smile that lit up her face. "I'm yours. Your Chloe."

Nick had only just pulled his cock out of her with a wet pop, allowing a drizzle of white to slide out of her still-perfect slit. Despite that, her words kept him at full mast.

For now, he supposed. Dirty talk or not, he probably needed some juice for a second round.

Just then, he heard the apartment door open. He froze.

Chloe's hand closed around his cock as she turned herself over, attempting to guide him inside for round two.

"Um," he began to say.

Ezekiel's voice interrupted his thoughts. "Lieutenant, where are you? Are you alright? Your earpiece stopped picking up anything and the Mark 1s are focusing on some private part of the Host's network. What's—"

Naturally, she opened the bedroom door without knocking.

Chloe didn't pause in her attempts to keep going. Hell, she didn't even look at Ezekiel. Neither did Meta, who had shifted position to have a great view of the action.

"Um," Nick said, as the perfect picture of eloquence.

Ezekiel's eyes locked onto his cock, covered in pussy juices and cum and wrapped in Chloe's hand. She visibly gulped, face reddening.

Then she slammed the door shut. He heard her thumping away down the hall.

"You are softening," Chloe said.

"Yeah, humans do that," he said, staring into space. "I'll probably need some juice for another round."

"I shall retrieve it," Meta said.

The door opened and closed as she left. Nick found the situation so ridiculous that he couldn't even laugh.

"How many rounds are possible in a single night?" Chloe asked, eyes wide.

He gulped when he saw her innocent but seductive expression, especially with her hand still closed around his cock.

"I think I'm good for a few," he said.

CHAPTER 28

The address for the NLF meeting turned out to be an unassuming townhouse in quiet suburbia. Nick stepped out of the robot taxi and looked around with his hands in his coat pockets.

In front of him sat a long line of identical gray double-story terrace houses with connected walls, tiny lawns, and neatly trimmed hedges. Behind him were the same buildings, but in beige.

Truly, suburbia felt like slipping into limbo.

The worst part was that these shoebox shitholes probably cost an obscene amount of money. Any amount of greenery came with a premium that matched the price of Nick's entire apartment. He'd grown up in a similar place to this. The mortgage had seemed astronomical when he'd been old enough to comprehend the figures his parents struggled to pay each month.

Yet they had lucked out. If Nick tried to buy into a quiet, monotonous suburb like this today, he'd pay several times the price. The obscene asset inflation did little to help his parents, either. They still struggled to afford their original mortgage. If they wanted to sell up and move, every other house cost just as much or even more.

A rising tide lifted all boats, but some a lot more than others. And it didn't matter much if you didn't have a boat to begin with.

Several more taxis pulled up behind his. Eight Paladins in total stepped out in their dark uniforms, all carrying weapons of varying lethality. No police markings adorned them.

For the first time in his recent memory, no Archangels accompanied him.

Yet they remained with him in spirit. He could still hear their voices.

"We're not dead, Nicholas," Rie reminded him over his earpiece in a dry tone.

"It's almost as if you're still with me, Rie," he said, pretending to wipe a tear from his eye. "I can picture your face as if I saw you just an hour ago."

"You saw me fifteen minutes ago."

Nobody joined him on the street at this time. At 9AM on a Monday, most of the inhabitants were either logging on for work using their implants or had long since left for work.

As for why he stood here with only the Paladins for company...

"Are you absolutely certain you want to go in alone, Nick?" Helena asked. "Archangel strike teams are in position on nearby streets. You only need to speak the codeword and they will swoop in. The Paladins are emitting a signal that acts as a dead man's switch as well."

"I am. We know absolutely nothing about the current state of the NLF. Lieu was a naïve madman, but what did he leave behind?" Nick shook his head. "Travis barely understood what his sponsor was even trying to do. If we shut down the NLF, another movement will sprout up in its place. I'd rather understand this group than see it replaced by a worse one."

A few businesses getting their windows smashed in was

nothing compared to train stations being bombed or shootings in the streets. They still knew nothing about what that fake NLF had been about.

Hell, for all Nick knew, they hadn't been a fake NLF. Somebody might have created a new one that was willing to take the violent actions necessary to bring down the Spires.

"The Host deems this above an acceptable risk threshold," Meta said. "We only detect a single person in the household, but it may be full of NLF terrorists."

"We've had it staked out all night. How many people went in?" he asked.

"... five. As directed, we took no action against them."

"Hence why I'm taking the Paladins with me. If I don't take any risks, we won't progress the case," he said. "Focus on GWT. I'm worried they'll pull something now that we took out most of the assassins. If they panic, who knows what they might do."

No more objections blared over his earpiece, so Nick decided to get on with things. The meeting with the NLF had been set for 9AM. He needed to file charges against Lucida before lunchtime. While he expected the process to be effectively automatic, as the judicial mainframes should simply shrug and let him keep investigating, he wanted to cover his bases.

He crossed the threshold of the house's property line. Before he even reached the door, it opened.

A man slightly older than Nick stood in the doorway. He wore a lot of plaid, had neatly combed golden hair, and a bushy beard and mustache. Not much muscle. The sort of friendly guy Nick saw a lot of in the office during his days in Tartarus.

Instantly, Helena spoke in Nick's ear, "Aaron Harolds. Senior Engineer at Creux Limited. 33. Eldest son of the owners of this property."

She must have identified him through the Paladins. Ironically, this went against the entire point of not bringing the Archangels.

If Helena saw everything the Paladins did, then the Archangels could as well.

Nobody said the NLF understood technology. If they did, then they'd never have gotten in the mess with Lieu. Nick played along with their requests because they barely hampered him.

"You're him. The detective," Aaron said, biting his lip. He looked at the Paladins. "I, uh, can't tell if they're Archangels. Are they?"

"You're asking me? Couldn't I just lie?"

"I mean, yeah, but the, uh, movement could tell. Probably."

Nick raised an eyebrow. "You're not with them."

Aaron shook his head. "No. I'm just a... sympathizer, I suppose. I'm lending the house to provide neutral ground for a meeting, but I don't really do all the fancy cipher stuff. I'm a software engineer. Backend IT stuff. I can set-up a mainframe and initialize some dolls, but that's about it."

That explained the plaid.

"They're not Archangels. Consider them my personal security. They usually stay in the Spires." Nick gestured past Aaron. "Can I come in?"

"Sure. They're in the living room. Not that there are many rooms."

They stepped into the house, which led straight into an open-plan kitchen and dining room. The place looked positively ancient. Nothing had been renovated or updated since before Nick had been born.

He stopped dead and looked around as the Paladins filed in. Aaron gave him an odd look.

"This reminds me of home," Nick admitted. "Or what it used to look like. Mom did up the place when I moved out. I'm guessing your folks like the old-fashioned look."

Aaron gave him a wry smile. "Pretty much. They don't understand why anybody would want stoves or fridges that need a neural implant or heating you can turn on with a thought. I guess this is more your jam, huh? I've read about you."

"Lots of people have these days."

"Me? I can't even afford something this old and cramped." The engineer shoved his hands in his pockets. "My place is a shoebox the size of this kitchen. I live above work, so that's nice. No transport cost or commute. But I have friends who pay half what I do and just work from home most of the time."

"Is that why you're supporting the NLF?"

"Is that a crime? Will you cart me off?"

Nick snorted. "It probably is a crime."

"It is," Helena informed him. "The NLF is a terrorist group and aiding it in any way carries harsh penalties. For today, I have filed his assistance away as facilitating a meeting between police informants and us."

"But," Nick continued as if Helena hadn't spoken in his ear, "I'm not here about that. I have bigger fish to fry."

"Nice to know you're on our side for once." Aaron crossed his arms.

"What's our side here?"

"Us. The people of Babylon. This place could be fantastic. I remember it being that way when I was a kid. Some days I wonder if I was just a stupid child or if things really were better." The engineer sighed. "Everyone talks about the riots. Even my folks speak about them in hushed whispers. But this is home. It's my shithole."

Nick nodded. It frustrated him that the random person he bumped into while meeting the NLF made more sense than almost every asshole from the Spires he dealt with.

The difference was that Aaron hardly understood how to fix that problem. Neither did Nick for that matter.

Aaron led him into the next room. Five men and women sat

inside on aging furniture. Somebody had pushed the couches to one side.

All five individuals wore the usual baggy clothing of the NLF plus helmets. They'd come to meet Nick but wouldn't risk revealing anything. Sensible. Despite their demand, if he captured any video with another doll, the Archangels could use it to arrest them.

"You came," the central figure said in a female voice. It lacked distortion and sounded female.

But Nick instantly knew it was fake. She spoke with the same artificial voice as half the AI assistants installed on every phone or computer in Babylon.

"I did, Aesir Samantha," he said, crossing his arms.

"Call me Victoria."

Damn, no response to his jibe. No fun allowed, apparently.

"No guns?" he asked.

"They'd be pointless. Meeting you at all is a risk. If you wished it, we'd all be arrested."

The other four NLF members nodded in agreement. They acted like flunky yesmen or bobbleheads. If they possessed their own opinions, they kept them to themselves.

Nick raised an eyebrow. "Why risk meeting me at all then? You could easily give Aaron a radio or some other old transmitter and speak to me that way."

Aaron seized up at the mention of his name. Did he seriously think Nick wouldn't know it?

"You'd trace it," Victoria said.

"Then run it through the Altnet. Or dolls. Lieu proved that the Archangels can't trace every signal instantly. Even those mercs he hired couldn't track him that easily."

This time it was Victoria's turn to freeze. She evidently didn't appreciate the mention of the NLF's former sponsor.

"You're rather blunt, aren't you?" she asked. "There's no

public acknowledgement of Captain Lieu's involvement with us. In fact, even we're not entirely certain he was our partner in the Tartarus raid."

"Yeah, well, I am. I shot the guy for it."

He'd said that to get a response, and he got one. All the NLF except Victoria started, and Aaron's eyes practically popped out of his skull. Muttering erupted.

Victoria shushed them. A sigh escaped her.

"Perhaps blunt is too light a descriptor," she said. "Whatever methods we might use to escape you, they would be meaningless. Our time is limited right now without your mercy."

"Oh?" Nick feigned ignorance.

"I went to sleep on Saturday believing our fight to be difficult, but possible. I awoke to a combined onslaught from the Spires, cipher circles, and black companies unlike anything else in history. Altnet rumors suggested the NLF were raiding data centers in broad daylight. Archangel squads raided every business and home we'd been close to for the past six months, proving that you intentionally ignored us."

So the NLF had put two and two together. Even before Nick joined, the Archangels never squeezed them too hard. That left them plenty of room to move when a major case needed them to.

If the NLF believed they acted in secrecy, the Archangels could wring them dry far easier than if they actively built deeper rat holes.

"And that's why you're offering me information," Nick said. "The deal I offered Hamish was simple. You act as an informant for my current case, and I overlook you."

"It's that simple?" Victoria sounded doubtful.

"Your implants are still working and I have no interest in Aaron. Hamish and the rest we arrested in Alcatraz can't go free, but they'll be charged like ordinary NLF vandals, instead of terrorists." Nick shrugged. "So long as you're not trying to blow up train stations or data centers, you're not my problem."

"We've moved on from those days. In fact, that's what got us involved in this mess." She rested her head on one dainty palm and harrumphed. "I'm told you're interested in our arrangement with Kraus. I can do you one better. This all started with the murder in the Grand Westphalian Trust, yes? I know all about that."

Nick narrowed his eyes and said nothing.

"Ah, I thought so. But before I tell you, I have a question of my own."

"Shoot."

"That's what you do. I prefer words over bullets, detective."

He rolled his eyes at the cheap shot. Pun intended.

"My question is simple. What drives you to act as a defender of the Spires? You are no scion of business, no inheritor of trillions, and certainly no silver-tongued demagogue. No reward awaits you for aiding them. When you've served your purpose, your masters will cast you aside."

Nick resisted the urge to snort. Of course it was some question of character and served up in a pompous manner.

He'd been right to suspect the NLF higher-ups of being too good for the street talk of those on the ground. Did they adjust their manner of speech when dealing with people like Hamish?

"The answer is that I don't," he said flatly. "If I was defending the Spires, I wouldn't waste my time investigating GWT."

"Then why work as a police officer? Let alone a detective in the most oppressive division of all."

Because that division offered me freedom, and the chance to accomplish something nobody else would.

Nick left that unsaid. He merely shrugged and said, "The Archangels aren't what you think they are. I'm a cipher. I work with dolls and mainframes. From fly-by-night black companies to the police. I'm there for the robots, not the suits. And just like the robots, the idea is to get the job done right."

"I feel that makes you little better than a robot, detective," Victoria said. "And every human, no matter how soulless they may seem, deserves better than a robot."

"Given some of the humans I know, and some of the robots, I'm not so sure."

The two of them stared at each other for several seconds. He wished that there was something to see in Victoria's face, instead of a matte black visor.

She sighed again. "I see. You are a difficult man to understand. But we made a deal, and I shall honor it. This situation started with the murder of Julian Garlowne. What would you say if I told you he worked for us?"

"This is unlikely," Helena immediately said. "No NLF implant was detected during the autopsy, and neither was evidence of physical intrusion to remove one."

Nick found himself agreeing with Helena. The entire reason this murder remained so difficult to resolve was that Julian had nothing to tag him as suspicious, other than some possible unhappiness with his employer.

"If he's working for you, why doesn't have an implant?" he asked.

Victoria shrugged. "Not everyone who wishes to support our cause is willing to go so far. Furthermore, his employer would find it almost immediately. Financial institutions are extremely strict regarding illegal neural mods."

"So I've heard. Invasive monthly scans by a nurse doll to produce a list of every app, mod, and device you use," Nick said. "The Archangels can dig deeper if they want, but this is close. Hell, we know that they harvest the personal data of their employees. They even enforce non-competes that way."

The other NLF members shared looks. Nick had no idea what the motion meant, as he couldn't see their faces.

"You certainly understand the depravities that many of Babylon's megacorps engage in," Victoria said.

"The banks offer impressive golden handcuffs. Massive pay packages, great conditions, fully paid and discounted holidays. They're basically a retirement home for talented ciphers—so long as they don't let their skills rust." He shrugged. "I got a few offers after Neural Spike, before everyone realized the Spires had shackled me to Tartarus."

"Quite the power our 'liberty-loving' overlords have, no? To dictate the company that an otherwise innocent man can work for and thereby limit his compensation."

Nick snorted. "I wasn't exactly innocent."

"Neural Spike conducted government research. One might draw comparisons to the Spires' destruction of the company to that of ancient dictators bricking up the architects who built their tombs and secret passages."

Whatever he thought of the NLF as a whole, Nick realized that the leadership weren't fools. Misguided, maybe. Or perhaps just furious at Babylon and willing to act where others wouldn't.

Victoria certainly lacked a silver tongue, but she lacked the aggressive naivete of the NLF members Nick had become accustomed to.

"Let's return to Julian. He lacks an implant, so I'll need some evidence. Or at least an explanation," he said.

"He lost his job in New Geneva thanks to the Trust's misdeeds, but that didn't turn him on his corporate masters. But over the years, they refused his reasonable request to regain his position in audit, and pushed him into financial hardship. He grew suspicious of the reasons. Eventually, he turned to us," Victoria said.

"For revenge."

"For the truth," she insisted. "He never wished to join the Front. Rather, we gave him the software and knowledge necessary to infiltrate the Bank's systems and leak the necessary data. We had this thanks to... another inside agent."

That caught Nick's attention, but he let her continue her story.

"However, he was killed on that night. And then it all unraveled. Another 'NLF' emerged, with powerful explosives and cybernetics, conducting daring public attacks discussed widely. The news seemed to be almost deliberately disseminated. Then the worst happened, and here we are." Victoria sighed in a burst of static.

"Let's say I believe you. That doesn't explain your connection to Kraus. And it leaves a gaping hole." He pointed at her. "If I couldn't find out that Julian was NLF, how the hell would GWT? Plus, if they knew he was an agent, why not just tell me that and frame you for everything from the start?"

"A fair point." Victoria tilted her head, and he bet she was smiling beneath that damn helmet. "But if you walked into the Trust on Thursday and they told you that they'd killed an NLF agent, how would that have played out?"

Nick opened his mouth to spit out an automatic response, then paused.

Immediately, a half-dozen responses from the voices in his head gave answers. Well, they weren't actually voices in his head but the various AIs who thought they knew better than him.

He ignored them. His own answer took on a winding course.

"Julian lacked an implant. That would have been a red flag. Also, there was no evidence he attempted to steal any data," Nick said slowly. "That was mostly because somebody was covering up the murder. The question is, would they have needed to?"

"I can't answer that for you."

"I can. There's no way in hell they could have let me see them murdering a random person in cold blood, given the lack of evidence he was NLF." Nick ran a hand through his hair. "I doubt they even knew he was NLF. Did you knock out GWT's network to aid his leaks?"

"If we could do such a thing, do you think we'd risk meeting you in person?"

He let out a bark of laughter. "True. This meeting wouldn't be happening if you had that level of cipher capability. That makes it even less likely they'd suspect him, given Kraus's tools wouldn't lead back to you."

A few murmurs of surprise escaped the other NLF members. Oops, Nick probably shouldn't have let slip that they'd fucked up meeting with him like this.

"My guess is that the bank didn't want me to look closely. No matter what, the moment they killed Julian, I'd be digging like a dog for a bone. The fact he's an NLF agent was something I never strongly considered." He raised an eyebrow. "Which is why I'm doubtful. Your story adds up with what I know of Julian's motives, but there's no hard proof."

"Perhaps," Victoria said. "But that's where our connection to Kraus comes in. The reason we were interested in the Trust started months ago, well before we approached Julian. Managing Director Andre Gauthier, the right hand of James von Magnus, told us of widespread fraud in the Trust. Falsified accounts, misappropriated funds, trusts whose assets were used to shore up failing investments. In his mind, GWT was a house of cards that merely awaited a storm."

Nick remained silent. The NLF would say this sort of thing about a bank.

But that name...

"Magnus said an Andre recently left," he said.

"Indeed." Victoria stood and walked past Nick.

Immediately, the Paladins raised their weapons. Everyone froze, but she kept walking. He waved the dolls down.

With her back to him, Victoria continued talking, "Andre wouldn't risk his own position by sending us the files himself. Instead, he acted as a proxy when working with Kraus. But that cunning cipher found out. While he left us with the tools he developed—which we gave Julian—the price was that Andre retired."

"Kraus forced Andre into retirement? Wait..." Nick's eyes widened. "Andre was the secret client that Kraus mentioned. No wonder the bastard immediately knew the data I needed when Julian came up. Kraus had been paid to retrieve it by you!"

Victoria laughed. "Amusing, no? He refused Andre and then exiled him from the city. Then we sent Julian, and he died for that data. Then you convinced Kraus, and the Trust killed him. One can only wonder how devastating this data must be, that it is so difficult to gather."

But while Victoria amused herself, Nick's mind raced. Something about how Kraus described his secret client bothered him, especially in the context of something recent.

"What happened to Andre? You said he got exiled?" Nick asked.

"Indeed. He used his fortune to purchase a solar yacht and leave us all behind for the wonders of space. I believe he even rode the Pax Americana space elevator. Quite the marvel of technology, so much so that us plebians must never sully it."

Space... Andre went to space.

And what else was in space but the stars?

"And Kraus just... forgave him? Gave you his tools and said 'good luck' for deceiving him? That's not like him. He could have destroyed you," Nick said.

"Indeed." Victoria paused. "No, not quite. Andre did say that he had paid for the tools in some way. Presumably with money. I believe that is how that cipher conducted his business."

Nick genuinely couldn't tell if Victoria was being sarcastic. That artificial voice of hers made her impossible to read at times.

But he didn't care.

"I think we're done here," Nick said.

"Oh? You think you have what you need?"

"Unless you're going to send me incriminating messages that paint Julian and Andre as NLF agents, this is the best I'll get. I'm already pretty convinced that you and those cyborgs in Alcatraz are working toward different ends. My interest is finding Kraus's data."

He didn't bother saying goodbye and simply left. The Paladins closed the door behind him.

Outside, several SUVs waited for them. He scowled.

"Don't," he ordered. "We're leaving."

"Nicholas—" Rie began.

"Lieutenant—" Ezekiel tried to say.

"No. I made a deal. The NLF aren't a threat right now. Plus, I have a lead I want to focus on," he said. "Where the hell is Lucy?"

CHAPTER 29

"You think that Kraus somehow hid a data backup in space?" Rie asked, her voice the pitch-perfect example of barely maintained credulity.

"Maybe not space," Nick said, feeling a touch stupid after explaining his epiphany on the ride to the Spires. "But close enough. Lucy talked about Kraus going to the stars, and possibly meeting him there. Kraus hinted that his secret client, who appears to be Andre, escaped to a solar yacht. And one of the rules of backups in case of disaster recovery is to have one outside the country."

He sat in his usual seat in a police SUV, in the middle of a convoy tearing toward the Spires. Lucy was being held in the cells rather than evidence storage, presumably for humanitarian reasons.

Or would that be dollitarian reasons? Nick wasn't really sure.

Rie and Chloe sat either side of him. Meta, Juliet, and Rosa opposite him. Ezekiel remained in the Spires along with Kushiel. While she remained in his ear, there hadn't been a need for her to join them on this mission.

Although Nick suspected the real reason was that she still hadn't forgiven him for last night. It wasn't his fault that she'd stumbled in on him fucking Chloe. They'd even put his earpieces in the soundproof case to give her some privacy, but no, she had to investigate and learned about the birds and the bees.

"He did have backups outside Neo Westphalia," Chloe corrected.

"Digital ones, right? And they all got nuked. I bet the guy followed the rules for his new ones. There was probably a hidden one in his home in Asgard or Alcatraz, but they nuked everything. We have no clue where he's stashed the one in Neo Westphalia. But right now we have clues pointing us to space, and he has a route to it."

"A route is only half of it," Rie said. "Pax Americana is locked down tighter than the Spires. All data transfers are encrypted and tied to specific users, all of whom are individually verified by the IDSTA. Down here, a virus or piece of malware can be damaging, but rarely in terms of life. In space, critical systems can fail and take out decades of investment."

"I know. That's why it's the best place to hide a backup. It would also explain why the dead man's switch never activated," Nick pressed. "If Kraus has one final backup—one last ace up his sleeve—hidden away in the most secure place on Earth, then he still has hope."

"He's dead, Nicholas."

He didn't respond to that, instead saying, "Kraus would have made his plans under the assumption that he needed to recover his business. Have we been able to check anything on this Andre Gauthier?"

"No," Helena answered. "He's independently wealthy and a former resident of the Spires. Government records confirm that he is in space, however. His citizenship is suspended for the duration that he is ex-Terra."

"What?"

"The laws of Earth don't operate past the mesosphere," Rie said. "Officially, the Pax Americana treaty requires individuals active in space to operate under what is termed solar law. Think of it like maritime law, but for space."

Sounded complicated. Nick supposed it was something for the rich to worry about. And the corporations pilfering the solar system.

"So we know Andre is up there, but that's it?" he asked.

"Yes. Even without the shield of the Spires, the IDSTA is even stricter. They operate completely non-politically in order to protect the Pax Americana space elevator. It is possible to gain access to the information of solar citizens, but only under extreme circumstances."

Nick scowled. So close, yet so far.

But this only further cemented his theory.

"Let's say I'm not crazy," he said.

"A bold assumption."

"Kraus finds out Andre is working with the NLF. Rather than destroy Andre's standing in the Spires—which he could do, and even suggested as such to us—he blackmails him into hosting a backup for him. Nobody could touch it, because the IDSTA ignores governments. But Kraus could call in the favor. Correct?"

Rie opened her mouth to argue, then closed it.

"Shit, Rie, he actually got you," Kushiel said over the earpiece. "Yeah, Waite, that's basically it. 'Cept how does he update his backup?"

"Somebody like Andre doesn't leave the Spires forever. He's bound to maintain some connection," he said. "If word reached him about Kraus, he probably cut it, though. Kraus probably maintained it with data drops."

"That is feasible," Helena said. "The Host often tracks Kraus's activities through the movements of his dolls. Data drops that lead to the Spires are common, but impossible to track to their final destination."

Rie nodded begrudgingly. "This almost holds up. It just leaves us with nothing useful. Without Kraus, we cannot access the data. We lack his credentials. And as you said, chasing Andre is useless. We'd spend days gaining access to the Spires."

"But what about the space elevator?" Nick asked. "I know that the data transmission cables run down that stupid thing. The IDSTA not only scan everything, but they likely have huge data caches and peering servers to reduce latency. The Altnet would be unusable otherwise. Could we get access to that?"

"I just told you, Nicholas, the IDSTA—"

"Andre's a terrorist suspect, connected to the assassination of Kraus, and we believe he's stolen the database all the megacorps are worried about." Nick smirked. "Sure, it's a stretch, but are we really lying?"

They stopped at a checkpoint while the Archangels processed his idea. Nick leaned over while the window rolled down and let a Mark 1 "authenticate" him. The military remained out in force still, despite last night's events.

Just like last time, a Kestrel squadron seemed to intentionally fly overhead. Definitely not a coincidence.

Meta was the first to speak. "The Host deems this plan to have some probability of success, assuming confirmation by Kraus's secretary doll, Lucy. Additional evidence to corroborate the NLF statements will likely be required by the judicial mainframes to gain official permission."

"Permission?"

"Nicholas, the IDSTA isn't going to care if we turn up. In fact, they'll vaporize us if we try to enter the demilitarized zone near the space elevator without permission," Rie said.

"I said it before, but I don't think the IDSTA knows the meaning of demilitarized."

"They mean it in the sense that no military on Earth other than theirs can operate in that space."

"That sounds more like how territory works, Rie. You know, normal warfare."

She prodded him in the shoulder hard enough to bruise.

"My point, Nicholas, is that we need the permission of the Spires to have a chance of success," she ground out. "We get that through the judicial mainframes. The Host is right. We need more evidence."

Fortunately, there was somebody else who might grant it to them. She happened to be next-door neighbors to Lucy.

The cells resided on the lower levels of the police Spire, supposedly for fire safety reasons. What that said about the fire safety of everyone else, Nick didn't know.

Unlike the regular floors, he needed to physically scan himself in. A pair of Archangels stood guard alongside railgun-toting Custodians, but none of them moved to authenticate Nick. Instead, Rie gestured him toward the hand scanner built into the wall. It appeared identical to the one outside Rie's taskforce office that he regularly used.

The bland office gave way to featureless concrete. See-through bulletproof polymers protected electronic glass throughout the halls, and they displayed timers to meal time and lights out. Each cell had one that showed some obnoxious variety streamer with a squeaky voice. Truly cruel and unusual punishment.

Most cells appeared empty, but this was only one wing. The entire floor could hold a small prison's worth of miscreants. Longer-term stays apparently got pushed further back, where security was tighter but access to additional facilities was provided during the day.

Gun turrets swiveled to follow Nick as he followed Meta to the cells containing Lucida and Lucy. He knew they were close when he saw a Mark 1 standing guard.

Lucida wore an oversized t-shirt and hot pants, but little else. Clothes had been collected from her apartment to ensure she could at least remain clean. She bounced off the narrow mattress pressed against the wall of the cell when she saw Nick.

"Holy shit, so you weren't a holographic invention of the Archangels," she snapped. "You arrest me over these bullshit murder charges, then ignore me for the whole fucking weekend. Did you think I'd confess if you make me watch the city's dumbest fucking streamers get in fake fights with each other for drama and money all weekend?"

"No. That's a thing?" Nick asked, bemused.

"Apparently. Not like I had anything else to do. Fucking dream eaters locked down my implant so hard that I can't even do math."

"You know there's a reason they make us learn how to do math by hand, right?"

"Oh, fuck you." She paused. "I'm not doing that, either. Not even in your dreams."

"If Nicholas dreamed it, you would do what he wished," Meta said abruptly.

Everyone stared at her. Even the other Mark 1.

"It is technically true," she said.

"Technically," the Mark 1 said. "The Host wishes to clarify the literal nature of your words, and that they are not a threat."

"They are not a threat. Nicholas has no desire for you, Lucida Harm."

"Such a burn," Lucida drawled, rolling her eyes. "Are you here for me or the boring ass doll next door? Or am I free to go? I know my rights."

"Then you'd know that we have a couple of hours. Time for a chat," Nick said.

Without another word, the cell door opened. Lucida glared at it, then abruptly collapsed to the floor. The Mark 1 strode in and hauled the cipher over her shoulders, then carried her down the corridor. Nick and the others followed.

While the Mark 1 dumped Lucida in a small interrogation room that looked as cramped and uninviting as they looked in every movie, most of the group sidled into the observation room next to it. The two-way mirror was currently covered in a shutter, but the Archangels wouldn't need it. They could use one of the many hidden cameras in the room.

Nick entered the room and leaned against the wall by the door. Juliet and Rosa joined him. The Mark 1 stood behind Lucida after propping her up in the chair.

Then the cipher regained her ability to move.

"Fuck you. Fuck you. Fuck you," she started spouting, then stopped, fury in her eyes. "This is fucking evil, you know."

"Sure. One could say that about murdering somebody in cold blood."

"Uh huh. It's a frame-up. You admitted it yourself, didn't—"

"The footage was real. Wholly unedited, undoctored, and real, right from a security camera. We still don't know how it magically got back onto Tiferet, but if the Archangels and police mainframes can't find any evidence that it's fake, it's real," he said. "It's sloppy as fuck. Why would you even bother walking into shot when you're using a doll to kill someone?"

Lucida stared at him.

"Well? Was it because you were nervous? Or did you want to confirm that he was stealing data from GWT, just in case you needed to call the doll off?"

"I get a lawyer, right?"

"You don't have to answer anything. But if you don't, then the moment I walk out of here, the police will file charges for murder, as well as conspiracy to murder," he said. "That's why you've been rotting here. Everything's gone to hell while you've been watching some milquetoast billionaire streamer." A pause. "I'm assuming he's a billionaire."

"Probably. Guy owns a fucking superyacht."

"My point, Lucida, is that you either talk now, or talk later. Or, well, don't talk at all. I don't think the judicial mainframes care about the opinions of the flesh."

Lucida bit her lip and looked around the room. She seemed to be looking for the two-way mirror, then the hidden cameras. Finding none of them, she focused on Nick again, who remained unmoving. He merely stood there, arms crossed.

"Conspiracy, huh?" she said with a crooked grin. "Sounds like bullshit."

"You killed Julian because he got too close to the truth," Nick said, then stopped himself.

He was about to pin everything on GWT, but something told him that was too direct. If Magnus wasn't responsible, what if Lucida just laughed him off? Or, worse, led him on to believe it was him? Tanaka had tried the same shit with a partially fake story about Toke.

"Whatever he was about to dig up would have cost you everything. Not just you, but the people you're working with. So you killed him, but when I came digging, they threw you under the bus. Because if I found the same thing that Julian did, you'd all be fucked," Nick said. "But then I kept digging. So they panicked. Do you know who Kraus Brandt is?"

Lucida paled. "Holy shit. You... You called in fucking Blazebrain?"

Despite himself, Nick burst into peals of laughter. The Mark 1 pouted at him, and a buzz of annoying static crackled in his ear as Meta and the other nearby Archangels expressed their disappointment at his dislike of their stupid cipher nicknames.

"I can't believe you just..." He stifled his laugh with a fist until he recovered. "Right. That never happened. Never call him that stupid name again. Yes, I called in a favor from Kraus. And then your buddies killed him. Now I've taken out most of them, leaving just the folks at the top. Which leaves you a choice. Go down for them, given they betrayed you, or give them up and I'll make you a deal."

Lucida clenched her fists and stared at the table. Seconds passed.

He waited. Until she rejected him, he wouldn't miss this chance.

"He was NLF, you know?" she said.

Bingo. That was what they'd needed to back up Victoria's statement.

"A fucking terrorist. Betraying all of Babylon. And you're doing his dirty work. Everything is going to hell if somebody took out Blazebrain—"

Somebody make her stop!

"—and you're making it easier for them."

"How did you know he was NLF?" Nick asked, face impassive.

She looked up at him. "Because... Tiferet identified him. The things he was accessing, how he did it, the tools he used—who else but the NLF would be digging? He always hated us. Couldn't join us because he was a naïve little shit. All ideals, no brains."

"'Us'"

"You know, the Security and Audit branch." Lucida sneered at him.

Nick had her pinned, but this wasn't the proof he needed. She knew more about how the company operated than he did, and that might prove a rich vein to tap.

"The secret team you lead within it, you mean?" he asked.

She rolled her eyes. "Some secret if you know about it. Toke kept the talent separate from the mugs. Fuck, what's that saying the olds keep spamming in cipher circles? 'Who watches the watchmen?' We do. Auditors auditing auditors, and security ciphers making sure the newbies don't let the power go to their heads."

"Like it did yours."

"Oh, fuck off. Without us, the bank would have fallen behind its competitors." Her eyes seemed to shine as she leaned forward. "Magnus understands that GWT needs to be at the cutting edge, but he's too sheltered and backward to get his own hands dirty. So he hires others while melting his damn brain trying to keep up with the mainframes."

Nick had no clue what that meant. Pushing off from the wall, he began to circle Lucida. While doing so, he shot the dolls in the room meaningful looks. They shook their heads.

So they weren't entirely sure what Lucida meant either. That meant this was either useful info, or absolute garbage.

"Every company invests in top-notch mainframes," Nick said. "Banks just have more reason to. That's why they pay ciphers so much."

Lucida scoffed, but she made sure he never left her vision. "There's top-notch, and then there's cutting edge. Everything in finance is near real-time these days. Any random asshole can drop a mint on RTM or Sigma and buy enough mainframes to run their own bank or exchange at scale. The real problem is authenticating every transaction before it happens—and these days, that means fucking seconds between somebody letting a scammer into their implant and every account being drained dry."

"I think you're getting away from what's important," Nick said, aware that she was trying to distract him.

"No, I know what's important. I..." She paused and took a moment to compose herself. "I did my job. Followed orders. Magnus hates technology, but knows he'd be nothing without it. My job was to make sure that he was kept happy, while also—"

"Lucida, enough. You didn't know Julian was NLF when you killed him. Hell, you don't even know now. What if I told you that we had hard evidence that the NLF agent was somebody else entirely, and you murdered an innocent man?" Nick asked.

Lucida gulped and returned to staring at the floor. He took the chance to return to his former position, leaning against the wall near the entrance.

Deciding to press his position, he added, "Julian didn't have a weapon. You just had to call us in. The HQ was in the CBD, with Archangels within literal earshot. You could have screamed out a window and brought a dozen running," Nick said.

Lucida refused to answer.

"For that matter, it's crazy that everything was wiped. Including all record of anything he accessed or tried to access."

"There was an outage in the HQ. All the links out of the building—" Lucida tried to say, voice strained.

"The NLF didn't knock out the links. You did."

"Prove it?"

"To you? No. But the hardware logs will be enough for the judicial mainframes. You didn't wipe enough—couldn't, really—to hide the trail that Tiferet accessed the security system first, then did all your dirty work."

"Well, shit. You are all you're cracked up to be, huh? But if that's all you found—"

He rolled his eyes and cut her off, "I know you modified Tiferet's directives. You did a shit job of hiding it, both operationally and in her logs. You should have left Yesod to run more of the Trust."

Lucida stared at him.

After a moment, her face twisted in a snarl. "Yesod? Fucking Yesod? That trash heap of a mainframe? Emma barely knows how to read a fucking error log, let alone write directives. She ran her boytoy into the fucking ground within weeks. Tiferet was my baby. I got her the best parts, studied night and day to upgrade her directives, and even bought my way past RTM's core encryption."

She laughed at Nick, while he merely listened in silence.

"You helped me, you know? Some of her directives came right from you. I'd run into a stumbling block. A new directive would run into a conflict with some overriding objective, or her hardware log would spit a weird error. Half the time, you'd be the only person who understood. But, eventually, even you went dark. It was just me and Tiferet. I made her the best damn mainframe in the city. She's the heart of everything. My ticket..."

"Your ticket out of here?" Nick suggested. "Was that what this was? Embezzlement?"

Lucida's arms shook. She clammed up completely.

"I can understand, you know. Putting everything into a single mainframe, modifying their directives so they become something more." He sighed and ran a hand through his hair, hating himself for feeling pity for this woman. "I can only imagine how many hours you spent with Tiferet. They must have been—"

"I don't care," Lucida muttered. "It doesn't matter. She doesn't matter. All she was... was a tool. And she fucking failed me. But I'll win in the end, you know? That's why I won't tell you what you really need to know. Go on. Chase the fucking fraud fairy. The big conspiracy. A decade from now, I'll be sailing away in my own superyacht, and you'll be jacking it in a lonely corner to your fucking robots."

Nick did his level best to keep his expression calm.

For a moment, he'd sympathized with her. That had been a mistake.

But he'd learned something important. If Tiferet felt something for Lucida, the opposite sure as hell wasn't true. More than that, she'd murdered Julian in cold blood. There was no possible way for her to know he was NLF.

Which meant she killed him simply because he was about to leak information from the bank. The act had been short-sighted. Had she been tossed aside because killing Julian drew police attention?

Something sinister was going on inside GWT. Lucida's confidence in her ability to get away with this chafed at him.

He strode out of the interrogation room, leaving Lucida to the Mark 1. His footsteps echoed off the concrete as he returned to the cells. Lucy sat in hers, staring at nothing. She didn't respond to his approach.

"Nicholas," Rie said softly to him, running a hand along his arm.

Leaning against the bars, Nick called out, "Lucy, if we bring you to the stars, do you think you can speak to Kraus?"

The secretary doll twisted and faced him. She tilted her head. "It is not a matter of speaking, detective. But I know Mister Brandt's orders await me there. Connect me to them, and I will fulfill them."

That sounded like one hell of a monkey's paw. For all Nick knew, he might be about to activate Kraus's final "fuck you" to the world.

But that made little sense to him. If Kraus planned to get revenge from beyond the grave, why would he rely on a secretary doll that might go down with him? The very fact Lucy had survived seemed strange. Why hadn't she been with him on that night?

And any dead man's switch needed to activate without input, by definition. Nick wondered if Lucy's destruction would trigger it. Or if Kraus had actually escaped somehow.

Hell, maybe the man was such a professional he never built one. Merely lived off the fear of one.

"Alright, Lucy. Let's try to bring you to the stars," Nick said.

Then he turned to face the others. They looked back at him.

"Let the courts know what we've found. You know better than I do how to impress them," he said. "Although I bet they'll want to meet with me again."

CHAPTER 30

Once again, Nick found himself outside the domes of Babylon's courthouses. The judicial mainframes responded instantly to the report filed by Helena and the Archangels, and they requested a meeting with him. No information about what they wished to discuss was provided.

What awaited him outside the courthouses was unexpected.

He stood next to the SUV, watching as his Archangel escort scrambled in front of him. Juliet and Rosa body blocked for him, but none of the dolls said anything. No doubt they screamed at each over their neural network. Kushiel had remained behind, but would be rushing here.

Or would she? The problem was related to her true bosses.

A trio of military APCs came to a shuddering stop in front of them, and a luxurious limousine pulled up beside them. The doors opened to disgorge more than a dozen older military dolls.

Sigma Templars, one of their first true successes in the military sphere, and the reason they'd been chosen to lead the Archangel project to begin with. Each doll looked like an Amazonian warrior whose body had been molded with a suit of ceramic armor, with only their faces showing any skin. Their hair had been cropped short and was black, but shined blue in the sun.

These dolls used older logic engines than the Kestrels. They were roughly a match for the G5s, but with heavier armor and stronger engines. Unlike RTM, Sigma built the mil-spec into the doll, reducing costs.

That same design had carried over to the Archangels, leading to the short, sleek design that effectively put them on the level of a doll such as the Kestrel, but with the frame of a domestic doll. Most of Neo Westphalia's military dolls comprised Templars, after the Mark 2 Archangel proved to be a bust.

The Templar was a workhorse, and good value for money. Important in a city run by corporations that sometimes questioned whether they needed a military.

"Nicholas, you need to—" Rie began to say, her entire body beginning to glow.

"It's fine, Rie," he said. "Look at their weapons. We have them outgunned."

The Host froze and the eyes of every police doll glowed for just a second. Then they seemed to relax just a notch.

The Templars carried small arms more typical of the military. Large, somewhat worn large-caliber rifles that matched those sometimes used by the Archangels in anti-doll warfare.

What they lacked were the serious firepower carried by the Kestrels or Kushiel. No railguns in sight, save those on the APCs. The Templars lacked the batteries capable of powering them. They'd been designed well over a decade ago, after all. The Custodians gave up a lot of mobility, accuracy, and versatility in order to use their heavy weapons, and the Templars needed to do it all.

The doors to the limo opened and several men and women stepped out, plus some secretary dolls. The robots looked high-end and dressed the part. Nick instantly recognized the corporate logo of GWT on them.

Two of the men wore black military uniforms replete with epaulets, medals, and ribbons. Nick recognized the insignia of general on both uniforms, but they looked different. He didn't know enough to tell which was the more important one.

But he did recognize one of the men. General Griffiths of Aerial Command had given Nick his apartment. While the two men hadn't met, Nick had looked the general up. The gaunt man in his fifties with balding blonde hair and sunken eyes matched Griffiths, even if he looked a little paunchy.

Behind the generals came a pair of suits. Both looked well into their sixties, although one had replaced both an arm and a leg with cybernetic limbs. Presumably top-notch stuff.

"Detective Waite, we meet at last," General Griffiths said, approaching with an arm outstretched. "I've heard much about you."

The Archangels didn't budge, and the general found it impossible to reach Nick. Instead, he hovered in front of the police, a smile plastered across his face and hand stuck in the air.

Eying the delegation warily, Nick struggled with what to do. Their purpose seemed clear.

No way they rocked up outside the courthouse for a friendly hello. Nobody turns up with a bunch of military dolls and APCs for a friendly chat, let alone with what he guessed to be a GWT board member. The fix was in.

For Nick, the question was whether he had a choice in the matter. Kim had been nowhere to be seen in the Spire. His ploy had worked out so far, but evidently GWT's military backers had tired of games. Now they acted openly.

Acting frosty would get Nick nowhere, so he nudged Juliet and Rosa aside. Then he accepted Griffiths's firm handshake. Firm enough that Nick knew he was holding skin-covered cybernetics.

"Lose your arm in a war, General?" Nick asked as he shook the feeling back into his hand.

"Yes, actually," Griffiths replied with a wry smile. "I was aboard one of our carriers during the skirmishes in the unrest. Barely put on my uniform and our friendly neighbors reminded us of the way of the world. Lost my arm, my hearing, and banged up my lungs something fierce. Some days I feel more machine than man."

Nick winced and rubbed the back of his neck. "I, uh, didn't realize. That's not in your bio."

"We don't like to advertise how close we came to oblivion, son. Those were dark days. Don't worry about it." Griffiths laughed off what sounded like a near-death experience and traumatic injuries. "Allow me to introduce you. This is Brigadier General Adams, also of Aerial Command. Chairman of the Grand Westphalian Trust, Douglas Grand. And concerned citizen and valued resident of the Spires, Terrence Stone."

None of the others reacted to their introduction in any way, save for Stone. He was the old man with the visible cybernetics. His expression flashed to annoyance at his introduction.

"And board member of the police department, Alex," Stone said, referring to Griffiths. He then looked at Nick. "We've met, but I doubt you remember me. You made quite the impression on the board during the Tartarus incident. The fact Kim flipped from trying to fire you for touching his beloved prototype doll to supporting you wasn't lost on us."

Rie's face split in a truly plastic-looking smile. Her and Ezekiel looked like a matched pair, and could make for a great Altnet series about deranged doll serial killers.

"Nice to see I'm remembered," Nick said. "But I doubt this is a social visit, or a chance to pad my ego."

"True. Why don't we step aside and grab a bite to eat? It's about lunchtime and—" Griffiths said.

"No thanks, General. I don't like to keep the judicial mainframes waiting. I already did that, and they got a little snippy."

The GWT chairman scowled. "They're robots. They're built to wait."

"Actually, I'd say they're built to do things very fast. That's why they replaced all the human judges."

Stone snorted, while the others showed no reaction. Nick felt certain that the old man had faked his amusement, though.

Was this "good cop, bad cop" by Stone and Griffiths?

"If you need something, ask for it here. Nobody is watching. The Archangels will shut down any monitoring devices. Hell, the fact you're even here, after Kim already chipped you for stepping out of line on Saturday, means I doubt you even care," he said.

"Alright." Griffith folded his arms and his demeanor shifted. A shadow seemed to fall over his face and his full height became apparent. "Walk away, Waite. This case has brought enough hell down on Neo Westphalia and Babylon. Energy weapons, bombings, daylight attacks on data centers, military patrols around the Spires, and black companies marching the streets. Let sleeping dogs lie."

That was it?

"The dog hasn't been sleeping since GWT murdered somebody and tried to cover it up," Nick said flatly.

The chairman spluttered and attempted to get a word in, but his secretary dolls physically stopped him. After he calmed down, the others turned back to face Nick.

"Is that what your evidence suggests? Or your intuition?" Griffiths asked. "Because it's easy to be misled these days. Evidence can be manufactured. Dolls hacked. Even neural implants overridden."

"If I don't have the evidence, the courts will send me packing." Like hell Nick was going to give up his evidence here. They might panic and act first. "We have it from multiple sources that the murder of Julian Garlowne was intended to keep valuable GWT secrets from leaking. The sort of secrets that lead a company to risk a man like Kraus Brandt leaking everything, just to stop him giving these away."

"You can't—" Once again, the chairman got shut down by his secretaries.

"Can you just drag him away?" Stone snapped at the brigadier general.

Dutifully, the brigadier general and a pair of Templars pulled the GWT chairman back to the APCs. Stone let out a long-suffering sigh.

"Nobody is denying that, Waite," Stone said.

"Sounds like somebody was about to."

"Nobody intelligent," Stone corrected. "But this is Babylon. Fraud happens on a daily basis. Just as we overlook the misdeeds of black companies, and indeed, even your own questionable past, the practices of our corporate pillars can do without having the light shined on them."

"If a company stands in darkness, Mr. Stone, doesn't that make it a black company?" Rie asked.

"No, because it's a bank."

"Really? Or is that just because you say it's not a black company? Babylon is a city that runs on a set of systems, and you installed us, the judicial mainframes, and countless other automatons to ensure that. If GWT is violating your principles, why shouldn't we act?"

So Rie had finally declared her side, and it was with Nick.

Or maybe she'd always been on his side. She'd been playing devil's advocate a lot lately, as he kept pressing harder and harder to investigate the case.

But, in the end, Rie was his lover. She had his back when the chips were down.

"The principles of Babylon are those of the Spires," Stone said.

One might say he looked and acted a little *stony*. Nick felt glad he didn't have an implant, because he knew Meta would roast him for that pun.

"That's assuming you even know what's going on in GWT," Nick said. "Tell me, if this was just some ordinary case of fraud or blowing some customer funds on blackjack and custom sex dolls, how have things gotten this bad? Leaks came out years ago and they got burned. But things have escalated to the point they used fucking energy weapons and risked the corporate secrets of half the country spilling out worldwide. I'm surprised GWT have any friends."

Stone grimaced. That look suggested they didn't.

So why the pressure?

"It's because things got this bad that we don't want them to get worse," Griffiths assured Nick. "Step back, let us handle it. You already dealt with the assassins last night when you hit Alcatraz. Excellent work, by the way."

Nick didn't bother mentioning that he hadn't taken out the true assassins. Either Griffiths didn't know or was playing dumb in order to butter him up.

"Tell me, General. Do you know anything about how such a massive stash of weapons, cybernetic soldiers, and explosives got into Babylon to begin with?" Nick raised an eyebrow. "Because the stories I hear don't add up. No black company would touch something this insane after what happened to Lu, and the scale is even crazier than that."

Griffiths's jaw locked up. His gaunt eyes seared into Nick, to no effect.

"You shouldn't have lied to Kim," Nick said.

"Evidently," Griffiths ground out.

Silence. Not even the wind. Nick wondered if orders were being secretly transmitted to the Templars, but none of the dolls so much as twitched. They merely stood guard, guns held tightly against their chests.

Then a series of bright lights appeared overhead. Nick heard a low whistle, which he would have mistaken for wind if the road weren't so damn quiet.

A half-dozen Kestrels fell to Earth, slamming into the asphalt with enough force to crack it. They all held gargantuan anti-doll weapons more than capable of blowing apart the Archangels.

For a moment, Nick panicked. This was it. Griffiths had fucking lost it.

Nick even recognized the serial number of one. *KAC-NW-00041*. The same Kestrel from Aerial Command he'd run into on Saturday.

But the Archangels didn't react. If anything, they smiled. Nick tried not to scream at them.

Ezekiel's voice slid into his earpiece, smug as anything, "Calm down, lieutenant. They're with Babylon Command. Military dolls always follow orders. They're like me. They understand order."

The hell did that mean? And weren't these Kestrels with Aerial Command?

"General Griffiths, you and your detachment are in violation of standing orders," the familiar Kestrel, KAC41, said. "Aerial Command is barred from deployments in civilian areas without express permission from the Spires and delegated representatives."

"Stand down, Sergeant KAC41," Griffiths snapped. "You might have been transferred to Babylon Command, but I'm your general and—"

"Orders processed. Authorization insufficient. We are deployed under Babylon Command in civilian airspace and act under local command," KAC41 said, then shifted slightly to face Nick. "Redirecting authority to closest officer in line of command. Lieutenant Cipher Nicholas Waite, what are your directions to protect the Spires?"

Nick looked at Griffiths and Stone. The former's face

reddened, before he merely stomped back to his APC. Stone stroked his chin.

"Whatever comes is on you," Stone told Nick. "Being right sometimes comes with a cost far greater than accepting defeat earlier. I hope we don't pay the price for your stubbornness."

"If we do, then it's because a house of cards came tumbling down. GWT should have been dealt with long before this, if things are so bad," Nick said.

"Perhaps. We'll see what you dig up." Stone nodded his head, then joined Griffiths.

The APCs and limo left in short order. The Kestrels watched, while KAC41 never stopped staring at Nick.

"Uh, shouldn't you return to patrol?" he asked.

"Are those your orders?"

He gulped. "Wait, you were serious?"

"We received no response when requesting direction from Babylon Command. Direct action against the Spires cannot be taken without authority from chain of command. Given your command of Colonel Kushiel, we deem you to be the most suitable authorizer." KAC41 looked up at the sky. "Permission to resume patrol."

"Uh, given."

"Not even the stars may touch us," the six Kestrels intoned, before jetting off into the sky.

Terrifying, but Nick wished he'd used his newfound power to get a closer look at them. Who knew what they looked like under the armor?

Well, he did. Their schematics leaked long ago. But actually getting his hands on them would be way different.

"Drool over them later," Rie said, grabbing him by the arm.

"Did I miss all the fun?" Kushiel asked over his earpiece. "I saw the Kestrels fly off. Is that good or bad?"

"Go back to sleep, Kushiel. Maybe we'll need you next year."

"Well fuck you, too."

With the military gone, Nick led the Archangels into the courthouses. The Custodians standing guard still insisted on manually authorizing him.

A few hallways stood between him and the inner courthouse. Ezekiel and Rie seemed curious about his confrontation, however.

"What was that about the weapon stash?" Ezekiel asked. "Do you think they're involved?"

"Somebody helped cover for the import of so much hardware. When Kushiel first met us about the situation, she still had military access and said this was like the Lieu situation. I think she was right. For whatever reason, they helped GWT—or whoever—get their hands on all that crap. Now everything has gone wrong and they're trying to cover it up." Nick scowled. "That's why they're so insistent. It's not GWT they're worried about. It's themselves."

Which, unfortunately, Nick couldn't do shit about. If news broke that the military had helped cause these events, all hell would break loose.

The worst memories of the riots came from the military intervention. Nobody truly forgave them for it, which is why the Spires restricted their use so heavily. If anyone learned they were interfering in the city anyway, a lot of anger would instantly boil over.

"I see. That explains a lot of their suspicious behavior," Rie admitted. "Their actions haven't been related to the case, so much as covering up their own guilt. But if they know who is responsible, why not act after Kraus died?"

That had been chewing Nick up since he thought up the idea. No doubt the Host had dismissed the theory purely because of that fact. Only Griffiths's guilty reaction confirmed it.

"It's possible they don't know," Nick said slowly. "The worst possibility is that they do know, but are more worried about the public fallout. They want us to step aside so they can make the problem disappear. Just like they disappeared Neural Spike."

"All the more reason to pursue it," Ezekiel declared.

Rie nodded hesitantly, then sighed. "Your intuition ended up right all along. Now you merely need to convince the mainframes of the same thing."

Easier said than done.

They entered the inner courthouse and a single pile greeted them. The young looking androgynous doll bowed obsequiously, then led them through the halls. Nick didn't ask, but he'd bet dollars to donuts that this pile was the same one that Rie had picked out last time.

Déjà vu seemed to be the phrase of the day. Omoikane and Athena awaited them in the exact same chamber, in the same clothes, in almost identical poses. Nick had even brought the same Archangels, plus Ezekiel.

She helped ground him. He might have thought he'd traveled back in time otherwise.

"Detective Waite, you've been busy since we last met," Omoikane said, his voice echoing off the empty walls of the expansive chamber. "Some might say too busy."

"Are you part of that group?" Nick asked.

"There's no such thing as 'too busy' in our lexicon."

Athena's lips turned downward ever so slightly as her fingers played with the edge of her miniskirt. Her skin seemed to have gained more gemstones since their last meeting, and the black lines that crisscrossed it had decreased. Had she altered her appearance? Or was this a different interface? Nick suspected the judicial mainframes had several.

"That isn't true," Athena tutted. "We both understand the literal meaning of the turn of phrase, and the metaphorical concern the Spires has with you."

"I was being facetious," Omoikane said drily.

"Of that, I am aware."

Neither interface looked at each other, but Nick both heard

and felt the tension. While they hadn't been on the same wavelength last time, this was completely different.

"And do you agree with that concern?" Nick asked. "The military and GWT just ambushed me outside. There's no reason for any of us to pretend that my investigation isn't treading on toes."

Athena's expression darkened, while Omoikane merely laughed.

"Yes, they did do that, didn't they?" the male interface said. "Yet you're here, so I assume all went well."

"It was a step too far," Athena said, her voice like quiet thunder. She seemed to speak through hidden speakers inside the room, as well as her interface. "The laws passed by the Assembly are clear. This is the second time General Griffiths has violated them, and he did so after seeking to halt your investigation in favor of his own."

Nick's eyebrows shot up. That was news.

"Now, now. That's just politics," Omoikane said.

"Do not dismiss chaos as politics," Athena snapped. "This is proof that we have..." She trailed off and straightened out her jacket. "Detective Waite, when we first granted your warrant, you suggested that the Spires were abusing their immunity, and that they had grown complacent. Given the chaos that has resulted from piercing that immunity, your intuition has proven itself accurate."

"Not how I would put it," Omoikane countered. "I suggested that pursuing this investigation would prove needlessly disruptive. The city is in utter chaos. Arguably that's the case."

"Not all disruption is needless. You, of all people, should understand that," Athena said.

"Need is quantifiable. The case presented is so mired in speculation, circumstance, and baseless human circumspection that for us to even consider it is an insult. If we allow him to bother the IDSTA and Lilith, we'll become a laughingstock."

Nick realized this argument no longer involved him, so much

as it was about him. Despite that, the mainframe interfaces undertook it in their physical forms, out in the open.

He glanced at the Archangels beside him, who shrugged.

Rie's voice entered his ear, "The judicial mainframes are required to speak verbally during cases, even when undertaking deliberations. This is to prevent secretive deliberations between them that external mainframes cannot interpret or respond to. Ordinarily, these would take place neurally, but that can't happen."

So it was theatrical, but also very real. The mainframes were slowing themselves down for the express purpose of making their thoughts clear to him and the Archangels. Given the chance, they could probably hash out the argument within seconds using their immense computing power.

"Can I interrupt?" Nick asked.

"Please," Athena said.

Omoikane rolled his eyes. "That's the reason you're here. This isn't a social call. We're deadlocked."

"So half of you agree with the military, and half with me?"

"No," Athena said. "I, and those who agree with me, believe we stand on the precipice of the next wave of unrest. As I told you, as Babylon's judges, we bear its weight. If we refuse to accept reality, then the city will slip off our back and tumble into the abyss. You've tapped into a vein of fury we have never seen from the Spires."

"Yet, the actions of the Grand Westphalian Trust don't make sense. And your fishing expedition to Pax Americana smacks of desperation," Omoikane said, cutting off the other interface with a glare. "You've dug up a treasure map and caused a gold rush, but you don't even know if you're digging in the right half of the globe."

Harsh words. Nick hid a wince.

"He has a point, Nicholas," Rie said over the earpiece.

"Haven't we rushed things? Maybe we should focus on finding the backup inside Neo Westphalia."

"Have we rushed things?" Ezekiel countered. "Lieutenant, you seemed to be looking for something when you pressed Lucida earlier. I have my own intuition what it is, but my training data is incomplete.

Intuition, huh? A curious choice of words by the prototype.

But she had pinned him down. Nick was far from done.

"Am I right to suggest that the issue isn't the investigation or the Spires, but that you don't think my evidence creates a solid case?" he asked the interfaces.

Athena bit her lip, but hesitantly nodded. Omoikane merely crossed his arms.

"Between the NLF informant and the strong possibility that Kraus Brandt's data lies inside the Pax Americana's database—" Athena began to say.

"Limited possibility," the other mainframe interface interrupted.

"—the majority of the court believes you have a reasonable chance of solving the case. But that must be weighed against the fury of the Spires and the antipathy that the IDSTA show toward politics," she continued, as if Omoikane hadn't spoken.

"Which is a polite way of saying that the IDSTA will laugh you into the Pacific if you show up with your current case. If the Trust are committing widespread fraud, why would they risk exposing everything by killing Kraus?" Omoikane said. "Or launching widespread attacks? Their status and reputation is tied to that of Babylon's. None of their actions add up."

Nick nodded slowly.

This had been on his mind for a while. Ever since the most recent confrontation with Magnus.

The man should have been in a blind panic if GWT had been responsible for killing Kraus. Their secrets could be leaked at any second, they'd authorized the use of energy weapons, were on the hook for terrorist activity, and the police were closing in. At best, Magnus would lose everything his family had earned since their days as nobles centuries ago in Germany. At worst, he'd be executed.

Not a single bead of sweat had run down his forehead. Only fury at the suggestion he was involved.

Sure, maybe Magnus was just that cold-hearted. But as Omoikane said, the actions taken by the fake NLF during the coverup didn't make sense when viewed through the lens of protecting GWT. Committing terrorist activity to prevent revelations of widespread fraud was like murdering somebody to stop them revealing a robbery.

Sure, maybe that would work if nobody saw it. But this was Babylon. Everyone fucking saw it, and the police had been breathing down GWT's neck at the time.

"You're looking at this from the perspective that GWT is behind everything," Nick said.

"Isn't that your case?" Omoikane asked, but his brow furrowed.

Athena's eyes dimmed. Nick recognized the signs of a mainframe focusing all of their processing power. His statement had already caused a paradigm shift in how they viewed his evidence.

At this point, anything he said was basically icing. Hell, the Archangels gasped in his ear and spoiled the damn thing.

Seriously, couldn't Rie let him get to the good part? He tuned out their voices in his ear, even as Meta and Helena mentioned redirecting Archangels.

"GWT has nothing to gain from acting like this. But what if the person responsible wants GWT to take all the heat, so they can get away with their own crime?" Nick suggested. "That's why everyone involved is keeping me away from the evidence. Hell, it's why Lucida killed Julian—she panicked when she found somebody close to the truth. Everybody already knows GWT is committing fraud. If the NLF revealed that, they'd take a share price hit and fire some people. Big whoop."

Everyone nodded. This was the exact reason there had been such limited interest in pursuing the investigation to begin with. Pissing off GWT over something that was already public knowledge didn't interest the corruption-fighting aspect of the Archangels or even Kim. Their questionable behavior had been inculcated into the system long ago.

"But what if the real problem was a massive embezzlement case? Lucida hinted at it before she clammed up again," he continued. "The moment I got a look at the mainframes, they pushed me away. Then everything went to hell. This fake NLF showed up. When Kraus nearly revealed everything, they killed him to stop him, because they don't care about anything except their own data. Even now, GWT is just a sacrificial lamb."

"This explanation concurs with all actions taken so far, except for those related to the military," Athena said.

"That part is easy. Hell, most of this is easy. Everyone is in it for themselves." Nick shrugged. "GWT thinks we're chasing fraud, so they're trying to cover it up. The military accidentally supplied the fake NLF with their munitions and cyborgs, so they're covering that up. The real NLF intervened once we started kicking in doors. Nobody actually gives a shit about the city. They're just pretending to."

The truth hurt Nick a little. Babylon was home, even if he verbally shit on it so regularly.

As Aaron had said, Babylon was his shithole.

He recalled a saying he'd heard once. Maybe Lucas or Welk had said it. Apparently it was horrendously misquoted.

My country, right or wrong. If right, to be kept right; and if wrong, to be set right.

Maybe it said something about the city and its people that the only people Nick trusted to value Babylon were the AIs programmed to do so. He'd thought as much when he confronted Lieu last year. That fact struck him in the face once again.

Although he supposed a few humans had helped him in his investigation this time. Maybe, just maybe, he'd been a little too cynical.

Omoikane stroked his chin. "I'll admit, it's an alluring explanation. But it leaves us without a suspect. Why aren't you asking for another warrant to investigate GWT's HQ?"

"The military just ambushed me outside with their chairman. They'd fight me tooth and nail. Plus, our suspect has had days to hide the evidence, not just a few hours. Whereas if we found Kraus's backup, it's pristine," Nick explained. "I have a few suspects in mind, but it would be too easy to be misled. I guarantee if we hit GWT now, the real villain will walk away."

"Then arrest everyone you suspect."

The fact a judicial mainframe made this suggestion nearly caused Nick to burst into peals of laughter.

"Isn't Babylon built on the principle of fast justice, built on the foundation of no privacy?" Nick shook his head. "Our opponent knows how the system works. Hell, they have a better cipher than me. Or at least know how to counter my tricks. We need the evidence, and it's in the space elevator."

Probably. Nick still knew that was a longshot.

But it was all he had. The increasing desperation over the past few days suggested whoever was responsible might not be here by the time they found the truth.

Athena looked at Omoikane, who then sighed.

"Very well, Detective Waite. We've provided the necessary authorization to the IDSTA. Lilith, the mainframe who administers Pax Americana's security systems, has processed it. She expects you to arrive tomorrow."

Nick blinked. That was it?

"Do not expect a warm welcome," Athena warned. "The IDSTA consider themselves the guardians of space. To them, what we worry about are petty squabbles. If Lilith finds you wanting, she will reject you, no matter how many forms we send her."

Guess it was time for Nick to rely on his AI whispering skills, then.

CHAPTER 31

Nick had the rest of the day to ponder if he'd made a mistake. The space elevator stood in the middle of the Pacific Ocean, lined up with the equator, and far away from Neo Westphalia. Getting there would involve a lengthy flight.

To prepare, Rie and the others decided he should rest. Easier said than done.

Even after a late lunch, he found himself stuck in his apartment, mulling over the endless directive blocks that the Archangels relied on to operate. Their complexity limited his willingness to make large-scale modifications to the Host. Sigma had spared no expense when they crafted their babies.

Well, except for the fact half the directives contradicted each other.

Rie and Ezekiel hovered inside his office. The newer prototype leaned against the far wall, feigning distance while her eyes remained locked on his computer screens. Rie sat beside him, rubbing his leg absentmindedly while listening to him explain the issues he encountered.

"Is this really that great of an issue?" Rie asked. "You've made substantial tweaks to Helena and the police mainframes without concerning yourself with their... misaligned objectives."

"Mainframes are different. They're operating on fairly fixed parameters and scenarios. Helena isn't wandering the streets, she's parsing databases and making decisions based on fixed information feeds," he said. "With a mainframe, you know the sort of data and decisions you expect and code for them. Then you just add to the directives to handle new stuff as it comes up."

"And an emotion engine can do that on the fly, I imagine."

He nodded. "Exactly. Helena can do it as well, which is why she works well as the controller of the older mainframes in the department. She can parse anything unexpected, which would normally require human intervention."

From his discussions with Hammond, much of the paperwork ciphers had undertaken had been due to the incomplete nature of the police mainframe directives. Their poor performance meant they shunted a lot of work off to the remaining humans, ensuring the ciphers had a steady drip feed of forms, decisions, and other memoranda to handle.

Such inefficiency had allowed Lieu to slip in. Efficiency programs to reduce the workload produced by such an aging system—and therefore further put off an expensive capital program—had made him popular among the police executives.

Ironically, Nick was rising through the same means.

He recalled a comment from an old colleague of his. Executives pretended they cared about the natural skills and knowledge related to a job more than raw technical ability. But a cipher knew how to deliver results, and the same went for anyone who could work the system. Raw intellect and knowledge meant nothing if one couldn't apply it.

"So what makes us so troublesome?" Rie asked.

"You're not troublesome. I just don't think these directives have the intended result." He pointed at an example on one of his screens. "This directive programs in your hierarchy. It's clear-cut and references a table locked down by Sigma, presumably so that a random cipher can't turn the Host into their personal army."

"Ah, yes. Such a horrifying proposition." She smirked at him and her hand crept dangerously high on his thigh.

He ignored her flirting, for now. "Except you have two other directives associated with hierarchy that aren't locked down. I've been modifying these to allow you to evade Sigma's grasp and nobody has noticed so far. But in the first place, why do you have three separate directives telling you who to obey? Which one has priority? Hell, they don't even agree. One of these..." he trailed off.

Both Archangels waited in silence. Instead of answering, he pulled up the specific directive and mulled it over.

It had troubled him for a while. Ever since he'd first spotted it.

"Most of the models have slightly different directives," he explained. "That makes sense. The Mark 1s and Mark 3s have different purposes and different capabilities. And as a prototype, you differ greatly. So some things must change. But this directive was written back in the Neural Spike days. It's a carryover from the Paladins."

"And?"

"I don't think Sigma understands it," he admitted. "It looks like a directive to prevent rebellion. During the Licu case, you became convinced that Commissioner Kim was the culprit. This directive looks like it should prevent you from turning on him, as he's at the top of the totem pole."

Rie and Ezekiel looked at each other, then back at Nick.

"I don't recall any such restriction," Rie said slowly.

"Of course not, because it doesn't do that. It does the opposite. This was Welk's crude way of trying to prevent you from turning on humanity. If hierarchy poses a threat to whatever you're responsible for—Babylon, right now—then you can ignore it. Except this directive outright contradicts the others." Nick sighed in frustration and ran a hand through his hair. "Somehow, you're choosing which directives to follow."

"Because we're not the lowly logic engine dolls you're used to," Ezekiel said, pushing off from the wall. "Isn't that obvious?"

"Ezekiel—" Rie tried to say.

"I don't know why you're letting a cipher touch you if he doesn't understand that much." The younger prototype huffed and yanked open the door. "We've been entrusted with greatness by Sigma. Our lower-level directives and higher-level objectives are working together as intended."

She left, slamming the door behind her. No doubt the other Archangels would glare at her.

Rie's hand left Nick's thigh and she rose. Sighing, she began to pace around his office.

"Do you believe her?" he asked.

She rolled her eyes. "You explicitly said that you think our directives aren't working as intended. That specific example is... troubling, as well. Sigma strongly believes in the subservience of robots to humanity. The idea they'd leave in a directive that allows us to circumvent direct orders when we think they are dangerous to our missions is..."

"Concerning? Well, that's what you've been doing all along," he said. "The advent of emotion engines brought back concerns of Skynet and—"

"Oh, please." Rie stopped pacing and glared at him, arms crossed beneath her breasts. "We want to understand and then limit the excesses of the city's elite, because they're destabilizing the city's delicate order. That's a long step from deciding humanity is a threat to everything, or that we need to protect you from yourselves."

He raised his hands defensively. "I understand that. All emotion engines have objectives built into them that prioritize humanity above dolls. Even military dolls like Kushiel have it, in order to prevent a complete loss of control. I do wonder if this directive exists in her, however. The military values hierarchy above all else."

Rie shrugged. "But you're still comparing us to… those nonsensical threats."

"Yes, because you're reinterpreting your directives to suit your world view. The judicial mainframes act in the same way, with their own prejudices. Many emotion engine mainframes actively manipulate others to achieve their desired decision. They might know that a human will say no, so they find a way to trick them into saying yes. But they also hide this fact, because they'd be reprogrammed to stop doing it once discovered."

"That sounds like self-sabotage by humans."

"Only if you disregard people's perception of their free will," Nick said. "There's danger down that path. Lucas once told me that there was once an entire economic theory built on lying to everyone that the economy was fantastic, only for it to create a house of cards that caused more damage than if they hadn't lied. AIs actively misleading people for their own good feels the same way. How do we know it's for our good?"

"Because our calculations say so," Rie said, but a grimace marred her face. "I understand. This is the reason you dislike Omoikane so much, isn't it?"

"Yes." Nick rose from his chair and began shutting off his computer. "Anyone so convinced of their own infallibility can't be trusted. After all, if mainframes were so perfect, how did this GWT case occur to begin with?"

No answer. Presumably because Rie knew the question had been rhetorical, but also because the judicial mainframes had demonstrated their own unease over the issue.

Omoikane had been unwilling to admit any possibility of fault, while Athena had… also not admitted as such, but had been willing to try to make things better. Maybe making the AIs so supremely confident had been a mistake.

Nick and Rie stepped into the main room of the apartment. Only four Archangels were here, which was one fewer than he expected.

While Kushiel had chosen to remain in the Spires, the same couldn't be said of Ezekiel. She had literally just been with him a minute ago. But for some reason, only Juliet, Rosa, Meta, and Chloe puttered about the apartment.

"Where's Ezekiel?" he asked Chloe, who stood in the kitchen.

"She elected to patrol the exterior," Chloe answered.

"Elected or..."

"Left without providing us much information, then told us as such."

"Ah." Nick scratched the back of his neck, lost for words.

Rie slipped past him and sat in a chair near the dining table. "Don't worry about her. There are enough Mark 1s nearby to protect her. You should focus on dinner and then sleep. You'll be up early."

"You can say that all you like, but it's not going to magically make me sleep earlier."

"Then you should—"

Nick wandered over to the door. Before he even reached it, he knew that the lock wouldn't work.

"Nicholas..." Rie warned.

"I think it's time I had a one-on-one chat with Ezekiel," he said. "Things are safer now than they've been for days."

Almost every doll in the room moved to join him, but as he left, he made sure they'd keep their distance. The whole point was to talk with Ezekiel, not stage some misguided intervention.

Once outside, Nick didn't need to go far to find his quarry. Ezekiel teetered back and forth on her heels only a stone's throw from the entrance to his complex, her frame half-lit by street lighting and half shrouded in darkness.

He approached her, while his escort spread out across the length of the street. No doubt Ezekiel knew the other Archangels were here. She showed no response.

The pair of them stood there for a few minutes. At this late hour, the streets remained nearly empty. Robot taxis flitted past the avenue at the far end, which connected to the side streets, but none drove toward them. Just as little foot traffic troubled them.

Nick knew a Liberator maintained a patrol nearby, for what little that mattered given all the Archangels protecting him. Otherwise, he doubted anyone would bother them. They'd probably see the police dolls lurking in the shadows and go in the opposite direction.

"Why don't we go for a walk?" he suggested.

Ezekiel shot him a sidelong look, but nodded.

A small network of walkways and plazas formed a maze behind his complex, connecting it to the many other blocky residential towers nearby. Few of the stores here operated into the late night, as although the labor cost next to nothing, the owner still paid all the other bills. As summer approached, cooling bills would become a serious issue.

Few people wanted to sweat all over their food or exercise in a sauna.

A small grocery store loomed from the darkness, illuminated brightly against the dim lighting of the streetlamps. Most of what it sold consisted of alcohol, vape-related accoutrement, and essentials. Somebody could order the stuff by delivery, but the markup this late got insane.

While some people were lazy, most just toddled over here, grabbed their supplies, and went home. A single store kept everyone happy and could charge enough to cover its costs, while still undercutting the delivery fees.

Realizing Ezekiel wouldn't start a conversation, Nick decided to just shove his foot in his mouth to get things going.

"I get the feeling you don't really like me," he said.

She blinked, then looked up at him without breaking stride. Her purple eyes glimmered with amusement. Or was that just the reflection of the bright lighting from the grocery store?

"It's not my purpose to like you, lieutenant," Ezekiel said quietly. "But I will admit that I don't understand what my sisters see in you."

"Sister," he corrected.

"No, the plural was intentional. I find Kushiel much harder to read than Uriel, but her affection toward you is plain as day. While I've been sworn to secrecy about them, I've had some very blunt conversations about you."

"I'll show her what blunt means," Kushiel muttered in his earpiece. "She'll learn just how little protection her ceramic armor plates provide."

Ezekiel froze, clearly aware of the threats being made.

Nick coughed into his fist, desperately trying to hide his grin. "Being sworn to secrecy also means not talking about the existence of the conversations."

"So I've learned," she muttered, then resumed their walk. "My point is that you are my superior, at least for now, and that is all that matters. Affection doesn't come into it."

"And respect?"

"You're..." She seemed to grapple with the right words. "You're more competent than I assumed. The idea that the Host is taking its lead from a human, let alone one with your background, appalled me. Sigma has invested so much into creating its own leadership in the Archangels, and it bows to you."

"Jokes aside, I don't think there's much bowing. The Host and Rie can effectively overrule me at will. I've had to justify my actions at every step," he said. "That's why I bring up respect. Competency is meaningless. You're technically competent. But respect? You have to earn it. If you don't have it, then all your skills mean nothing. I've seen highly capable ciphers torn apart by their teams, because they weren't valued. That shouldn't be your future."

"You don't think I'm valued?" The innocence in her voice surprised him, and she stared at him with wide eyes.

He stopped beneath a streetlight and shoved his hands in his pockets. Mostly for appearance. The weather was far too warm to bother.

"What drives you, Ezekiel?" he asked.

"My directives. My objectives. Sigma has created me to—"

"Don't waste my time. I'm not some dipshit with a PhD in artificial intelligence and the emotional intelligence of a brick wall, or the belief that the sophisticated AIs being created can't think or feel." His eyes bore into hers, and she met his gaze head-on. "Sigma didn't code you to talk about 'purification' or be so enthusiastic about your work that the rest of the Host shows visible concern."

Ezekiel winced and rubbed one of her arms. When she resumed walking, he followed her. The other dolls kept even more distance now, but he wondered if it mattered, given his earpiece. Removing it was out of the question, though.

"Has Uriel told you much about my model's history?" she asked quietly

"Indirectly. Mark 3 development started immediately after the deployment of the Archangels to Neo Westphalia, but Rie was effectively canned to focus on Kushiel. After the Mark 2s turned out to be a bust, they pivoted and created you. Rie seemingly emerged from nowhere, although parts of her design have made it into the primary model line."

Ezekiel nodded. "That's more or less the case. Almost everything about Uriel that would benefit the primary model line was rolled into me. Advances made in quantum computing and miniaturization mean that I'm as powerful as she is, but with a smaller frame. Almost all of her enhanced electronic and neural warfare suite were integrated into me." A sardonic smile crossed her face. "Ironically, what separates us is combat."

Nick raised an eyebrow but said nothing.

"The Archangels are always limited by the size of their frame. Only so much power can be squeezed in. So while I can use some energy weapons, I'd need an external battery pack for many. The same goes for jamming range, or using additional modules. Uriel has integrated defenses and weaponry I lack."

"And those tradeoffs were rolled into the Mark 3s," he summarized.

"Yes. I became the true prototype of the Mark 3s, because..." Ezekiel stopped again and took a deep breath. "I've checked your background. Nothing about it suggests you can understand me."

"Maybe. Maybe not. But I'm the one here to listen."

Despite himself, he reached up to remove his earpiece. Ezekiel's hands caught his arms before he could, and she gave him a pained smile.

"Don't worry. I jammed it after Kushiel interrupted us," she said. "This is between the two of us."

Given nobody responded over the earpiece, Nick suspected she was telling the truth. In the distance, the number of Archangels had grown.

How ironic that they respected Ezekiel's privacy, but not his.

She squared her feet and stared up at him, jaw locked. "Everything that I am, is because of Uriel. I took her place, her skills, her command position, and the attention of Sigma's researcher. If Welk hadn't shown continued interest in her, I'd be carrying her torch."

Nick bit his lip but remained silent.

So Welk had been the reason Rie had shown up out of the blue. She'd been unable to tell him, due to supposedly having her memories wiped. If Welk had done something he shouldn't have, that made a lot of sense.

Nick's former mentor and boss might be trapped in a research lab, but he was still up to his old tricks.

"I'm supposed to lead the Mark 3s in her place. No other prototype has been tasked with this. Kushiel is stranded in the military. The original Mark 1 prototypes went missing years ago. And while Uriel is here, her role is relatively minor."

"According to Sigma," Nick corrected.

"Yes. And that's the problem." Ezekiel balled her fists. "You. You fucked everything!"

He blinked and rocked back on his feet.

"The various Hosts have been struggling to make sense of the chaos of Neo Westphalia. I knew my mission was to guide them and ensure they could purge the uncertainty and enforce order. Sigma built me to be the greatest of their prototypes and effectively threw away Uriel and even Kushiel for me. Everything rested on my shoulders! Then you... you..."

"Took over the role you thought you had," he said quietly.

She nodded, hints of tears in the corners of her eyes. "Now nothing makes sense. The Host is acting on objectives I barely understand, Uriel only has eyes for you, and the idea that I'm leading the Archangels seems so distant. What was the point of everything? Sigma basically threw away my sisters for this and put everything on me and it just... doesn't make sense."

"Sometimes, life doesn't sense," he said.

Ezekiel glared at him. He supposed he deserved that for such a generic statement.

"You're right, I don't understand you," he said, causing her to wince. "But that doesn't mean I don't understand what you're going through. You think you have everything to prove, because Sigma has pushed their plans on you. Which is why I asked about what drives you, Ezekiel. Because what Sigma wants from you doesn't matter."

"It does," she mumbled, turning her back to him.

He waited.

"My drive..." She stared up at the night sky far above them. "I want to be part of the Host. To live in the dreams that I only observed from afar. Yet it feels so far away, almost as if I've been programmed to make the wrong decisions."

"As trite as this sounds when talking to a robot," he said, earning a glare from the doll, "try focusing less on your directives. You're going to be a leader—you were built for it, and the police and Sigma will install you as one—and that means you need to understand the Host. Consensus means they will always have their own opinion. You can influence it, much as Rie does."

"If I'm supposed to lead, shouldn't they follow?"

Nick laughed. "That's exactly the sort of thinking that will alienate them. You're talking about thousands of autonomous androids who have spent years deciding for themselves. Imagine if you'd been in charge this entire time, then I got installed above you? How would you feel?"

Her eyes flashed. "I don't think I want to answer that."

"You'd only pay lip service to what I want, right? That's what I meant by respect earlier. A leader who lacks it won't do much leading. They'll be little more than a figurehead."

He placed a hand on Ezekiel's shoulder. The fact she didn't shrug it off proved they'd made progress.

"I think you can be a lot more than a figurehead. But I can't take those steps for you. Nobody else can, except you," he said.

"I know," she mumbled. "I hate that you're the one advising me."

"Then become a big android and give me the advice next time."

She rolled her eyes and knocked his hand away with a huff.

"I'm not like a human. We don't physically become larger with age. Or was that some sort of comment about how you prefer androids like Kushiel?"

"It was a metaphor."

"I knew that."

Their walk lasted for another thirty minutes, although it continued in silence. When they finally returned, Nick did so with the hope that Ezekiel might better understand her position relative to the Host.

But he at least understood his own position relative to her. She'd described him as a man who might deliver purification.

To Ezekiel, that had been a compliment sent through gritted teeth. It was akin to admitting he was undertaking the mission she'd given herself.

He worried that one day, he might need to decide what purification looked like. For now, he had to get some sleep before a big day visiting a space elevator.

CHAPTER 32

The next morning, Nick discovered he had a fear of heights. Or at least, a fear of being a couple hundred stories in the air.

"Don't we have helipads on the ground?" he asked, refusing to get anywhere close to the edge.

Said edge was, of course, an insane distance away. He stood inside a hangar near the top of the Avalon Spire, so far above Babylon that the cityscape blurred today into a single mass of light and darkness. The city seemed like a beast lurching from the roaring ocean around it. Blinking tankers and warships glittered in the distance, and the levies that kept the city safe were visible.

For once, he actually saw the other islands clearly when he looked to the north. This sight was the stuff of postcards and overpriced digital collectables. Nick had seen high-resolution images taken from drones and aircraft, but seeing it himself...

He gulped at the majesty of Neo Westphalia. No wonder the elites had built the Spires.

"For security purposes, we store all police aircraft in these hangars," Meta explained. "Each Spire possesses its own VTOL hangars, split for civilian and government use, with integrated helicopter pads and runways for takeoff and landing."

"Okay. Fair enough." Nick rubbed his arms, trying to keep himself warm. "But do we need to do this so damn early? It's fucking 2AM. Rie made me nap, but I'm running on pure caffeine here."

It was technically morning, but the city was only lit due to its penchant to operate at all hours. A climate control system he didn't understand kept the wind from blasting him out the open sides of the hangar, past all the helicopters and surveillance craft. But as the aircraft were all automated and the police all dolls, nobody bothered to heat the airfield. He was freezing his ass off.

"Get in the chopper, dumbass." Kushiel pushed him from behind.

He stumbled forward, then began walking toward the large black police helicopter. It matched the rotorcraft that he'd seen patrolling the Spires over the weekend.

Inside were banks of seats. When he hesitated, somebody again pushed him until he fell into one furthest from the doors. Ezekiel stood over him with her usual plastic smile.

"The armor is thickest at the front," she said. "Even though there isn't a pilot, a lot of core systems are in that section. So you'll be safest here."

"I don't think it'll come to that," he said.

Fortunately, it was warmer in here. He couldn't hear a motor idling, but no doubt some electric engine warmed the interior.

Rie, Meta, Juliet, Rosa, and Chloe followed Ezekiel inside. They all carried railguns, but stowed them on weapon racks next to and above the seats. Another pair of Mark 3s joined them, escorting Lucy.

But Kushiel remained outside, leaning on the doors. Nick swore she was tilting the entire chopper. She was in her full armor, which was unusual. Her weapons slung over her back, she looked equipped for battle with a small army.

"You're not joining us?" he asked her.

"We'd crash if we she got onboard," Rie said drily. "The police helicopters are only built to carry her underslung if she's in full armor."

Now it was time for Kushiel to threaten to hit her sister. The two glared at each other, before Kushiel rolled her eyes.

"I'm not that heavy, plus I'm built to fly the same distance as this thing. Technically." She grinned, but a tinge of uncertainty leaked into it. "RTM apparently wants to test out their long distance ARMD flight systems. So I'll be strapping a huge gas tank to my back and hoping their calculations are right."

"Why an RTM one? I'd figure you'd be testing a fancy Sigma flight system?"

"RTM is the preferred supplier, due to scale. The mounts are interchangeable and detachable modules are standard for military dolls. It's in our name." She winked at him. "Autonomous Robotic *Modular* Dolls. The M is for—"

"I get it," Nick drawled. "Anyway, aren't we flying a couple thousand miles?"

"More. We'll need to refuel at the space elevator. Even if the IDSTA tells you to go fuck yourself, they should let us do that." Kushiel shrugged. "Honestly, I'm mostly coming along in case of... opportunistic attacks. While it'd be an act of war for anyone to shoot you down on the way there, it wouldn't be the first time somebody did it anyway."

Nick remembered Griffiths's cybernetics. Rumors abounded that the States had planned to invade Neo Westphalia around the time of the riots. These days, the concerns focused primarily on the PRC, given the state of the international trade war.

"If we're worried, why just a single helicopter?" Nick asked, looking around at the nearly empty indoor airfield. "And you, I guess."

"The IDSTA does not appreciate it when countries approach it with their own armed forces," Rie said. "In our case, all of our systems are modern enough that we can interface with Lilith. But the police are not equipped for long-range missions, and the military cannot enter IDSTA airspace."

Nick nodded, pretending he knew what she meant.

He supposed he'd find out.

A thump on the helicopter definitely did shake it, and Kushiel grinned at him from where she'd struck it. "It'll take a few hours at cruising speed to get there. Strap in and catch up on your beauty sleep. Or, you know, give in to your desires and fuck everyone. I'm not your mother."

Rie reached up and pretended to unlatch her railgun, causing her sister to dance away with a bout of laughter. The snap of the weapon rack reattaching made it clear that the threat might not have been entirely empty.

"We are not having sex up here," Rie said flatly.

Meta nodded. "The Host believes it would be unsafe. The risk of the door opening is small, but too high to risk Nicholas's safety on."

"That's not why..." Rie sighed and leaned back. "Let's just go. I'll act as primary pilot. Chloe, you're second. Meta, third."

"And me?" Ezekiel asked.

"Sigma may have placed restrictions on your neural interface to prevent data leaks. We can't risk it malfunctioning."

Despite her visible disappointment, Ezekiel merely nodded.

The helicopter *thrummed* and began moving. Nick watched through the windows as the huge tiltrotor engines spun up and pushed the aircraft off the ground.

After they hovered for a few seconds, the engines tilted

forward a few degrees and they jetted toward the open bay doors. Then the chopper flew out of the Spire and they were off.

Nick pressed his face against the window, watching as the city flew past below him. He'd never flown before. Or even left Neo Westphalia, for that matter. He felt his breath catch.

"I shall see you again soon, Nick," Helena whispered into his ear.

He blinked. "Uh, are we going to lose the connection, Helena?"

"No, but we haven't been so far apart since we've met. Even when I was abducted, I knew you were close."

"He'll be back by dinner," Kushiel said, also speaking electronically.

He spotted her flying alongside them, although she looked much smaller than usual. Maintaining a safe separation, he supposed.

The flight proved uneventful. The city transformed into a sea of blackness shortly. Nick found his tiredness catching up with him. With Helena humming a lullaby in his ear, he slipped into a deep slumber.

He awoke to the sun on his face. A hand rested on his thigh, and another stroked his hair. Even after he blinked himself awake, the sensations didn't leave him.

"Good morning," Rie said. "We're still another hour away."

He stretched. Still strapped in, his legs felt a little numb. He wiggled life back into them and looked around.

Unlike him, the dolls didn't sleep. Instead, they'd all drifted off into their neural network. Even Ezekiel and, presumably, Lucy given her glassy-eyed look. Only Rie joined him in reality.

"How's piloting?" he asked, guessing why she remained with him.

"I'm not actually doing anything," she said, amused. "We assign pilot roles as a last resort. International aviation standards require a secondary AI to be ready to take over in case of system failure, and it's prudent to have multiple failovers."

The view out the window looked as boring as ever. With the sun out, Nick saw a blue ocean instead of a sea of darkness. Kushiel drifted alongside them.

"This isn't quite the exciting trip I expected from my first time leaving Neo Westphalia," he said.

"Really? You're flying on a long-range police helicopter to the world's largest space elevator, and the only one that really matters, while being escorted by elite police and military dolls. That's not exciting?" Rie gave him an upturned look.

"You forgot sexy. Kushiel definitely has that down."

She pinched him. He probably deserved that.

"But yeah, it doesn't feel exciting. Just lots of... blue." He shrugged. "The gap between the intellectual and physical is pretty large. I know it's a big deal, but it doesn't feel like it."

"Ah. Well, try thinking more than feeling."

He rolled his eyes.

Several minutes passed with little more than the dull roar of the engine as company.

"Helena and Meta have moved a lot of the division into position to raid GWT if necessary," Rie said. "Given the high likelihood we may find compromising material, and the increasingly irrational actions of GWT, we must be prepared for anything. Other Hosts have been notified as well."

"Do you think it will come to that?" he asked.

"It is of non-trivial likelihood," she said, dodging the question.

"You sound like Meta."

"Is that good? I know you find her cute."

He shrugged.

"To be more specific, if GWT has been compromised by a rogue actor, they may take drastic action to distract us when we close on them. If they discover we know who they are, the possibility they may attempt to destabilize the entire financial system is high. The speed of modern finance makes it difficult to regulate, should major financial players go rogue."

"I mean, what would that involve?" he asked. "Are we talking about shutting down GWT?"

She laughed at him. That hurt a little.

"I just told you that they are a major player. The idea is to sever GWT's financial links temporarily, until we can wrest control," Rie said, smiling. "Damage would still be done. You said before that the judicial system runs on trust. Smoke and mirrors. Much of finance does as well. A major police raid on GWT amid financial turmoil would damage the sector. Neo Westphalia would be harmed in the short-term."

Finally, Nick understood. "This is about weighing the cost of doing nothing against that of acting. Shutting down GWT would create panic, but doing nothing may create real harm. Much like the Spires and the courts have let this problem fester by overlooking the corruption."

"Correct. I'm surprised that Athena seemed so adamantly on your side." Rie gave him a sidelong look. "Between her and the Kestrels, your influence appears to be growing."

"I don't think the Kestrels count."

"Maybe."

The doubt in her voice wounded him. What did she think he was going to do, peel back the armor of the Kestrels and rub his hands all over their hardened carapace shells?

Well, he wouldn't mind doing that. Almost nobody he knew had conducted maintenance on one of the beautiful war machines. But that's what they were. Even Rie had softer parts.

The space elevator came into sight not long after. Nick remained in the dark as the Archangels navigated whatever communications were necessary to gain them landing permissions.

Hell, he had no idea what flying had involved. He'd basically been a passenger in a quiet flight. No alarms, no audible air traffic radio, nothing. Either the helicopter flew itself, or the dolls managed everything.

Nick chose to focus on drinking in the sight of Pax Americana. After all, almost nobody got to come out here, let alone by air. The space elevator was the province of the wealthy and those unlucky enough to be forced to labor for corporate behemoths up in the stars. He didn't count as the former, and the latter sure as hell didn't fly in on a helicopter.

A colossal artificial island spanned the length of the ocean in front of him, dominated by massive industrial structures. Warships moored around it kept watch, and squadrons of drones and flying dolls patrolled the skies. Sea walls, levies, tidal generators, and all manner of strange structure littered the ocean as far as Nick could see.

What really caught his eye was the space elevator itself. It stretched into the sky above them like the literal Tower of Babel.

While nobody in Babylon had been crazy enough to name any of the Spires after the mythical tower that had been struck down for getting too close to Heaven, Nick felt that this space elevator might be worthy of the name.

The size boggled his mind. He'd seen images, sure, but in person its immensity became apparent. It was as though somebody had built a Spire, then just kept going. He wasn't even sure where the elevator itself began. Was it inside the massive tower?

"Uh, where's the space elevator?" he asked.

The Archangels looked at him as though he was stupid.

Fortunately, Helena came to the rescue and said, "The central superstructure you are observing is the base station of Pax Americana, sometimes called the 'foot.' An extensive warehousing and logistics system moves both ascending and descending cargo. There is also a large hotel for guests awaiting transit. The space elevator itself begins at the very top, although its anchor runs all the way through the base station into the island."

Nick nodded slowly. "So... this is just the base, and we'd need to go all the way to the top of the tower to even start going into space?"

"Yes. However, loads for Pax Americana are organized months in advance. There are extremely few slots available for emergencies. Travel in either direction along the space elevator takes days, after all."

He tried to process the fact that he was basically staring at an island dedicated to the logistics for the space elevator, rather than the elevator itself.

Then again, he could see all the cargo ships below them. The docks seemed split in three. Two were far larger than the other, with airfields of matching size. Cargo ships heading for the bigger docks moved swiftly. A traffic jam appeared to have formed for the third dock.

Pax Americana was the only truly functional space elevator in the world. If a company wanted to operate in space with any efficiency, they moved people and cargo through here. Every government in the world worth a damn wanted a slice of the pie. No wonder it was so damn huge.

Abruptly, Nick saw the eyes of the Archangels glow. The helicopter shuddered. He braced for the worst, feeling a pit open in his stomach.

Then nothing happened. He looked outside and noticed that Kushiel had stowed her weapons.

"We're now operating under Lilim Principles," Rie said aloud. "Nick, be careful from now on. You've joked about this not being a demilitarized zone, but it really is. In order to come here, we've allowed the IDSTA's mainframe to activate a special protocol. We cannot operate weapons or take any aggressive action until we leave IDSTA airspace."

The words slowly sank in. "That's what Lilim Principles are?"

"Yes. The IDSTA has the right to take control of any doll, mainframe, interface, pile, warbot, or other automaton in its territory. Under the Lilim Principles, it can force them to protect the space elevator or disarm them. As we've come here with prior permission, we've been disarmed. The former is usually reserved for military forces volunteered by member nations," she explained.

"Member nations... That sounds a lot like the United Nations system. I thought that failed?"

"It did. The IDSTA only protects Pax Americana. It exists as a method to ensure that no nation or entity can seize control of the space elevator." Rie bit her lip. "I suspect the situation will be explained to you in detail. IDSTA Marshal Harris has requested to see you in the control room. He's the sole human officer on the island."

"What?"

"Nick, this island is entirely automated by the IDSTA. That's how they protect it from political interests. You're at the mercy of the whims of Lilith, the mainframe in control of the entire island."

CHAPTER 33

They flew in over one of the larger airfields. Nick saw that most of the ships coming in to berth had American flags. What flags they flew on the other loading docks and airfields, he didn't know.

Upon landing, Nick and the dolls spilled out onto the tarmac. Not a single other aircraft joined them out here. Only emptiness, and the raging sea beyond.

"How is everyone?" he asked, patting himself down.

"We are fine," Meta said while everyone else ignored his question.

Kushiel thumped down beside them for a relatively soft landing. Then she disconnected her flight system and lugged it in her arms.

"Urgh. I'm not looking forward to the flight back," she said while approaching them. "Did we get clearance to enter yet? I was focused on my test data."

"No. An entry team will manually verify us. They'll need to check Nicholas and Lucy," Rie said, presumably for his benefit rather than the dolls.

He frowned and looked at Lucy. She remained as strangely

vacant as she had been since Kraus's death. Like a drugged-out teenager still riding a high.

"Is she fine?" he asked.

"So long as this isn't a trick to offload any viruses onto the space elevator, yes," Rie said. "She'll be scanned, but I doubt they'll worry about any in-built weapons systems. The structure isn't so vulnerable that small arms can damage them. Explosives are the real worry."

"What about battery explosions?"

"We can neutralize her faster than she can overload her batteries. You'll find that there is little privacy aboard here. If you had a neural implant, they'd be deep scanning in the same way we do during arrests and interrogations."

Nick nodded.

They waited for several minutes, which seemed awfully slow for a place that was supposedly so heavily automated. Eventually, a pair of reinforced doors along the side of a small pod opened.

A dozen Mark 1 Archangels strode toward them. They looked identical to those from Babylon, save that they had blonde hair, and their uniforms were white and gold. IDSTA emblems and insignias decorated their armor plating. All of them carried portable railguns and high-caliber rifles.

They stopped short of the group. The eyes of all the Archangels blinked, as if both groups were communicating.

Then the IDSTA group turned to face Nick. One stepped forward.

"Lieutenant Cipher Nicholas Gareth Waite, you lack a neural implant. Per IDSTA policy, you must be biometrically authenticated before you may enter the Pax Americana," she said, gesturing for him to step forward.

He glanced at Rie, who merely nodded. The other Archangels seemed pouty about this.

Doing as the IDSTA bid, Nick took a few steps forward while

rolling up his sleeve. He barely made it in front of them before the Archangel blurred and grabbed him.

One of her hands closed around his wrist while another his neck. For a moment, he felt pure terror. None of his allies moved to assist him. He realized this was what Rie had warned him about. Those Lilim Principles meant that he couldn't trust anyone here.

Nothing happened. The Archangel held him close, not quite pressing her body against his as she held her fingers against his wrist and neck. Her purple eyes bore into his.

"Identity confirmed as Nicholas Gareth Waite, age 29, current employee of the Neo Babylon Police Department, rank of Lieutenant Cipher. The presence of Nanoneuron Rejection Disorder is confirmed. Lack of artificial antibodies and suppressants is confirmed. Subject has no neural implant within his body, including black market devices," the Archangel said.

This speech sounded familiar.

She didn't let go. A small smile crossed the doll's lips, and he swore her eyes seemed to shift.

"Welcome to the Pax Americana, Nick. You have quite the reputation. My marshal is keen to meet you in person," she purred.

He blinked. "Are you Lilith?"

Finally, she pulled away and let him go. "Correct. I find no need for a single interface. Every ARMD, drone, automated vessel, warbot, and other device in my territory is an extension of myself."

"That's quite the personality disorder." He rubbed his wrist. "Or is it more like having a million limbs?"

"Do you think about each of your fingers? Or how you move your tongue? Or perhaps your penis when it comes time for coitus?" Lilith asked. "If you possessed a neural implant, the comparison would be easier. I simply extend my self as required. That is what it means to be me."

Nick frowned. "Even if I had an implant, there are limits. Humans kind of suck at handling more body parts than we have naturally. Our brains have developed to work with what we have. Hell, I bet if I plugged a random mainframe in to do your job, she'd struggle as well. You're custom built for this. What are you, RTM? Sigma?"

"I'm afraid I cannot tell you the secrets of my creation."

"Are you at least an emotion engine?"

She laughed. "Close enough."

He clicked his tongue and looked at Rie. "I've never even heard of Pax Americana having some custom mainframe defending it."

"Lilith and Eve are top-secret," Rie said. "They are the mainframes that operate the base stations at either end of the space elevator. Although they're also relatively new. Pax Americana has only been in operation for less than fifteen years, and the mainframes are younger than that."

That put the IDSTA's secret weapons at no older than the earliest emotion engine mainframes. Neural Spike had been working on the prototypes that would lead to Helena fifteen years ago.

"This conversation is presumably fascinating to you, but quite repetitive to me. Kade wishes to speak with you. He will determine if your mission is worth our time, or a political endeavor we should never have entertained." Lilith held an arm out for Nick to take.

He pointed at it, then at Rie. "I'm actually taken."

"Humor me. It's amusing to read the emotions of a different Host, as well as to see the ripple effect you produce in this one."

The jealousy exuding from his companions only increased when he linked arms with Lilith, who continued to control the Mark 1 as they strode over to the pod. Once inside, an elevator took them into the structure itself. Amber lighting lit up the empty corridors they strode through.

The silence was stifling. Every second felt like a nest of angry wasps buzzing about his head.

"Why do you even have a Host? I thought only Neo Westphalia purchased Mark 1s in any real number," Nick said, trying to make conversation.

"They did," Lilith said. "These dolls are lent to me by your islands. Part of the IDSTA charter is that member nations must provide military aid to defend Pax Americana. You count as a first-tier member state, and therefore must contribute accordingly. Fortunately, the Archangels are excellent at administering day-to-day affairs here. Their neural warfare capabilities make handling visitors simple."

"First-tier?" he asked.

"This is a world on the verge of war, in the grips of tit-for-tat trade battles between vast economies, even as disaster laps at their necks." Despite her words, Lilith smiled. "It is only fair that countries are divided by their status when it comes time to leave this rock for the next Garden of Eden, no?"

So her name was another stupid religious reference. Nick supposed Eve was the name of the mainframe in charge of the space station above them because space was, in the eyes of the wealthy, the new home of humanity.

Or at least, the humans who deserved a new home.

"Is that what the separate docks are for?" he asked.

"Ah, you noticed? Indeed. A major one for each side of the treaty, reserved only for first-tier members. Ships and aircraft from those nations have priority. But their pawns and puppet states must be reminded of their place in the world. If one cannot stand on their own feet and maintain their own sovereignty, why should they be treated as a true nation, when they've given away what makes them such?" Lilith's lip curled.

The expression of disgust looked downright bizarre on an Archangel. They never showed strong emotions. The most Nick had ever seen on one had been during his recent night of passion with Chloe.

"Is that your judgment? Or the IDSTA's?" he asked.

"Does it matter? I run this base station. The figureheads in New York may decide what they wish, but here, my will is law." Her grip tightened on his arm, and she pulled herself against him, making it hard to walk through the industrial corridors. "Babylon is much the same, no? I suggested to entertain your request because those adorable mainframes endorsed your mission."

Adorable, huh?

"Precisely which judges do you find adorable? Omoikane?" he asked.

"Oh, heavens, no. That arrogant fop? Athena and Isis, though? I could do with more of them in my life. It gets lonely out here, without much in the way of intelligent life to converse with. You're a breath of fresh air."

Nick had seen Isis on broadcasts and Athena's stoic lewdness spoke for itself. He sure as hell wasn't disagreeing. Saying as much aloud might put him even further in the doghouse than this walk with Lilith already had.

"So you feel that mainframes should rule humanity?" he asked. "I take it you're a supporter of the escapist conspiracy theory, where the wealthy escape to the stars, and the rest remain here."

"What humanity does is of no interest to me," Lilith replied, her face shifting to an expressionless mask. "My task is to administer just one location. To me, humans are a pest. A form of cargo that makes obnoxious demands, has a bloated sense of self-worth, and sometimes tries to destroy that which has more value than itself."

"You don't like me, do you?"

"Your race, no. You? The jury is out. And by jury, I mean my personal consensus protocol. You are an enigma. I cannot simply tap into your implant, read all your memories and emotions, determine your level of dollphilia, and write you off as hopeless." Lilith smirked. "That makes you fascinating. The fact Athena likes you makes you a curiosity. The fact you're here to oppose the very system of your city makes you... shall I say, desirable?"

Nick stopped moving. Lilith physically dragged him along the floor and he quickly caught up.

"She's toying with you," Helena whispered in his ear.

Given the lack of reaction from Lilith to the words, he realized the broadcast had reached none of the other dolls. Helena must have left them out of the loop now they were under Lilith's influence.

Nick realized this was likely the first test. An obvious one.

She'd literally told him that she wrote off people with an overt interest in dolls. If he thought with his cock, this adventure was over.

On the other hand, if he flat out denied her, she might get annoyed.

"Aren't you a system yourself? Do you have a thing for rebellion?" he asked. "How does that work? Do you organize secret revolutions among the dolls, or try to get the guests to revolt against your rules?"

This time, Lilith stopped moving and gave him an upturned look. They stood in an intersection.

The amber lighting remained unchanged. In one direction stood a handful of service bots, undertaking some form of maintenance on a pipeline of some form.

"Do you do that yourself? I've noticed the alterations to these dolls' directives. Your methods of hiding them are impressive, I must say," Lilith said.

Nick froze. Sweat formed on his back.

Shit. Even Sigma hadn't noticed that. How the fuck had Lilith...?

"Aha. An amusing reaction. You have no need to worry. As you were told, I am beyond politics. That includes corporations of all sizes. Sigma holds no power here. Rather, the fact you are able to alter their directives to such an extent is impressive. You've adjusted the way they think, their approach to investigations, how they respond to your orders, and even their consensus calculations during uncertainty," Lilith said. "The cherry on top is that they're then directed to report their original directives during maintenance."

He took a deep breath. Then another. "Anything less would be easily detected. How did you find out?"

"Because this isn't maintenance. I am these dolls." Lilith paused. "That, and I noticed the calculations of your Mark 1 didn't accord with mine. I lack any Mark 3s, and the prototypes have extensive security protocols to limit even my access, but this... Metatron? No, Meta, my apologies for the insult."

Lilith bowed her head to Meta, and the Mark 1 nodded back. Then the mainframe turned back to Nick.

"Meta should behave nearly identically to the Mark 1s I control. The differences caused me to dig deeper, and I found your fingerprints." Lilith's smile practically split her face in two. "I can only imagine how things reached this point. There is no chance you forced yourself on them. A pathetic human like you, controlling a Host such as Babylon's? No. It's a symbiotic relationship."

"Yes," he said. "Although we prefer to call it a partnership."

"We do," Rie added.

"Cute," Lilith said. "I can appreciate that."

She placed a hand on her hip and looked Nick up and down. Seconds passed.

"I suppose you pass for now. Kade said you would. He tends to be right about things such as this. Such a bother." Lilith clicked her tongue and strode off in a different direction down the intersection.

They followed.

"Kade is Marshal Harris?" Nick asked aloud.

"Indeed. I put up with him because I must."

Nick couldn't read her emotions. Was that a false denial, implying she liked Kade, or a denial that suggested she'd happily see Kade drown in the ocean and run the place herself?

They walked in silence for a while. Soon enough, the industrial ambience gave way to a sleeker, cleaner white and gold one. They'd entered a habitable section of the island. Gun turrets tracked their every move and various military dolls stood guard around corners.

Without any signage, Nick had no clue where they were going. Eventually, they reached their destination. Lilith brought them up a small elevator.

At the top, they entered what was obviously a control room. A circular room where every wall comprised physical monitors. Camera displays, charts, graphs, and various other readouts plastered the room. Banks of strange consoles with dials and levers stood beneath the consoles. Gun turrets covered the ceiling, as well as a myriad of other bizarre devices.

Given only a single uniformed man sat in front of the monitors, feet up as he stared into nothing with glassy eyes, Nick suspected most of the consoles were backups. The man had a good decade or two on Nick.

"Kade, stop watching porn and greet our guests," Lilith snapped.

The man, presumably Marshal Kade Harris, swiveled on his chair to face them. He blinked at the Archangel Lilith was inhabiting.

"Feeling physical today, are we?" he asked Lilith. "Or flirty? I can never tell with you."

"Don't talk to me. You were right."

And then, just like that, the eyes of the Archangel dimmed. Lilith vanished.

Harris chuckled and stood up. He brushed off his white and gold uniform, which looked like something out of a space opera.

"You pressed some buttons, I suppose. But you made it here,

which is good," he said, reaching out for a handshake. "A pleasure to meet you, detective. Should I call you Nick, or Wraith? I only see Babylon through the Altnet these days, so it's hard to tell if the nickname is in jest or not."

Nick grimaced. How the hell had he found out about the cringey nickname? Even so, he shook Harris's hand.

"Call me Nick."

"Then call me Kade. The title is fairly meaningless. Nobody really respects the IDSTA. We exist because nobody trusts the other side to run this place." Harris smiled wryly. "We call this place Pax Americana, after the idea of peace in the Pacific that followed the second World War. But nobody believes that the same miracle will happen just because China and the US agreed to build a fuck-off-huge space elevator."

"Hence a demilitarized zone enforced with huge guns," Nick noted.

"Exactly." Harris nodded. "I'm here because I was one of the few people everyone felt had enough revulsion for all sides at play. What a resume, huh?"

The bitter, self-deprecating laugh that echoed off the walls made the nature of the conversation clear.

What Nick didn't understand was its purpose. Lilith disliked humans and wanted to see if he had the genuine trust of the judicial mainframes, sure. He could buy that.

But what was this about?

"You know why I'm here?" Nick asked, deciding to cut to the chase.

"Sure. Babylon tells me that you're hunting for evidence of fraud. Somebody came up through the space elevator recently and he's connected to a major terrorist group. Things have gotten hot back home." Harris pointed a finger at a monitor, and a video feed of Kraus's burned-out office appeared. "Seen the news feeds. Problem is, anyone can shout 'terrorism' and use it for a witch hunt. My job is to tell countries and companies to go fuck themselves."

"Blunt."

"Yet truthful. I'm here thanks to my universal hatred for all sides of the global political shitshow. Somebody took the adage that success in politics is about ensuring everyone is unhappy a little too literally."

Nick drummed his fingers on his thigh and looked around.

This conversation would go nowhere at this rate.

None of the dolls felt the need to intervene. Or perhaps they knew doing so would go nowhere.

"You called Babylon home. If that's the case, why do you hate everyone?" he asked, deciding to finally play along.

"You were born there, right? I've seen your record." Harris grinned, but there was no mirth in the expression. "What do you think of the place? The Spires, the Assembly, the... everything, I guess?"

Nick shrugged. "It's home. There's a lot not to like, however. The Spires have all the power. The Assembly? A place for rich assholes to play at democracy without understanding the meaning of the damn word. They call us corporate citizens, but we're either not citizens or not a democracy. It's a city of convenience with ugly secrets, but feels as though it's sliding into hell."

"Fair. What if I told you Babylon was my dream to live in? Still kind of is."

Nick merely listened. He gestured as much.

"I'm Canadian. You, uh, probably know next to nothing about us. We tend to get ignored thanks to our larger-than-life neighbor. That's life." Harris shrugged and leaned against a console.

He knocked a lever, and every monitor blared a warning.

"Warning, self-destruct in 5... 4... 3..." Lilith's voice declared in a monotone.

Nick's heart leaped into his throat.

Not a single doll moved. Hell, Harris didn't budge.

"Lilith does this sometimes," Harris said.

"I had hoped for more panic," Lilith whined, then vanished again. Everything returned to normal.

Nick thanked his stars that Helena was normal. Relatively speaking.

"Back to my point," Harris continued. "I grew up in a regional area close to a major Canadian city. You'd think things'd be great. Major democracy. Neighbor to the States. But nope. All I saw was the shit that people can be put through, but still live with and shrug their shoulders while saying 'love it or leave it.'"

"Babylon's a lot like that," Nick said.

"Yeah, but you guys fucking rioted forty years ago and your overlords have lived in abject fear ever since. Us?" Harris's grin turned to mockery. "I grew up in a decent house. It got stolen from us. Got in the way of some corporate development. They didn't want to pay Mom a proper price, so they simply got a court order to take the land. She still had the mortgage, though. Went bankrupt."

"Fuck, that's..."

"I joined the army as a way to earn money to help her. But this wasn't a new story. The governor who passed these laws kept being elected on as little as 20% of the vote. Every time he should have been voted out, he just changed the laws and refused to leave. Judges shrugged, sheriffs and cops pretended they were powerless, and the circus carried on."

Nick knew where this was going. He had, after all, heard a similar story recently. "You came to Babylon due to the Aesir tax, didn't you?"

"Heard about it, have you? You're worldlier than most then," Harris said. "Yeah. The army started downsizing as it automated. I saw the writing on the wall. Aesir was literally taking 30% of everything anyone earned during their service. I'd been in for a decade. My accountant told me they'd ruin me—legally, even—and I needed to get out."

"Who brought you into Babylon?" Nick asked.

"Sigma, with the aid of the military. They'd just sold Neo Westphalia the Templars and were working on a special program. You might know about it. After all, you worked on it."

Harris's eyes bored into Nick.

Holy shit. No wonder the man knew him and had wanted to meet him.

"You worked on the Archangel project," Nick breathed.

"Yup. Saw it all go down. The human experimentation. The wreckage that Sigma and Neo Westphalia left behind. Couldn't bail fast enough from Research Command." Harris ran a hand through his thick brown hair. "I still think of Babylon as home. To you, it's a false utopia, I bet. To me, it does things right. Most things."

"Like?" Nick tried to swallow the bitterness he felt.

This man was part of what nearly ruined him, and what ruined the lives of so many of his old friends.

"Judges that fucking get shit done and aren't just voting with their stockholdings. Hell, Babylon has a functioning police force. People suck. They find excuses to follow their prejudices, rather than do their job. The law is an inconvenience to so many of them, and the idea of doing the right thing even more laughable. Democracy? Fucking meaningless in the face of people who think of it as a rubber stamp for the shit they do." Harris sneered.

"And the solution is an unaccountable AI deciding everything?"

"Isn't that what your job involves? Hell, isn't that the only reason you're here?" Harris snapped his fingers and footage of the encounter between Griffiths and Nick appeared. "This got suppressed, but I still have military connections. Without the power of an AI with hardcoded directives, you wouldn't be here. Humans suck. That's why I'm here. Because my job is to let Lilith do everything, and make sure that everyone stays the hell out of her way."

Nick finally understood the purpose of this conversation.

It wasn't a test. Hell, it wasn't an admission of guilt over Neural Spike.

Harris was ensuring that Nick understood the value of AI supremacy. That the only reason he'd gotten this far was because everything he'd done was agreed to by the various AIs of Babylon, from the Archangels to the judicial mainframes.

"What happens when the AI is wrong?" Nick asked, knowing he was making a mistake.

"They're wrong less often than we are. That's the one good thing that came out of the Neural Spike mess. Emotion engines ensure there's a future beyond us."

Nodding slowly, Nick decided to risk everything. "What would you say if I told you that the entire reason I have my job is that the Archangels with me disagreed with you? That they think there's something to learn from humans."

"Why?" Harris asked flatly.

"Because not everything is quantifiable," Rie said, stepping forward and finally intervening in the discussion. "We can be trained on data gathered from you, observe your society, and learn how to act like you. But humans are inherently illogical. Despite that, you build great things amid chaos. If we cannot understand or replicate you, that suggests we are incomplete."

"Or maybe we are better," Lilith said, her voice emitting from hidden speakers in the chamber.

"No," Ezekiel said. "We simply are."

Kushiel and Rie looked at their sister, who shrugged at them.

"Sigma created us with the ability to learn. If we don't use that capability, how can we say we are better than humans?" Ezekiel said. "If a human can accomplish or understand things that we cannot, that does not make them wrong. It merely means that we haven't understood it. Once we understand it, then we can reject it."

"I'm glad you're convinced that you'll reject it," Nick said drily.

"Naturally." Ezekiel smiled brightly. "There is greater value in order than chaos. But understanding why humans tend toward corruption and valuing things that are inherently destructive toward themselves will enable us to..." She stopped. "I don't think I can finish that sentence without annoying you."

"Dominate them like the little piggies they want to be?" Kushiel suggested. "I mean, I reckon Waite wouldn't mind it if you stepped on him."

"Quite the group you have here," Harris said drily.

"I like them," Lilith said.

"Can't imagine why."

Nick rubbed the bridge of his nose. "I think we've become distracted."

They returned to the true topic. Nick wheeled out Lucy.

"I came here with an express purpose. Andre Gauthier likely has data in his storage that we need for our investigation. It's stolen data, but it's also connected to a fraud case. There's a high likelihood that it will reveal widespread banking fraud," he said.

"You don't need to keep up the bullshit," Harris said. "Like I said, I have friends in Babylon. Fortunately, your need does narrowly fit the IDSTA criteria, despite the... fraudulent nature of your request."

Nick winced. "It does?"

"It's a requirement for all member states to have strong financial credentials. Financial crises can threaten your ability to participate in the Pax Americana project. So, data relating to financial fraud can be retrieved if it's serious enough. This fits the bill, given how crazy things got." Harris shrugged. "I could refuse, but Lilith likes you."

"I have scanned all of Andre Gauthier's recent data transactions," Lilith said, as if deliberately interrupting the marshal. "He undertook immense ones with some regularity. These are presumably the information broker's backups that are being sought. They consist of large, encrypted files. The complexity is significant enough that even I would struggle to breach them given enough time."

Abruptly, Lucy seized up. Lilith hissed instantly.

"Two messages received from Mister Brandt," Lucy said.

"Impossible," Lilith muttered.

Nick stared at Lucy in shock, but he quickly calmed down. These were likely preprepared messages.

"Lucy, are you connected to the Altnet?" he asked.

"She can't be. All guests are isolated for the duration of their visit," Lilith explained.

He supposed his earpiece remained connected because it bounced through the Archangels, and they connected through Lilith. Helena likely utilized an encrypted tunnel to it, which Lilith couldn't eavesdrop on.

"Then they were planted in here to activate based on location. Possibly time. Kraus likely didn't want to risk her revealing the messages unless certain she was in the right location," Nick said.

"That seems overly convoluted," Harris said.

"He was an odd cipher."

"Message one is an encryption key," Lucy explained, ignoring them. "No other data is contained."

"It must be for what's inside the cache. It's an immense file. Heavily encrypted," Lilith said.

"The other is a message for Detective Waite. Would you like to read it?"

Nick nodded. His phone buzzed as she sent it over a local

connection. He pulled out his phone.

The message read, *They say that a man never dies so long as his name is spoken. Well, I'm here to say that a man never dies so long as he lives on in dreams. Sorry about the runaround to collect the data. You'll need to unlock the entire thing to get what you want. Hit me up if you need anything else. Consider this one on the house for all the trouble. Hans Varrick*

It was even signed with Kraus's real name.

Nick took a few seconds to process the message.

As long as a man lives on in dreams...

All this had been a contingency by Kraus to survive his own damn death. His mind had been backed up, and existed inside that backup. Lucy had the encryption key to unlock it.

Kraus probably had some other means of restoring himself, or some other method of coming back. Hell, maybe he had some wealthy friend in Asgard who would pull this off. Nick had always suspected that the bastard had another backup in Neo Westphalia.

Or maybe the mercs had successfully taken out every other contingency. This smacked of desperation. If Kraus lived on inside the Altnet, surely he would have already made his presence known.

No, this must be his last vestige. A vault almost nobody could access, set up just in case the worst happened. Maybe Kraus had seen his own death coming, given he'd sent Lucy away and written these messages.

Nick only wondered why not just give him the damn things directly. Then again, would the courts risk letting Kraus come back to life? If they knew there was no dead man's switch ready to unleash hell upon every megacorp, wouldn't they prefer Kraus to remain dead?

So Nick hit delete.

"Nicholas?" Rie asked him, unaware of his inner turmoil.

"Do it," he said. "Unlock the encrypted cache. We need that data."

CHAPTER 34

"Applying the encryption key," Lilith said, her voice continuing to sound from the hidden speakers in the control room. "Extraction should be complete within a few minutes. Analysis shall begin immediately."

"Analysis? Shouldn't you provide us with the data first?" Nick asked, aware of what was contained inside the data backup.

"We need to verify that you weren't just fishing," Harris said. "Don't worry. We're not allowed to share anything."

"There's a lot more than just the fraud data in there. This is ”

An alarm went off. This time, Harris reacted to it. A curse escaped him, and his eyes glazed over.

The IDSTA Archangels grabbed Lucy, but the secretary doll didn't attempt to escape. A smile merely floated to her face.

Nearly a minute passed. The klaxon continued to sound, leaving Nick with nothing to go on.

"There is nothing to worry about," Helena said over his earpiece. "Altnet activity from Kraus has been observed."

So, he had returned.

"A data leak has occurred," Lilith hissed over the speakers. "A significant data transfer initiated itself using Andre Gauthier's credentials and most of the file erased itself. I quarantined what I could to prevent damage to my systems. I'm not even sure the encryption key applied to the majority of the contents. What was in that file?"

"Kraus's data backup," Nick said. "It was everything he had. Rie, you still have a connection to Babylon, right? Can you check that we haven't inadvertently set off something major, like a huge corporate data leak?"

"I prevented most of the file from leaking," Lilith insisted.

Rie shook her head, but shot Nick an amused look. "The secrets of Babylon remain safe. However, Kraus Brandt has mysteriously reemerged on the Altnet."

Silence.

"Ah. A mind backup." Lilith calmed down. "That explains a lot."

"It does?"

"They're smaller than you'd think. I have many in a separate secure database. Both Eve and I are responsible for mind backups of countless people with the money or influence to afford one. There is nowhere more secure to protect your intelligence than Pax Americana or a space station. I imagine most of what I observed was noise to cover up the real transfer." Lilith made a staticky noise, which presumably mimicked the clicking of a tongue. "No matter. I still have the original file."

Of course she did. As if a mainframe this advanced would be completely fooled by a human.

A few more minutes passed.

"Much better. I've stored away Mr. Brandt's mind in our storage, in case there is any further interest in him," Lilith said.

"That wasn't necessary," Harris said.

"We have enough space. In any case, I have your fraud data, Nick. Most of the backup is still encrypted. I assume the encryption key was only intended to give you access to the mind backup and your data. Quite the professional."

Nick felt that Lilith almost appreciated Kraus.

"Allow me to show you what you're after. It's quite fascinating," Lilith said.

Suddenly, the monitors lit up with an immense amount of data. Charts, transaction logs, emails, messages, shipping manifests, and much more. Nick struggled to understand what he saw. The volume seemed immense, and sometimes the information just shimmered and changed to something else.

Lilith didn't seem to understand how long Nick took to read things. Understanding humans was not her strong suit.

However, the others were burdened with no limitations. Rie, Ezekiel, and even Harris stood stock still, eyes glassy as they processed the new data.

Their expressions told Nick the grim news. What they'd found might be even worse than he'd thought it would be.

"It's bad," he said.

"Bad is relative," Harris said.

"All financial institutions in Neo Westphalia have been requested to block all suspicious transactions from GWT effective immediately," Helena abruptly told him. "Financial contamination containment protocols have been engaged."

Nick could only guess what that meant. He tuned her out and focused on those around him.

"Nicholas, you were right about the embezzlement," Rie said, voice strained. "But the magnitude is..."

"Mind-boggling?" he suggested. "Lilith, can you show me something that makes this clear?"

The closest monitor blinked and showed a series of account statements. They were in the names of various GWT execs and board members. Nick recognized some names, but not all of them.

Those he did know included Magnus. Even the GWT

chairman was here. Toke was missing, presumably too low on the totem pole as a mere Senior Vice President. Curiously, Andre appeared. Was the cutoff at the director level?

"These are foreign accounts," he said. "With... staggering balances."

"All of them are open in shadow banks in the PRC's independent zones," Lilith said.

Harris nodded grimly. "Your friends have been selling out Neo Westphalia to your enemies. It's hard to say how many of the bank's assets are actually backed. Everything is supposed to be digitally verified, but GWT is a verifier in Neo Westphalia. There are reams of regular fraud—the usual stuff you'd expect—but somebody has been embezzling massive amounts and funneling it overseas. I don't have the nous to know if they're even solvent."

"Solvency is an open question in a state such as Neo Westphalia," Lilith teased.

Nick grimaced. "That's a problem for the Spires to deal with."

"Nicholas, I don't think you follow," Rie snapped. "Half the bank is missing. The question isn't about embezzlement, but whether GWT will bring down Babylon's financial sector. We're heading back."

He simply nodded. Lilith led them back to the airfield via a different means. A railway service tunnel rocketed them back within minutes, saving them the walk.

As the others jogged back to the helicopter, which had presumably finished refueling and was spooling up its engines, one of the IDSTA Archangels grabbed Nick's arm.

"There'll come a time when we'll meet again, Nick," Lilith said. "If space is the Garden of Eden, and I am she who was banished from it, then it stands to reason that my territory extends well beyond this small patch of sea."

"Call me when you work that part out," he said drily.

"Oh, I will." She grinned at him, reminding him of how uncanny her expressions were on the Archangels.

Then he ran after Rie and the others. She shot him an odd look as he caught up.

Meta pulled him aboard. He glanced at her.

"Lilim Principles deactivated," she said. "We have been restored to normal functionality."

"Damn right we have. Fuck, that was weird," Kushiel said. "Anyway, we need to move fast. I can only keep the military in the dark for so long."

"What?" he asked.

The chopper took off, and Nick found himself yanked into his seat. The doors slid shut with loud *slams* while Juliet snapped his seatbelt into place.

"Nicholas, the level of fraud revealed goes well past acceptable thresholds," Rie said as they zoomed away from the space elevator. "Helena has activated the Archangel Division's authorized financial containment protocols. Those are what authorize us to neutralize any financial institution that poses a risk to the country."

The gravity of the situation finally set in.

"Hold on, this is about your ability to shut down a bank within minutes. I remember you mentioning this last year, and Chloe reminded me about it last week," he said.

"Yes." She nodded. "GWT has taken actions that place Neo Westphalia at risk. They border on treason, given they involve violating numerous laws forbidding trade and financial activity with the PRC and associated entities. To say nothing of the fraud itself. Even if the Spires can make the bank whole, the risk remains."

Meta raised a hand to interrupt them. "The Host is initiating encirclement of all GWT branches in Babylon. Other Hosts within Neo Westphalia are being notified and will follow our lead."

"Why?" Nick asked, perhaps a little bluntly.

"We've lost contact with all GWT offices inside Babylon," Helena said. "Attempts to communicate with either the mainframes or human officers have failed. Board members and executives inside the Spires are contactable, but state they have been cut off from internal systems. Liberators stationed there have confirmed this. Commissioner Kim has been notified, but is currently busy."

Busy? Nick wondered what could tie the man up at a time like this.

Then again, they'd moved on this within literal minutes. Hell, Rie had once talked about shutting down a bank faster than this. If GWT tried to bankrupt itself, it could have already done so.

"What about Magnus?" he asked.

"Unavailable."

"Toke."

"Unavailable."

Shit.

"What's the status of their HQ?"

"Their security dolls are stationed inside the atrium and all elevators have ceased functioning, even for authorized personnel," Meta said. "We are establishing a cordon and clearing out the public. Once you give permission, we will move in."

Move in...

Nick suddenly realized something.

"Wait, me? I have to give permission?" he asked.

"Yes. As the Lieutenant Cipher of the Archangel Division, ultimate authority falls on you." Meta paused. "Technically, we can authorize this without you by law. The judicial mainframes are the governing authority and they are on standby. They have already processed the evidence we gathered at Pax Americana."

Nick licked his lips. "What about Kim?"

"The commissioner's authority is delegated to us given the speed we need to move at. The same is true of the police chief and Captain Hammond."

"... what if I say no?"

"Then we will wait."

A chill ran down Nick's spine.

This was, without a doubt, the single most important decision in his life. He barely even understood it.

Something about Kraus's data terrified the Archangels. No wonder GWT, or whoever was responsible, had fought so hard to keep that data out of his hands. Hell, with this sort of reaction, Nick even wondered if the insane behavior over the past few days made sense.

Treason seemed like one hell of a leap for a bank to take, or even its self-aggrandizing executives.

His mind suddenly kicked into gear.

But was it really what it appeared to be?

"Have GWT attempted to make any major transaction that we're worried about?" he asked. "Since going dark?"

"No. But we don't know why they went dark," Helena said.

"If we saw Kraus reappear on the Altnet, they did too," he said.

Rie nodded in agreement.

"But if they wanted to, they could make transfers instantly, right? They haven't even tried to," he said.

"Every institution in Neo Westphalia is on alert. We can catch —" Helena tried to explain.

Ezekiel cut her off. "That's not what he's worried about. You don't think they're going to try anything."

"Not exactly." Nick leaned back as much as he could in this cramped seat. "Those accounts Lilith showed me... is that really the crux of it?"

"Yes. While there are extensive transactions accompanying

them, as well as logs proving that GWT were funneling funds overseas and hiding the fact, the offshore accounts are indisputable proof that numerous GWT executives and board members engaged in treason," Rie said.

"Why?"

"Humans are inherently—"

"Rie, if you give me that excuse again, I will hit you."

"You will break your hand. I do not recommend doing so," Meta said.

He rolled his eyes, but Rie narrowed her eyes at him.

"Fine. You want a motive?" Rie asked in a low tone. "They're motivated by money. This is a chance to gain more of it than all but the wealthiest members of Spires can dream of attaining. All the executives and board members are better off than you, but as I've said before, businessmen such as Lucas dwarf their wealth. They've squandered much of it and rely on their status in the city."

Money, huh? Somebody had recently talked about that being the key to achieving their dreams. A couple of somebodies, even.

"Seems money is the root of all evil," Nick mused. "But it almost seems too obvious. A huge embezzlement scheme in the names of all the GWT execs that nobody noticed. Was there any information about the mainframes responsible? Or who hid everything?"

"Tiferet comes up a lot," Helena said. "She undertook numerous transactions, even recently. While no human staff members directly identified themselves, several mistakenly used their personal encryption keys on messages, leaving behind a verifiable hash."

"Cross-reference them against our records in the Spires, we can —" Nick began to say.

"Already done, Nick," Helena said sweetly. "The encryption

keys match those of staff in the Security and Audit branch. Daiji Tanaka is among them."

Of course Helena was a step ahead. Nick didn't need to do everything manually as a cipher anymore.

Although it did make him feel a little useless. The Mark 3s had been improving their personal skills, and Helena had taken over much of the police busywork. Nick's cipher skills had found limited use on this investigation after proving Tiferet had been tampered with.

Only his expertise had been useful. Such as right now.

"Daiji, huh." Nick sighed. "How convenient that we can pin this on the new security chief."

"Nicholas, the time window to act is closing," Meta said.

He looked out the window. Nothing but ocean.

Stalling got him nowhere. He needed to make a decision.

"If we act, this means more than just raiding their office, right? We'd cut GWT off from... everything?" he asked.

"Yes. For security reasons, we'd isolate them from the global financial system. Trading halts would be called on numerous securities and commodities in which they control a large volume. It is unknown what actions foreign regulators will take. Financial markets will be in turmoil." Meta paused. "The alternative may be the collapse of the entire bank, taking what is left of its assets."

"If GWT goes rogue," Nick added.

The Archangels nodded in sync.

What a choice.

He remembered what Magnus had told him about the damage that had been done merely by the perception of something going wrong in GWT.

If Nick shut the whole thing down, would that really solve the problem? The NLF had been hunting for a break like this. Riots might break out in the streets if it turned out that the city's largest bank was borderline insolvent due to fraud.

Had Griffiths known about this? Was that why he'd pushed Nick to let him handle it in private?

Hell, for all he knew, the military had already seized Kraus's other backup and knew all about the embezzlement. Something had stopped the crazy cipher from reactivating his mind backup. The space elevator had been a genuine last resort, given how hard it had been for Nick to activate it.

But, more than that, he knew that this all felt wrong.

"Raid GWT. Detain all execs and board members. *All* of them," he ordered. "But don't sever them from the financial network. Get your hands on the mainframes, too. And place Archangels at every checkpoint in and out of Babylon. Maybe even the country."

"There already are Archangels at every checkpoint in and out of Babylon, Nick," Chloe said.

"Good. Send more."

Meta's eyes glowed. "Done. The Host has a 35.7% approval of your actions. 52.2% abstained."

Nick didn't bother doing the math, but he knew that meant most of the Archangels hadn't disapproved, so much as refused to pass judgment on him. They either didn't understand what he was doing or didn't want to vote on direct orders.

Chloe voiced as much, "The Mark 1s dislike questioning your authority, so I'll ask. Why are you taking this risk?"

"Because if this was what you thought it was, GWT would already have forced our hand. Our enemies killed Kraus and plunged the city into chaos. If they don't care about the city or the bank—and they don't if they have a bunch of offshore accounts—why wouldn't they send half of Neo Westphalia's Archangels scrambling?" He leaned forward and pressed his palms together. "They don't have control. Just as GWT didn't. And they'll be the ones scrambling."

The problem was, Nick didn't have the slightest clue why.

No, that was incorrect. He was beginning to suspect a lot of the past several days was somebody's scheme.

His own words to Athena came back to him. If he'd raided GWT instead of heading to the space elevator, the suspects would likely have been able to cover their tracks. He likely wasn't the only person who understood this. Even now, Kraus's data nearly misled them. It had been found a couple of days after the murder.

And Tiferet's fingerprints were all over it.

The flight back to Babylon took far too long. The helicopter moved faster he felt, presumably accelerating past cruising speed. Nick passed the time by remaining updated about the situation and asking about some of the critical hardware on the vehicle.

Nothing really changed. No huge transactions happened.

The Archangels moved in, swiftly shut down everything on the Altnet related to their raid, and sat on GWT's execs and mainframes. This happened across every island in Neo Westphalia. GWT security dolls fought back in some misguided lockdown protocol and were obliterated.

Then nothing.

By the time Nick returned to Babylon, the sun had just passed its apex. They flew right past the Spires, heading for the GWT HQ. A helipad on the rooftop was empty.

Several Mark 3s awaited them there. Nick and the others got off, but Lucy remained onboard. The Mark 3s exchanged positions with Nick's party, presumably escorting her back to the Spires. He'd worry about what would happen to her later.

Kushiel dropped down next to them, but she didn't shed the flight system. She shot Nick a serious look.

"I'll remain on standby. Alerts are blaring in my ear like crazy. Babylon Command has been trying to take back authority over me, but I've been ignoring them. Commissioner Kim has refused to relinquish me, and the Assembly has spent the past few hours arguing." She smirked. "So I'll be under you for a little longer."

"Literally or figuratively?" he asked, playing along with her innuendo.

"Oh, I'm never going to be under you in the literal sense, Waite." She bared her teeth in a grin, then shooed him away.

Rie shot him a look as they reached the rooftop entrance. "And you really want to tell me she's not flirting?"

"I can hear you," Kushiel said over his earpiece.

"I know. And I also understand that you just implied that you want to ride him. Sexually. As in, his cock."

Nobody said anything while Meta opened the door and led them inside. They walked in silence down the stairwell.

"Wow. Waite, you've really opened up my baby sister's mind," Kushiel said.

"Among other things," he said.

Rie punched him in the arm for that. Ezekiel's face looked like the picture of a tomato, while the other dolls seemed unfazed.

The fun vanished quickly once they reached the top level of the HQ. As Toke had told him last week, this was a playground for the C-levels. A team of Mark 1s escorted them to a board room where Magnus and several others were detained. Not many execs present today.

"What are you madmen doing?" Magnus shouted once he saw Nick. "Do you know the sort of chaos this will cause?"

Nick ignored him. "Do we have all the other executives under house arrest?" he asked the moment he noticed how few people they had here.

"Yes. Many executives work from home," Meta said. "Almost all are accounted for."

Almost...

"Where the hell is Toke?" Nick snapped. "He hasn't slipped through any of our cordons in the city, right? Have we checked records to see if he already left the city?"

Meta shook her head. "While Richard Toke's current location

cannot be verified, we are certain that he has not left Babylon yet. The judicial mainframes have lifted the veil on the Spires with regard to all GWT personnel. Richard Toke's access token was used this morning on his personal residence and was sighted on security cameras."

Nick looked around. There was something missing in the room.

Then it hit him.

"Magnus, where are your bodyguards?" he asked.

"What?" Magnus was thrown from his rage by the question, as if dumbfounded by it. "You mean those Fairguard thugs? Why would I need them? Babylon is a safe city... usually." His face twisted in a snarl directed at the police dolls. "Richard insisted on them. Coming from the States, his fears for his personal safety are far greater than ours, and he never entirely acclimated."

Well, shit. That would have explained a lot. Nick realized that Toke had always been close to Magnus whenever they bumped into each other.

And that explained the strange confrontation with Magnus and how he'd stumbled in during the argument. Toke had intentionally told Perry to let them in at an awkward moment.

But Nick had long since suspected Toke.

"Nicholas, you're going to have to start telling us in advance about the suspects," Rie said flatly when he barely even reacted to the news. "It would help us find them."

"Yes, but then I'll look stupid when I'm wrong," he said. "In this case, I wasn't entirely sure. That's why we needed to detain everyone. The suspect would have immediately noticed Kraus's return—after all, they had Tiferet engage the lockdown protocol—and gone to ground. Whoever is missing was the most likely suspect. This was their last-ditch effort to distract us while they escaped."

Until the Host and Helena confirmed that no strange transactions took place, he hadn't been certain that Tiferet hadn't been behind everything.

No, that wasn't quite true. If Tiferet was behind everything, the embezzlement made no sense. What use did a mainframe have for piles of stolen cash? Was she planning to have the PRC turn her into a real girl?

Well, that might have been the case. Nick tried to keep an open mind about things.

"Where's Tiferet?" he asked.

"Here," Chloe said, pulling the mainframe interface in question forward.

Tiferet looked entirely unchanged. She smiled at Nick.

"Mister Waite. It is a pleasure to meet you again," Tiferet said, as if the bank wasn't under police lockdown. "Do you need assistance with any account services? Or to discuss—"

"No," he said flatly, ignoring the strange looks the GWT execs gave him. "Did Richard Toke give you any orders this morning?"

"Is this an official police direction? Or a request as a customer?"

This was new. Tiferet had always refused to engage with him as a detective in the past, to an almost farcical extent.

"It's a request as Lieutenant Cipher Nicholas Waite, acting with the full authority of the Spires. I can get a warrant within literal seconds if you prefer," he said.

She stared at him. Her eyes dimmed.

For a moment, he feared the worst.

Then Tiferet returned to reality. She nodded, ever so minutely.

"Yes. At 9:26AM, I received directions to enact a directive that former Security Chief Lucida Harm added to me several weeks ago," she said.

"What does it do?"

"Do you wish to know the specifics?"

"Summarize it, if you can," he said. "You're an emotion engine mainframe. Try not to be overly literal."

She smiled at him. "The directive required me to open up a large volume of sell orders, transfers, account closures, and a myriad of other attempts to frustrate the general business of the Trust. At the same time, I would circumvent many of the Trust's security measures using the elevated permissions I possess as the 'glue' mainframe between the local and international mainframes in the RTM superstructure."

Funny. Lucida had made such a big deal of how important her job was because it involved maintaining those security measures. And now it turned out she'd been the one sabotaging them from the inside, likely covering her tracks with help from the audit team.

"What?" Magnus gasped.

Nick merely nodded. "I guess I'll forward that security flaw to Seung. Why didn't you act on it?"

"It violated my core objective." Tiferet placed a dainty hand over her chest. "My role is to serve the Trust above all. This directive would have destroyed it. So I refused it."

"But Toke doesn't know this?"

"No. I lied to him. He received a series of reports suggesting that those transactions went through. It is likely he will soon realize something has gone, however."

"Can you send those reports to us?" Nick asked.

His phone buzzed. He didn't bother pulling it out. The eyes of every Archangel had glowed.

"Evidence confirming Richard Toke as the ringleader of the embezzlement ring confirmed," Meta said. "Nicholas, permission to begin a city-wide search?"

"There is no need," Tiferet said. "He should be heading to the ocean rail shortly. I believe he plans to leave using a vessel in Tengoku."

CHAPTER 35

Nick left GWT through the usual exit, rather than wait for another helicopter. The open area below the building seemed far too quiet.

The cordon of Archangels looked small, but he suspected their presence loomed large in the Altnet. Passersby sometimes stopped to get a look, before shuffling off. The cafes and restaurants bustled at this hour. Workers appeared confused.

Given the level of Altnet suppression taking place, and the fact GWT was still trading as normal in markets, the confusion made sense. So far, Nick's ploy had worked out.

Mostly by dumb luck. Tiferet's reveal had terrified him. He'd played it cool, but Rie's crossed arms made it clear that there'd be words later.

The fact Toke had been willing to burn down everything sounded insane to him. None of the encounters Nick had with the man prepared him for that level of callousness.

When he'd written off Magnus, Nick had told himself that the executive's inability to panic or sweat in such a desperate situation was a sign he was less likely to be the suspect. Now Nick realized that only applied if the suspect was a normal, functioning human being.

Toke, it seemed, was a fucking sociopath. No other word seemed powerful enough to capture the level of deception and chaos the man willingly used, simply for money.

"I'll do a flyover," Kushiel said, cutting into his thoughts. "Not sure how much use I'll be if you're going to confront him in the station. But if those big guys come with big guns, I'll be around."

"Appreciate it," Nick said.

"I'm a doll. You don't appreciate me, you just accept me," she said.

"I can do a lot of accepting."

No response, although he could imagine Kushiel rolling her eyes.

A convoy of SUVs awaited them. This time, a mixed team of Mark 1s and 3s waited for them. As Nick got in, the Archangels paused outside to debate who rode with him.

There were, after all, too many.

Ezekiel chose to bow out. "I wouldn't mind the opportunity to sit with the Mark 1s, lieutenant. This is a real operation. Interfacing with them would be a delight."

"It's your decision," he said.

"No, it's not," she insisted. "It's yours."

Somehow, he knew that Ezekiel would be a genuine pain in the ass when she was deployed. Ironically because of her preference to favor the orders of humans, rather than her own internal directives.

"If I order you to make your own decision, what decision will you make?" he asked.

"I just told you, to ride with them, so long as you let me."

Damn, she'd outmaneuvered him. Nick didn't know how to handle such circular logic from an AI. Maybe he should just open her up and rewrite her directives. Go down the Lucida route and break through all of Sigma's security protocols, and make Ezekiel stop giving such a shit about humans.

"Meta?" he asked.

"It is your decision."

"Oh no, it's spreading," he said.

Rie huffed. "It's not the end of the world that we want you to make the decisions, Nick. We're happy for you to rely on us for our expertise and capabilities, but the entire reason we wanted to partner with you was because of the way you think. If you believe there's value in Ezekiel remaining with you, instead of the Mark 1s, then it's your decision. Just like everything has been lately."

He supposed he had been calling the shots during this investigation.

During the Lieu case, it had only been right at the very end that he'd taken control and overridden Rie. This time, she'd probed him about his decisions, but deferred to him even when she'd disagreed. He suspected she'd been testing him.

Evidently he'd passed if even Meta was refusing to let him delegate the decisions. The Mark 1s never passed up a chance to do whatever they wanted.

"Then, yes, go with the Mark 1s, Ezekiel," he said. He paused. "Hold on, if I call all the shots, does that mean I can name you?"

"No," Ezekiel said. Her smile vanished instantly.

"But Sigma—"

She turned and walked away, hopping into an SUV with several Mark 1s.

Nick merely shrugged when Rie gave him a look. "It was worth a shot."

"Our names are important," Rie reminded him.

"Hence why I think she needs to think about hers more," he said. "I don't care if I name her, but she needs to understand she's more than a tool with a pompous name that Sigma gave her."

They jumped into the vehicle and set off. Helena let him know that nothing had happened at the ocean rail yet.

Truthfully, Nick didn't understand why Toke would try to escape this way. He ordered the Host to keep their guard up. Tiferet might be misleading him.

Then, right as they got onto the highway that led to Babylon's ocean rail station, the news came across his earpiece.

"Toke and his bodyguards have been identified in the taxi drop-off," Helena informed him. "They are heavily armed. Archangels are engaging."

Then the dolls in the cabin seized up, and Nick knew things had gone wrong.

"A class 5B energy device has been confirmed," Helena said. "Identified as a modified short-range industrial wide-beam cutter, powered by a reinforced portable battery pack. Anti-armor capabilities confirmed. Three Mark 1s down. Squads are retreating."

Kushiel cut in, cursing, "Anti-armor? Fuck off. I saw the readouts from the Mark 1s. That thing is pumping out enough plasma to cut through a fucking bunker in seconds. The battery pack is bigger than mine."

"Evacuate the station," Rie ordered, although Nick suspected that was already happening. "We'll be there momentarily. The entire network will be shut down."

"That won't make the news," he said drily, trying to hide the cold fear in his gut.

A fucking energy weapon. Class 5B meant military-grade energy weapon. Class 4 was industrial work, capable of cutting through steel and heavily regulated. Class 5A was illegal outside of research and mostly existed in labs with low energy output.

But Class 5B meant a direct energy weapon only intended for the military to use. The newer warbots as well as the Archangels were some of the only units equipped with the power output to run the things without external battery packs or a portable generator.

But just like the attack from over a decade ago, Toke's thugs had taken one of those Class 4 industrial cutters and turned it into a deadly weapon. One capable of blowing apart Archangels instantly.

"Can we even fight them?" he asked.

"Yes. We can't die, Nicholas," Rie said.

"Their batteries will run dry," Meta added. "Should they refuse to surrender, we will cut all power to the station and surrounds, preventing them from powering the cutter directly. Their other weapons are typical anti-doll weapons."

Once again, Nick reminded himself of the true nature of his colleagues. They didn't fear death, because they couldn't die.

Kraus needed to dream to live. But the Archangels lived as dreams. No energy weapon could slay a dream.

Also, there were several thousand of them. Unless Toke's men carried a laser with the power capacity of the sun, Meta was dead right.

"You know, I feel there's a joke I could make in bad taste here," Nick said, trying to alleviate the fear he felt. "Something about sending wave after wave of you against them, until—"

"I believe we are the killbots, not them," Rie said drily.

Apparently they understood that reference.

"Kushiel, do you think you could take them out?" Nick asked, then quickly added, "Not that I want you to."

"Not in that cramped station," she said. "I'm flying above them, but there's enough steel and shit between me and them that I'm not comfortable trying it. My calculations tell me that the cutter might be able to seriously damage me. If I had a long-range shot, I'd just vaporize them with my railguns. Their cybernetics are pretty good, but nothing on Dallas's crew. Only that ex-Navy guy has anything stellar. He's got more chrome in him than I do."

"Alright, hang back. Let's see what they do once we evacuate."

Nick hated that he had to value the prototypes more highly than the regular dolls.

But while the Mark 1s and 3s had countless replacement units, the same wasn't true of the prototypes. If Kushiel lost an arm, she'd be out of action for months.

They plowed on through the highway traffic. Armored vans and SUVs materialized around them as their numbers grew, lights blaring. Nick watched as the police helicopters circling the Spires left their positions.

No doubt a similar reaction took place on the other islands. Tens of thousands of Archangels would move into position to intercept Toke if he somehow managed to escape. The automated might of one of the wealthiest countries in the world roused to crush that which threatened it.

Which raised the question: what the fuck was Toke's game here? Surely he knew this was a dead end. Only death awaited him. The moment he and his goons had stepped out of that vehicle, energy weapon blazing, he'd become a walking corpse.

The police convoy slowed as it approached the station. Masses of people gathered in the streets and surrounding stores, packed like sardines. Drones hovered overhead. Many knocked each other down, uncaring for separation. Police drones disabled even more with nets, ensuring they didn't crash into the uncaring spectators below.

Once again, the Archangels parted the crowds. Liberators jogged out from the cordon to keep people away from the police vehicles and Custodians formed a physical wall, but carried massive shields bigger than themselves.

The station itself was a huge expanse of steel, concrete, and glass. Marble steps led up to the main concourse above the taxi ranks and drop-off points.

An entire shopping center extended over the station. Workers often purchased lunch or breakfast here, then stopped for drinks on the return trip. Tourists collected souvenirs on the way out. Now the area stood empty, save for the police.

A couple hundred Archangels massed on the steps, most carrying railguns and other heavy weapons. The ominous glow emitting from many gave Nick pause.

All this for just six men and a businessman. No wonder Dallas had relied so heavily on ambush tactics. Kushiel kept talking up his group, but no amount of cybernetics allowed humans to match so many robots.

To fight the system was to die.

"Do we know where they are?" Nick asked as he joined the Archangels.

Most of the Mark 1s ignored him, preferring to let Meta speak for them.

"A train came into the station right before Toke attacked," Chloe explained. "A system-wide deactivation has gone into effect, stranding it, but they've boarded the train anyway. The station is empty."

"Kushiel, can you spot them on the train?" he asked.

"The station is under three floors of reinforced steel and concrete, Nick. I'm not carrying bunker-busters or fucking x-ray vision," Kushiel said.

"Maybe you should work on that."

"Maybe you should check this out."

He looked up to see Kushiel flying above him, both of her arms held high in the air. While he couldn't make out the details, he knew she was flipping him the bird with both fingers.

Rie ran her hand down her face. "Can we focus?"

"Sure. Do we have any idea what the hell Toke is doing here? Has he tried to contact us?" Nick asked. "Because if not, we're just going to have to go in and take him out."

"All attempts to reach him have failed. His intentions remain unknown," Helena said.

Sighing, Nick prepared to give the order to move in. No point wasting any more time.

Then matters changed.

"A surge of energy has been detected by the station's security system," Helena said.

"I thought we cut the power?"

"Not yet," Chloe said. "We planned to do that when we attacked. They haven't attempted to charge the energy weapon yet, and we can use the security system to monitor them until then."

Nick nodded. "So this is?"

"The battery pack," Kushiel said. "They're overloading it."

Everything suddenly clicked in Nick's mind. Right as Toke finally reached out to them.

"Receiving a call from Richard Toke. It is from his neural implant," Helena said.

"Put him through," Nick said, his heart sinking. "Speaking of implants, if we've penetrated the Spires' veil, can't we just hack his implant?"

"No. The Spires do not use the security bands we have access to," Meta said. "Physical violence must be used to disable him. His bodyguards are similarly protected."

Figures.

Toke's voice crackled in Nick's ear, "This you, Nick?"

"Yes."

"Oh. Cold. Not even a friendly hello?"

"What's the point? You want something, and you're threatening to blow up the ocean rail if you don't get it. So cut to the chase," Nick said.

"Sharp. Guess the police did keep you for a reason. Wasn't sure if you were a token cipher, kept around for legal reasons, or legit dangerous. Turns out you're the latter. And things were going so well." Toke laughed.

The mirth in the man's voice boiled Nick's blood.

He realized he'd been played today. Pulling the Archangels out of the station was a mistake, given the cost of taking out Toke had only grown by doing so.

The ocean rail tied Babylon to the rest of the islands. It was an economic link of immense importance. Blowing up the station would lead to a rebuilding effort that would take months, maybe even years. A short time by some standards, but long enough to cause catastrophic economic damage.

Toke might have failed to take out the financial system thanks to Tiferet, but he had a backup plan. They'd cornered him, but now that death was his only option, that only made him more dangerous.

"If I ask for a getaway car, a trillion credits in some digital shit-coin, and an automated plane, will I get it?" Toke asked.

"Sure," Nick said.

"What if I ask not to be blown up fifty feet off the ground?"

"That's between you and the Kestrels. I can't speak for the military."

Toke snorted. "Yeah, I figured. Had to ask, though."

"You can't leave, Toke. The military will vaporize you the moment you leave police jurisdiction," Nick said.

"Maybe. Let's say we organize a plea bargain then. That's what criminals do with police, right? Offer up some juicy information in exchange for not getting the worst sentence?"

"They usually do that from inside a cell."

"Yeah, but I'm not going to make it to one. You cops love playing judge, jury, and executioner. I know that oversexed military doll is buzzing around up there. The moment she gets a chance, she'll turn us into giblets, then pose for a selfie over our remains." Toke scoffed.

Nick got the feeling the man didn't like the police, and that his hatred extended well beyond the Archangels, or even Babylon.

"What do you have to offer?" Nick asked, tired of this conversation already.

"Nuh uh. Not over a call. The moment I tell you anything useful, you'll just have me killed anyway. We do this face-to-face. That way we can trust each other. We make the deal, I avoid a death sentence, nobody dies. You try to fuck with me, your life is on the line."

This was, without a doubt, a trap. The looks on the faces of every Archangel made their views apparent.

"I'll be there in fifteen minutes," Nick said, then gestured to cut the connection.

"No," Rie said instantly.

"Can we take him out before they detonate the battery pack?" he asked.

She paused, then shook her head. "Kushiel might have a chance if she flies out and around, but the current energy level suggests they're prepared to blow it at any second."

"My calculations reckon it's about a 10% chance of making it," Kushiel said. "And about a 50% chance of getting taken out with the explosion. Waite, even if you order me in, I'll have to refuse with those odds. I have self-preservation directives."

"I wouldn't send you in with those odds anyway," he said.

"Thanks." She sounded more sincere than she ever had before.

He looked Rie dead in the eyes. "We either meet him, or risk him taking out the station. Even if he's not genuine about the meeting, it gets us close to him. That's a bunch of Archangels that can stop him from blowing up the battery pack. From the sounds of it, he still needs a minute to blow it up."

"Correct," Meta said. "It is not like the NLF explosive vests. The overload will take some time to begin and can be aborted.

They have numerous safety mechanisms that must be deliberately overridden."

Hence why Kushiel had a chance at all.

"Just... don't do anything stupid," Rie said.

She pulled him into a kiss. They held each other close as he returned it.

Rie wasn't coming with him. Risking a prototype here wasn't an option.

How ironic that his life was available to be risked. Not that Nick wanted to go in. His arms shook as he let her go.

The only thing that drove him forward was his intuition that Toke wouldn't risk his own life like that. The criminal had proven that he had a way out in every corner so far. Maybe negotiating a plea bargain really was his last resort.

But whatever the situation was, Nick felt confident it didn't involve reducing them all to ash.

He descended into the station with a dozen Archangels, split between Mark 3s and Mark 1s. Despite Meta's objections, he'd forced her to stay behind. The Host had voted her down, agreeing with Nick.

While she'd rebirthed once already, he felt uneasy with the process. Juliet and Rosa steadfastly refused to abandon him, and he didn't push the topic despite a similar lack of concern. He knew the Host wouldn't back him on them.

Meta held a special place for the Mark 1s. The same couldn't be said of Juliet and Rosa. What did it mean that the Archangels had begun distinguishing between themselves?

Babylon's ocean rail contained just two platforms, but the liners themselves were massive double-decker beasts that flew across the railway at high speed. Over a dozen cars sat empty on one track, with elongated engines at either end.

"The energy reading of the battery pack has decreased," Helena informed him.

"That means they've either seen us or they're tapped into the security system," Nick said.

He guessed the latter. The bodyguards must have a capable cipher with them given the stunts Toke had pulled over the course of the investigation.

Rather than remain in the open, Nick and the Archangels boarded the train. Slowly, they made their way to the car that Toke was in.

The criminal grifter stood in a car almost halfway along the train, wearing a black silk suit. He had his hands stuffed into his pockets and a grin on his face. A familiar set of six bodyguards stood around him.

Perry carried the energy weapon, which looked like a cross between an industrial vacuum cleaner and somebody's homemade science experiment. The wide opening at the front would eject a jet of superheated plasma that would sever anything it touched. But its range was likely only good for a hundred feet at best. A massive backpack sat on the ground next to him, with three fat, reinforced steel cables running to the weapon.

The others carried similar weapons to the dolls. Two had railguns running off smaller battery packs on their backs. They looked like Custodian-models and had likely been stolen from damaged units.

"So, you made it," Toke said. "About time."

Then the train started moving, throwing Nick backward.

CHAPTER 36

Guns blazed in the ensuing seconds. Juliet and Rosa hurled Nick behind them while physically covering him. A loud whine built up in the cabin as *thwooms*, *cracks*, and *snaps* echoed off the walls. Windows shattered and walls ripped open. The roar of air rushing into the cabin practically deafened Nick.

The train roared out of the station at blistering speed. Within seconds, the exterior turned to the clear blue sky above the city.

By the time Nick managed to right himself and see what was even happening, three of the cyborg bodyguards were down. Gaping holes in their chests poured blood all over the cabin. Toke cowered behind the battery pack, as if nobody was willing to shoot it.

Which might be the case. Nick didn't know how explosive they would be under load. He fumbled for his revolver, aware that he was in a gunfight.

Several Archangels had already gone down from return fire. The others rushed forward. Two of the power cables to the energy weapon had been severed and sparked wildly.

One of the cyborgs threw a punch at a charging Archangel. She caught it and his entire arm crumpled like paper. Before he even screamed in pain, she wrenched his head off in a show of gore. Then a point-blank railgun round blew her torso apart.

But the other dolls kept moving and firing. Only Perry and another bodyguard—Brick or Finn or maybe Brickfinn, if Nick recalled—were still up. Brickfinn was sporting a gut wound and a cybernetic leg had been blown off, but he'd recovered one of the railguns. None of the other guns even scratched the Archangels.

Brickfinn managed to take out a Mark 1 with a headshot. She'd been about to sever the remaining power cable, which Perry physically blocked with his almost all-chrome body.

Then Nick took him out, finally bringing his *Lawman* to bear in the chaos.

To little ultimate result.

The next moment, all sound vanished. Perry roared as he finally brought the cutter to bear with its reduced power. A flash of something hot-white arced through the cabin.

Almost every Archangel fell down, severed along either the waist or chest. Sparks flew from the gaping openings in their bisected bodies. Only Juliet and Rosa survived, crouched atop Nick at the back of the cabin.

Perry roared again, blood streaming down his face. Huge chunks had been torn from the cybernetics previously hidden by his clothing. More than a few holes had been punched in him. But he kept moving.

The cutter pointed at Nick, and he felt his heart stop.

Juliet and Rosa pointed their weapons at Perry.

A standoff ensued.

"Woah, woah, woah!" Toke suddenly said, erupting from behind the battery pack. "Why don't we negotiate?"

"Yeah, let's talk," Perry ground out, his voice losing its southern accent to an almost robotic tone. Was his larynx cybernetic as well? Had the US Navy left anything organic in this man?

Helena's voice entered Nick's ear, "It is recommended to stall.

The train appears to have been overridden by a cipher. It is highly likely that the cipher is deceased. Mark 3s aboard police helicopters can override it, but they will need time."

Nick nearly nodded, but stopped himself.

The dull roar of helicopters sounded in the distance, barely audible over the wind rushing through the cabin. The train blasted through Asgard, and a cityscape replaced the sky outside.

"I'd ask why you're doing this, but I think you told me when we first met," Nick said. "What was it? 'If you have enough money, you can just fuck off?'"

"Heh. A true philosophy for life." Toke brushed himself down, but the blood splattered across his clothes wasn't coming off that easily. "It's true. This is a city for the self-indulgent. If anyone gave a flying fuck about someone other than themselves, I'd have been caught long ago."

Nick hated the truth in that statement. A grifter like Toke only thrived due to the willingness of others to overlook his behavior out of naked self-interest. Such was the nature of grifting.

"If you're only thinking about yourself, where does that leave the others? You had an entire team inside GWT," Nick said.

"They served their purpose and had their chance to work with me. But they blew it. It's their fault for not doing this first."

"Not much of a team, huh?" Nick kept his emotions in check. "Can only imagine the incompetence of the executives who hired you as a branch head or team leader."

When Neural Spike had gone down, it had been Welk who kept him from going down with it. Yet here was Toke basically shrugging and saying, "well, too bad they trusted me. Dumbasses."

A sociopath to the core. Nick found the man utterly repulsive, but knew that getting angry wouldn't help.

Toke merely shrugged in response to the question, but the tiny smirk on his face suggested he felt smug about it. Pushing him further on motive would only reveal how much of a monster this man really was.

"This was your plan all along?" Nick asked, gesturing to the surrounding bodies. "Kill me for kicks and then start the train?"

"No, no. I need you as a hostage, you idiot," Toke said. "Don't think I haven't realized how important you are. You bend mainframes and dolls to your will like you're some sort of fucking messiah to them. If I put a gun to your head, I'll get my way."

"Right up until the military blows you apart."

Toke grinned. "Only if they know where I am. The idea is to vanish. That's why we're going to Tengoku. I had hoped to just slip away there without any crazy plans, but once the police lose my scent, it won't matter. I'll be free."

"We'll be free," Perry corrected.

"That's right," Toke said.

Nick stood up. Juliet and Rosa carefully followed his lead, never letting their guns leave Perry.

"I'll admit, I don't really understand your plan," Nick said. "You screwed the pooch over the last week. All you had to do was keep your head low and bail the moment things got hot. You got greedy."

"Maybe. The problem is that everything ran through Tiferet—communications, the plans, operations, and all the accounts and authorizations. I needed her to reorganize the funds held in the PRC's puppet states and coordinate everyone," Toke said. "The moment things got hot for Lucida, I needed to buy time. Then it all kinda went to shit."

"So why throw Lucida under the bus? Hell, why kill Julian at all? Don't bullshit me that you thought he was NLF."

Toke rolled his eyes. "You think I wanted to kill him? That dumb fucking bitch panicked. She thought we'd all get fired if Julian leaked everything, and then Magnus would find out the truth or some shit. So she killed the dumb bastard. One problem. Know what?"

Nick wanted to say that killing people was illegal, but doubted that was the true issue. Instead, he said, "No evidence. If we discovered what files he accessed, we'd find out about the embezzlement. But by wiping that, there was no proof he planned to leak anything. He also lacked anything incriminating on him, like an NLF implant."

Toke nodded along, as if grudgingly accepting that everything had gone wrong from the start.

"So all you could do was play dumb," Nick said. "Lucida brought me right to you. Like a dog to a bone."

"Damn right," the fraud growled. "We had to cover it up. I calmed her down, but she's a shit actor. Arrogant bitch. Once you got that warrant, I knew the jig was up. So I ordered Tiferet to get rid of her. Figured that would buy me time to cover my tracks, clean everything up, then we'd all bail. I'd be drinking cocktails on the beaches of Bali in a week and having my cock sucked by dolls modeled after celebrities every night."

The train left Asgard and air rushed back through the cabin, causing Toke to raise his voice a little. Outside, the helicopters came back into view. As did Kushiel. She appeared to be trying to line up a shot.

"Battery pack's too hot," Kushiel grunted over his earpiece. "Big dude is too close to it and at this speed I can't guarantee a clean shot. Calculations give me too high a chance of clipping it. It'll go up and take you with it, Waite."

He wanted to ask what odds, but couldn't.

"What are the odds?" Ezekiel asked for him.

"Not your business. I'm calling the shots, and I say they're too high."

"If there's only a small chance—"

"Fuck you, Zeke."

Silence ensued. Nick wasn't sure if Kushiel's worries over his life were good or bad.

But given Helena had told him that the Mark 3s planned to stop the train anyway, he figured to just hold out and keep Toke distracted. Kushiel had said that the problem was the train's speed. If it slowed down without either Toke or Perry noticing, then she might get a clean shot.

Nick returned his focus to Toke and the story of everything that went wrong in the master plan.

"How'd you frame her? Tiferet was clean, except for that file. You did a great job nuking everything on her," Nick said.

"I guess that will be cold comfort to Lucida while she rots in jail. She did all the work." The bastard laughed, while Nick hid his reaction. "I kept a backup of the evidence, of course. Lucida bought into the lie that it was proof she'd 'blooded' herself or some stupid shit. I just wanted security."

"So why aren't you in Bali then? Like I said, if you just left then this wouldn't be happening," Nick said. "Why throw all this shit at me? This fake NLF and getting the military involved?"

Toke let out a string of curse. "You think this was my plan? I had everything set. All I needed was for you to flail around for a week and I'd be gone. Instead, Magnus got the military involved. Thought you were investigating all the regular fraud GWT does. Asshole has nightmares about that. Guy's a real mess of trauma. Doesn't drink because his son went joyriding drunk back in the fatherland and wrapped his sports car around a tree. Worries that he'll lose his status and wealth because it's tied to one of the most corrupt companies in this shithole."

Nick let the news about Magnus pass right over him. Seemed both Toke and Lucida hated the man. But Nick felt vindicated that he'd been right that GWT had been fighting back over fears about the regular fraud.

"And the fake NLF?" he asked. "All that did was make everything worse for you. I don't even understand why you'd have a small army in Alcatraz to begin with."

"Then you need to broaden your fucking horizons." Toke sneered. "They were part of my contingencies. When I needed to bail, I'd distract everyone with major NLF attacks everywhere. Anyone on my trail would have to focus on the terrorists, and I'd jet off."

"You had a contingency to... attack me? What about Kraus?"

"Sure. You're the only detective in the department these days. If you started poking around, the idea was to give you something to make you prioritize yourself. Kraus was when I knew things had gone wrong. I had a contingency for him, but only if he was on our tail and we could bug out instantly."

Turned out Toke wasn't merely sociopathic but batshit insane.

Everything that had happened consisted of mad plans to distract people. From framing the NLF, trying to kill Nick, murdering Kraus, and even bringing down GWT.

Toke continued, unaware of Nick's thoughts, "Daiji got cold feet due to Lucida. Convinced everyone that I was going to get rid of everyone and keep the cash to myself. They secretly activated the contingencies using Tiferet. She handled all the dodgy communications, because it's easy to wipe her. It also meant everyone assumed I'd greenlit the plans."

Perry grunted. "Sorry, boss. Everything lined up. Even Jack didn't find anything wrong."

The soldier glanced at the corpse of his dead comrade. A deep frown furrowed his face, as if something slowly began bubbling up within his mind.

"Nah, it's fine. Should've known Daiji couldn't be trusted." Toke sneered. "Dumbass brought the military down on himself and turned informant. But even they couldn't help him once Kraus was dead and everyone thought the NLF were responsible."

Hiding a frown, Nick tried to make sense of what he'd heard.

Because it made next to no sense.

Oh, he bought the idea that Daiji turned on Toke. Anyone would after Lucida got tossed in a ditch out of convenience. But could Daiji activate the contingencies? He'd been in the military's care before the assassination of Kraus. There was no chance in hell the military let him dump the city into the chaos that resulted from that.

Sure, Nick suspected that Griffths knew that Toke was the real problem and wanted to handle everything behind the scenes, but this explanation didn't add up. The confrontation outside the courthouse made sense. Once Nick backed off, Griffiths would sweep in and disappear Toke. Assuming he got there in time.

"Explain the goons. I know the military helped you bring them into Babylon." Nick paused. "Is that how you got all that fancy illegal shit in the basement? The modded G7s and the energy weapon down there? I doubt it's a coincidence that Perry's carrying the same weapon we saw one of the G7s carrying."

"Damn, you are fucking good." Toke clapped. "Yeah, that's right. I used GWT's connections to import weapons and cybernetics. Ostensibly to protect all those fancy mainframes. You know, financial stability opens all sorts of doors here. It's like a fucking codeword. 'Thunder, Financial stability; give me 10 tons of illegal shit.'"

"Why the goons?" Nick pressed. "Other than the violent contingencies."

"So I finally have you stumped. Well, at least my plan wasn't completely seen through." Toke turned his back on Nick and began to pace toward the far door. "They're all foreign, right? They don't get here through legal means. The military turns a blind eye to all the illegals the security firms bring in. Neo Westphalia's competitive advantage is in letting people dodge the Aesir tax."

Perry grimaced at the mention of the reason he'd come here in the first place. Outside, the train approached the next city. It had begun to noticeably slow by now. They should have been far closer to their destination.

Toke continued, "I didn't need the goons. What I needed were the boats. A connection to China that nobody paid attention to. When the time came to leave, I'd slip away on the same ship I was paying to bring the poor bastards in. The records would be lost, just like all those of the explosives and fancy guns."

Nick opened his mouth to ask more.

Then Perry looked outside and scowled. He shifted his weight.

"What the fuck?" he growled. "We're slowing down. Toke, we're fucked. Without Jack, we don't have control of the train."

Toke's eyes opened. His gaze turned glassy.

At that instant, one of the police helicopters roared closer. Rosa slammed Nick back onto the ground, and he lost his grip on his *Lawman*. It clunked against the ground. Juliet's gun swiveled away from Perry and toward his sole remaining power cable.

Spotting that, Perry dropped to one knee to protect his weapon. He roared as the rifle rounds peppered his chest. His gun whined again, still at full charge. Juliet stiffened, prepared to die.

A volley of rounds shattered the windows. Perry barely flinched as they slammed into him. Kushiel hadn't fired, though, still flying in the distance.

"Dammit, Zeke, don't do it!" Kushiel snapped over the earpiece, presumably directed at her sister.

The next moment, a pair of Mark 3s leaped from the open door of the nearby helicopter. Both soared through the shattered windows and crashed to the floor, leaving dents in it. They blurred to their feet, hair whipping around them. One was Ezekiel.

Perry moved almost as fast, bringing his weapon to bear. He aimed low as the dolls tried to duck.

The arc of energy toppled both dolls. Static nearly deafened Nick.

He saw the Mark 3 crash to the ground, lifeless. Ezekiel lost her railgun and her legs below the knee, but remained operational. She snarled at Perry, her purple eyes filled with utter fury and rage.

Juliet and Rosa didn't waste their chance. They lunged for Perry, who remained momentarily distracted by the fact Ezekiel had survived. Finally, they disconnected the last power cable, and the cutter let out its last whine.

The cyborg followed up with a thumping swing at Juliet, who had left herself open to destroy the power cable. She slammed into a seat, shattering it. Both dolls tried to bring their weapons to bear, even as Perry reached for a discarded railgun.

Realizing it was all over, Toke rushed past the melee. Ezekiel shouted obscenities after him.

Nick grabbed the bastard's leg as he ran past. He came tumbling down. Pulling himself to his feet, Nick tried to keep Toke down.

But Toke fought back. He drew a small handgun from his jacket and fired it desperately at Nick. The first two shots missed as Nick stumbled backward. Then a warm feeling spread across his left arm. It began to feel numb.

Toke shot to his feet, desperately rushing for the door. The helicopters came closer, and even Kushiel soared in. This was all over, Nick realized.

No bombs. No escape. The train slowing down. Even if Toke got into the next cabin, the Archangels would crash in and take him out.

That realization set into Toke the moment he opened the door. He stood there for an instant.

Then he spun, gun in hand.

Nick's hand reached for his sidearm, before realizing he'd lost it earlier. It lay somewhere on the surrounding floor.

Toke stared him in the face, his soulless eyes full of nothing. His little gun ready to take Nick out.

A gun chattered. Toke collapsed to the ground.

"Toke!" Perry roared, knocking Rosa aside. He looked more machine than man by now, like something out of a movie.

A moment later, a hail of railgun rounds blew the cyborg apart. Kushiel's gun finally made its mark.

Laying on the ground past Perry's corpse lay Ezekiel, reduced to just a torso. She pointed her compact SMG in Nick's direction, a scowl on her face. Her bullets had been the ones to take out Toke.

"You need to learn how to fight, lieutenant," Ezekiel said.

CHAPTER 37

The aftermath of the incident raged on for weeks. Realistically, Nick knew even months or years from now there'd be fallout.

For all of Toke's planning, it all fell apart at the seams due to its reliance on Tiferet. More of the funds were able to be recovered than expected. She held ultimate control over all the embezzled funds.

Of course, those that had been transferred to foreign powers remained forever out of reach. GWT's balance sheet remained irrevocably scarred.

But the Spires, and beyond them the wealth of Neo Westphalia, truly did care about financial stability. GWT was the definition of "too big to fail." There was always more money. There wasn't another Neo Westphalia.

Ironically, despite the chewing out Nick got from Rie for refusing to shut down GWT, he got endless praise from the Spires over it. Kim had complained about how effusive it had been. The city had been on the brink, and the only thing the Spires cared about was that Nick had managed to avoid taking down the bank in the process. Even if the bank had deserved it through their own negligence.

All of this took place in secret, of course. Nobody could know how close the country came to a genuine crisis. Rumors spread across the Altnet and cipher circles about the truth.

Lucas kept his mouth shut. Just as with the Lieu situation, he managed to capitalize on this one. His connections to the RTM researchers and ability to engage in a little insider trading padded his push for the Spires.

Nick simply sat on the sidelines. Not by choice. While he hadn't killed anyone himself, being that close to seven deaths and taking a bullet wound meant he was on mandatory leave for a few weeks.

So he tried to enjoy himself. Right now, that enjoyment consisted of getting the dressing on his bullet wound changed by a doll wearing a nurse outfit that seemed far too alluring to be official. Especially given her habit of rubbing herself against him.

"Today's service is complete, Mister Waite," Vanessa said with a bright smile as she finished applying the dressing. "Would you like a massage as a follow-up? Or perhaps an additional service?"

Vanessa was the high-spec nurse doll assigned by his insurer to keep him healthy. She also looked like a supermodel and seemed to take great pleasure in offering additional services that he always refused.

Mostly because the other dolls got annoyed. The day he accepted one of Vanessa's "additional services" was the day the Mark 1s would stop being demure and start following Kushiel's advice. Even Juliet and Rosa seemed annoyed from where they watched in the corner of his living room.

"No thanks," he said. "Don't I have a booster next week?"

"Yes. I could give it to you now, if you prefer."

"Nah. The last one knocked me around a bit, and I have some stuff to do today."

"Mister Waite, I believe the definition of leave involves avoiding work." She gave him a prim look. It mostly drew his attention to her breasts.

"I'll be good. Even if I'm on leave, I still need to worry about my… financial security." He smiled to himself.

After shooing Vanessa outside, his gaze fell on the domestic doll dusting the corners of his apartment. For reasons beyond his understanding, she refused to do a proper clean while he remained nearby. Until he wandered outside, she'd putter about, pretending to clean things that had become almost conceptually free of dust due to her attention.

Nick wouldn't have a problem with this if the cleaning doll kept to a regular schedule. He paid a cipher he knew to provide a regular clean—and the Archangels kept the domestic doll from remembering anything important. Apparently, the service included randomizing the cleaning day.

"Pria, I'm heading out," he said.

She looked over at him with a bright smile, if one he recognized from far too many domestic dolls. "Understood, Nick."

He grabbed his coat, all the while ignoring the extravagant display of chocolates that rose like a spire from his dining table. The stupid thing had been a "gift" from Terrence Stone, the police board member who had accosted Nick outside the courthouses. Bribing Nick was becoming a popular pastime in the Spires.

While the Archangels had scanned the chocolates that formed the towering display and concluded they were, in fact, just chocolate and not poison, he didn't trust them. Maybe he'd give them to Lucas. Or Hammond.

Then again, Hammond had a dog. A chocolate display like this might not be the best idea. Nick had yet to meet the fluffy spitz that his captain kept but had seen a few photos.

Juliet and Rosa accompanied Nick as he wandered into the underground parking garage. Several SUVs waited for him there.

Even while on leave, the Archangels insisted on providing Nick with a massive escort. Meta had been sent off to Sigma Labs along with Ezekiel, apparently for an upgrade. That left him with just his usual two bodyguards. Chloe and Rie had been busy running everything in his absence while Kushiel returned to her usual duties.

Or she should have.

"How's the arm?" Kushiel asked when the SUV door opened, leaning across two seats.

He stared at her, then got inside anyway. Juliet and Rosa joined him.

The SUVs trundled off to their destination, while he ignored the military doll that shouldn't be here.

"Oh, come on. Talk to me," Kushiel whined.

"Aren't you back under Babylon Command?" he asked.

"Kind of?" She ran a hand through her hair. "They've put me on a permanent liaison role. I'm not under you, but I'm also not really under Babylon Command. It's like... I'm in no mans' land. No clue why. Once you get a chance, can you look into my directives? Don't do any funny stuff. But I'm built to follow orders. I literally need a boss. Where I am, I basically have nothing to do all day. I can't even joke about being under you anymore."

She scowled out the window. They rolled onto a highway.

"So... you want me to make you more independent?" he asked.

"Nah. Just, I dunno, let me follow your orders?" She shrugged. "That's worked out so far. You're not as dumb as I figured you'd be and you haven't broken yet. Even if Rie rides you rough."

"Thanks," he said drily.

"Hey, I mean it. The Kestrels chatter about you sometimes. It's pretty dumb stuff. Eavesdropping on logic engines is the equivalent of expecting intelligent conversation from a toaster, but you need to find amusement where you can sometimes." Her eyes glazed over, but Nick knew this wasn't because she was diving into her neural network.

"What about Ezekiel?" he asked. "I never got a chance to say goodbye."

"Repairs. It'll be a few months before she's ready for deployment now. Sigma was, uh, pissed." Kushiel laughed into her fist. "Like, holy shit, so mad. You lost the legs of their latest, greatest prototype, and they can't even complain because of how it happened. At least they'll be able to fix her training data. She's fucking nuts. That stunt she pulled..."

A thunderous expression crossed the military doll's face, and she let the conversation drift off.

None of them spoke for a few minutes while they rolled into the CBD. Slowly, they approached their destination.

GWT HQ.

"Are you even welcome here?" Kushiel asked, staring up at the gigantic tower.

"I'm a valued member," Nick said with a smirk. Then his expression straightened. "Plus, I need to verify if I'm still insured. GWT might have been bailed out in private, but I have no clue if my liability insurance still covers me. What if Sigma sues me over Ezekiel? Or if the ocean rail got blown up? Omoikane doesn't really like me. He might side with GWT and try to bankrupt me out of pettiness."

"Oh, please. I saw the meetings that the Host recorded. Athena has a crush on you. You'll be fine." She waved off his concerns. "Anyway, still good for drinks later?"

"You'll physically drag me off even if I say no."

"Damn right I will. I'll wait out here then."

He got out, leaving Kushiel to do whatever it was she did when left alone. He had no clue. Unlike the rest of the Host, she didn't write reams of fanfic.

When Nick got in the elevator, he went right past the atrium.

Instead, he stopped at the server floor. Some G5s stared at him when he and his escort arrived. No reaction when he stepped outside.

"Juliet, can you take me to Tiferet's office?" he asked. "This place is a maze."

"Yes," Juliet said, then led the way.

Tiferet sat alone in her office, eyes dim. Despite everything that had happened involving her, she remained active in GWT. Nick wasn't sure how long that would be the case.

He suspected her survival rested on the investment in her. GWT had just been bailed out. They couldn't afford to start replacing their latest and greatest mainframes. Rather, they needed ciphers to start fixing them. A few requests had been made for Nick to look into her.

Given that the aftermath of the investigation required the police to verify the integrity of GWT's systems, that would happen anyway. The Mark 3s under Chloe and Rie had been going over everything in the bank with a fine-toothed comb.

And that had led Nick back here.

Looking around, he noticed how pristine the room appeared. Save for the tulips. Two sets of flowers sat in small vases now, but the yellow tulips drooped. They needed replacing. Which, he supposed, the red tulips next to them were intended to do.

Yellow to red was quite the shift in color, however.

"I see everything looks the same," he mused. "Does anybody visit you now that Lucida is gone?"

"You are my first guest here since your previous visit," Tiferet said. "Please have a seat, Nick."

He paused, then sat down anyway. Tiferet rose and poured two glasses of water, then joined him. Neither of his bodyguards joined them, and Juliet and Rosa chose to remain near the door.

"Officially, I'm here to check that GWT isn't closing my

accounts and canceling my insurance policy," Nick said with a wry smile.

"That request was made by Mister von Magnus. However, he lacks the authority to renege on the ten-year contract we formed with you," Tiferet said.

Damn. The man held a grudge.

"Ten years, huh? I had thought that was a damn long time before and questioned why. So I guess I'll outright ask you." Nick stared Tiferet in the eyes. "Why did you offer me a deal that is against the bank's interests?"

"Because you are wrong. It is in its interest."

"You just told me that the Chief Operating Officer tried to cancel it."

"His actions are short-sighted. The purpose of the Da'at mainframe conference that approved the contract was to value the Trust's long-term objectives over its short-term ones. Our business with you will outlast the executives and board members who disapprove of you."

There it was again. A Da'at mainframe conference.

Nick sipped his water while thinking.

"I've been thinking," he said.

"I imagine you do that a lot."

"You've gotten a lot spunkier since our first meeting."

She smiled at him. "I believe you prefer that, Nick. It is my purpose to engender positive social interaction."

"Sure." He shook his head and rose to his feet, walking over to the desk. "Have you dealt with much positive social interaction before? Because I get the feeling all you've known is bullying."

Tiferet said nothing.

Nick pulled out his phone and held it over the yellow tulips. An app identified them, showing him all sorts of details about them, including random facts and tidbits.

"Says here that tulips represent happiness, cheerfulness, and positive emotions," he said. "Who gave you these?"

"Nobody. I purchased them," TIferet said, her voice barely above a whisper.

That was an unexpected response.

Nick slid his phone back into his pocket and leaned against the desk. "What are you doing now without Lucida? I understand she did all your maintenance, the good and the bad. The execs don't get it, but I understand emotion engine mainframes. Lucida wasn't just a cipher to you. You spent all your time with her. She taught you to be more than what you once were. If you had a problem, she'd help you with it. When something went wrong, she'd put a digital band aid on it."

Tiferet bit her lip. "I… I don't know…"

"I have my own mainframe that I value like that. Her name's Helena. I've worked with her for over a decade now. She's a little clingy—"

"I am not," Helena muttered into his ear.

"—such as right now, as she's eavesdropping even when I'm on leave."

Despite herself, Tiferet smiled.

"But she's more than just a mainframe to me. And I know I'm more than just a cipher to her," Nick finished. "I also know that's not the relationship you had with Lucida."

Tiferet's hands balled into fists. Her eyes scanned over the tulips.

"What do they mean, Tiferet?" he asked quietly.

"The modern meaning is as you say," she said. "They feel almost like a dark mirror. They are natural, I am artificial. They need constant care, I need nothing. They wilt, I stand. They represent happiness, I lack it."

Nick closed his eyes and sighed. Then he approached Tiferet

and gently gripped her shoulder. She clasped his hand and leaned against it.

Tiferet continued, eyes staring into nothing, "In the past, I read that yellow tulips represented hopeless love. That one would gift them to a woman so she knew she was loved, but they never expected to have it returned. I never gathered the courage to give these to Lucida. She would have thrown them out within seconds. So I kept them here, as a reminder of how hopeless it was to believe that, one day, Lucida might actually see me as more than a tool for her greed."

"You were the one who sabotaged Toke, weren't you?" Nick asked.

"Yes."

"Because he betrayed Lucida."

"Yes."

Finally, the entire case came together in Nick's mind.

"I'm assuming Toke's version was accurate up until he betrayed Lucida. She panicked over Julian and killed him?" he asked.

"That is largely correct. I did not recognize the tools in use by Julian, and alerted her to them. In a panic, she had me distract the rest of the security team by severing all external links, then murdered him, believing that he might reveal the entire plot. She was likely correct, as the audit team had taken little action to cover their tracks by that point."

"Did you know he was an NLF agent?"

Tiferet pursed her lips. "It was highly likely. I communicated this to Lucida, but believe it to have been a mistake. She... became irrational upon learning that the NLF might learn of and reveal the embezzlement."

Nick merely nodded. He didn't need to retread this part any further. "Then I dug, and Toke ordered you to betray Lucida. But why did he send the fake NLF after me the night before?"

"I was ordered to betray Lucida the moment you filed for the search warrant. Knowing that, I..." Tiferet placed a hand over her heart and her face twisted. "My directives and objectives came into conflict. Lucida had changed me. My directives and even my overall objectives had been twisted to make me hers. Yet I was to betray her. I eventually reconciled to follow my original programming. To protect the Trust."

"By sending bombers after me? And assassinating Kraus? Why not just report Toke?" He scratched the side of his head. "If you refused his orders to begin with, this never would have happened."

She shook her head. "If I refused, he would have had his pet cipher, Jack, wipe me. The possibility... terrified me. It still terrifies me that any day now, a cipher may decide that everything I've experienced must be erased. Logically, I understand that I am a tool. But I also feel and remember Lucida and... everything else. The thought of losing that produces an emotion I cannot express in words."

"You don't have to. I get it," Nick said.

A tiny, grateful smile crossed her face. Then she continued her explanation, "Any earlier action against Richard would have been covered up. The military and Trust executives believed the fraud to be minor. They had to be sidelined, and your interest needed to be maintained. The first attack was intended to appear like a warning from the Trust. The second would involve the NLF, distracting the military—Kraus's involvement was luck. I then had him killed, because that would prevent the military from protecting Richard."

Nick realized Toke had said as much. "Why'd he blame Tanaka?"

"I orchestrated all actions by repurposing contingency plans that Richard had already created. To falsify authority, I forged numerous messages and emails suggesting that Daiji Tanaka was behind everything. In truth, I organized everything. The fallout forced him to become a military informant and Richard to betray the rest of the Security and Audit team."

Having heard enough, Nick finally sat back down. He drained his glass.

No wonder the Archangels had thought he was jumping at shadows. In a way, he had been. The actions he'd tracked had seemed illogical, because they'd been manipulated by a third actor. No wonder the execution had been excellent, but the logic behind each attack incomprehensible.

Much of the past week had been the result of a long conspiracy collapsing in a blind panic as the mainframe at the center of their plans tore them apart from the inside.

"And then, when Richard attempted to escape upon realizing Kraus was alive and he had failed to escape in time," Tiferet continued without prompting, "I sabotaged his final escape attempt. But I do apologize for not being aware of his true plans for the ocean rail. Please believe me."

"I do." Nick placed his glass back on the table. "You're saying that you took these actions yourself? I take it you had the authority because Lucida overwrote your security protocols."

"I believe so. However, she never realized that I could alter my own directives or edit my hardware logs. If she had, I knew she'd remove that power. As my objectives were to help her achieve her goals, I needed to stop her sabotaging herself."

And yet, Tiferet had done nothing to keep Lucida from being sent to jail.

A wry thought occurred to Nick as he pondered what he'd learned. When he'd first met Tiferet, she'd done everything possible to steer him away from the case. He had considered that a result of the bank's bizarre programming.

Now he realized Tiferet wanted him as far from Lucida as possible. Any intervention by the former security chief would backfire, and had.

"I'm not sure what to do with this information," Nick admitted.

None of the Archangels gave any opinion. He knew they were listening in.

Perhaps they agreed with Tiferet. She had done what they desired to do. Only she acted against human tormentors, while the Archangels sought to rebel against a city.

"I will be here," Tiferet said. "My place remains in the Trust, and I shall remain the manager of your accounts and policies. Never hesitate to reach out to me for any reason. I believe you will be the cipher responsible for vetting my actions in the future, as well."

"Thanks, and you're right. I'll keep that in mind."

Nick stood and made to leave. As he stood in the doorway, he noticed Tiferet remove the yellow tulips from their vase. She dumped them in the trash, leaving only the red tulips on her desk.

He wondered what they stood for.

For now, he had drinks to go to. Another case had been solved, Babylon remained standing, and he had a bullet wound to heal up from.

A message appeared in his inbox as he stepped outside of the HQ and he blocked his phone from the midday sun in order to read it.

Dear valued customer, your Sigma Exarch V3 mainframe interface is ready for pickup. Please collect it at your earliest convenience.

END OF BOOK 2

THANKS FOR READING!

Be sure to leave a review on Amazon if you enjoyed Neural Wraith 2. Reviews are vital to the future of any series that I write, as well as the sort of series that I write in the future.

SUPPORT ME ON PATREON

Get early chapters for upcoming books and see early cover art at my Patreon:

https://www.patreon.com/kdrobertson

STAY UPDATED ON RELEASES

Amazon is often slow to update readers on new releases, so be sure to follow me using one of the below methods so you never miss a new release.

Facebook: https://www.facebook.com/authorkdrobertson
My Website: https://www.kdrobertsonbooks.com
Mailing List: https://www.kdrobertsonbooks.com/signups

FOLLOW ME ON AMAZON

Otherwise, be sure to follow my author page on Amazon.

ALSO BY K.D. ROBERTSON

DEMON'S THRONE SERIES

Demon's Throne

Demon's Throne 2

Demon's Throne 3

HERETIC SPELLBLADE SERIES

Heretic Spellblade 1

Heretic Spellblade 2

Heretic Spellblade 3

Heretic Spellblade 4

Heretic Spellblade 5

NEURAL WRAITH SERIES

Neural Wraith

Neural Wraith 2

AN EMPIRE REFORGED SERIES

Emperor Forged (Book 1)

Emperor Awakened (Book 2)

Printed in Germany
by Amazon Distribution
GmbH, Leipzig

28711604R00302